MW00989150

C.H.U.D. LIVES!
A TRIBUTE ANTHOLOGY

COMPILED BY ERIC S. BROWN
EDITED BY JOE MYNHARDT

Let the world know:
#IGotMyCLPBook!

Crystal Lake Publishing
www.CrystalLakePub.com

WELCOME TO ANOTHER CRYSTAL LAKE PUBLISHING CREATION.

Thank you for supporting independent publishing and small presses. You rock, and hopefully you'll quickly realize why we've become one of the world's leading publishers of Dark and Speculative Fiction. We have some of the world's best fans for a reason, and hopefully we'll be able to add you to that list really soon. Be sure to sign up for our newsletter to receive two free eBooks, as well as info on new releases, special offers, and so much more.

Welcome to Crystal Lake Publishing—Tales from the Darkest Depths.

OTHER ANTHOLOGIES BY CRYSTAL LAKE PUBLISHING

Or check out other Crystal Lake Publishing books for more Tales from the Darkest Depths.

SPECIAL THANKS TO:

Producer Andrew Bonime for granting us the rights to this franchise. Frances McFetridge for making this happen. Eric S. Brown for bringing this project to our attention. As well as Theresa Derwin, Kairam Ahmed Hamdan, Tim Feely, David Lars Chamberlain, Curtis M. Lawson, Kevin Holton, Mark Spears, Ethan Harris, Roger Venable, Kris Majury, Eli Chaffin, Rob Voss, Michael Stokes, R.B. Wood, Jennifer Tuck-Ihasz, Tom Deady, and Kevin Ashton for their continued Patreon support.

TABLE OF CONTENTS

I.N.T.R.O.D.U.C.T.I.O.N.

Dave Drake

EGREGIOUS: MY PERSONAL RESPONSE TO C.H.U.D.

THE WORD EGREGIOUS means "out of the herd." It doesn't imply bad or good: it implies different. *C.H.U.D* is that in spades.

Even an occasional movie-goer like myself runs into a few films which differ from the rest of their category only in being an order of magnitude better. In the '60s there was a fad for biker flicks: I recall hearing about one which involved the Hell's Angels going to Vietnam and winning the war (I sincerely wish they'd really managed that before I was drafted). There was no chance at all that I'd decide to see a movie like that, but—

A coworker at my summer job told me that he and his wife had just seen *Born Losers* at the drive-in and that it was great. My wife and I saw it, a little doubtfully, and it was a hell of a movie. There was a gang of outlaw bikers, but that was incidental. The film was about people, and about what family means; about what you believe in and how far you're willing to go for those beliefs.

DAVE DRAKE

A few years later—1969—I was in Army Language School in El Paso. The Motion Picture Ratings System had just been applied, and response of the El Paso paper had been to refuse ads for X-rated films. Unless you were at the theater, you didn't know that such films were showing.

A buddy of mine and his wife saw *The Best House in London* and told us that we had to see it. I didn't need to see an X-rated movie, but my buddy had been getting his PhD in Old English at Princeton when he was drafted, so his opinion counted.

My wife and I saw the film. It was hilarious and extremely witty, at least to people with enough knowledge of High Victorian history and culture to get the jokes. There were bare breasts, but that was true of British TV also. *The Best House in London* was no more a porn movie than Ovid's *Amores* was a Night-Stand Reader.

And then there was *C.H.UD*.

Again, a friend brought the film to my attention. This time it was Karl Edward Wagner, whom I was seeing six days a week during the '80s. Karl spent most of his time watching television as an alternative to writing. This was before the explosion of cable channels, but Karl took both HBO and Showtime; and I think it was on Showtime that he saw (and recorded) *C.H.U.D.*

Karl watched a lot of bad movies (I recall him watching *Xanadu* multiple times), but he knew they were bad. He said that *C.H.U.D* was exceptionally good, and we all watched it one night when we were having dinner at his house.

C.H.U.D was a low-budget monster movie the same way that *Born Losers* was a biker movie: in name only. *C.H.U.D* is about people. The characters talk the

2

INTRODUCTION

way people talk and they have the motivations that real people have: little motivations. The villain is trying to cover a departmental screw-up. The cop is concerned about homeless people disappearing, but not particularly for the people themselves: it's for what the disappearances imply for the taxpayers like his wife. The journalist wants a story that will make his name, the successful photographer wants to find a story that will give his life meaning.

C.H.U.D is truly an exceptional—egregious—film. When Eric asked me if I were a fan of *C.H.U.D*, I immediately said that I was—even though I hadn't seen the film since that night 30-odd years ago in Karl's living room.

Before I wrote this essay, however, I got the DVD and watched *C.H.U.D* again. This reinforced my positive reaction to that first viewing, but there was one surprise also. In the cut I saw from cable TV, the end credits run over the diner scene: the cops and waitress chatting on a foggy night as shapes appear outside the glass—and finally press against it and are seen clearly. On the DVD, that scene is in chronological order.

I suppose chronological order is the better choice (and presumably the director eventually decided that also), but running the scene as a flashback has its virtues also. It demonstrates how much thought the people who made *C.H.U.D* gave—and how many risks they were willing to take—to keep *C.H.U.D* from being just a low-budget horror movie.

They succeeded.

Dave Drake
david-drake.com

INTERVIEW WITH THE LATE ANDREW BONIME
(a few months before he left us)

BY ERIC S BROWN

Tell us some about how *C.H.U.D.* came to be and where the idea came from.

Bonime: As a producer I used to get tons of screenplays submitted to me. I usually didn't read them unless they came with a recommendation. I initially didn't read *C.H.U.D.* because it was of the horror genre. It was not something I was interested in doing. I felt it would demean my credibility. My first wife worked at Random House and she had obtained the screenplay written by Shep Abbott from a friend and pleaded for me to read it. I told her I felt that it could ruin my reputation. She said to me "If YOU do it, it won't be bad." So I realized if I did it I would have control and felt I could make it into something great.

INTERVIEW WITH ANDREW BONIME

What were some of the high points of filming *C.H.U.D.*?

Bonime: The process of building the underground set was very gratifying because the effect we wanted was fully realized. Most people thought that the set was more realistic than the actual underground tunnels.

What were some of the worst things you faced during the filming?

Bonime: The worst things stemmed mostly from contractual misunderstanding. For example, the music used in the film was originally temp music selected by Doug Cheek. I had an expensive and elaborate score written specifically for the film which ultimately became the final soundtrack. The most frustrating part had to do with the CHUD's themselves. Time and money forced us to use rubber makeup which limited the mobility of the CHUD's to a very comic effect and detracted from the horror mood I had wanted to set. Also the distributor editing moved whole scenes out of order, which was grossly insulting. For example, during the test screening when Lauren (Kim Greist) shouts "Help me" somebody in the film's audience (one of the extras) shouts back, "Call the Ghostbusters." The distributor insisted we leave it in the film. The *Ghostbusters* movie had just been released, not realizing that the Ghostbuster line changed the tone of the entire last half of the film. Not the absolute worse was that over one weekend Kim Grant went to the beach and got a pretty bad sunburn, when Doug Cheek (director) specifically told her to stay out of the sun. Any skin coloration changes would change the matching of Kim's makeup. Luckily this was not too much of a problem.

How does it feel to have created a horror classic that, after all these years, still has a huge fan base?

Bonime: Perplexing in the least, but flattered none the less.

What do you think makes *C.H.U.D.* such a beloved film among horror fans?

Bonime: I think it is a combination of the film's anti-establishment stance, and its tongue in cheek approach. Parnell Hall, the film's "rescue writer" could never take the plot seriously, especially the so called acronym for CHUD: Cannibalistic Humanoid Underground Dwellers. He thought that line would get a laugh every time it was uttered. So he came up with an alternative ending: Contamination Hazard Urban Disposal. This created a complex plot line.

Do you think there will be a *C.H.U.D.* remake, and what are your thoughts on that?

Bonime: I truly can't say. On one hand I have been involved in three attempts to remake the film, and found a strong passion for the remake. On the other hand, I have also found complete misunderstanding of the essence of *C.H.U.D.* and what makes it unique. Simple iconic symbols, such as the manhole cover, clawed hand reaching up from below and government and quasi government agents with nefarious plots have been ignored. I can't see these two sides coming together. But not a day goes by that I don't get a phone call or an email expressing interest. If someone came to me tomorrow and they said they had the money and distribution and wanted the two elements for the remake, I'd sign up immediately as producer. However, it would take a commonality of vision and sensibility between myself and the driving force of the new entity.

How did you feel about *C.H.U.D. II*?

Bonime: In my contract with the distributor my conveyance of the rights for *C.H.U.D. II* was conditional based on my approval of the film. The company producing the film had to give a video tape showing the entire film including my credit. Upon review I was to withhold or accept my credit. I chose to retract my credit. Most of the other creators (writer, Director, etc.) made the same choice.

Do you have a favorite memory in terms of dealing with the cast of *C.H.U.D.*?

Bonime: Yes, John Heard liked to indulge and showed up on the set quite late owing to his fondness to the spirits. One day during one of these absences I sought to make peace with him and put my arm around him and said, "It's alright John, you're a star." John turned to me and with his classic impish grin said, "No Andy, the stars are all in heaven, I'm just an actor."

CHUD are iconic, classic monsters, but if CGI had existed then, what would your vision of them have been? How different would they have looked?

Bonime: When we were developing creatures for *C.H.U.D.* we didn't take budget into consideration, nor schedule nor calendar. It's hard to tell what a CGI would look like. But based on our budgetary research I can say that a Canadian corporation would have affected large pieces of the film. It would have affected the creatures, hallucinations, fantasy sequences, and other effects not even in the script currently would have been utilized throughout the screen play.

Do you have a favorite character in the movie?

Bonime: Yes, Graham Beckle for his beloved intensity, and his sidekicks Gog and Magog.

How involved were you with *C.H.U.D.*'s soundtrack?

Bonime: Because the music was so integrated to the soundtrack I had produced, you couldn't separate out the two. For example, some of the music effects were produced by resampling the sounds of the tines strummed with a quarter across the strings of a grand piano. This gave an underground drippy sound. To supervise all of this I traveled to Liverpool and London to work with Liverpool's highly popular pop group OMD (Orchestral Maneuvers in the Dark), Martin Cooper and David Hughes.

INTERVIEW WITH ANDREW BONIME

If you could remake the movie today, how would it be different?

Bonime: In many ways better, in many ways worsc. The plot would be more coherent, the tech more cohesive and the art more scientific.

D.O.G. W.A.L.K.E.R.

ROBERT E WATERS

FLORA BOSCH ANSWERED the blare of the alarm clock with a hand shaped like an angry claw, reaching out from beneath a warm sheet. She grabbed the clock and considered ripping it from the wall. Instead, she gently touched the snooze button and rolled over. Just ten more minutes . . . just ten more. But ten would lead to twenty. Twenty to thirty. And she'd be late again. She reached out for her husband Marty. As usual, he wasn't there.

Flora cursed below her breath and forced her eyes open. The ceiling was as empty as it always was, a dirty beige with a red-and-white flower wallpaper trim along the base of beige walls. She sighed and wiped sleep from her eyes. The blare of the clock was replaced by a rambunctious bisou-poodle mix.

Bull yapped her way into the room and jumped into Flora's lap. What a silly name for a female dog, but Flora had promised herself that she'd keep at least one memory of her grandfather, a bare-knuckled boxer of the twenties whose stage name had been Bull. The little dog was much like her grandfather: fearless and persistent, and perhaps a little dense, but always kind.

"That's a good girl," Flora said, accepting sloppy kisses. She smiled. "Did Daddy let you out this morning?"

Of course he didn't. He always forgot. Captain Martin Bosch was a career police officer for the NYPD. His job was his life, and recently, he'd been pre-occupied more than usual by a case dealing with the homeless, or as they often called them at the station, under-grounders. 'I didn't want to wake you,' he'd say at night when she wondered aloud why he hadn't said goodbye on his way out. But she knew that was false. That excuse was just a cover. There were other reasons why he left without saying a word.

She gently set Bull aside and climbed out of bed. A crack of sunlight from the window spread across the room. She opened the curtains and felt the warm sun on her face, neck, and chest. The muffled, controlled chaos of the New York streets gave her comfort, though sometimes she longed for a beach, a Manhattan, and a tanned Cuban pool boy to bring it to her. She breathed deeply, closed her eyes against the hot light, and dreamed of careless days in the Caribbean.

Bull's scratching at her ankle reminded her of reality.

Flora rubbed her face again, yawned, and stumbled into the bathroom. She eyed the matching dry toothbrushes in their little stand beside the dripping faucet, the half-empty toothpaste tube teetering on the edge of the sink. She shook her head. Marty had bolted quickly this morning. He had even left the toilet seat up, something that he was trying to be better about. She leaned against the sink and looked at herself in the mirror.

No makeup. Dark circles forming below her brown eyes. A small pimple on her left cheek. Messy brown hair. Pale lips. She was no pinup, that was for sure, but she never had been, and that had never seemed to bother Marty, to his credit. Flora Bosch was just a typical, normal woman in New York, trying to better herself with school, work, and family. Well, she really had no family other than Marty and Bull, but one day . . . maybe.

She removed her tank top and panties. She leaned into the tub and turned on the hot, then cold, splashing her hand through them both until she had the desired temperature. She turned on the shower, then stepped back and closed the curtain until the room was filled with steam. She climbed in.

Flora stood there, for several minutes, leaning against the linoleum, letting the water warm her body. Her wet dark hair matted against her face, and she lowered her head to let the water trickle into the tub. She watched as the water swirled around the drain and disappeared somewhere into the New York sewer system. She grabbed a bar of soap and began scrubbing.

Her face, hair, and shoulders were nice and lathered when the alarm clock, set to snooze, blared again. *Damn!*

She peeked out of the shower. "Bull, can you turn that off?"

Bull only replied with a cocked head and a yap that matched the incessant trill of the alarm. Flora reached for a towel. She wiped soap off her face, turned off the water, stepped out, and cursed. She walked into her room dripping water and struck the alarm like a hammer.

It was going to be one of those days.

The man across from her on the subway was homeless, an under-grounder. He was Jamaican, or perhaps Dominican? She could not tell how much of his color was based on skin and how much was based on soot. His hair was long, but rolled up like a Rastafarian might have it, though it was difficult to tell since it was tucked under a thick bola falling apart from dry rot. His face was covered in a grey beard. His burgundy trench coat was holey and singed with some kind of green substance, like puke maybe. He dozed. He smelled of smoke and sour fish. Other passengers avoided him. Flora fought the urge to move.

But she felt comforted and secure behind her satchel of textbooks, and besides, what kind of teacher would she be if she could not show strength and empathy when faced with an uncomfortable situation? How could she mold impressionable minds if her own character was suspect? It wasn't as if she hated or resented the homeless—not at all. But Marty's investigation of their mysterious disappearances of late was giving her pause, forcing her to transfer her leeriness to this poor man who lay before her, all twisted and folded up in his fitful sleep. And who was he really? Had he been a singer? A dancer? Was he a veteran? None of the above? He had not been born homeless. He had had a mother and father. Everyone did. Who was he?

Perhaps when she got her degree and found a steady teaching gig, she'd join the chorus of voices that spoke out against the plight of the homeless. There were a number of writers and photographers in the city who were doing wonderful exposés about them, and maybe her students would be proud of their teacher if she took action, and follow her lead. But she wasn't a teacher. Not yet, anyway.

Flora worked hard to be one. This was her third part-time semester of classes at New York University. She was close to finishing, but not quite there yet. Summer courses had helped her keep up with other classmates, and even a few night classes, although Marty didn't like her being out in the dark, not in a city like this. They had argued strongly about that, and finally she had relented, taking instead another day class to make up the time. She worked part-time too as a library assistant in the local branch, but only on and off, to help bring a little extra money into the house and to help pay for classes. Marty's salary, though not ideal, covered their modest lifestyle. It was enough to get by.

Flora was tired of just getting by. She was worried that someday, she'd end up just like this broken, lost man in front of her. But how could that be? She was the wife of a police captain. She was white. She was privileged. What could possibly go wrong? Perhaps this over-concern about her future was just her guilt for not studying for the test last night.

She took out a book and began running over the answers on the practice test in chapter four, "How to Prepare a Multiple-Choice Quiz for Middle-Schoolers." Make it fun and challenging, not too easy, but not too hard. How does one prepare a multiple choice quiz in one's own life, Flora wondered, as she worked through the answers. Pick one: Stay with Marty. Leave Marty. Stay in New York. Go home to Pittsburgh. None of the Above. All of the Above. Flora did not like those options, did not like having to make such definitive choices, for how could someone make such a choice in a complex world? Life was never as simple as one stark choice with a Number 2 pencil.

She tucked her book away, looked up, and saw the homeless man staring at her. She startled, caught her breath, then settled. He wasn't moving. He was just staring at her, expressionless, vacuous.

"Where do you live?" he asked her.

Don't give them your address . . . Marty's warning about speaking to strangers rang in her mind. "I live— not too far. Where do you live?"

"Everywhere."

He smiled and turned away, tucked his head behind the lapel of his dusty coat, and slept some more.

Flora hugged her satchel, thought of Chester, and prayed that the train would stop soon.

★★★

Flora was frustrated. The test was harder than she thought it would be, and it covered subjects that were not on the study guide. She thought about folding it up, setting down her pencil, and walking out, but she knew Chester would try to stop her.

Professor Chester "Chesty" McNamara was the son of a late ex-Marine cum history professor, with a concentration in military history. He had named his son after the great World War Two Marine "Chesty" Puller, hoping, she supposed, that his son would grow up to be a great soldier. What he got was a lanky, overly hairy, curly-locked, bookish man who had marched against war in the '60s. Flora loved his smile.

"Are you okay, Ms. Bosch?" Chester asked, keeping up appearances.

Flora shook herself from her daydream and nodded. "Yes, sorry." Then in a whisper, "It's a little harder than I expected."

Chester smiled. Flora melted. "Perhaps we can discuss the answers," he said quietly, letting his long fingers run along the edge of her desk. "Over coffee?"

All she could do was nod.

Two hours later, Flora rolled out of Chester's bed and scrambled for her clothes. She had no time for a shower, not another one. Her hair would not endure any more hot water today. She'd have to risk just a quick cleaning with a towel. Besides, she wouldn't see Marty again till dinnertime, if then.

"What was your problem today?" Chester asked, turning over and letting the sheet slip to his waist. "You're usually very sure of yourself."

"You changed the questions. You had stuff on there I hadn't studied."

"All of it was from previous chapters," Chester said, trying to reach for her.

Flora moved away. "You promised an easy test."

Chester chuckled. "I have to mix it up once in a while, you know, to keep you students on your toes."

"Or ten toes up, right?"

Chester groaned at the attempted insult-joke. He slid over to her side of the bed. "Come on, you know we don't do it for that. I treat you like everyone else in the classroom."

Flora sighed and sat back down on the bed. She rubbed sweat off her neck and shoulders with her towel. "I know. I'm sorry. I'm just . . . having a bad day."

"Marty?"

She hated when Chester brought up her husband, especially in this setting. He had no right. But how could she complain? Here she was, in another man's bed, trying to clip on her bra. How could she demand any respect or sanctity for her marriage?

Chester took his long fingers and worked the clip on the back of her bra until the hooks fell into place. Flora adjusted herself and stood, grabbed her dress, and wriggled into it.

Chester smiled and leaned his long body halfway out of the bed. "You have beautiful feet, do you know that?" He tried reaching for them. "Beautiful little toes, smooth—"

"I have to go," she interrupted, "I'm sorry. I have a busy day. I have to go to the bank, the grocery store, the—"

"When are you going to tell him?"

She paused, her fingers on the buttons of her dress. She stared at him, his question hanging in the air between them. A light smile spread across his lips. She tried smiling back. It was a question he asked almost every time, and he deserved an answer. Any other man would have kicked her out by now.

She fought back a tear and finished dressing. "Soon. Very soon."

★★★

In Flora's heart, her promises were no lie. She really meant to tell Marty about Chester, and to make a clean break. Always in the moment, there beside him, sharing that moment, she knew it was the right thing to do. But standing now in the grocery store, staring at another price hike on 2-percent milk, the chance was slipping away. It would devastate Marty, throw her life in disarray, and what good would it do anyway? This thing with Chester was just temporary.

That's what she had said four months ago when it started. One hundred and twenty days and one pregnancy scare later, it was still on. Just a passing phase? She couldn't tell herself that either. It had started so simply. She had stayed after class to discuss questions on a test. The next thing she knew, they were getting coffee. The next, she was in his bed. It was easy at first to deny her feelings about it. Now, it wasn't so easy. She loved Chester. There, she said it. But she still loved Marty, too. Didn't she?

She reached into the refrigerated case and grabbed a pint of milk. She put it in her basket and continued walking down aisle after aisle, seeking bread and bologna, some cheese, a bottle of wine, birthday candles, and a cake mix. It was Chester's—no, Marty's—birthday soon. And she needed a ham. Yes, Marty liked ham, especially the kind baked in brown sugar.

She reached the meat section. She set her basket down and looked through the processed meats. Bacon, salami, other brands of bologna, kielbasa, linked sausage. The sausage made her queasy; it always looked to her like intestines, and as a child, her brother would tease her about it, chase her around the store with links dangling, grunting like some feral beast, moaning like a zombie, until their father would box him around the ears to make him stop. She could laugh about it now, but then . . . Flora made a mental note to call her brother and say hello. It had been awhile.

Ah, there was the ham! Honey-baked, glazed, spiral cut. The best. She smiled, reached into the cooler, and pulled one out. It was wrapped in plastic, cool but not frozen, nice and fresh. She lifted her basket, placed the ham in it, and walked away.

Her path was blocked by a homeless man.

Not the same one that she had met on the train. This one was shorter, white, and did not have a burgundy coat. But his eyes watered, and his dirty skin oozed in places—a green, corpuscle-like flow from spots on his neck, his cheeks. It reminded Flora of the dried-green patches on the other homeless man's coat. The man reached out with surprising speed and grabbed her basket.

Flora screamed and let the basket go. The milk and ham tumbled to the floor. The cheese skid across the linoleum. The wine bottle shattered, leaving a pool of blood-like liquid at her feet.

A clerk tried grabbing the man. "Sir, what are you doing? You can't—"

The homeless man knocked him away with ease, growled something Flora could not understand. She backed away. The homeless man followed. Then his foot struck the ham like a soccer ball. He stopped, seemed confused, his eyes dripping some indiscernible goo. He leaned over, grabbed the ham, growled something again, then turned and walked away. In his flight, he knocked over a kiosk of baked beans, but kept going, toward the door.

Flora stood there in shock. Her heart pounded. The clerk who had been tossed aside had recovered and was screaming for the police. Others in the store did the same, as Flora watched the man knock aside those who tried stopping him. The entire store was engaged in the flight of this man, but were helpless, or afraid, to stop him. Flora didn't blame them. The man was deranged, perhaps sick.

She began picking up her food. The wine was a lost cause. The others she scooped up and put back into her basket.

She heard a shot. She dropped the basket, and like everyone else, she funneled outside to see where it had come from.

The homeless man was on the pavement, writhing like some tortured soul. A policeman stood over him, his pistol trained at the man's back. One bullet had already blown a hole through his torso, another most certainly in the chamber and ready. Flora knew about the NYPD. The police officer—she looked, but didn't know him—wouldn't hesitate to end the matter with another round.

He didn't need to. The man's writhing stopped cold, and with a final tortured gasp of air, he died.

The crowd gathering was thick. The officer tried to keep them away. Sirens blared in the distance as other officers arrived. Flora walked around the dead man until she was, at a good distance, facing him. He still held her ham. He clutched it like a baby. He had begun to eat it, but he hadn't torn away the plastic. He had bitten right through it. Pieces of ham and bits of plastic were stuck in his mouth. His eyes were open wide, and for a moment, all that Flora could see in those dead eyes was Marty's face.

She turned and ran, not caring about her food or the basket. Let them rot on the floor, she thought. This was all too much. Too much . . .

She had spent hours in the park, until the sun set. She walked. She sat. She watched ducks waddling around a pond, watched children fly kites, laugh, and play with dogs. She watched intently as two young lovers kissed on a bench on the other side of the pond until they seemed to notice her. Then she got up and moved. She picked a few flowers, gave them to an old woman hustling along with a cane. The sweet smell of the petals brought a smile to the lady. Flora was pleased. It was nice to bring a little simple joy into the life of someone she did not know. There was so little of that these days.

Flora returned home around eight. It was dark. Marty had been waiting.

"Where's your satchel?" he asked as he greeted her at the door.

Damn! She had left it at Chester's. "I left it at school. I'll get it Thursday."

He gave her a peck on the cheek. She could smell brandy. Marty wasn't a drunk, but a brandy by eight o'clock meant a rough day.

"How's the investigation?" she asked.

"What investigation?"

Images of both homeless men came to her mind. Images of chewed ham and torn plastic. She shivered, rubbed her arms. "The homeless thing you mentioned."

"Oh." His expression turned sour. She was worried. It wasn't going well. She could tell. "Okay. We have a few leads, but it's difficult. Something's going on. Just can't put my finger on it."

She thought of Chester's fingers. "Well, you'll figure it out. You always do."

Marty nodded. "Anything interesting happen in your day?"

Many things, she thought, but didn't bring them up. Not even her homeless encounters, which might prove useful to his investigation. They were too unsettling. Marty would have to work it out, whatever it was, on his own.

She took a step toward the kitchen and right into a puddle of dog urine.

"Darn it, Marty!" Flora snapped. "Why haven't you taken Bull out?"

"Sorry," he said, putting up his hands in submission. "I just got home."

Flora shook her shoe. "Yeah, just got home, but you've had time to pour a brandy. Not time to walk the dog."

"Hey, back off! It's been a rough day. I'll take her out after dinner. I promise."

"Yeah, like you promised last night to take her out this morning, but you didn't. You make a lot of promises, Marty. When are you going to keep them?"

She began to cry, hard. She turned from him and put her hand over her mouth to muffle the sobs.

"Hey," Marty said, gently putting a hand on her back. "What's going on? Why are you so upset? It's just a little dog pee. It isn't toxic waste. I'll clean it up. I promise. And I'll take her out right now."

Flora rubbed her eyes, shook her head. "No, that's okay. I'm sorry. It's been a rough day for me, too." She turned to face him, tried to smile, tried to wipe away the image of Chester in her mind, the faces of the homeless men. "It's my fault. Let's start over. You clean up the mess, and I'll take Bull out. I'd like to get a little air anyway."

"No, I can take her out."

Flora shook her head and wriggled off her shoes. She walked over to a pair of white sandal flats. They were a little old and worn, but they were quite comfortable. "That's okay, let me do it."

"I don't like you walking around this neighborhood in the dark," Marty said. "It's dangerous."

"I'll be fine," she said, snapping a leash onto Bull. "I won't go far."

He tried objecting again. Flora gave him that look she often did that told him the discussion was over. Sometimes, it worked. Sometimes, not. This time, it did. "Okay," he said. "But remember what I told you."

She nodded. She walked to the door, opened it, then said, "Marty, when I get back, I have something I want to talk to you about."

"What is it?"

She almost told him, right there, but she paused, took a breath, and said, "When I get back. Okay?"

Marty shrugged. "Okay. Just don't be too long."

He smiled at her. Flora tried smiling back, but it was half-hearted at best. She wrapped the leash around her hand, gave a wave, let Bull out first, then followed.

★★★

Marty had always told her that if she were going to be walking at night, if at all possible, to walk in the middle of the street. Walking on a dark sidewalk, with access to alleys and side-streets, invited arms to reach out and grab you. At least by walking in the street, you'd be able to see an assailant and have some time to react. Not much time, of course, but seconds could matter. It was the kind of practical advice that her husband was known to give out, and it was something that she always tried to follow.

Flora let Bull drag her along. The sweet little thing had already done its business two fire hydrants ago, but she had kept walking, another block, maybe two. The cool night air was refreshing, and although Flora's legs were tired from all the walking she had done in the park, she kept going. One more block, and then she'd turn around and go home. And tell Marty what she needed to say.

I've met someone else. I'm leaving, Marty. Could she actually say it? Could those words, those exact words, come out of her mouth? She felt that queasiness again that she often felt when looking at linked sausage, the kind of sinking feeling in her stomach that she had felt when she thought she was pregnant with Chester's baby. That was a false alarm, thank God. False alarm . . .

Then she had another thought. Why should she say anything? Why ruin her marriage? Sure, it wasn't the best situation, but compared to the lives of other women she knew, it wasn't so bad. And who was Chester, really? She didn't know much about him, save for how he got his name. Was he sleeping with other students? He might be. He had that kind of arrogant swagger and charm that many academics had. No, there was no reason whatsoever to blow things up . . . not yet, at least. The semester was coming to a close soon. She would wait it out and see what happened. And if Chester finally got frustrated with her refusal to tell Marty of their affair, so be it. That would say less about who she was and more about him.

No, wait it out, Flora. You have all the time in the world.

But what would she tell Marty when she got home? She had told him that she wanted to discuss something. He would expect that conversation. What would it be? Then she knew. Of course! She'd tell him about the two homeless men she had encountered. Tell him about the green substance they had both had on their bodies. He would definitely be pleased with that information. He'd be happy, she'd be happy. The evening would go well.

She turned a corner and let Bull guide her into the middle of the street. And for the first time all day she was truly happy. She had a plan and a life. Perhaps it wasn't the best life in the world, but she would handle it, day to day, and take care of the little things, all the minuscule details that defined who she was and what she was all about as a human being. Flora Bosch was happy, and that mattered more than anything else.

Ahead of her in the middle of the street, a manhole steamed. Bull pulled her along at a good pace. This would be the last street, she promised herself. Then she would cut back toward home and prepare a great meal.

She was so distracted with her decisions that she let the handkerchief in her hand drop to the street. She stopped by the manhole and knelt to pick it up. Sweet little Bull pulled up beside her and waited.

She heard the scrape of the manhole cover as it opened. She felt the claws of a hand that reached out of the manhole and grabbed her calf. She felt the sting of those claws as it cut through her flesh and drew blood. She turned and saw the deep green-gray arm yank her hard toward the cover.

She screamed, lost her balance, and was pulled into the manhole. She tried letting Bull's leash go, but the arm was too strong, too swift, and she had no time. Bull followed her right into the sewer.

The last thing Flora Bosch thought about as she was being ripped apart was the incessant blare of her alarm clock.

T.H.E. D.W.E.L.L.E.R.S.

NICK CATO

THE NAME WAS Samantha's idea and the "artwork" was Frankie's. Tommy didn't care for the name at first, but over the last year, since they had become a band, he grew to love all it latently implied. Punk rock, at least in New York City, had taken a backseat to hardcore and heavy metal, but The Dwellers were faithful to their late 70s-styled sound. The name suggested they were an unflinching underground band, and that's just how Tommy liked it. It may have been closing in on 1984, but Tommy and his band had quickly mastered a sound that would've fit in the scene perfectly seven years earlier.

The Pyramid Lounge wasn't too crowded. It sucked to be the opening band, but Tommy knew this was how they paid their dues. The Dwellers played better than four of the five bands on tonight's bill, but he knew they still had to deliver, even if their audience was a bartender, the soundman, and whoever straggled in during their set.

Tommy plugged in and tuned up with Samantha as

best he could over the music blaring over the PA. When they were satisfied, Samantha leaned her bass against the amplifier and walked over to the bar. Tommy belched as he watched her, and tasted the knishes. The slight regurgitation was vile and he turned around to face his amp thinking he was going to puke. But he took a deep breath through his nose and was grateful the taste and his desire to hurl subsided.

Samantha placed a bottle of beer on top of his amp.

"Thanks," Tommy said. He took a sip and felt better. There were now about ten people in the club, one face he recognized from Mental Decline, the Queens-based hardcore band scheduled to go on after them. *I'll show these guys hardcore*, he thought as the music on the PA began to lower.

This was it. This was The Dwellers' first club show after a year and change of countless appearances at their friends' basement parties and street fairs.

Most of the small crowd came close to the stage, and Tommy intended to make a lasting impression on everyone there, including the bouncer who sat by the entrance, peeking over to see what this new band was made of.

Samantha stepped to her microphone and said with a playful sneer, "Thanks for showing up so early."

The audience chuckled.

Tommy leaned into his mic and said, "We're The Dwellers," then stepped back with his guitar hanging just above his knees, legs spread, and ripped into the opening riff of their first song. After a few bars, Frankie and Samantha came in right on cue, and by the time Samantha began singing the first verse in her snotty, high-pitched tone, Tommy was more than pleased. Everyone who had come up front were bobbing their heads to their music. Even the bouncer nodded in approval.

A couple of their friends arrived just as the opening number ended, and stood front and center, fist-bumping Samantha and Tommy.

By the third song, the audience had doubled, no doubt by people who had been hanging out front, waiting to hear if the opener was worth their time.

Tommy gave it his all, as did his band mates. After the fourth song everyone applauded and whistled. Tommy was a bit disappointed no one had started slam dancing, or moshing as the hardcore preferred to call it, but hoped that would change as more people began filing in.

Samantha thanked everyone, then began their next song with a catchy bass riff.

When Tommy and Frankie joined in, Tommy felt severe heartburn, but he ignored it and waited until they went into a brief bass/drum breakdown, at which time he was able to quickly take a swig of beer.

It seemed to help, and Tommy came back in blazing as tight and fast as he could manage without losing control.

The burning in his chest was distracting, but not enough to ruin this important show. Everyone there were cheering them on, and Tommy would be damned if he was going to let some indigestion stop him.

And then the backs of his eyes tingled. Tommy figured it must've been the lights that were a bit too close to him, so he stepped toward center stage and dragged his mic stand along with him.

As The Dwellers started another short song, Tommy thought about this morning as the tingle behind his eyes started to . . . burn.

★★★

"You're going, and that's the end of it," Wilson said, slamming his fist on the kitchen table. "You're twenty-four years old and barely working. You need money. You can't even afford the piss ass amount I'm asking you to stay here! How do you expect to ever be on your own?"

"Okay, okay. I'll go. But it better not interfere with my gig tonight," Tommy said.

He ducked as his father swung his hand to slap him in the head, and just barely missed. "Speak to me in that tone again and you're out of here. Do you understand me?"

Tommy stared his father in the eye. He was afraid of the old geezer, and knew better than to challenge him to a fight. Not only would he lose, but his old man would throw him out, and he couldn't afford to leave just yet. He finally lowered his eyes and said, "I understand you, yes."

"Now go get dressed. John will be here soon to pick you up. It's only going to take about an hour and you'll be getting paid a full day's salary. You'd have to be crazy to pass this up."

Tommy walked into his room and shut the door. The walls were covered in black and white fliers for various punk shows, including his first club gig tonight at The Pyramid Lounge. His clothes were thrown about and one wouldn't be able to tell which were clean and which needed laundering.

"Hurry up. He's outside beeping already."

He had no idea what his father had for him this time, but wished his part-time job at the corner deli paid a little more. He wouldn't have to listen to his dad complain every second they were together, and he'd be able to move in with one of his friends or maybe even get his own apartment, regardless if it was a rat hole far away from the nicer Bronx neighborhood where he grew up and still lived. To be away from his dad would be a blessing any way it came.

He threw on a pair of black jeans and a ripped black T-shirt and covered it with a gray hooded sweatshirt. It was 7:10 AM and they needed to be on the lower east side of Manhattan by 8:00. Chances are they'd just make it, and his father would blame their lateness on him and maybe even attempt another slap to his head for good measure when he got home.

One day, Tommy thought, *I'll be able to tell him where to go.*

★★★

Tommy followed John to the backroom of an unmarked warehouse where a couple of other guys his age stood listening to two men dressed head to toe in white hazmat suits. They had arrived at 8:03, and hopefully his old man wouldn't find out. These people were a bit too strict.

"Now listen carefully," John whispered as they joined the small group. "I don't want to re-explain everything once we get in the tunnel."

But Tommy barely heard a word being said. Something about storing barrels in an old area of a downtown subway station. He knew he'd have to wear one of those stupid looking white suits for safety reasons, but what occupied his mind as the men spoke was their location: this place was only a few blocks away from CBGBs, a legendary club he'd dreamed of playing at since he was a kid. Tonight's show at The Pyramid Lounge would be cool enough for the time being, and it, too, was located just a few blocks east of where they now stood. He thought of the classic bands who played at each venue, and zoned out.

"Tommy Wilson, are you with us?" one of the men asked, snapping his fingers in front of his face.

Tommy saw John's face redden. "Yeah I heard you. But this place stinks. What's in those barrels anyway?"

"So you haven't been listening! If we weren't on such a strict time constraint I'd be sending your ass home, regardless of who your father is."

Tommy wanted to say something smart, but instead said, "Sorry."

"Now listen up. I'm only saying this one more time."

As the man spoke, Tommy listened but was more worried about remembering his songs at tonight's gig. He couldn't wait to get this crap over with so he could go home and start tweaking the set list.

★★★

"How'd everything go?" Wilson asked as he stuck his head into Tommy's room.

Tommy stopped strumming his guitar, which wasn't plugged in as his amp was packed up and ready to go. "Pretty good. And they paid us already in cash."

"Feels good to have something in your pocket, right?"

Tommy pulled the roll of bills out and handed a couple to his father. "Is that cool for now?"

"Yes, it's cool for now." He tucked the money in his jacket pocket. "John called to say you guys were done in about forty minutes?"

"Yeah, it was quick. But those friggin' barrels were heavy. What the hell's in them, anyway?"

Wilson came in and shut the door behind him. "None of your concern, son. They're only being stored there temporarily until we can ship them out to our location in Arizona. You'll probably have more work in a couple of weeks when we get the order that the new facility is ready."

Tommy thought his father was a bit crazy. He knew the barrels contained some kind of waste that most likely wasn't being stored legally. But he didn't push it. He had a fat wad of cash on him and, after the gig, he intended to treat his band mates to a good time out. If his dad didn't mind risking his sweet job with the Nuclear Regulatory Commission, why should he care?

"You understand?"

"Yeah. But next time your people should make them lighter. My shoulder's killing me."

Wilson walked over, squeezed his son's shoulder, and said, "Big guy like you? You'll get over it."

Tommy wanted to crack his guitar over his father's head but thought better of it. And as his anger began to subside, he felt a burning in his chest and had to sit down.

"Oh come on. Don't tell me I just hurt you?"

"No, you didn't."

"Then what's the matter?"

Tommy burped under his breath, then said, "A little heart-burn I think."

Wilson smiled then turned and reached for the door. "You'll be fine." Before leaving, he added, "Good luck with your, uh, show tonight."

He shut the door before Tommy had time to say thanks, so he flipped the bird instead.

★★★

"Tom! I think your friends are here," Wilson yelled from the living room.

"I'll be right there," Tommy said as he slung his guitar's soft case over his shoulder and pulled his Peavey amp behind him on a dolly.

Frankie met him at the front door and took the amp. "Thanks, man."

Wilson said, "Try to keep it down when you get back later. I don't need your mother waking me at five in the morning."

"Okay," Tommy said as his father came over and looked into his eyes.

"You smoking that crap or something?"

"No. Don't you think the whole house would smell if I did?" Tommy expected his dad to give him a slap, but instead he stood back.

"You feeling okay?"

"Fine, why?"

"Just wondering. You look tired. This morning wasn't that bad, was it?"

"Are you kidding? Easiest money I've made since the last time you sent me to work with John."

Wilson nodded. "See you later."

Tommy and Frankie left the apartment as Samantha beeped outside in her dad's station wagon.

THE DWELLERS

★★★

Wilson made sure his son had left before he picked up the phone. He went into his room and looked at the flier for Tommy's gig, then jotted the name of the club down.

"John? Yes, it's Wilson. Someone else sound like me?"

"Not a soul."

"Tommy's band is playing at some place called The Pyramid Lounge. You know where that is?"

Wilson heard pages shuffling, then John said, "Hang on a sec. What was the address again?" More shuffling, then he added, "Ah yes. That's that dive bar right next to that soup kitchen I was telling you about."

"Well get a truck in the area. I'm not taking any chances."

"What's wrong?"

"Just taking precautions is all. Is there a problem with this?"

"None at all, sir. I'll be in touch."

"Get there early. I think Tommy said his band goes on first. But hang around until you see him leave for the night. Understand?"

"Understood."

Wilson sat down in the living room and poured himself a half glass of Scotch. He wasn't worried the barrels hadn't been sealed properly, but knew even being around them for too long could possibly cause complications, at least in their lab animals. And he wasn't taking any chances.

Especially after the look in his son's eyes as he left for his show.

★★★

The crowd had finally started slam dancing. Tommy ignored the burning behind his eyes and closed them, happy to at least have caught a glimpse of the enthusiastic crowd going nuts to a song he had co-written. It felt great, even as the pain in his chest increased.

When the song ended, he heard Samantha say in his ear, "You okay? Your eyes are tearing?" She started the next song with yet another fast bass riff as she waited for an answer.

Tommy opened his eyes. His pupils were gone. He heard his band mates playing but it sounded *deeper* than it should have. His body felt as if someone had removed his skull cap and tossed a blazing torch inside.

He was on autopilot. He could feel himself playing in time with the next song, yet he couldn't remember how or why. And by the middle of the track, Samantha walked over and yelled in his ear, "I hope you weren't poisoned by that food cart."

"Just keep going!" Tommy said as he took a step back and dropped his guitar. He shook his head, got his bearings back for a few seconds, then stumbled to the front of the stage where he threw up into the first row of slam dancers. When he was done he felt his eyes widen.

Someone who had been puked on jumped up on the stage and said, "Not feeling too good, buddy?" then punched Tommy square in the jaw.

But the person's fist caused Tommy's face to split open. The punk jumped back into the crowd wide-eyed as Tommy's face fell to the floor, revealing a distorted, olive green head with two glowing, over-sized eyeballs. The internal burning engulfed Tommy as he watched the two halves of his head hit the floor. His vision zagged in and out, but as the realization he had just been punched in the head grew clearer, so did his eyesight. People who had just cheered him on were now screaming and pointing in his direction. He looked down and noticed his arms had become veiny, thick stalks ending in larger than normal hands. His nails had grown to lethal-looking chiseled points.

The punk who had punched him wailed a beer bottle at Tommy's head, but it bounced off, unaffecting whatever it was he had become.

Tommy reached into the crowd and grabbed his attacker, pulled him back onstage and opened his mouth to reveal a couple of rows of razor-sharp teeth.

The punk screamed as Tommy bit into his shoulder and severed the guy's arm from the rest of his body.

He heard Frankie and Samantha scream when he turned to face them. They yelled things at him but his hearing had become heavily obscured. They sounded as if they were speaking a foreign language under water.

Tommy reached for Samantha and felt incredibly hungry, even as he chewed on the punk's shoulder. She escaped his grasp and headed for the front door along with the rest of the panicked audience.

But the main (and only) exit busted inward.

Tommy saw a bunch of men enter the place and start shooting.

Bodies fell. He saw the bouncer fall to the ground after trying to take something away from one of the intruders. And when he saw Samantha spin around with two holes in her forehead, he couldn't control his rage.

Tommy approached the gunmen. He couldn't tell over the intense burning behind his *new* eyes, but he figured there were at least a dozen heavily armed men, and he decided to do whatever he could to avenge his band mates'—and audiences'—deaths.

He managed to punch a hole in the chest of the closest gunman, and felt satisfied the guy didn't have a second to even scream.

Bullets entered Tommy's mutating body, but he kept on, hoping to at least take one or two more of these bastards down.

And in the back, standing near the exit, he noticed the guy who had been in the tunnel with him earlier today. He noticed his father's buddy, John, and it was at that moment he realized his illness wasn't due to any food cart, but to the barrels he had helped store not too far from where he now stood taking on gunfire.

He hated his father now more than ever. He wondered as a series of bullets ripped into his stomach, if one of those damn barrels had in fact been leaking or not properly closed. Perhaps he had damaged one when he put it down?

Either way, Tommy's mind was consumed with hunger, rage, and grief. He wished his father was here so he could use his powerful new hands to rip his head off and smash it into the back of John's skull.

But with each thought more bullets entered his changing body, and before long he felt himself fall to the ground, having only killed one of the intruders.

The burning behind his eyes stopped as he looked

up from the ground and saw a few gunmen aiming their weapons at his face. And he heard whatever members of the audience who were left begging for their lives as more gunshots went off.

★★★

Wilson answered the phone at 10:14 PM. "Yes?"

"We need to get those barrels moved immediately."

"You know that's not possible. What happened?"

John explained the quarantine and extermination of everyone inside The Pyramid Club. John's people were already spinning it to the press, claiming a gunman had entered the club and killed everyone inside until the NYPD arrived with their special tactics group and took control of the situation.

"Very good."

"Maybe so, but this is going to be a real scandal, Wilson, if even one person saw or heard what really happened."

"Well, did anyone?"

"How would I know? I did everything that was expected of me. There weren't many people hanging outside the place, aside from some skeevy looking guy a few doors away who runs some soup kitchen."

"Excellent. Then let's just think positively. And Tommy?"

John paused a moment, then said, "He changed. Just like the dogs at the lab." He waited a few moments. "This is really bad, Wilson. We really need to move—"

"You did good, John. Leave the rest to me. And try to take it easy. Your job is done. For now."

"Yes, sir."

"Meet me with the others at my office in an hour. You all need to be checked for contamination."

"We'll be there."

Wilson hung the phone up and took another sip of the Scotch that had been sitting on the night table. He remained calm and collected. It was a trait his bosses liked about him. But he knew the NRC needed to act fast before this situation somehow grew beyond the walls of some stupid dive bar.

His professionalism allowed him to feel a brief sorrow for his son, who he loved despite the annoying path he had been on since barely getting out of high school.

Wilson had a job to do, and he needed to get down to the office despite how late it was.

T.H.I.S. C.I.T.Y. W.I.L.L. E.A.T. Y.O.U. A.L.I.V.E.

RYAN C. THOMAS

"Kirby isn't a homicide, he's a missing person. I can't tie up the whole force just because some guy decided to . . . walk out on his wife."—**Captain Bosch**

THE RAINS HAD done nothing to wash the graffiti off the sides of the buildings. Ron Kirby stared at it like he did every other day. Disgusted. It wasn't even legible. Bunch of swirls and symbols that were supposed to be the code names of the neighborhood kids, but it all just looked like alien screed. Damn kids. They were as annoying as the rats that flowed in and out of the dumpsters behind that dirty diner on Cleveland and Kenmore. Food there was atrocious; the burgers were hockey pucks and the coffee was tar. Not to mention it was a cop hangout, and those idiots were just itching to give upstanding citizens like himself a hard time. Only reason to go in there was the cute waitress, but even she got old after a while.

Vandals. Bad food. Corrupt cops. And rats.

It was all getting old, growing tiresome. It all

seemed to weigh down on him, this city, this life. Especially his wife, Greta Kirby. She was always whining about something. All week she'd been up Ron's butt about why he was coming home late. She suspected an affair. He knew it. But the truth was not so tawdry, just depressing. The truth was he'd been laid off from his job in the meat packing district two weeks ago and had yet to find another one. All the jobs at the Chelsea Pier were taken, and the storehouses were over-employed. It would change during the winter, he knew, since there was always someone who got tired of the cold, but that was a ways off. Rent was due now. Rent to keep living in this trash heap of a neighborhood.

He turned from the graffiti, looked up at the sky, looked for a familiar face in the night clouds. God, an angel, someone to hear his pleas. "C'mon, just give me this gig tonight."

He couldn't tell his wife he was jobless because she'd just call him a loser. She'd done that enough lately. He was tired of it. All he wanted was a new job, a better paying job, one that would put extra cash in his pocket.

His marriage was strained, sure, but that didn't mean he couldn't salvage it. He still loved his wife, after all. Still remembered their wedding day, how young and angelic Greta had looked. Her working two shifts at the laundromat had put so many lines in her face she looked like a road map, but he saw past the aging. He still remembered.

If he could just get this new job, some money, he could buy her something nice. They could start over. She wouldn't think he was a loser.

"Try the night shifts," his buddy Carlo had said. "Some places pay more. No one wants those shifts, the roaches come out in swarms, the drifters steal your food, but they offer incentive."

"Know what, Carlo? You might not be as dumb as you look."

That's what he'd been doing these past weeks. Interviewing at night. Problem was the bars were never closed in this city, and bad interview after bad interview had landed him in whiskey and vodka and passed out on a park bench, crying. Greta had told him she'd called the police a few times, worried about him. But he'd played it off with talk of overtime and double shifts and falling asleep in the break rooms. She mumbled something about other women, and he told her not to worry about what he was doing.

He decided to walk tonight. He was feeling okay about himself. The law of averages said he was due for good news. Greta had been asleep on the couch when he'd left. She looked peaceful for once. He didn't want to disturb her. He kissed her forehead before grabbing his coat.

He passed the Cleveland Diner. Two bums were drinking against it. It made him angry. They seemed to be coming out of the woodwork lately, these lowlifes. Through the front window he watched the waitress cook some eggs. She looked pretty. She usually did. Maybe he'd stop in after the interview, have some celebratory sausage.

The subway was at the end of the block. He noticed more bums hovering around the stairs. Boy, they were just everywhere lately.

"Outta my way," he told them, shooing them away like flies.

"What's your problem, mister! We ain't hurtin nothin."

"You smell. You're dirty. Get a job!"

"Whatever, mister. I wouldn't go down there, I was you. Bad sounds down there. It ain't right."

Ron Kirby ignored them, descended the stairs into the station. The humid air of the underground subway system washed over him. The stench of urine and grime. He removed a token from his pocket and paid the turnstile. The MBTA worker behind the token booth didn't even look up from her magazine.

As the train arrived, he noted he was the only one on the platform. Nothing new about that, it being kind of late, except that as the doors to the train opened he swore he heard a scream come from out of the blackness of the tunnel.

★★★

"You're certainly qualified, Mr. Kirby, but unfortunately, we're just too full right now. Can you come back in a couple months?"

Ron held back the desire to pound his fist on the man's desk. "But you told me on the phone you could use some extra help."

"I realize that, but I misjudged our output. These things, they're not always so easy to tell from one minute to the next, but I ran the numbers again . . . Like I said, in a few months—"

"In a few months I'll be homeless and divorced."

"I'm sorry to hear that. If I could offer you something I would. I swear. But I just can't fit it into the budget now that I see the new numbers. Give me a call in two months, we'll take another look at our schedule."

Biting his tongue, Ron Kirby stood up from the plastic folding chair that had been placed in front of the hiring manager's desk, and thought about walking straight to the bar. Never before had he wanted a drink so badly, and he always wanted a drink.

As he exited the warehouse, he thought, no. No bar tonight. Tonight I'm gonna go home and tell Greta about everything. I owe her the truth. She'll hate that I lost my job, but I'll tell her I still love her, and that I still find her beautiful, and that I'm aware I drink too much, but that I'm going to get my act together. I'll tell her that first thing in the morning I'm going to scour the city for work. If I have to be a rat catcher in the subway, that's what I'll do.

He looked at the sky, looked for a friend. "Okay, I get it now. You're telling me it's time to start new. I get it. And you know what? You're right. You always are."

He was angry, but he knew it was time to throw in the towel, put pride to the wayside. With resignation came acceptance, and with acceptance came hope. His life would be different come morning, and that was a good thing. He was adaptable. He could learn new trades. Life was about new experiences. Yes, he thought, this is a good thing.

When he got off the subway train it was almost two in the morning. Greta would have moved to the bedroom by now. Most likely she had noticed he was gone and would be furious when he came in, but he'd deal with it.

The train rumbled off into the tunnel, disappeared from sight. He was alone on the platform once again. The stained subway tile stared back at him apathetically. Here too, someone had sprayed graffiti in nonsensical fonts. The lights overhead flickered, a surge from the trains scouring the underground. He faced the rails, watched a rat scurry along the far wall looking for a hole to escape into. *I know the feeling,* he thought. The rat continued on along the base of the wall and disappeared into the blackness of the tunnel.

"Rat catcher," he whispered. Sure, why not, it was still a job. As long as he could make things right with Greta, what did it matter? Perhaps he'd ask the woman in the booth how to apply.

But the woman in the booth was gone. The window was cracked and a single rivulet of blood was dripping down it on the inside.

"What the . . . "

He moved to the side of the booth, saw that the door was open. The hinges looked bent. Inside, the booth was empty. No woman. Just a tuft of hair and a broken necklace. The magazine she'd been reading earlier was spread open on the ground, like a bird that had been shot out of the sky. A single dot of blood on the page.

Maybe it was nothing. Maybe she went to the bathroom. Maybe some bum threw a rock at the window and she went to get a manager. It could be anything.

He jumped as a scream wailed out of the tunnel. The hairs on the back of his neck went rigid.

"Hello?" he mumbled, his eye darting back and forth between the booth's empty interior and the darkness of the train tunnel. The scream had sounded almost human, but could have just as easily been a train in the distance.

He scanned the platform again, as if people might suddenly appear and help him. But no one came. He was alone with the rats and cockroaches. And an MBTA booth that looked suspiciously like there'd been a possible struggle.

As if by divine intervention, one of the homeless men from the top of the stairs appeared. "See what we mean. Things aren't right down here."

Ron grabbed the man by his crust-covered collar, pointed at the booth, putting two and two together now. "She's hurt. Don't just stand there, go call the police! Go!"

The bearded man's eyes went wide, as if he was more afraid of Ron than the darkness of that tunnel. "Don't go down there, mister."

"Go!"

Ron shoved him, and the man took off up the stairs.

He stood in the dark, thinking of Greta, about how she was going to be so angry with him in the morning. But maybe not if he proved he still had something to give. Maybe this was his true calling, public service, helping the little man. Sure, he didn't much like people, but he liked feeling worthy. He knew now he was destined for something better than shipping and receiving, he knew the world was waiting for him to play to his real strength. The scream came again. Distant, lonely, full of agony.

I can do this, he thought. I can be useful. I can help. I have something to give.

He made his way to the end of the platform, looked down into the dark tunnel, saw the tracks curve away into nothing. He listened, making sure no train was approaching. Then, cautiously, he lowered himself off the platform, made his way along the rails, keeping close to the wall. Every few feet there was a niche he could duck into if the train came, though it looked like it would be a very close call—any loose clothing would easily be snagged by the train and he'd be dragged across the tracks until his face was rubbed off.

This is insane, he thought. What am I doing?

But the scream came again, far off. "Hello!" he yelled. "Can you hear me? The police are coming! Whatever is going on down there better stop!"

He inched forward, smelling urine-soaked concrete and dirt. He moved quicker now, feeling along the wall for the indents, praying he didn't need to press inside one. This time of night, the train only came every twenty minutes or so. He still had at least ten. That should be enough to get to the next station.

But as he found himself deeper in shadow, he felt a hole in the wall. Air rushed out of it, stale and stinking of trash. This must be one of the passages the homeless used to get around. He knew there was no parallel train to this one, so whatever was in the hole must be an access passage of some sort. Or it could simply be an abandoned tunnel; the subway was full of them.

He stuck his head inside, seeing nothing but black. Without a flashlight, he was blind. Best he could do was shout that help was on the way. "If you can hear me, the police are coming!"

In response, he heard the gurgle of a choking victim. Fear raced down his back. This was a bad idea. He thought he had it in him to show the world he was a contributor, but just like his interview, he was realizing he was useless.

He turned from the opening and looked back the way he'd come. It was lighter, and he could barely make out an opening in the distance. He should just head back. Wait for the police. He wasn't useful after all.

And to make it worse, now he was in the middle of a subway track, one of the stupidest things a New Yorker could do.

He heard shuffling on the other side of the opening. He heard labored breathing, wheezing, what sounded like wet gulps for air.

Don't be a wimp, he thought. Think about Greta, think about how proud she'll be of you for once. Go in there and get that woman. Take her away from whatever sick homeless mole person was harassing her.

Okay, he decided, I'll just peek inside, see what I see.

Tentatively, he stepped inside the hole in the wall. Once on the other side, he felt hot air against his neck. Someone was right next to him. He turned.

Two glowing eyes met his.

His neck exploded in pain.

Greta would never believe him.

He saw her face as his mind swam.

It was blotted out as a massive green claw covered his face.

This city, he thought, it always gets you in the end.

D.A.T.E. N.I.G.H.T.

DAVID ROBBINS

THE PURPOSE TO *life is to live.*

Angela Swinton repeated her mantra over and over as she put on eyeliner and applied her lipstick and gave her hair a last brush. It helped to keep her focused. Otherwise she might weaken, might lose her resolve and not go out.

All done, Angela stepped to the full-length mirror on her bedroom door. "The purpose to life is to live," she said, and smoothed a crease in her dress. She didn't look her age. In low light she would look even younger.

Taking her purse from the table, Angela paused to reread the Post's headline: C.H.U.D. SWEEP NETS THREE MORE MONSTERS. She shuddered and bowed her head. "I must be very careful."

Locking the apartment, she went down the hall to the elevator. It stopped at the second floor and Mrs. Ferguson joined her. Ferguson was taking her trash down, in her frumpy bathrobe, no less.

"Angela, dear. It's been a while."

DATE NIGHT

"It will be two weeks tomorrow."

"How do you remember things like that?" Mrs. Ferguson said. "You must have a really good memory. Is that why you're a teacher?"

"I teach because I love kids," Angela said. "When I was eleven I lost my little sister. She ran into the street and was struck by a car. I cried for a month. She was so precious."

"I'm sorry for you," Mrs. Ferguson said. "Losing someone close is always awful."

Angela felt compelled to tell her more. "Later, after I married, we couldn't have kids no matter what we tried. Teaching was a way of making up for that."

"You have a husband? I don't believe I've ever seen the two of you together."

"The C.H.U.D.'s," Angela said.

"Oh, you poor dear."

"Not really. We never did see eye to eye. A bunch of them ate him alive in the subway."

"Did you see it?"

"Every last bite."

"What a strange way of putting it," Mrs. Ferguson said. "Well, here's the lobby. Take care." She trundled out.

Angela slung her purse over her shoulder. She would have liked to wear high heels for the added appeal but she chose loafers instead. Loafers were better for running.

Mrs. Ferguson was at the double doors. She had set the trash bag down and was fiddling with a key ring. "Here you are again." She stopped fiddling. "Wait. It just hit me. You're going out on the town this late?"

"Why not?"

"Are you serious?" Mrs. Ferguson was aghast. "It's past eleven. Those things hunt at night."

"The city has gotten rid of most of them."

"Dearie, don't you believe it. I hear stories all the time. People disappear right and left, and the government hushes it up. No one with a shred of common sense goes out at this hour."

"You're emptying your trash."

Mrs. Ferguson pointed. "The bin is three steps from the door. I'll be perfectly safe." She opened the doors and grabbed her trash bag. "Don't get eaten."

"I'll try not to."

At the end of the block Angela stopped and took several deep breaths. She was a little jittery. She always was on date night. The empty streets didn't help any.

"The purpose to life is to live," Angela resorted to her mantra, and kept going. She had the illusion of being in a city of the dead. Buildings loomed like giant tombstones. Grated storefronts and entryways reminded her of cemetery gates.

In the deathly quiet her footsteps seemed unnaturally loud.

Four blocks would bring her to Riverside. There would be traffic, and people. She started to pass an alley when from out of its depths came a flurry of thumps and a gurgling that ended in a gasp. Stopping, she peered into the shadows and glimpsed movement.

Angela ran. She couldn't say for certain it was a Cannibalistic Humanoid Underground Dweller—as the government or somebody had branded them—but she couldn't say it wasn't, either. She didn't stop until she was sure she wasn't being pursued.

Angela's purse strap had slipped from her

shoulder. She slid it back and continued on, but hadn't gone far when she heard a grating noise, as of metal on a rough surface.

Out in the middle of the street, a manhole cover was rising.

Angela willed her legs to move but they wouldn't.

Huge, inhuman hands, ridged with deformed sinew, slowly lifted the heavy cover. Under it, a pair of eerily glowing eyes swiveled back and forth. The creature was looking for something to eat. Make that someone to eat.

Smothering an outcry, Angela flew faster than before. The C.H.U.D.'s were immensely strong and had dagger-like teeth and sharp claws, but they were so heavy with mutated muscle, they couldn't move all that fast. She glanced back and saw the thing had clambered out of the manhole but instead of coming after her, it turned and lumbered into the night.

Angela didn't stop until she reached Riverside. She was sweating and her side ached but she didn't care. Now her night could truly begin.

Taking a few moments to put herself together, Angela moped her brow and rearranged her dress. As incentive, she took her perfume out and sprayed a little here and there.

A passing car honked.

The club was only a block down, atop it a blazing sign that announced to the world Anything Goes.

"I couldn't agree more," Angela said.

A doorman in a lavender jacket opened the door for her and she was enveloped by the pulsing thrum of the music. A guitar launched into a riff that shook the rafters. Attached to them were strobes that flashed in rainbow hues. Out on the dance floor writhing forms gyrated, while randy satyrs and nubile vixens lined the bar.

Bobbing her chin in time to the music, Angela moved to the near end.

"Well, hello, gorgeous."

Angela couldn't believe her luck right out of the gate. He wasn't much over twenty with a mop of brown hair, his eyes devouring her as if he had a sweet tooth and she were candy.

"Hello yourself," Angela said. It was as clichéd as it got but her need trumped the banality.

"That's one hot outfit."

"Glad you like it," Angela said as seductively as she knew how.

He grinned and squared shoulders he didn't have. "I'm Lance."

Angela said the first name that popped into her head. "Janis."

"Pleased to meet you. Can I buy you a drink?"

"My knight errant."

"Your what?"

"Never mind." Angela told him what she wanted. When the drinks came, she beckoned him closer.

"Nice perfume," Lance said.

"What do you do for a living?" Angela asked to keep him from getting ahead of her game.

"I work at a broker's. Moving up the ranks, as they say. You?"

"I'm a teacher. I work with special needs kids."

"Special needs," Lance said, as if he knew what that meant. "I have a special need of my own," he added with a leer.

DATE NIGHT

Angela was wary of jumping the gun but she took a gamble. "Listen. I didn't come here for small talk. I came to hook up. You interested?"

"Hubba, hubba, hot stuff."

Wondering if the guy managed to pick up more than two women a year, Angela suggested, "What say we quit the bump and grind? I have a place about eight or nine blocks from here."

"Lead on."

She welcomed the night air. They were barely outside when Mr. Hot-to-Trot tried to cop a feel. She warded him off with, "Cool your jets, naughty boy. We have a ways to go. I promise the wait will be worth it." She offered her arm.

"Whatever you say, sexy."

Angela knew he was being magnanimous because he was confident he would score. She headed up Riverside, taking her time. She always enjoyed this part: the suspense, the thrill.

"You got quiet all of a sudden," Lance said.

Gazing skyward, Angela admired the stars. "You ever wonder what we're here for?"

"Huh?"

"Our purpose in life."

"How would I know?" Lance said. "I sell stocks. I watch movies. I go to clubs. I guess you could say my purpose in life is me."

"There's a lot of that going around," Angela said. "I think our real purpose is to make the most of what we have."

"And I have you," Lance said.

"Not yet you don't." Forcing a laugh, Angela kissed him on the cheek. "To keep you interested."

"No worries there."

"I didn't think to ask. You're not married, are you? No kids or anything?"

"Puh-lease. I'm having too much fun to tie myself down. There's me and only me."

Angela grinned. "That's more than enough."

They were almost to the light. It changed, and Angela firmed her hold and practically pulled him into the crosswalk. He slowed slightly as they neared the other side and stopped once they reached the sidewalk.

"Hold on."

"Something the matter?"

"Where are you taking me?"

"I told you. My place."

Lance regarded the street ahead with trepidation. "I thought we'd be heading uptown, not this way. It's awful run-down."

"Are you a mouse or do you have a pair?" Angela teased. "I get around fine."

"I don't know."

"I'll protect you," Angela said, and giggled. "Think of me as your very own Wonder Woman."

"Who?"

Clasping his hand, Angela tugged while puckering her lips invitingly. "You coming or not?"

Lance hesitated, then said, "We only live once, right?"

Angela picked up the pace. This was the dangerous stretch. The C.H.U.D. she had seen earlier was likely still around, and there might be others.

Lance kept glancing right and left and hung back a little where the gloom was deepest.

Luck favored them for five and a half blocks.

Angela was hoping they would make it all the way when the chuff-chuff-chuff of heaving breathing, startlingly near, galvanized her into gripping Lance's wrists and pulling him down a flight of steps into a recessed doorway.

"What are you . . . ?" Lance blurted.

"Shhh," Angelia whispered, putting her finger to his lips. "Don't you hear that?"

Lance did. The whites of his eyes showed and he pressed back against the door.

The sickly sour odor of the C.H.U.D. filled the air. Angela's blood turned to ice as a pair of feet appeared on the sidewalk above. Slimy, obscene caricatures, they squished slightly with each step. She held her breath as the creature came abreast of their hiding place.

And stopped.

The C.H.U.D. sniffed a few times, its hideous feet turning from side to side as the creature tested the wind.

Angela felt Lance tremble violently. He was terrified. It wouldn't take much to make him bolt. She saw him open his mouth to scream and clamped her hand over it to keep him from giving them away.

The C.H.U.D. uttered a low growl.

Please, please, please, Angela prayed, go away. It's not just for me.

A dreadfully tense minute ended when, with a grunt, the C.H.U.D. shuffled off, its ponderous steps gradually fading.

Lance angrily pushed her hand from his face. "I've had it," he whispered. "I'm getting out of here. You're going to get us killed."

Angela pressed against him. "You'd let a little thing like that spoil our night?"

"Little?" Lance was incredulous.

Angela touched her lips to his neck. "In this part of town, you learn how to survive. Besides, we're closer to my place than we are to the club. Do you really want to go all the way back when in a few blocks we'll be safe and cozy and can have our fun?"

"Well . . . " Lance said, and he looked her up and down yet again. "Your place is close?"

"Cross my heart," Angela said, and did, knowing his eyes would be drawn to her chest.

"All right. But you better be worth it after all I'm going through."

Taking his hand, Angela cautiously climbed the steps. "The coast is clear. Are you up to running the rest of the way?"

"Sure," Lance said without much enthusiasm.

Angela was in good shape. She had to be, as many risks as she took on her excursions. She ran full out, knowing he would be intent on keeping up and not have time to think about much of anything else.

Lance stayed beside her until she veered into an alley. Glancing apprehensively at the towering walls, he said, "How much farther?"

"We're there."

The door had not seen a new coat of paint in decades. Angela fished the key out of her purse and inserted it.

"This dump looks deserted." Lance was staring at the dark windows on the upper floors. "How many people live here, anyway?"

"A few." Angela opened the door and gestured for

him to precede her. "What are you waiting for? A Cannibal to come by?"

Lance scooted past. A single bulb lit the entry. He moved to the stairs leading up and looked at her expectantly.

Shutting and locking the door, Angela stepped to the stairs leading down. "I'm in the basement." She descended, swaying her hips more than she normally would.

Lance was scowling when they reached the third sub-level. At the fourth, he halted. "How much lower does this go?"

"One more floor. Is there a problem?"

"Yeah. A big one. You might have heard of it," Lance said sarcastically. "It's called the Underground. It's where all that toxic waste was dumped. You know. The stuff that turned those homeless people into those Humanoids. The lower we go, the closer we'll be to where they live."

"I know all about the Underground," Angela said. "I used to teach down there."

"What?"

Angela placed her hand on his arm. "I told you I was a teacher. Before the outbreak I conducted classes for the kids of those homeless people. The State paid me a pittance but it was worth it. They were so eager to learn. So precious."

"Good for them," Lance said.

"Come on. You've made it this far." Angela continued down to the last landing. She unlocked the door and switched on the light. "After you."

"What's this?" Lance said. "I thought you were bringing me to your apartment?"

The furnishings consisted of an oak desk, an old couch with thick cushions, half a dozen bookshelves, and a folding table piled high with pens and paper and other supplies.

"This is where I taught out of," Angela said. "I stay here overnight now and then. It's quiet and we won't be disturbed." She grinned and winked. "That couch is more comfortable than a bed."

"I guess it will do."

"Would you like something to drink?" Angela said. "A beer? I have some in a small fridge."

"Would I ever," Lance said, looking around. "Where?"

Angela indicated a door at the other end of the room. "In the back. I keep it stocked for occasions like this."

"Occasions?" Lance said and snorted. "You sure do talk like a teacher."

Angela crossed to the door. Instead of a lock there were three large bolts and a latch. She threw each bolt, then worked the latch. Sticking her head in, she turned to him. "The light has gone out. You don't happen to have a flashlight, do you?"

"I don't believe you, lady" Lance said, coming over. "How hard can it be to open a fridge and take out a beer in the dark?" He chuckled and stood in the doorway. "Damn. You're right. It's pitch black. I can't see a thing."

As he was talking, Angela took several swift steps back. Extending her arms, she ran at him as fast as she could and slammed into him with all her might. Lance yelped in surprise. There was a thud and another sharp cry and a string of curses, ending in, "What the hell?"

DATE NIGHT

Angela reached around and flicked the switch to the spotlight.

A short cement lip ended in a sheer drop of more than ten feet to subway tracks so old and rusted, they hadn't been used in a century. Past the tracks was another high wall, cracked and pitted from long neglect. The circle of light was the only illumination in the black maw of a tunnel that receded into the unknown.

Lance stood by the rails, a hand pressed to a leg, grimacing and gazing about in bewilderment. "What is this?"

"An abandoned spur," Angela said.

"No. I mean, what is this? Why'd you knock me off? What are you up to? Are you some kind of sicko?"

"I keep telling you," Angela said, bending and picking up an object near the door. "I'm a teacher."

"What's that you've got?"

Angelia held it by the handle, gave it a slight shake, and it clanged. "A cowbell."

"A what?"

"In the old days farmers used them to call in cows for milking," Angela explained. "And teachers used them to call their students to class." She shook harder, the cowbell's loud peals echoing and reechoing down the tunnel.

"Get me out of here, dammit. This isn't funny."

"It's not supposed to be."

"Lady, if I ever get my hands on you . . . "

Angela went on clanging, paying no attention to Lance as he tried, again and again, to jump up and catch hold of the top of the wall. She watched the tunnel in both directions, and it wasn't long before the first of the glowing eyes appeared. More quickly followed, none over three feet off the ground. Soon there were thirty pairs or more.

Lance shook a fist at her. "Stop with that bell."

"I might as well."

Lance saw the eyes. Recoiling, he looked the other way and saw more. Sheer terror contorted his face. He made a desperate leap but again fell short. A sob escaped him and he screamed, "Why? Why? Why?"

Angelia smiled benignly. "They were such adorable kids. I used to call them my little cuddles. Now I call them my little C.H.U.D.DLES. Get it?"

Lance wasn't getting anything. Keening hysterically, he hobbled over the rails to the opposite wall and frantically tried to climb it. He was still trying when the mutated children reached him.

Angela always found this part fascinating. How the children closed on their meal and tore at him with their teeth and claws. How they shredded his clothes and the flesh underneath, blood spraying and spattering all over. Lance fought but was helpless against so many. He shrieked and screeched as they ripped and rent and tore at their meat. A small creature ripped an ear off and hungrily chewed. Another buried its fangs in Lance's belly, and when it straightened, intestines dangled from its mouth.

Angela stayed until only bones remained. The mutations looked up at her and raised their small claws and hissed and snarled as if begging for more.

"Soon, my little C.H.U.D.DLES," Angela promised, and blew them a kiss.

S.T.R.A.N.G.E. G.O.D.S.

CHRISTOPHER FULBRIGHT AND ANGELINE HAWKES

A **GUTTED DOG**, flies swarming the carcass, lay stinking in their path. The three of them avoided stepping in the gore.

Suppressing the rising vomit in her throat, Addy choked. Her skirt bunched in her hand, she stepped over rusted cans and shredded cardboard. "Are we almost there?"

"Gettin' there," came the gruff response. Jake Last Name Unknown served as their sewer tour guide. It was a tenuous arrangement. He only agreed to the job in exchange for money and a promise of free food at the church pantry.

Addy had been visiting the underground labyrinth for a few months. This time she came to the odorous maze with both Jake and a social worker assigned to partner with Addy's church in order to match charitable programs with the "undergrounders," as the homeless beneath the city were called. The social worker was interested in the physical needs of the homeless; Addy was focused on the spiritual.

Deep in thought, Addy fondled the crystal hanging around her neck. A metallic crunch jolted her, as the social worker kicked some sort of electronic device and almost lost her balance.

"Watch where you're goin', Lady!" Jake snapped.

"What's this?" Addy picked it up, ignoring Jake's rude tone. It looked like a Geiger counter.

"You find that junk all over down here." Jake looked at the broken device in Addy's hand. "You'd be surprised what we find. Lately, there's been a lot of those scientist suits. Mostly ripped up."

"You mean hazmat suits?" the social worker asked.

"Yeah, that's the word." Jake glared at the woman but avoided eye contact with Addy. "Sorry I'm not a fancy college degree like you. I don't know all your big words."

"Hazmat isn't a big word. You don't have to have a degree to know it. If you're seeing a lot of hazmat suits, then someone must have dumped hazardous trash down here. Maybe a medical facility? That seems dangerous."

"Lady, everything down here's dangerous." Jake laughed. His teeth were rotten, neglected by time and misfortune. He stopped short, looking around as if finding his bearings. The sewer passages converged on the tunnel before them. There were six options. He sniffed and scratched himself. "I think it's this way."

"You think?" The social worker sounded perturbed. "Could get awful gritty down here if you take us in the wrong direction."

"I'm sure Jake knows where we're going." Addy laughed, lightening the conversation. At the very best, Jake seemed bi-polar. He switched from polite above ground, to erratic and mean here below. She didn't want him refusing to take them any farther due to the other woman's words. Addy's mission was to cleanse the dirty energy beneath the city. She needed Jake.

Jake frowned, his thick uni-brow furrowed.

"It's okay, Jake. You're doing a wonderful job!" Addy encouraged.

Jake chose a tunnel and pointed with a grunt, indicating they should follow.

This tunnel was narrower. Dark sludge glopped along in a putrid stream around their feet.

"Stop here, please," Addy said. She reached into her bag, pulling out a bowl and a bottle. She set the bowl on the sewer floor and poured water into it.

"What's that?" Jake asked.

"Salt water. I'm going to cleanse the energy in this tunnel." Addy closed her eyes, meditating. She removed the crystal from around her neck. She moved it through the air like she was writing while waving her empty hand in a circular motion. Occasionally, she stopped to flick her hands toward the bowl.

"Now what're you doing?" Irritation was evident in the man's voice.

"The water is neutralizing the dirty prana." Addy swept the area five more times, flicking her wrist toward the bowl at the end of each sweep. She exhaled slowly as she worked to clean the energy.

"What's a prana?" Jake asked, resting against a jutting pipe.

"It means life force. Comes from the Sanskrit."

The social worker's eyebrows arched in annoyance as she addressed Addy, "Will this take long? I need to get on with it. I have a full load today."

"Not long." Addy hummed and waved. Hummed and flicked.

"I seen someone do that at your church. Before we have sandwiches."

"Yes, at the Church of the Healing Prana, we keep a clean life force. We draw positive energy from nature. This city is choked with dirty energy and if we don't cleanse it there will be diabolical consequences."

"You done yet?" Jake asked.

Addy poured the water into the sludge and dried the bowl with her skirt. She put the items into her tote and the crystal around her neck.

"Is that expensive?" Jake jabbed the air in front of her neck with his grimy finger.

"Clear quartz. Every stone cleanses—"

Jake lunged and yanked the cord, snapping it.

"Ah!" Addy shouted, taken by surprise. She grabbed her neck.

"What the—?" the other woman interjected.

"Both of you, shut up. You—give me your rings."

"These are for—"

"I don't care what they're for, you loopy nut job. Give 'em here!" Jake pulled a knife from his jacket.

"Here, take them!"

"And you—give me the purse!" Jake grabbed the strap from the social worker's shoulder.

"Hey!"

"Shut it. Both of you. Over there." Jake shook the knife toward the left side of the tunnel.

Addy looked frantically around. There were tunnels going in either direction, but both faded into ebon shadow. There were no lights in one corridor. The other tunnel was blocked by Jake's bulky frame.

The tunnel behind them hummed with an occasional electric light and ended in a metal grate. They were trapped.

Jake took a roll of duct tape from a pocket. This robbery was premeditated.

"If you need money, we can get it at the church. Money and sandwiches? I'm the chief healer. I—"

"I don't give a crap if you're the Queen of mother frickin' England, lady, shut yer pie hole and move over there NOW!" He stood before them, a burly menace.

Addy began to chant loudly, faster and frantic. She waved her hands, praying for safety. She summoned protecting spirits, tapping into the sewer's energy. As she moved her hands, a presence filled the tunnel. A rank odor permeated the air. The terrified social worker shrieked and cowered behind a trembling Addy.

In front of them, behind Jake, a diabolical being emerged from the darkness. The demon spawn, black and abhorrent, outstretched mutant arms, roaring a primal sound. Addy watched in horror as the shadow-beast opened its great maw, uttering a guttural screech as it was suddenly joined by a second creature.

Jake jerked around, staring at the monstrosities clawing and flailing wildly as they shrieked hideous howls which reverberated throughout the tunnels.

Addy shrank against the wall, still chanting, chanting, chanting, as the abominations pounced on the man, ripping him limb from limb, savaging his flesh as they feasted. Blood sprayed the tunnel, spurting into the river of sludge which turned from black to crimson at their feet.

2.

Karen sat a bowl of soup in front of the man. His disheveled head was down, face buried in the sleeves of his dirty coat. The soup's aroma stirred him to consciousness. He lifted his face, studying the bowl.

"Hey! Dr. Alexkavich? Valerius Alexkavich?" She immediately recognized her professor of Eschatological Studies. He was one of her favorite professors and had been absent from classes for two or three semesters now. No one really knew what happened to him.

"Who's asking?" Val said between spoonfuls, but then he set down the spoon, as he recognized his former pupil. "Karen?"

"Yes, it's me. Holy crap! Do you know how worried everyone has been?" Karen paused. There was a stereotypical brown bag and bottle perched on the table next to his elbow. She lowered her voice as she sat across from him. "I'm so sorry about your wife."

"Yeah. Me, too."

"It's just, one day, well, you were just gone—"

"Had to get away." Val ran his hand through his dirty hair. "It was all too much."

"Did the police—"

"Exhausted all leads. Found her car. Her body was never found."

"I'm so, so sorry." Karen handed him another bottle of water. "So, you've just been living here at Reverend Shepherd's then?"

"Mostly underground. Come here to eat. Sometimes sleep."

Karen nodded, and then hesitantly, "Uhm, I don't know how you feel about this, but, well, I've been going to these meetings. I, um, I was feeling wrong about life. You know, about my purpose? What I'm supposed to be doing? So, I met this cool chick named Zah. She runs these meetings in the heart of the city." She laughed. "Well, really it's an abandoned part of the Victorian era sewers, but Zah says it's the heart of the city where the city's energy lies."

Val watched her as he ate.

"Anyway, I've been going for a few months. Zah helped me find peace. Now, this might sound really messed up, but we worship two gods named Gog and Magog. They are ancient gods for a modern era. They bring purpose. There are different levels of purity humans need to reach to let go of their old lives and find their true paths."

"Like destinies?"

"Yeah. Just like that. I've been working to achieve the level of 'Purification of the Soul.'"

Jaded, Val smiled. "So, what, you get a trophy?"

Karen laughed nervously. "This is serious, Dr. Val."

"I'm sorry, go on."

"So, tonight, I will give myself to the gods. There's a ceremony: a union. The gods take my mortal vessel, make me pure, and allow my soul to live on a higher plane."

"Give yourself to them? Like what? Some sort of kinky sex? Sounds like a harem or something."

She shook her head. "I've never seen the ceremony. Yes, there's sex, but that's okay. It's pure. I think you should come. You won't be able to stay for the ceremony, but you can come for the message of peace and meditation before it. I think it could really help you."

"Gog and Magog, huh? Which class did I have you in?" He frowned. "In the book of Ezekiel, in the Christian bible, Gog and Magog play a role in the apocalyptical myths. Any of this ringing any bells?"

Karen shook her head.

"During the end of days, Gog and Magog, along with Satan, lead armies against the Judeo-Christian god, Yahweh." Val sat straighter, seemingly concerned. "So, these friends of yours named their gods, Gog and Magog? Here's a bit from the book of Revelations: 'The beast that comes up from the Abyss will attack them . . . and kill them. Their bodies will lie in the street of the great city.' So, you have two gods—or imposters in suits, I don't know—down in the sewers, that this Zah person has named after two guys who are best friends with the Devil. I'm not sure how you think any of this is a good idea."

"It's not like that. It's not an abyss. It's clean."

"Hmm. Ancient cultures considered the abyss to be a subterranean dwelling for hordes of demonic warriors. You've got a meeting place underground, in the sewer, and two faceless gods, you've never seen, named Gog and Magog . . . and some 'cool chick' named Zah leading this circus. This equation doesn't add up to 'inner peace,' Karen. This sounds like some bad crap to me." Val put his spoon into his empty bowl.

"Just show up and listen to Zah's message. You don't have to come back if you don't like it."

Val shook his head. "Nope. Sorry. I hope they give you what you're looking for. I really do, but I've got enough situations in my life without adding more crazy."

"I—"

"Hey!" A.J. Shepherd shouted from across the room. "Karen? Are you serving soup or picking up a date?"

"Yeah, sorry, okay." Karen turned back to Val. "Well, think about it. I'm here for the next couple of months, if you change your mind."

3.

Through the shadowed tunnels he crept, following just behind her, just to the side of her, quietly, so she couldn't hear. Val side-stepped the human excrement, and the carcasses of rotting rodents, jumped over trash and forgotten pieces of someone's life. Karen was ahead, carrying a lantern, illuminating the filth-encrusted tunnels in a half-circle of battery-fueled light. The daft girl was humming some Top 40 number as she leapt over a dead rat.

The tunnel opened into a massive cathedral-like chamber. The old Victorian brickwork reminded him of medieval archways, beautiful craftsmanship. One look at the floor, bathed in feces and urine, reminded him, lest he forget, he was in a sewer. Karen mingled with the crowd, and then he lost track of her.

Val crept to a balcony-esque sewer pipe, far above the people. Dropping to his hands and knees, he stared down at an improbable scene. An altar stood in the center of the cavernous room, created from heaps of containers pulsing an unearthly green. He strained to make out the black letters on their sides: Contamination Hazard Urban Disposal. He whistled softly to himself. Hazardous Waste. A stone slab had been placed on top of the stacked containers. In the dimly lit room, the glow reminded him of a big green light stick—the kind you buy for kids during camping trips. His attention drifted from the obviously toxic altar to a larger than human-size statue made from some combination of radioactive sludge and clay. It was crude, looked like a child had formed it, but he could make out a hideous, frog-like being, which must be the representation of this Gog and Magog Karen had told him about. What sort of lunatics did she get mixed up with?

Aside from the pulsating frog-man statue and the makeshift altar, the rest of the room was lit with torches or flashlights. A metal barrel, which provided the most light, was ablaze close to the statue. As he studied the congregation of fools, he noticed they began to cluster, sitting on mats or old blankets. Their hands raised above their heads, the collective hive began to chant. They leaned against walls or lounged against each other like Romans of old, eyes closed, their words a monotone-ish hum.

Val took a swig from the bottle in his pocket. The warmth of the drink spread through his body, prompting him to take another drink, and another. He crawled into the darkness of the high tunnel, making sure he was out of anyone's line of vision. Figuring he was here for the long haul, he rolled onto his back, against a dry wall. The chanting continued, a blend of syllables and music, lulling him to sleep.

4.

Drip, drip, drip.

Val opened his eyes and stared upward into the darkness overhead. From some unseen location, cold water dripped slowly upon his face and down his neck beneath his collar. He rolled over onto his side and grew aware of a pounding beat emanating from the chamber. Thu-thump. Thu-thump. He could feel it through the bricks. Thu-thump. Thu-thump. The air around him pulsated like a heartbeat. Down below, drums were beating slowly, but now, quickening. The monotone chanting which lulled him to sleep began to crescendo into a cheering tone. Val lay on his stomach and inched forward, staring into the vile sanctuary. Standing behind the altar was a woman wearing an elaborate, wooden frog mask. It was painted dark green and would have been comical had it not been so terrifying a setting.

The mask. The name. "Zah is short for Zhaba!" he uttered. Zhaba was Russian for frog. So, the priestess of this wretched little congregation seemed familiar with at least one Russian word. More scripture from the Christian book of Revelations filled his mind: Then I saw . . . evil spirits that looked like frogs . . .

"My god, what is this?" Val whispered. The hairs on his arms stood as if electrified as the drums and chants continued. The woman in the mask, her black robes crudely stitched from rags, stood with arms upraised, behind the green-glowing altar and the worshipping cluster of misguided converts.

Frenzied, they began to remove their clothing,

gyrating around the toxic slab. Val couldn't take his eyes from the spectacle.

Then, he gasped.

Being led from the shadows, dressed in a white gown, was Karen, suspended, obviously drugged, between two acolytes also wearing frog masks and clad in black. The drums beat louder.

Karen couldn't even stand. The two acolytes brought her before Zah. Behind her, twisted laymen dragged forth three more women, also semi-conscious.

"It's time, my children!" Zah spoke in a loud voice. As she spoke, the followers dropped to their knees, raised their arms and swayed to the drumbeats.

"After many good works, these believers have attained the level of 'Purification of the Soul!' They are ready to complete the final step in their life transformation. Tonight, you will bear witness as they give themselves, body and soul, to our most holy gods, Gog and Magog."

The crowd chanted Gog and Magog, Gog and Magog, in a soft repetition.

"When purification has been achieved, Gog and Magog purify the soul of filth and misfortune. The gods come from the Abyss to purge this city of all that is unclean!"

A curtain was pulled back.

Val covered his mouth, stifling a scream. He struggled to remain silent in his revulsion.

Emerging from behind the curtain, were Gog and Magog, the blasphemous duo of destruction worshipped by these fiends. Standing about seven feet tall, they were black, frog-like in appearance, mutated limbs stretching longer than they should, with glowing orbs for eyes and mouths boasting jagged fangs which snapped hungrily for victims.

The commotion was sheer chaos as the monstrosities were released from their chains and allowed to fall upon the helpless women in white. Blood spurt through the room, flowing in torrents over the altar and in rivulets running in the mortar between the bricks on the floor. The crimson rivers spread, reaching farther across the chamber until the floor around the altar was red. There was nothing remaining of Karen and the other women save puddles of flesh when the beasts were finished.

Zah stood behind the ghastly scene, words of praise flowing from her masked face.

Abruptly, Gog and Magog dropped the grisly remains of their feast and looked up at him. They smelled him over the briny blood, over the unwashed supplicants, and over the stench of the sewer.

Zah and the others stopped chanting, staring upward to see what their demonic gods spied.

Instinct told him to run. Val dropped his bottle and turned into the tunnel, fleeing into the darkness. Gog and Magog leapt, supernaturally, from the chamber floor up into the pipe previously occupied by Val. The two creatures were close as he ran through the maze of pipes.

"Gog! Magog!" Zah's voice echoed through the concrete and brick corridors, calling her monstrous gods back to her. There was a familiarity to her tone: as if he knew her, had always known her. Her words felt comforting, strangely calming.

The two gods of the abyss halted their chase and turned around.

Val continued his flight, running, running, until, in the sludge of sewage, in a downward leaning tunnel, he lost his footing and slid, slid, like a cesspool waterslide, through the endless artificial night, and was spewed out onto a hard floor below.

Hands in the darkness, pulling him, lifting him. His feet dragged behind. His arms—jelly. The pounding drum matched the beat of his heart and the pulse of his blood. Thu-thump. Thu-thump. And then blackness swallowed him.

5.

"Hellooo," a woman's voice said a little too loudly.

Val rubbed his face with his hands, and then touched the side of his head. His skull felt as if he was being hammered with repeating blows.

"You took a nasty tumble," the voice said.

Val focused on the blurry face hovering above him. He sat up slowly. "Where am I?" Looking around, the realization sank in. He was still in the sewers. Old, red bricks separated by crumbling mortar created a cell. One end was walled up as if workers had sealed it a century earlier. The other end was blocked by a makeshift, crude wooden door. There were large gaps between the slats, allowing the prisoners inside to see the corridor leading to their cell. Nearby was another holding pen. Val could just make out the slumbering shapes of the miscreant gods, Gog and Magog. Their snoring was animal-like.

The woman smiled. "Don't look over there. You'll just worry yourself sick. How do you feel?"

"Cold. Wet. My head hurts. Where am I? How long have I been here?"

"They dragged you in here night before last. From the blood on your head, we figured you fell during the chase." She held up three fingers. "How many fingers am I holding up?"

"Three."

"Good. My name's Ellie, what's yours?"

"Val." He looked around the cell. "How many of you are here?"

"Well, there's me, and four others. With you, we're six." Ellie sat on an old rug and rested her head against the wall.

"Six?" Val rubbed his forehead. "Are you part of that crazy church out there, or what?"

"We're the 'or what' part. When there are no new converts to feed the beasts, they come get one of us."

Val groaned. "Who is this priestess anyway?"

"She calls herself Zah."

"Yeah, I got that part. Who is she? Where'd she come from?"

Ellie shrugged. "I don't really know her. Spent about an hour with her before all this madness happened. I think she was into the occult or something. I'm a social worker. I teamed up with her to come into the sewer. I was working on getting the undergrounders food and medical care. She was interested in cleansing the sewers of negative energy."

"Sounds like my wife," Val laughed.

"Anyway. She was a little hippy dippy, but I think she went over the edge when Jake, this homeless guy who led us into the sewers, pulled a knife on us and tried to rob us."

"That made her go coo coo for Cocoa Puffs?"

"Not exactly. She started chanting some hocus pocus protection spell, and suddenly our pals over there," Ellie nodded toward the sleeping gods, "showed up and ripped Jake to pieces, ate him in front of our eyes."

"Wow."

"Yep. Wow. I took off into the sewers—but those things—they obeyed Zah. Maybe she did summon them? I don't know. Maybe they think she fed them? This whole thing is nuts."

Val looked her over. She was skin and bones. "She feeding you people?"

"Not so much. We've been catching rats. Conway over there, he has a lighter. We start a little fire and grill the ones we catch."

"How long have you been here, for Cripe's sake?"

"Not sure. For me, a long while. At least a year, maybe? I'm just trying not to go insane. The waiting for death is the worse part."

Conway chimed in. "Crazy woman comes in here, or sends her goons, and grabs one of us and feeds us to those things right in front of the door there. You never know, when you see them coming, if they're coming to feed us or to feed us to those monsters."

Everyone grew quiet.

"So, what's Zah's plan, do you know?" Val asked.

"We've pieced together information. Zah wants to create a "pure race." She thinks her pets over there are unsullied by the evil of men. She brings women into the congregation, feeds them some line of level of purification and crap. Then, she presents them to Gog and Magog. She's been hoping they'll mate with the women, but so far, all the two do, is eat them. The few men you see in here were undergrounders who showed up in the wrong place at the wrong time. About Zah, one day she was wearing regular clothes, the next day she showed up wearing the frog mask and that crazy black mess of a robe. Obviously, sewing isn't in her skill set."

"Why are you still alive?" Val looked at her suspiciously.

"I don't know. My only explanation is she has some sanity left and hasn't killed me because we pseudo-worked together. I'm not an anonymous kill." Ellie shrugged.

"So, let me get this straight. Hippy chick, Zah, and you go into the sewers. Jake tries to rob you. Zah summons demons. Gog and Magog show up. Eat Jake. Zah wigs out. You're a prisoner. Zah creates an entire religion around these two mutants, and here we are?"

"That's about it, yeah. Sounds like a bad horror movie, huh?"

Val laughed. "Unfreakinbelievable."

Every head snapped toward the corridor leading to the door as they heard the clank of chains and echoing footsteps.

"They're coming. They're coming!" Conway cowered in the corner.

"Get back!" Ellie shouted.

6.

The door burst open, and several acolytes stormed into the cell. Seizing upon the closest person to the door, they dragged the unfortunate woman through the doorway, screaming and kicking.

Val listened in horror as he heard chains clanging to the brick floor. The woman continued to scream. She fought to break free from Zah's henchmen. Gog was being led by a dog-leash type chain right to their cell. Then Zah dropped the chain, and the monster descended upon the shrieking woman like a ravenous dog. Legs, arms, flesh, gore, and blood flew through the air, decorating the walls and floors with scarlet. The beast dropped to the floor and licked the spilled blood before Zah ordered him to come away.

The commotion died as Zah and her murderous cohorts left. The heavy breathing of the satiated god filled the air. The pile of steaming gore was left gelatinous upon the cold floor.

Val's heart beat wildly. "Why does she do it?"

"They get uncontrollable if she doesn't feed them every few days. She can really only control one at a time. Except for during the ceremonies, she usually only brings them out individually. She feeds them new converts or one of us. Occasionally, she throws a new person in here, like she did with you." Ellie pointed at him.

Val pulled his shirt over his face. The stench from the mutilated corpse was pungent and he fought the urge to retch. Conway wasn't so successful, emptying his mostly bile-filled stomach into the farthest corner of the cell.

"A few days ago, Tara, over there, heard a couple of Zah's people talking. Zah heard on TV that cops are canvassing the city due to a rash of missing persons. Zah's running scared. The cops might be onto her. Or onto the sewers anyway. It's going to be harder for Zah to feed her Pure Race Puppets," Ellie said sarcastically.

"She's going to be picking us off pretty fast if there aren't any more religious suckers."

"This is crazy. Why don't you people break out? Escape?" Val said, anger in his voice.

"We're half starved and half mad," Conway growled.

Val was so thirsty, his tongue stuck to the roof of his mouth. He spied a trickle of water running along the wall and shamelessly lapped at it, not caring if it might be sewer water. Once his mouth was wet, he turned to the terrified group. He was sweating profusely. The ache in his guts was unbearable—both from hunger, but more from the DTs. He shuddered. It was going on two days, with no liquor. He knew even worse was yet to come. If he was going to stand a chance of getting out of this hellhole alive, he had to act quickly.

"We have to team together and rise up, or none of us are getting out of here. Would you rather go out fighting, or go out as a meal for those two bastards?" Val rallied the trembling prisoners.

"We don't have any weapons," Tara said.

"Sure we do. We have bricks, we have wood, we have Conway's lighter. Most of all, we have desperation and fear. Are we going to do something—together—or are we going to sit here for another day, another week, another month, listening to the rats in the walls, and the panting of those demons in the dark?"

"How do we know Zah doesn't have more of them?"

Val grew serious. "Revelations 13:11: Then I saw another beast coming out of the Earth."

"Yeah, thanks for that buddy. I thought you were trying to instill us with hope and rainbows," Conway quipped.

"No rainbows, my friend. I'm not even sure there's much hope, but I know I don't want to go out on some dinner plate. I've got a plan. You people decide if you're going to be lambs or if you're going to bring the slaughter."

7.

Zah came through the corridor, her black gown flowing behind, with Magog eagerly pulling on his chain, leading her like a hideous mutt.

"She's coming!" Tara whispered.

Light illuminated the cell in slivers through the slats in the wood door. They extinguished their makeshift torches. Darkness hung heavy and dank around them save for the golden shards penetrating the black.

Zah unlocked the door, and threw it open, allowing Magog to enter the room first.

Val snapped from his detoxing anguish into sudden lucidity. The prisoners fell into position as rehearsed. And then they struck.

Some jumped Zah. Grabbing the chain, they twisted it around Zah's neck. Magog turned around, pulled by the resistance of Zah, and by the tugging caused by the prisoners. The shrieking mutant lashed into the darkness, swiping at whoever came near, his bellows shredding the stillness of the sewer.

Val knew they had to work fast. It was only a matter of seconds until Zah's people would hear the echoes of the attack through the tunnels and come running. The other prisoners held bricks, wood, whatever they could muster to use as weapons and began to pummel Zah. Magog pulled Zah into the corridor, back into the light of the hall torches.

Zah grasped the chain tightening around her neck, clawing at it, trying to pry it free. Magog reeled in the chain, bringing the priestess closer and closer.

"No, Magog—" Zah croaked between gasps and gurgles.

The demonic god did not listen, but fought to bring the flailing woman to his fanged mouth. Some of the prisoners made a run for it—disappearing into the sewer. Others clung to the chain, fighting Zah in a desperate attempt to kill her before she ordered her beast to kill them.

Magog yanked the chain violently toward himself. Zah was thrown into his chest, eyes lit with horror. Struggling with the beast made god, she was bent backward, her wood mask, tumbling over her head, onto the filthy floor.

Val gasped. "Addy!"

His wife looked in his direction, her horrified eyes meeting Val's, recognition and sanity, fleeting sanity, kicking in just for a moment, before Magog ripped her head from her body.

8.

Val stood rigid, frozen to the floor. Addy's headless body flopped in a spreading pool on the sewer floor as Magog disemboweled her, tossing loops of intestines like Christmas tree garland through the air.

Ellie grabbed Val's arm. "Come on!" She yanked him toward the tunnels.

Val allowed himself to be pulled. He ran, blindly, holding onto Ellie, weaving through the pipes, barely lit in some areas by buzzing electric lamps, groping along wet walls in other corridors until they found the light.

Behind they heard more screams as Magog found another meal. "No!" the voice echoed. It was Conway.

Ellie pulled him harder.

They heard the racing of feet—Zah's acolytes running to let loose the demons from the abyss. Screams, more screams, as the acolytes lost their protected status and joined the prisoners as Meat.

They kept running. Val heaved Ellie into a higher pipe, and she helped him scramble up after her. Running. More running. The ground was slippery with sewage. Rats ran beside them as if sensing the danger rapidly encroaching.

They reached a familiar part of the sewer. "This way!" he said, taking control and guiding Ellie toward a far passage.

"The Reverend. There's a hole," he panted. "It comes out into the soup kitchen. Close."

They were almost there. The light was brighter. Reverend Shepherd had installed shop lights so the undergrounders could find their way into the soup kitchen.

"Here it is!" Val squirmed through the opening and reached for Ellie.

Half in, half out, she shouted. "Val!"

One of the creatures had her leg. It wailed and gnashed razor sharp fangs, as Val played a dangerous tug of war with Ellie's body.

Too late.

The demented wretch from Hell sank sharp teeth into her soft flesh, severing her leg from her torso in one vicious bite. "Go!" she screamed. "Save yourself!"

Val shook his head. "No. No!" He pulled her, but the beast was too strong. Ellie slipped from his grasp, her flesh slick with sweat, sewage, and blood.

"Go, Val!" Ellie faced her killer as the spawn of Satan crumpled her like a paper doll, blood spurting over the lamps, turning the white light in the room, pink.

9.

Val huddled in a fetal position in the corner of Shepherd's kitchen. He slept fitfully for a few days. Reverend Shepherd didn't wake his visitors. He just tossed an old blanket on them and let them sleep.

When Val finally stumbled to the table, he slurped the waiting bowl of soup like a starving man.

"Whoa, there! Slow down. You'll choke." Shepherd ladled more soup into Val's bowl. "I don't know where that girl, Karen, disappeared to. She signed up for a couple months of volunteering. Gotta do everything myself—"

Val grabbed the knife beside his bowl and slipped it into his pocket.

The Reverend frowned. "All you undergrounders wanting weapons. What's going on with you?"

Val continued to eat, gnawing at his bread.

Reverend Shepherd went around the room, trash bag open, cleaning up paper cups, cardboard pizza boxes, and soda cans. He placed the bag against the wall. It hung open; a bundle of black rags wadded inside, a broken, wooden frog mask tumbled out.

Val jumped to his feet. "Revelations. Revelations. It is written: The beast that comes up from the Abyss. It will kill them. Their bodies will lie in the street—"

"Come on, Val, settle down. Eat your soup."

"It is written!"

"Sure, Val. Sure. It is written: Have some more bread." The Reverend smiled, tossing a roll onto Val's plate. Then he hauled the trash to the dumpster.

L.O.S.T. A.N.D. F.O.U.N.D.

GREG MITCHELL

1984

"**C**HECK AGAIN."

Barbara Dean tucked in the small, squirming frame in the overlarge bed. Stuffed animals sat protectively around a six-year-old girl whose bright blue eyes gazed up anxiously at her mother.

"Cindy," Barbara groaned. "We've been over this."

The girl pulled the covers to her chin, holding her favorite stuffed friend—Mr. Higgins, the sad-eyed, brown dog—to her tiny chest. Barbara surrendered with a sigh and raised her hands. "Okay, honey. I'll check again."

Barbara crouched to the floor and lifted the edge of the thick, fluffy comforter. With little interest, she scanned the dark space beneath her daughter's bed, spying nothing but one displaced shoe and a naked Barbie doll. Satisfied, Barbara rose to meet Cindy's probing glare. The child was breathless with anticipation, and Barbara smiled, desperate to comfort her frightened daughter. "The coast is clear."

Cindy lowered her blanket. "You sure?"

Barbara kissed the girl on the forehead. "Now go to sleep. Gramps will be here in the morning to pick you up. You two are going to have such an adventure! I'm actually kind of jealous, but don't tell Daddy, okay?" She winked and Cindy nodded, a grin finally replacing her worried scowl.

Cindy rolled over, snuggling up with Mr. Higgins, and Barbara quietly exited, pulling the bedroom door partly closed. Monsters-under-the-bed was a new one, and one that Barbara had not expected. She'd thought Cindy was too old for such fears. But over the last few weeks, Cindy had become increasingly convinced that some creature lurked down there, ready to attack as soon as the lights were off. At first, Barbara suspected Cindy was just creating excuses to forestall her bedtime, but now she considered that it could be her daughter's anxiety about her upcoming trip that was producing these macabre fantasies.

Barbara's father had made preparations to take Cindy to New York City to see the sights while Barbara accompanied her husband on a business trip. Cindy seemed excited about going to the big city at first, but as the date neared, the talk of lurking monsters increased. It was, after all, the girl's first time to be so far away from her parents—and for a whole week. Barbara just hoped Cindy could shake these fears long enough to enjoy the Big Apple.

Though Barbara had her own reasons for being apprehensive about Cindy's upcoming tour of New York.

She descended the carpeted staircase and crossed the living room, passing the stereo that softly played

LOST AND FOUND

Dan Hartman's "I Can Dream About You." She slipped the cream-colored phone receiver off its wall mount and punched in the numbers scrawled on a notepad nearby. While she waited, Barbara twisted the cord, her heartbeat accelerating.

"Come on," she muttered. "Pick up."

Art Finkle sat low on his orange, moth-eaten couch—the one with the broken springs that he'd rescued from a corner somewhere down past Lafayette. The ratty old thing still smelled of cat urine. Nevertheless, Art did his best to ignore the smell as he reclined his head against the misshapen headrest, taking a long puff of his glass pipe. From the small TV set, the soothing explosions and boisterous hero music of *The A-Team* proved the perfect soundtrack for getting high.

"I ain't gettin' on no plane, fool!" Mr. T decried to George Peppard on the screen.

"I don't get it," Tina interrupted, her long, slender legs arched over Art's lap. She wore only a tank top cut from an old sweatshirt, plus silky panties, and dabbed at her toenails with red polish. "See, he always says that, but they always end up getting him on the plane."

Art ignored the comment, putting in another rock of crack and lighting it for his girlfriend. She took a hit and rolled her eyes back in ecstasy.

Fred, the third party in the room, sat on a red bean bag chair across from the couch. The burnt-out ex-hippie was fat with age, his long unwashed hair balding on top, revealing a shiny dome. Fred was a relic from decades prior, still sporting the same tie-dyed shirt he swore he wore to Woodstock. The dude was a bum, passed from one pad to the next, crashing on his friends' couches all across Lower Manhattan or residing at Reverend Shepherd's soup kitchen. He was a leech, and Art's patience with the loser was fleeting, but Tina had a soft spot for the pathetic old man.

A cloud of sickly sweet reefer smoke swirled about Fred's head as he chugged on a fat blunt. His eyes were nearly shut in quiet contemplation as he blew out a fresh fog of fumes. "It just goes to show the ruin that comes from our best laid plans," he pontificated in a slow drawl. "About how we are so quick to abandon our convictions when faced by the pressures of our peers."

Tina regarded him with something like amazement. "Yeah . . . Yeah, that makes sense."

Nodding at Mr. T on the screen, Fred raised a finger. "And on that note, I have a confession to make."

Fred lifted his leg and unleashed a slow, agonizing, wheezing fart. Instantly, a dreadful new tang pierced the already noxious air. The hippie sighed in relief, while Tina pinched her nose and Art gagged.

"Aw, man!"

"Sorry, bud," Fred grinned. "Those enchiladas were barking. Been holdin' that one in way too long."

The phone on the stand by the couch rang. Tina waved away the poisonous odor and reached over to answer it. Still coughing, she snapped, "Hello?"

Art swallowed hard, glowering at Fred. "Not cool, man. Not cool at all."

Fred snickered and returned his attention to the television.

Tina spoke quietly into the phone, "Uh . . . o-okay. Y-Yeah, sure, hold on a second."

LOST AND FOUND

She pressed the phone to her chest, her voice a harsh whisper. "Art, it's your sister."

Tina might as well have said that Barbara was in the room with them, for Art sprang up off the couch— "Hey, watch it!" his girlfriend objected—and shuffled about the room, disturbing the weeks' worth of beer cans and takeout boxes that littered the filthy floor. Panicked and overcome with a sudden, irrational anger, Art snatched the phone from Tina's grip and stepped away from the party.

He flapped at the blaring set. "Turn that down, huh?" Fred did, and Art tried to compose himself before answering. "Hey, uh, what's up, sis?"

"Just checking in to make sure that you remember that Dad and Cindy are coming into the city tomorrow night."

Art panicked, his eyes scanning the nudie calendar tacked to the far wall. "That's tomorrow?"

A disappointed sigh emanated from the other end. "Oh, Artie . . . "

His cheeks flushed. "Aw, c'mon, Barb, nobody calls me 'Artie' anymore."

"And nobody calls me 'Barb,' either."

"Look, I, uh, I didn't forget. Just messing with ya. Okay?"

"Please clean the place up," she scolded. Art nudged an empty beer can with his sock. "I don't want Cindy seeing your . . . lifestyle. Maybe Dad shouldn't, either."

He frowned, indignant. "Yeah, well, excuuuuse me. We can't all wear ties and loafers to the office every morning like Bill. Or afford cruises!"

"It's for work," Barbara groaned.

"Fancy work, then. Paid vacations. You married well, Barb. You really did. Maybe the rest of us ain't that lucky."

"I will not apologize for my life, Art. There is no shame in never having smoked or drank or done drugs or slept around. I married a good man who takes care of his family."

"Fine! Well I ain't gonna apologize, neither! You don't know how hard it is over here!"

"Made harder by the fact you sit around high all the time."

"I do not!" he railed, realizing he still clutched his pipe. He set it down, fuming.

"Artie, I'm sorry . . . I didn't call to fight with you. Cindy is really looking forward to getting to know her Uncle Art. You haven't seen her since she was a week old."

"I know, I know," he grouched.

"We all miss you. This trip means a lot to Dad, too. You didn't have a chance to make up with Mom before she died—"

He rubbed his brow, feeling tears threaten to emerge. "I know. I get it, alright?"

"I'm not putting all the blame on you. I'm just saying—he wants to see you. He wants to get to know you again. I do, too."

Art released a heavy breath. "Yeah. Okay."

"Have fun, okay?" she chuckled, trying to lighten the mood. "Take care of my kid. Show her a good time."

"Yeah, sis. Yeah, I will."

"I love you, brat."

Despite himself, he smiled, warmed by the sentiment. "Yeah. Love you, too."

LOST AND FOUND

★★★

Cindy sat cross-legged before the television set downstairs in her checkered shirt, jean overalls, and sneakers. Mommy had already packed her small red duffel, which rested beside her on the floor. In her lap, Mr. Higgins lounged as the two of them watched *The Smurfs*. Mommy was full of smiles, talking about the trip, asking Cindy a bunch of questions: "Are you excited? What do you think you will see? Won't you have so much fun?" Cindy didn't think so. She didn't want to leave. She didn't want to be away from her home and her room and her toys. Most importantly, she didn't want to be away from Mommy and Daddy. Just last month she'd turned six years old, and Cindy prided herself on being a big girl now—but the thought of leaving her parents reminded her just how little she really was.

Tears built in her blue eyes, but she blinked them away. Mommy didn't want her to cry. Besides, Mommy seemed nervous enough—Cindy didn't need to make it worse for her.

Mommy rushed through the living room, calling to Daddy in the other room as she put on her earrings. "Bill! Have you seen my black heels?"

"In the closet, I'm sure," he returned.

Mommy nearly tripped over her. "Cindy! Come on, turn this off. Gramps will be here any second—"

The doorbell rang. "There he is!" Mommy exclaimed. Then she shouted over her shoulder, "Bill, Dad's here."

Mommy shut off the TV and guided Cindy to her feet. "Come on, sweetheart, there's nothing to be scared about, alright? You are going to have the most amazing time in New York. I promise!"

Cindy slumped, but nodded, and followed her mother to the front door. Mommy opened it, and there was Gramps. He wore a beige plaid suit jacket and slacks and a tie. He had a kindly face and a single bald spot that parted an otherwise full head of salt-and-pepper hair. At the sight of Cindy's mother, he beamed and opened his arms.

"Daddy!" Mommy squealed.

"There's my girl," he growled, hugging her tightly. "How are you, sweetheart?"

"Good, good. Running late, but good."

Releasing her, he peered into the living room, spotting Cindy. As usual, he bent forward, meeting her at eye level. She always liked that about her grandfather. "Hey, honey! Are you ready to take a bite out of that Big Apple?"

Cindy shrugged, and Gramps rose, facing Mommy.

Mommy rolled her eyes and lowered her voice, though Cindy could still hear her perfectly fine. "She's a little jittery. I think she'll be fine once you get on the plane."

"Oh, I'm sure, I'm sure." To Cindy, "Well, the cab's waiting on us! You ready?"

Cindy clung to her mother's leg, frowning. Mommy rubbed her back, still talking to Gramps. "I called Art. He remembered you were coming."

Gramps raised his eyebrows. "He remembered?"

"Well, he remembers now."

"Ah."

"I think this can work, Dad. I think he wants it to work. Just don't kill each other, okay?"

Gramps lifted his hand dramatically. "Scout's honor."

"Oh!" Mommy left Cindy's side and rushed to the phone, yanking a sheet of paper off the nearby pad. "Here's his number, just in case you need to call him."

"Yes, Mother," he groaned, then grinned. She did, too.

"Love you, Dad."

"Love you, sweetheart."

Mommy crouched down before Cindy, smoothing out her long, brown hair. "Okay, sweetheart. Have a good time."

Cindy tried not to cry, and instead held her stuffed dog closer. Mommy ruffled the animal's fuzzy head. "You keep Cindy safe, do you hear me, Mr. Higgins?"

In Cindy's mind, the dog barked happily in agreement.

★★★

Art popped a cigarette in his mouth and lit it in a hurry as he marched down the sidewalk the next morning. Tina matched his brisk pace in her bright red cowboy boots, balancing the sack of groceries he'd just spent his last twenty bucks purchasing.

"Hey, slow down, will ya?" she whined. "You really think you need all this stuff?"

He took the cigarette out of his mouth and gestured wildly with it. "Ha! You don't know Barb. Trust me, she has ways of finding stuff out. Can't have that kid coming over and not have anything to feed it, yeah?"

"Her," Tina corrected.

He slid to a stop. "What?"

"The kid. She's a 'her,' not an 'it.'"

"Whatever!" Huffing, he moved on, smoking like a train. "The heck am I supposed to do with a kid? I ain't exactly the fatherin' type, you know?"

Tina rolled her eyes and smacked her gum. "I know."

"And my old man?" He barked a sarcastic laugh and took a long, harsh pull from the coffin nail. "Man . . . What was I thinkin' agreeing to this?"

"Gee, I don't know, maybe you wanted to be decent to your sister? For once?"

Art shot her a scowl. "Ah, whatta you know, anyhow?"

Tina sighed. "Nothing, Art. I just carry the groceries."

He relaxed into a soft smile. "Hey, I'm sorry about that. You're great." Catching up to her, he wrapped an arm around her slender waist.

She blushed and shrugged. "I dunno, Art, I think maybe this could be good for us."

"Yeah?"

"Yeah. Maybe see what it's like to have a kid around. A little one, ya know? Family ain't so bad, right?"

Art gently pulled her to a stop and leaned closer until their lips were nearly touching. "You thinkin' you gonna set me straight?"

"Maybe. You got a problem with that?"

At last, they met in a kiss. It lasted only a moment before they were startled by an abrupt clang from below. Art looked underfoot, realizing he was standing atop a drainage grate. And there, in the dark, for just a fraction of an instant, he thought he saw two glowing eyes peering back at him.

"Art? Art, what is it?"

He shook off a shiver in the summer heat. "Uh . . . nothing." Gripping Tina's arm, he led her away from the grate. "C'mon, we need to quit foolin' around and get home. We gotta tell Fred he's gotta find somewhere else to sleep tonight."

Fred stood on the steps of the apartment building, his mouth agape, arms extended to receive something. "B-But, c'mon, dude . . . "

"Sorry, Fred," Art said hurriedly, tossing him his ratty, rolled-up sleeping bag. "My Pop and niece are on their way. Me and Tina gotta get this place cleaned up."

"But I can help!" Fred whined.

Art smiled anxiously, "See ya around, Fred," and closed the door. Fred remained in the same stupefied posture, holding his sleeping bag, shut out on the street. At long last he turned to face the pedestrian traffic, watching people shove past, too busy with their lives to notice him.

The sun was setting, and Fred knew he'd need to find a place to stay for the night. He shuffled through his mental Rolodex, checking the list of his buddies—but he'd burned too many bridges. He'd overstayed his welcome one too many times, laughed too loudly, partied too hard, or smelled too foul. Maybe he'd go down to the shelter and stay with Shepherd; that had always been a haven to him in the past.

Carrying his bag, he slumped down the street, wondering what had become of his life. He had no family who claimed him, no girl, no kids, or a house.

No job. No friends—not real ones, anyway. Art and Tina were good people, but they had each other.

Who do I have? Fred considered.

Where had he gone wrong?

Sadly, now was not the time for grim personal reflection. Dark was coming, and he needed to get off the street. New York was not a safe place to be these days. Sure, there were always predators about—dope dealers and pimps and gangbangers. But something else was going on out there lately. Street folks were disappearing left and right, leaving no trace. People of his particular societal standing were getting scared, fleeing the subway tunnels and sewers, even seeking to arm themselves against some unseen threat. Fred had never been one to think too long or hard about anything, and he couldn't guess who or what was behind it all—but he sure didn't want to discover for himself. He lived by a simple code: Leave me alone, and I'll leave you alone. He would stay out of it—

A stirring in the filthy alley beside Art's building. A trashcan careened to the ground, a pile of cardboard boxes shifted. Fred paused, hearing a faint cry coming from the mound of trash.

"Hello?" he probed, stepping into the alley. Was someone hurt? "Hey, dude, come on out. Fred ain't gonna hurt you. I'm headed down to the shelter. You wanna tag along?"

Fred lowered his bag to the ground and eased forward. He imagined who he might find hiding under the heap. Maybe another hard luck case like him, a guy with nowhere to go, no one to care for him. Or maybe he'd find a beautiful blonde like Heather Locklear who would be forever grateful to him for rescuing her.

LOST AND FOUND

His smile broadened, and Fred quickened his step. "Come on out, now. Let me help you."

The trash shuffled and sloughed off like a spent cocoon, and the thing that emerged from it was definitely not Heather Locklear. Fred stammered back, petrified. "No . . . No! NO!"

Round, lidless, glowing eyes were the last things Fred saw before a claw raked across his face, slicing through flesh and muscle, bone and brain matter.

The hour had grown late. The streets of Lower Manhattan were slick with rain, and loose trash rode on the cooling breeze. Dilapidated buildings marked with graffiti and the wailing of police sirens in the distance were constant reminders that Cindy was unsafe. She squeezed Mr. Higgins snug, never straying more than a foot from her grandfather. The flight to New York City had been okay—and she got to have a snack on the plane. The rest of the evening had been spent with Gramps showing her every sight he could scrounge up, recalling his own youth spent growing up in the city. Cindy had nodded as he recounted his wistful stories, ever checking over her shoulder, dwarfed by the immense size of the buildings, deafened by the honking and shouts and catcalls and chatter. The people—there were so many people! All shapes, sizes, colors, and temperaments, pressing against one another in an impenetrable wall of humanity, shuffling her back and forth. She had wished that Mommy could hold her hand, but at least she had Mr. Higgins. He would have to do.

Gramps, however, seemed to be having a

wonderful time. There were moments he seemed to have forgotten Cindy was there at all. He laughed as he recounted the names of his buddies and all the shenanigans they'd gotten into on these same filth-ridden streets. He was so caught up in his visions of yesteryear that the hour slipped away from him, as well as his sense of direction.

Now it was dark, there were less people about, and the wet streets took on an eerie shine underneath the harsh streetlamps. Cats screeched from shadows and dogs barked and snapped from unseen folds of Cindy's surroundings, and she imagined all sorts of monsters out there in the dark.

She walked closer to Gramps, whimpering, "Where are we?"

Gramps' brow was dotted with sweat, his moist eyes scanning the deserted block, his mouth hovering between a smile and a scream. His look of sheer indecision and panic told the child all she needed to know.

"We're lost, aren't we?"

"What?" he blurted in a frightened laugh. "No, honey, no, we're, uh . . . well, this is a shortcut to your Uncle Art's. It's, uh, well, it's just been awhile since I've been down this way and, uh, things are a little different than what I remember. That's all."

Cindy hugged Mr. Higgins tighter. "I want to go home."

"Aw," he brightened, patting her on the back to soothe her fears. Instead, the gesture jostled her, and she released a small shriek. "Now, none of that. Your uncle is excited to meet you! He's been looking forward to this, so we can't let him down, okay?"

LOST AND FOUND

Cindy relaxed her arms at her side, trying to calm her worry. Gramps grinned for her, then spotted something up ahead. "Ah, there! Crosby and Spring."

Emboldened, Gramps quickened his pace, taking Cindy by the hand and hurrying her toward the intersection of Crosby and Spring Streets.

"Now I remember!" he cheered, laughing a little too loudly. "Right where I left it, huh?"

They came to the curb, and Cindy saw a lone phone booth across the street, illuminated from above by a streetlight. It seemed a beacon of safety, at least to Gramps, and he herded her for it, heedless of the street they were crossing.

"There it is," he mumbled to himself in relief. "Look both ways . . . before any cars come . . . No cars coming. Remember that."

They came to the glass box, and Gramps couldn't get in fast enough. "Honey, I wanna go in this phone booth, and . . . " He pushed his way inside, fumbling in his pocket for the scrap of paper Mommy had given him. "We'll have to wake Uncle Art. Find out where we're going. Come on in, dear. Close the door . . . "

Cindy did as she was instructed, squishing herself inside the booth. Not willing to turn her back on the night for a single moment, she and Mr. Higgins kept watch as Gramps continued to fill the tiny room with empty talk. "Just wait a minute . . . Stay there."

He inserted his change and began to dial, still mumbling to himself, making gentle reassurances that they would be alright. Cindy tuned him out, her attention drifting toward the street. The sound drew her notice first: a clanging, then grating, metallic sound. Cindy pressed against the glass and watched with rapt fixation as the manhole cover in the middle of the street shifted, scooted . . . raised. But not of its own accord. Rather, a slimy, green-black claw slowly appeared from the darkness beneath, gripping the manhole cover and sliding it aside.

The girl gaped in horror at the misshapen thing that rose from the depths.

Art snoozed on his couch, the TV set still blaring, flickering in the dark like a fluorescent campfire. The window in his small, adjoining kitchen was open, allowing the sounds and smells of the street to waft in, encapsulating him in pleasant familiarity. Art had never felt entirely comfortable in suburbia like Barb. The quiet was maddening. He needed noise. The traffic, the shouting of New York was a breath of fresh air. The city was alive, and being inside of its beating heart, he always felt a simulacrum of life, if not just distraction from his own pitiful existence. Contrary to what his holier-than-thou sister believed, he didn't like living in a drug-induced haze all the time. Yet, whenever he tried to rise above, reality had a way of slapping him down. It almost seemed that the cosmos didn't want him to get anywhere in life. But he could, he knew it, if he was just given the chance to prove himself.

Among the smog-drenched smells, a new odor slipped inside his open window. Even though Art was asleep, his nose began to twitch, but it wasn't until the crash in the kitchen that he awoke. Art rose off the couch, heart thundering, surveying the cramped, darkened apartment. "Wassat? Huh?" He sniffed the air and winced. Smelled like raw sewage.

LOST AND FOUND

Art gazed deeper into the shadows of the kitchenette, trying to discover the source of the fetid stench. There was something like a shape, something hunkered over—a shadow that stood out from the rest.

"Wha . . . ?"

From the black, the torn remnants of Fred's sleeping bag flopped before his feet, illuminated by the dim glow of the TV. Art studied it, wiping sleep from his eyes, then returned his focus to the shape in the kitchen. "Fred? Aw, come on, man, I told you, you can't sleep here. Not tonight."

Fred did not answer him, but remained crouched. Art frowned, confused, and searched for the lamp next to the couch. Before he could switch it on, the phone rang abrasively. Art retracted in fright, huffed, and snatched the phone off the receiver. "Yeah?" he yawned.

"Art. Art, I-I'm sorry to wake you."

It was his dad's voice. *Crap*, Art thought. *What time is it?* He checked his watch against the TV's glimmer. "Pop? What happened? You were supposed to be here hours ago."

His dad stammered, apologetic. "Yeah, yeah, we're here. We're here. Ah, but, ah, we, uh, we got on the subway downtown—"

Art heard his father's rambling explanations, but was distracted by more noises coming from his shadowed kitchen. Fred began to groan, rising to a slow stand. Art clamped his hand over the receiver and hissed at his frequent roommate. "Fred, man, really. You gotta get out. My Pop's on the way—"

"We're lost, Art," his dad was saying. "We're—"

★★★

In the phone booth, Cindy's eyes swelled in stark terror as the creature from the sewer shambled closer. She covered her eyes, quaking in her sneakers, repeating what Mommy had always said. *There are no monsters, there are no monsters . . .*

But when she reopened her eyes, however, she saw the truth. There were monsters. One was coming for her right now. It was tall and lumpy, with a long, veiny neck and a pulpy, bulbous head. Its asymmetrical face leered at her, two ping-pong shaped eyeballs shining like mini-fireballs. A V-shaped mouth pulled back to display jagged rows of crooked, glistening fangs. Rather than fingers, the monster twitched shiny wet flippers, their ends tapering off into sharpened bone.

"We're lost, Art," Gramps said over her shoulder, and she tugged on his coat, pointing frantically to the street. She wanted to scream, to beg him to save her, but she was struck dumb by the impossible sight.

Gramps glanced up from his phone call, his mouth going slack with disbelief when the creature flung aside the door to the phone booth. One of those slick, strong claws plunged in, grabbing Gramps by the throat. Cindy buried her face in Mr. Higgins' fluffy back and dropped to the ground, scooting away from the sounds of Gramps' terrified shrieks. She pressed against the far end of the booth and watched her grandfather being dragged into the street. He clawed and pleaded for mercy as two more deformed, gelatinous devils rose from the sewer. They crowded around the frightened man, taking a leg or an arm—and pulling.

Splorch!

As her guardian was rent asunder, his red insides adding to the greasy sheen of the stained Manhattan backstreet, Cindy could only stare on. The monsters lifted Gramps' quivering organs to their hungry mouths, as the phone dangled by its cord before the paling face of a poor girl too numbed by madness to even scream.

★★★

In Art's apartment, the smell became stronger, nearly strangling his senses. His eyes watered, the reek so overpowering that he was only barely aware of a desperate howl on the other end of the phone. "Geez, Fred! What, have you been eating Mexican food again?"

Then, from the receiver, he heard a tiny voice. "Mr. Higgins . . . " a small girl begged. "Please help . . . "

Art leaned in, sticking a pinky in his unoccupied ear, hoping to hear better. "Wassat? Pop, you there? H-Hello? Hey, who is this?"

The line went dead. "Hello? Hey, who—?"

Art moved about the house, trying to get away from an exceptionally raucous commercial, and pulled on the cord for slack—only to discover the line was severed, yanked clear from the wall. "What the . . . ?"

He held it up, and his eyeline caught the shadow in his kitchen limping for him. "Fred, man, what are you—"

Art finally switched on the lamp, coming face to face with a dripping, swollen shape, roughly in the outline of a man, but largely abhorrent and blasphemous. Art jerked back, a scream loosed from his mouth before he could contain it. The tar-skinned creature reared back with an elongated, muscular arm and swung. Art stumbled back onto his couch, sparing his head, but not the lamp. It took the brunt of the thing's anger and shattered against the wall, leaving no light but the sporadic flicker of the TV. The beast roared through its teeth, and Art shouted again, this time drawing Tina from the bedroom.

She wobbled out, her teased hair a wild mess, rubbing her eyes with the back of her wrist. "What's all the noise about?" Then she saw. Froze. Shrieked.

Art, from his crashed position on the couch, shooed her back. "Tina, get away from there!"

But his warning was too late, as the oozing fake-man in their apartment turned its lethal talons toward his girlfriend. Tina screamed, backing away into their bedroom, but bumped against the wall, halting her progress. She threw her arms up to shield her face, but the humanoid fell upon her in an instant, biting and snapping and snarling. Tina's shrill cry was replaced with the agonizing echo of crunches and slurping.

Art was instantly blinded by tears, by grief and confusion, and he tumbled off the couch onto the floor before scurrying to his feet. "No!" he cried, as if the sound of his sorrow could turn back the clock those few moments to when Tina was still alive and everything made sense. No, his life hadn't been perfect, but he'd had her. He'd had her!

"NO!" he blubbered, roaring himself hoarse. Art charged the hunched thing even as it feasted on Tina's throat. Her glassy, lifeless eyes reflected the moonlight cutting through the open kitchen window. Why had he left that window open?

The beast hugged Tina's limp body to its maw, her blood smearing its grotesque, inhuman face and spilling down its slippery front. Art reached for the nearest thing he could grab—his square glass ashtray—and swung it against the back of the creature's malformed melon. The corner caught with a muted *thunk*, but the animal did not give up its meal. With one powerful swipe, it backhanded Art, clipping him on the chin. His teeth clattered against one another as he was cast back into the living room. Art collapsed into the TV set, smashing the screen, plunging the apartment, and Art's mind, into total darkness.

Cindy wasn't sure how long she sat in the phone booth gripping Mr. Higgins before the policeman showed up. He asked her a bunch of questions—who she was, what she was doing out so late alone, where were her parents. She tried opening her mouth to speak, but words seemed lost to her.

"Monster ate him," was all she managed.

What followed was a blur of activity. She was taken to the 9th Precinct, where she was placed in a special room for questions, they said. More police officers milled about her, asking her the same questions again and again, making phone calls, whispering to one another. They wanted to know who her parents were, but in her terror she'd forgotten. Forgotten their names. She could barely recall their faces, or her bedroom, or her life before this terrible night. Cindy did her best to reach back into her memories, but they stopped short at that phone booth. That phone booth was all she knew. That, and faithful Mr. Higgins, who whispered to her words of comfort, trying to call her back to herself.

Hours passed in the station, until the morning shone in through the windows. Cindy remained seated at the table, only able to shed a single tear, her eyes barely blinking, her mouth only now closing. The shock was still fresh, and she couldn't grieve yet. Gramps wasn't dead. It was a joke. He was playing a trick on her. He would walk through that door at any minute, and they would go back to the way things were.

"Honey? You want a drink of water?"

Cindy barely glanced at the sandy-haired policewoman who took a seat beside her at the table. The woman's hair was pinned up out of her face, and she wore a heavy sympathetic expression.

"Can't you tell us anything?" the woman asked again. Again and again and again, all the same questions.

Cindy stared at the wall. "Monster ate him."

"Your grandpa, right? You said your grandpa. Where's your Mommy? Do you know?"

Cindy did not. Mommy had taken such great pains in having Cindy memorize her phone number and address for when she would start first grade in the fall, but she had forgotten all that. "Their eyes glowed in the dark," she replied, sullen.

The woman smoothed Cindy's hair, frowning. "It's going to be okay. You're going to be okay."

LOST AND FOUND

★★★

Art woke up on the floor, his head stinging. He touched his temple and brought his fingers back to find their tips dotted with red. He groaned and stood, but the room continued to shift and spin, and he felt nauseous.

"Tina . . . " he croaked, moving for their bedroom, disorientated. Had he passed out last night?

Then he saw the torn remnants of Fred's sleeping bag, and in the late morning light he glimpsed a sticky splash of blood along the polyester. He next looked to the kitchen, where the overturned tables and chairs brought back the reality of the night before.

"Tina," he gasped. Her blood and chunky remains were spread about the kitchen, splattered on walls, flung against their refrigerator. There was nothing left of his love but a smear leading from the sloppy mess in the kitchen to the window.

★★★

Red-faced and sweating, Art burst into the police station. "Help! I need help!" Even so early in the morning, the precinct was a circus—with beat cops hauling in their perps, detectives hustling past, and phones ringing in concert—and Art's pleas went unheeded. He pushed his way through the winos and prostitutes escorted by boys in blue, sidling up to the front desk. "Sergeant! You have to help me!"

"Well, well, if it isn't our old pal, Art Finkle. Y'know, we usually gotta bring you in—you don't typically stroll in yourself."

Art nearly threw himself across the counter.

"Someone—some *thing*—killed my girlfriend Tina last night!"

"Whoa, whoa, back up—"

"Please! Do something!"

The Desk Sergeant leaned on a beefy forearm. "You tweakin' again, Finkle?"

"No!"

Down the hall, Officer Crespi trotted down the stairs with a little brown-haired girl in tow. Art knew the cop—they'd had run-ins in the past. Crespi was a macho meathead in a tight uniform and Ray-Ban shades. With his perfectly coifed head of dark hair, fake tan, and sleazy too-white smile, the guy looked more like a stripper in a cop's uniform than an authentic upholder of the law.

Nevertheless, Art suspected he might be his last hope. "Crespi!" Abandoning the Desk Sergeant, Art bumbled down the hall, manic. "Crespi, man, I need your help!"

Crespi rolled his eyes. "Finkle? C'mon, pal, I got better stuff to do than put up with you. You're lucky the Captain's already taken off—he'd have you locked up for sure after that last stunt you pulled."

Art gripped Crespi's collar. "Will you listen to me?"

Crespi lowered his brow into a stern posture. "Take ya hands offa me, Finkle."

"I'm sorry, I'm sorry. Tina's dead. This . . . this thing came into our pad . . . claws and dripping with slime, and its eyes glowed, man!"

Crespi exploded in laughter, and hollered to the rest of the 9th Precinct. "What is this? There, like, a convention going on for the crazies?"

At the cop's side, the little girl muttered, "Their eyes glowed in the dark . . . "

Art and Crespi shot a look at her. Dropping to one knee, Art took the child by the arms. "What did you say? Did you see them, too?"

"Leave her alone, Finkle. She ain't got nothin' to say to you."

"Wait, wait! Little girl, what do you know? What did you see?"

The girl sunk her chin into a stuffed dog she held against her chest. "Monsters ate Gramps."

"We brought this one in last night," Crespi volunteered with a disgruntled grimace. "Kid was alone in a phone booth—over on Crosby Street. Can't figure out who her parents are. She had some luggage. Must be from outta town, as best we can figure."

"Mommy said there aren't monsters. She was wrong."

"Yeah, honey," Art breathed, grateful that someone believed him. "Yeah, I think she was."

Something about the child struck Art as strangely familiar. The shape of her eyes conjured vague memories. He felt he should know those eyes somehow.

Crespi tugged on her sleeve. "C'mon, little girl." He held up a crumpled slip of paper, and Art glimpsed a phone number scrawled on it. "Let's try this number again. See if we can't find out who you belong to."

A peal of stark terror ripped through Art's senses. He yanked the slip from Crespi's grasp, ignoring the cop's heated protests, and unfurled it to stare at the handwritten number, horrified. He gaped at the girl. "Where did you get this?"

"Mommy gave it to Gramps."

"Give it back, Finkle, or so help me—"

Art's wide eyes met the cop's glare. "Crespi . . . it's *my* number."

★★★

Once more, Cindy found herself in the quiet room upstairs where the police asked her questions. Only, this time, she sat without police escort, her only company the man across the table from her. He was unwashed, with a sweaty face and damp, messy hair. His clothes were oversized and mismatched, and had a strange odor. He was as quiet as she had been when she arrived. Tears had dried on his cheeks, and he stared at his hands in silence.

All in all, he wasn't taking the news very well.

"Pop is . . . " He blew out a long sigh and shook his head, fighting off tears again. Running his fingers through tangled hair, he swallowed, then looked at her. "So you're Cindy. Your mom is Barbara? My sister."

Cindy nodded.

He forced a tired grin. "I guess that makes me your Uncle Art."

Cindy considered him. She couldn't remember ever meeting her Uncle Art, only hearing Mommy and Daddy arguing about him downstairs at night long after she was supposed to be asleep. She didn't know why, but she knew that Mommy was always upset whenever "Uncle Art" entered the conversation. Still, she'd only known him by reputation, and seeing him now was akin to meeting the Tooth Fairy in person. It was unreal, but then again, her entire world was unreal right now.

"I don't know what to tell you, kid." He hung his head, rubbing his face anxiously. "I'm sorry."

"What will happen to me now?" she ventured, her voice little more than a whisper.

"What? Ah, you'll be fine. Don't you worry about that. These guys, they'll take good care of you. They'll be sure you get back to Barb—to your mom."

"Will you stay with me?"

He tittered, his cheeks flushing. "Me? Nah, kid, I don't think . . . Nah, nah, your Mommy and Daddy will be here before you know it, and I . . . I shouldn't be. I've got . . . I just can't, alright?"

Cindy frowned, a sob hitching in her chest.

"Aw, don't look at me like that, kid. You don't know me. I got . . . I got bad habits. I'm not a good guy, you ask anybody." Uncle Art stood, pacing. "This just . . . this isn't my scene, ya understand. I can't be here. I gotta—I gotta think, is what I gotta do. Tina and Pop . . . monsters coming up outta the sewers. I can't . . . I'm sorry, kid."

The tall, handsome cop that had talked with Cindy earlier entered the room, one hand still on the doorknob. "Alright, Cindy, we finally got in touch with the travel agency and got word to your parents. They're docking in the Bahamas, and they'll catch the first flight to LaGuardia. I got a car downstairs. A real nice officer is gonna take you to the airport to meet them, okay?"

Cindy nodded, gathering her red duffel and faithful Mr. Higgins.

Uncle Art headed for the door, rambling. "You, uh, you take care, Cindy. You tell your mom, well . . . You tell her I'm sorry about all of this. She'll understand."

The cop stopped Uncle Art. "Where you goin', Finkle?"

"Anywhere but here, Crespi." He offered one last pathetic look in Cindy's direction, dipped his head in shame, and pushed his way out the door. "Anywhere but here."

★★★

Art removed the yellow police caution tape and shut himself into the dark solitude of his ruined pad. Between filling out reports and waiting for the cops to contact Barb, he'd spent the entire day at the station. The sun was starting to set, orange rays illuminating the wreckage in his home. Tina's blood was everywhere, the furniture was destroyed, and now there were little evidence markers littered here and there, from when the cops had come to investigate.

He closed his eyes to the horrid sight, only to be met by the image of little Cindy in his brain, staring up at him, begging him with those big blue eyes—Barb's eyes—to stay with her.

Why didn't I stay?

"You shoulda stayed, you idiot . . . "

Art took his face in his hands, huffing in aggravation. He couldn't face Barb, not with Pop dead and her kid almost dead. They were coming to see *him*, he thought. And that was only because he'd spent the last ten years avoiding them all. Even after his own mother had died, he refused to go to the funeral. Bad blood, he'd told himself at the time.

I didn't even go to my Ma's funeral.

Art slid to sit on the floor, trembling. He was a failure in every way that had ever counted. Only Tina had ever been able to see past all that to the man he could be if only someone gave him the chance.

LOST AND FOUND

Cindy gave you a chance. You let her down.

He moaned and picked himself up off the floor, then moved to the couch. Giving a heave, he slid it to the side, revealing an air vent on the floor. On hands and knees, he pried off the grate and scrounged around inside, finally pulling out his pipe and stash. Furious, he dropped a rock in the bulb and fished in his pockets for his lighter. He put the crack pipe to his lips and clicked the lighter, but the flame didn't take. Again and again he thumbed the wheel, creating sparks but no fire.

Art released a growl and hurled the crack pipe to the floor, where it smashed with a *pop*. He rested his head against the wall and took a deep breath.

"C'mon, Art," he sighed, imagining what Tina might say if she were still here. "Do the right thing. For once in your life, do the right thing."

★★★

Cindy rode in the back of the police car, seated behind the cage, as the squad car pulled away from the 9th Precinct. The man driving was an officer she hadn't yet met today, but he talked a lot, as though he were afraid of the quiet.

"We'll get you to your mom in no time," he was saying. "She's going to be real happy to see you, I bet!"

Cindy hugged Mr. Higgins, quietly watching the neighborhood pass by, when the police band crackled, "Attention all units, we've got reports coming in from all over of some kind of attacks from Lafayette to Spring Street. Captain Bosch is calling in all available units to be on the lookout."

The driver yanked the radio off the CB. "Come again, dispatch? What kind of attacks?"

"Bosch didn't say. Something about creatures coming from the sewers!"

Cindy leaned forward in her seat, glimpsing the road up ahead. A manhole cover had been slid aside, and emerging from the dark pit, she saw—"No . . . no, no . . . "

But her driver remained oblivious, still laughing incredulously into the radio. "You serious?"

Cindy pointed ahead and screamed. "Watch out!"

The cop looked up in time to see one of the monsters stand tall. He hollered a curse and jerked the wheel. The cruiser careened off the road, avoiding the black-gooey shape, but plowing headfirst into the corner of a rundown brick building. Cindy squealed and crashed into the floor, landing in a heap. Mr. Higgins told her to get up, that it wasn't safe. That she had to get out.

Groggy, Cindy rose. Two rubbery clawed hands slapped against the glass. The deformed beast with engorged, glowing eyes pressed its face against the window, snarling. Cindy pulled Mr. Higgins to her, shrieking at the top of her little lungs. She looked to her police escort for help, but he was folded over the dash, covered in his own blood and glass from the shattered windshield. Two more dripping creatures dug their hooks into his lifeless body, hauling him clear of the wreckage. He landed on the ground with a dull thud, and immediately the monsters shredded through his clothes and flesh.

Cindy shook her head in hopeless dread. "Mommy! MOMMY!"

LOST AND FOUND

The devil at her window reared back its veiny head, then slammed it against the window, busting out the glass and pelting her in tiny particles. Cindy fell back and crawled toward the opposite door, out of the thing's reach. It stuck its head inside, its blood-stained jaws salivating. It snapped at her with needle-like teeth, drawing more petrified cries from her throat.

She heard snapping bones and popping tendons, and, impossibly, the beast's neck extended like gooey elastic. The head moved closer to her as the creature's long tongue unfurled, licking the air around her. She tried to back farther away but ran out of room. The tongue writhed like a snake, sliding along her soft, delicate cheek, leaving a trail of foul-smelling waste on her flesh.

Cindy sobbed hysterically, beating at the monster with Mr. Higgins. Her puppy fought bravely, pummeling the thing's head until it halted in frustration, if not surprise. Freed for a moment, Cindy howled, "Mommy, help me!"

"Cindy?" a voice called from the distance. "Cindy!"

It wasn't Mommy. It was—

Art Finkle tumbled out of the taxi, gaping at the three sludge beasts attacking a wrecked squad car. Already a cop was splayed out on the ground, torn apart by the things that now devoured his insides. But there was one more trying to get inside the car—from which Art heard small, heartbreaking screams.

"*Cindy!*"

He swiveled to the driver. "Stay here!"

But the cab driver reached back and closed Art's

door from the inside. "Forget it, pal!" he exclaimed, then floored the gas and sped away. Art cursed after him, but there wasn't a second more to waste.

Sidestepping the creatures that were content to feast on what remained of the cop, Art directed his attention on the beast angling for his niece. He winced, not sure what to do—then leapt on the thing's back with a wild, "Hyah!"

Instantly, he gagged at the horrible stench. Wrapping his arms around the spongy form, he pulled and twisted. "Get away from her!"

He managed to pry the thing loose, and it withdrew a hungry head that chittered at the top of a spindly tentacle. The long neck twisted, as the head redirected its hate against him. Art's eyes widened at the unnatural display. He readied a colorful obscenity, but the head—those teeth—shot for him like a cobra strike. He dodged out of the way, but the head reared back and struck again. This time Art let go, dropping back onto the seat of his pants with a shout.

The beast's neck shrank to a normal size again, and the slime monster stalked for him, flexing its claws.

"Cindy!" Art said. "Cindy, crawl out of there! Get out!"

The child popped up, watching the unfolding scene with a terrified gaze.

Art fumbled backward, crab-walking away from the lumbering monster until his fingers slipped in warm goo. He jerked to the side and saw that he'd just crawled himself onto the beasts' dinner table, joining the dead cop. Gore squished in between his fingers, and Art shuddered in revulsion.

A claw landed on his ankle. Art's pursuer surprised him, slowly reeling him in with incredible strength.

LOST AND FOUND

"Uncle Art!" Cindy cried from inside the car.

Art breathed hard, kicking and squirming, but unable to get free. He flopped about like a beached fish, finally spotting the cop's discarded sidearm—still in its holster. Art flailed and thrashed, reaching for the gun. The two snacking creatures regarded him, and with whatever intelligence they possessed, must have recognized what he was trying to do. They dropped their raw meal and reached down for him. Art beat and slapped at their hands, all the while focusing on that gun. Claws tangled into his jacket and shirt, starting to pull. He heard tearing fabric and imagined his skin was next.

"No!" he roared in a fit of desperation, reaching one last time, wrapping his slick fingers around the gun. "Aha!" He wrestled it free, monstrous hot breath washing over him.

He aimed the revolver at the nearest pair of glowing eyes and put a bullet right between them. A river of fluorescent green goop spilled out of the fresh opening onto Art's face. He spat and choked, scrambling free and wiping off the sludge. The beast he had shot continued to gurgle and spasm until its eyes went dark and it tipped over like a stone. The other two stared at their fallen brother in surprise, then stretched their lumpy arms toward Art. He backed against the squad car, the pistol still aimed at them, and waved for his niece.

"Cindy, come on! Come on!"

He used his sleeve to clear out the jagged edges of glass, and Cindy crawled out the window to him, clambering up his torso to wrap around him like a monkey. He clutched her tight with his free hand, her legs squeezing around his waist. She whimpered into his shoulder, "Thank you, thank you, thank you," and he felt bulletproof.

So this was the path of the righteous man.

Emboldened he said, "I've got you, kid. You got nothing to fear now. Uncle Art's here."

The creatures advanced, but Art's fear was gone. Calm as the breeze, he stiffened his gun arm toward them and fired—*Bam-Bam! Bam-Bam!* With expert precision, he plucked the two creatures like ripe fruit. They bled green where they fell, the hell-lights slowly fading from their bulging eyes.

And then it was over.

Art and Cindy hugged each other, both trembling. Eventually they relaxed, and Art set the girl down. He heard the squall of tires, and suddenly the taxi that had abandoned him rounded the corner. The driver poked out his head anxiously. "Hey, uh, you two alright?"

Art grinned.

The cabbie nervously stuttered, "G-Guess I couldn't leave, huh? What kinda guy would I be? You two need a lift?"

Art glanced down at the little girl whose hand he clutched. "LaGuardia Airport."

"Y-Yeah, sure, pal. Get in. Geez, how'd you do all that?"

But Art was no longer listening. Cindy stared at him intently, the fear gone from her at last. "Are you going to stay with me now?"

He smiled. "Yeah, honey. Yeah, your Uncle Art ain't goin' nowhere."

She hugged his leg tight, and he warmed. "Come

on, honey. Let's get out of this neighborhood. It's bad for my health."

The girl and her stuffed animal eagerly made their way to the taxi, but Art looked back for a second, surveying the grisly aftermath of his battle. He popped open the cylinder on the revolver.

One bullet left.

The nightmare seemed over, but he clicked the cylinder closed and tucked the gun in his waistband as he joined Cindy. Best to take the gun with them.

Just in case.

T.H.E.Y. A.R.E. C.H.U.D.

ALEX LAYBOURNE

THE SUBWAY STATION was empty. Even the echo of the group's footsteps seemed dulled somehow. Everything pointed to the tunnels not wanting to admit them into its deeper, dark belly. The five men stood together on the platform. Each held a flashlight, cutting five distinct beams of light through the murky gloom. The sign announcing their location, Chambers Street station, shone under the power of their beams.

The power had been cut in an attempt to keep whatever it was that had been causing such havoc on the streets, in check.

"Jenkins, keep your lights on the tunnel. Phillips, Moore, Hagen, I want you to keep the sides and rear lit up as best you can. I don't know what's down here, but Bosch was spooked, and I won't be taking any chances," Sergeant Gregory Mallory instructed his men.

"Aye, Sergeant," each man responded in turn.

None of them moved too fast, eager to keep as tight a unit as possible. The trains were canceled, yet there was an irrational fear that held them from climbing down onto the tracks.

"Are we sure about this," Phillips asked.

"We've got our orders," Mallory answered.

He looked at Phillips and then beyond him to the rest of the team. Even through the plastic visor of their hazmat suits, it was clear to see Hagen's pale, sweat-soaked skin.

The Geiger counter attached to Mallory's hip crackled. His sudden detection pushed all five men even closer to the edge of their nerves.

"That thing makes me nervous," Phillips said.

"Would you rather get cooked by whatever is down here? I ain't acting as no miner's canary," Mallory snapped. "Bosch said they found a number of these things down here, and the last group reported off the chart readings once they get in deep."

"Yeah well, Bosch says a lot of things," Phillips answered, his nerves jangling on every word.

"Did you hear they found his wife? I heard she looked a real mess," Hagen said, speaking up for the first time since they'd entered the sewer.

"Why do you think they sent another group of us down here? Bosch is sure that whatever killed his wife lives down here," Mallory said, adjusting the dials on the Geiger counter.

"Do you believe that?" Moore asked.

"Maybe. I mean there's enough homeless folk living in these sewers, and they are all acting mighty aggressive lately," Hagen answered, taking ownership of the question.

"Did you hear they attacked a diner? Killed two of our own," Phillips said, his fear manifesting as anger.

"This city is going down the drain, and we are down here hunting monsters,"

"Alright ladies," Mallory said, "that's enough tongue wagging. Let's head through the tunnel. We need to move south, that will bring us around behind the group that lost contact." Mallory tried in vain to hide the quiver in his voice. "Just keep it slow and steady."

One by one, the men dropped down onto the train tracks. They moved in a diamond formation, with Jenkins taking the lead. The largest of the group, and a veteran of the Vietnam war, he had volunteered to take point, when they were still above ground. Behind him, Hagen brought up the rear. Between them, Mallory repositioned the flamethrower over his shoulder, as the counter gave another loud crackle.

They were flanked by officers Philips and Moore, two exceptionally tall and thin men. An odd looking couple, they were force veterans and neither known for backing down from a fight.

The tunnel loomed ahead of them, the darkness too much for their flashlights, reducing the effectiveness down to not much more than an arms' length. The four men surrounding Mallory were armed with their trusted .38 Specials, while Phillips and Moore also carried a shotgun each, and it was this they clutched against their chest as they walked.

Without warning, the darkness before them began to move, a shadow appeared and emerged, staggering toward them. Feet shuffling, barely able to lift themselves to keep the momentum rolling.

Moore raised his shotgun, and only Mallory's quick reactions stopped him from blowing a hole through the chest of the homeless man staggering their way.

The man was caked with semi-congealed blood. Too much for it to have come from just him. He staggered and stumbled, seemingly oblivious to the presence of the five officers.

The man tripped and fell to his knees on the tracks. Only then did he look up and see the men staring at him.

"It will all fall down," the man said, his lips flapping over largely toothless gums. "It will all fall down."

With that said, the man started to crawl away on his hands and knees, doing so until he reached the steps to bring him back up to the platform. Only, instead of doing that, he crawled under the metal steps and pulled himself into the fetal position.

"What the heck?" Jenkins said, turning away from the tunnel's gaping maw to watch the man.

"Never mind him, we've got a job to do," Mallory answered, his voice echoing inside the large helmet he wore.

The five men left the station and entered the tunnels. The conditions felt cramped, the walls too close for comfort. Slowly, their eyes adjusted, as they were absorbed into the dark, becoming another part of it.

They didn't make it far before they found the first bodies. The two men lay atop one another, their flesh torn open as if savaged by wild beasts. Flesh and bone shone in bright contrast when the flashlights swept over them.

"What happened to them?" Moore asked, crouching down to take a closer look.

"What on earth is living down here?" Hagen added.

"Don't get too close." Mallory leaned closer to the bodies and the Geiger counter went mad, erupting in a burst of crackled alerts that echoed around the tunnel, only adding to the shock.

The five men jumped back.

"I'm done with this," Moore said, turning to leave.

"You cannot abandon your post, officer," Mallory said. "We are here to protect this city. That is our duty." His words were harsh, but his tone soft. "Now there are five of us, and we have the advantage on whatever this thing is. We have the advantage in numbers and in intellect. So pull it together, and let's go get this thing."

Moore didn't say anything, but nodded and turned back toward the group. Abandoning their formation, they pressed onward, journeying deeper into the dark. They found several more bodies along the way, before the tunnel rounded a corner, sending them deeper into the underground network beneath the city.

"You know what I don't get," Hagen spoke.

"What?" Mallory asked, not interested in conversation, yet happy for the noise.

"If those bodies were radioactive, why isn't that counter going nuts now?" Hagen asked, turning suddenly to sweep his flashlight behind him.

"Your guess is as good as mine,' Mallory replied.

"Alligators," Moore said, dryly.

"Very funny, asshole," a terrified Phillips replied, tightening his grip on his shotgun.

The darkness continued ahead of them, when a rumble of what sounded like thunder rolled through the tunnel.

"I thought you said the trains had been canceled," Phillips yelled.

"That's not a train," Hagen answered. "Hit the deck!" The vet threw himself to the floor as the wave of the explosion hit them. The walls and floor of the tunnel shook, bringing clusters of brick and mortar crashing down around them.

When the tremors settled, the darkness was a dusty haze. Even with their flashlights, they could not see more than a few feet in any direction, even lost to one another. "What on earth was that?" Jenkins asked, his voice groggy.

"An explosion," Hagen answered. "I'm guessing the gas mains caught and blew. Only thing I could think of that would shake us down here like that."

"Looks like we are stuck here, boys," Moore said. He shone his flashlight against the rubble that blocked the tunnel behind them.

"Where's Phillips?" Mallory asked, looking around.

The four men grouped together, each taking it in turn to shout out. When Phillips didn't answer, they spread out, fearing he had been injured. The dust began to settle, and their eyes could pick out objects in the dark.

"I've got something," Hagen called out. Bending down, he picked up Phillips's rifle.

"Do you think he got trapped on the other side?" Jenkins asked, pushing against the blockage to see if they could maybe dig their way through.

"I don't think so, look," Moore called to them.

He stood by the far corner of the wall where a bloodied arm protruded from the mass of rocks and collapsed subway walls. Black shaded blood oozed down the rubble, and along the twisted metal tracks.

"Somebody get ahold of dispatch, they need to know what's happened," Mallory said, taking charge. "We need to keep moving. I don't want to get trapped down here if something else blows."

"What do you suggest, Sarge?" Hagen asked, his focus still on the wall, scouring it for weak points.

"I'm not getting anything from dispatch. Not getting anything but static," Jenkins spoke up.

Mallory sighed and threw his hands up in mock surrender. "That calls it, we are heading topside. There has to be a maintenance shaft along here somewhere."

None of them wanted to leave Phillips behind, but they understood the need to get to safety. Their formation abandoned, their only goal was to get out of the subway. Moving at a quicker pace, they missed the first burst of static from the Geiger counter, and only when an ear-piercing cry came barreling down the tunnel toward them did they pay it any mind.

"Look sharp," Mallory said, bringing up his flamethrower. "If that thing wants to come at us, then it will get what it deserves."

The scream grew louder and louder, and the Geiger counter growled off the charts, yet nothing emerged from the darkness.

"Get your lights on the walls, it has to be here," Mallory ordered, turning around in a tight circle, swinging the barrel of his fire spewing weapon like a club.

"Nothing," Moore said.

"All clear here," Hagen shouted back.

The screech fell silent and the Geiger counter

calmed in an instant, ticking over slowly like an idling car before it finally fell silent.

"Keep moving," Mallory ordered. "Where's Jenkins?"

"Sergeant, I've got something you're going to want to see," Jenkins' voice came in a whisper.

"It must connect to the sewer systems," Moore said, as they stared at the hole in the wall.

"Must have been knocked loose when the gas mains exploded," Hagen said. He stood back from the wall, the beam of his torch shining directly into the center of the hole.

"I don't think so, I mean look at it. There's no other damage to this wall." Jenkins' voice sounded calmer now that the others had joined him.

"What are you trying to say?" Moore asked, "You really think something broke through the wall into the sewers?" He lifted his flashlight to highlight Jenkins' face. The light reflected from the plastic facemask, obscuring him in the reflected glare.

"Or something broke out of the sewer and into the subway station," Jenkins said, reaching out to push Moore's arm away.

"Enough of this, there are plenty of homeless people living down here. They probably did it as a way to get quick access to the surface," Mallory said, once again rising above the rest, and using the authority his rank gave, to push the group on. "I'll take a look what's back there, you children stay here and argue about who made the hole."

The gap in the wall was smaller than a man, so Mallory needed to stoop down low in order to push his head and shoulders through the gap. It was narrower than they thought, but when Mallory stepped through with one leg and then disappeared completely, they agreed with the sewer line connection.

★★★

"Sarge, you got anything through there?" Hagen called, crouching down to call through to the other side of the wall.

They got no answer, but a few moments later they heard a crash of something falling, and the crazy growl of the Geiger counter as it once again exploded with noise.

There was one scream, not much more than a cry of alarm really, for it was cut short before it had time to develop into anything more substantial.

The three men jumped back, weapons in their hands. Behind the wall, something growled and slammed against the bricks. Panicked, Moore fired his rifle, the roar of the shot echoing around them like cannon fire. Bricks and mortar crumbled and the hole spread open, allowing Mallory's body to fall back toward them.

Blood pumped from the stubby wound that was his neck, spraying the trio with gore. The body fell to the floor still shaking with the final throes of death.

"His head," Moore cried out, "where's his head?"

"Fire," Hagen roared, obeying his own order the second he gave it. The guns exploded in a barrage, decimating the wall, creating a hole large enough for a car to pass through without issue.

"Hold up, hold up." Jenkins waved his arms at his fellow officers, who ceased their fire and stood panting, trembling with a mix of fear and adrenaline. "I don't see anything,"

Jenkins approached the gaping wound they had carved into the tunnel wall. He paused for a moment before leaning over the threshold to peer inside.

"Don't go in there, are you crazy?" Moore gasped.

From behind them, in the underground tunnel, the sound of approaching footsteps pulled their attention away from the wall. Both Hagen and Moore turned to face the noise, their weapons raised.

"The coast is clear," Jenkins said, his voice echoing from the other side of the hole. "There has to be a manhole cover we can use, just climb the ladder, pop the cover and we are done."

"Hagen, get back here," Moore called in a frantic whisper.

Hagen had not moved far, but already the darkness was obscuring his form. The opening in the wall seemed to pour an extra density into the darkness, as if it somehow leached it from the other side as a way to force their direction.

"Guys, come on, let's get out of here," Jenkins called, his voice already confirming he had started walking through the sewers.

Stepping over both the body and, a few meters into the sewer the head of their sergeant, the two men followed.

Hagen stopped to collect the flamethrower. "I'm taking this with me."

The straps were broken, cut clean through, but Hagen was strong enough to hold them with one arm and swing the hose with the other. After a moment of hesitation, Hagen bent and collected the Geiger counter from the floor. He did not think it was broken, and after a quick inspection, it came back to life.

"Wait up," Hagen called. Looking ahead he could make out a figure ahead of him. "Hey, Moore, wait up."

The figure kept walking, and Hagen gave pursuit. The floor in the sewer was slippery, and several times Hagen felt his feet slipping beneath him. The idea of wading through the shin-high sludge that flowed through the central reservation of the tunnel made his stomach turn. Yet up ahead, he heard a splash. The figure disappeared.

"Moore, you alright? Did you slip?" Hagen hurried to the point where he believed the splash to have originated. He shone his torch over the floor and could see signs of footprints in the slime.

Turning to shine his light on the water, Hagen screamed. Two bright eyes reflected the beam. The face around it was a blur in the darkness, but the stench that came from the creature was overpowering. The Geiger counter exploded with sound as a clawed hand grabbed Hagen by the face.

He choked and coughed as long claws dug into his head, punching through his skull to lock in place. The skin of the creature's hand was pressed hard against Hagen's face, and the slime that seemed to ooze from its body ran into Hagen's mouth and down his throat. Hagen still had a pistol on his hip. He managed to draw the weapon, and fire, even as his body began to shut down, as the long claws found their way into his brain.

The creature screamed as the bullet tore through its flesh, carving a wide path through the soft, partially melted tissue, the same way a warmed knife would slice through a stick of butter. Snatching back its arm, as it fell back into the sludge of the sewer, it yanked away the front half of Hagen's skull.

THEY ARE C.H.U.D.

Bone snapped with a crisp, delicate sound, and the flesh tore with the painful simplicity of sheared paper or cloth.

Pain registered in Hagen's mind, even in the final seconds, where his eyes saw the majority of his brain pass before him as it tumbled from the space that had once been closed by his face. Hagen dropped to his knees, his body weight crushing the grey blob of brain matter with a wet squelch before he tumbled into the sewage and disappeared beneath the surface.

★★★

Moore heard Hagen's calls and saw the form moving behind him. He assumed Hagen was following him.

He didn't want to stop because he needed to keep up with Jenkins, who it seemed moved at quite a pace when given the chance.

Moore heard the splash, the gunshot, and the screams. It was the latter that stopped him from turning around. Self-preservation came easily to Moore, who had joined the force after his disciplinarian father gave him a choice between that or the military.

"Jenkins?" he called out. "Jenkins where are you, buddy?"

Something splashed in the water. Moore jumped, and his mind screamed alligator.

He saw nothing and was calmed. Continuing to walk, his eyes half focused on the sewage river, he didn't see the figure standing before him. Moore walked into the back of the figure and stumbled backward.

"Jenkins, blimey man, you could have answered

me," Moore began, his words falling short when his eyes adjusted and focused on the creature.

Naked as the day it was spawned, the blackened flesh hung loose and saggy on the creature's frame. His large, hairless head played host to a melted, hideous face. Yellow eyes that shone like searchlights in the dark and a festering maw of a mouth, filled with double rows of needle-like teeth, were the only discernible features. Two holes served as a nose, and they opened and closed like blinking eyelids as the creature stared down at Moore.

Moore went for his gun, but the other creature was too quick. His mouth latched onto Moore's throat from behind, tearing away a thick chunk of flesh and gristle. Moore screamed in pain, but all that came out was a strange, bubbling whistle.

The two creatures descended on him, tearing into his flesh, ripping Moore apart and yanking out the succulent and juicy fruits that were contained within his body. His skin burned and blackened from their touch, the heat of their radiated bodies cooking his flesh, bringing it out in blisters that swelled, burst and infected in a matter of seconds.

Moore's death finally came when one of them found his heart and shoveled it into their mouth in a single chomp.

★★★

"Bosch had better pay me hazard pay for this," Jenkins said as he stood looking at the blocked off section of sewer. It did not look as if it had come from the explosion, but rather like something had created it.

There was enough room for the sewage to flow

through, for there were no signs of a build-up. Jenkins stood close to knee deep in a strong flowing current of sewage. His mind was torn between tracking back to a spot where he had noticed another hole in the wall, or submerging himself and trying to swim through to the other side.

Neither option seemed particularly appealing, and while he was leaning more toward the concept of trying to swim it, the knowledge that even something as thick as sewage could flow through gaps in a human body could not have kept Jenkins from going through with the idea.

Instead, he turned around and made his way back to the crack in the wall. It went beyond the sewer, and away from the underground tunnel. He had no idea where it led, but it seemed as if his hand was being forced. Like a rat in a maze, his free will was being stripped from him, and he was left at the mercy of whatever waited for him at the exit point.

He waded through the sewage and found Moore's body as it floated up to him. The hollowed out body stared with dull, lifeless eyes.

Jenkin's felt his skin crawl as the echoes and banging of the city's sewers came to life around him. Every noise became a possible threat. Gripping his pistol in a white-knuckled grasp, Jenkins climbed out of the sludge and onto the far side of the sewer wall. He could make out a figure limping its way toward him. He knew it was not Hagen, the gait did not match. Jenkins reached the crack in the wall and squeezed his way through.

The space was close—tight and claustrophobic. The walls were rough and abrasive, tearing at the material of his hazmat suit. Yet Jenkins pushed on, soon emerging into a wide and open space. The air was stale and the stink of the sewer seemed even stronger. Pools of it had gathered, seeping through the cracks in the wall, but without the movement of the current, it had grown stagnant.

Jenkins moved slowly, pausing at every crack and crunch that came from either his footfalls or from whatever lay ahead.

There was only one way for him to move, once again the path being presented to him rather than his to choose.

Certain that something was still following him, Jenkins pushed on, certain that he would find an exit point. The tunnel was strewn with debris, old shopping trolleys, and empty containers and packages lay over the floor. Blankets and other items of clothing scattered at regular intervals, along with signs of fire-pits, told Jenkins he had found one of the tunnels used by the city's homeless.

He remembered the Captain had told them the tunnels connected to a downtown soup kitchen, somewhere, but he just didn't know where.

Moving forward, the tunnel widened with side passages sprouting on both sides of the central tunnel. Sticking with the larger route, so long as it showed signs of life, Jenkins kept himself moving at a brisk pace, certain that he was still being followed.

A scream rang out, and stopped him. It came from inside one of the side tunnels.

Everything in his body told him to move, to keep walking, but he was an officer of the law, and the people under the city were just as vital a part of it as anybody else. They needed his protection, too. They did not need to be the seedy secret any longer.

Hurrying to the tunnel, he paused. There was a heat wafting through the tunnel's entrance, and on it floated the strong aroma of rotting fish. Jenkins paused, once again ignoring the voices of self-preservation. He took a breath and moved in, unaware of the hand that swiped for him, the fingers just missing his shoulder as he slid through into the tunnel.

Another scream came, and Jenkins knew he was close. He held his firearm in a white-knuckled grip. He had never had the need to fire it before, but something in his gut told him that was about to change.

The tunnel came to a natural end, with a railing blocking the end, and a flight of steep metal steps on the left. The stairwell gave way to a large square level which provided access points to multiple sewer passages that created a junction of sorts. Jenkins reasoned that they were beneath the treatment works. It made sense given how far the group had traveled and their starting location. It was either that or one of the other properties on the industrial estate.

Moving to the edge, leaning against the railing, Jenkins looked down into the darkness. He could hear people moving, shuffling and grunting. The noise was like a strange chant to his ears. Raising his flashlight, he moved to light up the scene below, when a hand clamped over his mouth, catching his startled cry and turning it into nothing more than a muffled grunt, covered by the noises from the level below.

"Shhh, quiet. They will bring it all down on you," a voice whispered. "They will bring it down. Our world, this is our world, they don't belong, but neither do you."

There was a madness to the voice that was terrifying, yet at the same time, Jenkins felt no urge to fight. Turning, he stared into the wide, white eyes of a homeless man. His long hair and thick beard were a tangled mess revealing little of the face beneath it.

"Quiet," the man said, removing his hand from Jenkins' mouth.

"What is down here?" he asked, his voice trembling.

"They are C.H.U.D." the man answered, his words even more chilling than his madness.

Jenkins could not help one last glance, turning to peer at the shuffling forms below him. His flashlight clanged against the metal railing, the echo rolling out like a battle cry. In an instant, the floor below him was alive as dozens upon dozens of glowing eyes turned their way toward him. Shrieks and snarls turned into hungry growls and wails of excitement.

The homeless man grabbed Jenkins by the hand. "Run!"

A few moments later they were sprinting through the main tunnel, the ground trembling behind them. The cries of their pursuers echoed around, bouncing from the walls, overtaking them, giving the impression they were surrounded.

Jenkins chanced a look back over his shoulder and saw creatures straight out of Hell itself closing the distance on them. Their slick, green bodies, looked wet and rotten, while their shambling gait added to the horror of their hellish appearance.

Up ahead of them, the tunnel ended, yet Jenkins' new friend did not slow down.

"Through there." He pointed to a sewer grate. The

relative light of the early evening was a comparable ray of sunshine after the darkness of the tunnels.

As they approached, the hinges creaked and the grate opened. Jenkins and his friend spilled out into a run-off viaduct on the edge of the industrial estate, just beyond the chemical plant. The fresh air had never tasted so good to Jenkins, who crashed to his knees and missed the gathered, rag-tag army of the city's homeless. They stood in numbers almost a hundred strong, armed with everything from knives and guns to bats wrapped in barbed wire and even car door shields and planks of wood.

"What is this?" Jenkins asked.

"This is our home. You don't belong down there, and neither do they," the crazy man spoke, taking a large machete that was offered to him by a large bodied woman who Jenkins recognized from a prostitution arrest he had made a few weeks previous.

"We can help," he tried to speak, but the breath in his lungs would not cooperate.

"This is our home, and we will fight for it." With that said, the army entered the tunnels, and as the sewer grate was pulled closed behind them, Jenkins fell to the floor.

Exhausted, the only survivor and a long way from the precinct, he lay back and allowed his body control to return. From deep within the sewers, he heard the mixed screams of pain, both human and C.H.U.D.

C.H.A.D.

MICHAEL H. HANSON

THE EXPLOSION DOWN the street woke me up and I stumbled from bed to window. Splitting the blinds I saw a veritable bonfire in the middle of Kenmore Street, roughly three quarters of a block away and far too close to the La Esquina Diner. I could just make out the silhouettes of a woman and two men quickly walking away from the fire and disappearing down Cleveland Place. A moment later a series of loud rumbles seemed to echo from every direction and were immediately followed by tremors that shook my apartment and knocked me off my feet onto my back.

Another series of tremors struck and twice I bounced a full two feet into the air. A few seconds later I stood up, made it to my telephone, and poked nine-one-one but instantly realized the line was dead.

"Just perfect," I muttered to myself, "break up AT&T and what do you expect?"

Distant shouts from the main hallway caught my attention and I quickly pulled on a T-shirt, worn Levis, and kicks before venturing forth to figure out how bad the damage was.

Overhead lights flickered as more of my panicking fourteenth floor neighbors stuck their heads out into the hallway.

"Dave," a familiar female voice yelled, "was that a friggin earthquake?"

I spun around and frowned at my next-door neighbor Jinny, an attractive toll-booth operator at the Lincoln Tunnel who was sporting a blonde mop of bed-hair and was wearing running shorts, sneakers, and a wrinkled Terminator T-shirt.

"I don't think so, Jinny," I replied, "I saw an explosion just down the street. I'm guessing a gas main ignited."

"And Koch keeps saying he's going to upgrade the city's infrastructure," Jinny said. "Should've known he was full of it."

The hallway rapidly filled with all of my neighbors, an eclectic mix of old and young married couples, and singles of every age and gender. Everyone began speaking at once, most asking for answers.

"Listen up," I shouted as the hallway quieted, "I think one of the underground gas lines exploded about a block away. I don't know about the rest of you but I'm not sure how stable the building is after all that shaking. It's up to you what you want to do, but I'm heading down to the lobby in case we need to be evacuated soon."

"You're a taxi driver, David," Barney, a semi-retired Chiropractor yelled out, "what the heck does a cabbie know about high rise architecture?"

I rolled my eyes, shrugged at Jinny, and headed toward the nearest of the two exits that lead to the two stairwells at each end of the building.

I reached the exit and hurriedly started walking down the stairwell. A glance back showed me that about half of my fourteenth-floor neighbors had decided to take my advice.

Several minutes later I stepped out into the main lobby, and complete chaos.

A mix of two-dozen police officers and firemen were flooding into the small clearing of the main lobby of the first floor from the front entrance of the building. Screams and shouting flooded through the front doors and I could see several fires burning in the distance.

Parked cars were in flames, and in the dancing and flickering light the outlines of people could be seen running in all directions, not to mention strange silhouettes of seemingly misshapen people.

The policemen and the firemen rapidly formed a semi-circle before the front door. The cops were leveling pistols and shotguns directly at the entrance, and the firemen were all holding axes and fire hooks at the ready, like a group of Vikings readying for combat.

The front glass doors and windows of the high-rise exploded inward. Shards of glass flew in all directions, one piece lightly scoring my left cheek. A couple of my neighbors whose reflexes were not quite as fast sustained multiple lacerations followed by their screams of pain.

Macabre creations, things out of some twisted nightmare, charged into the lobby. Each one was nearly seven feet tall, vaguely humanoid with two arms and two legs, sporting long fingers with vicious talons, but worst of all were their faces, horrid caricatures of humanity, with overly large glowing yellow eyes, and mouths packed with overlapping rows of rat-like teeth.

Their scarred and scaled skin was dark green and smeared with some kind of glistening mucus secretions.

The first two waves of horrors, about three dozen of the monsters, were brought down by a rain of point thirty-eight revolver rounds and twelve gauge shotgun blasts, but unfortunately the cops had to stop to reload and another wave of the monstrosities charged inside.

The firemen moved forward and toed the line hacking at the invaders and taking a bloody toll. Bright green blood oozed and burst from the dispatched creatures, spilling onto the lobby floor and making it a slippery nightmare to navigate.

A minute or two later it appeared the city employees were more than holding their own, and victory was nearing when, without notice, two dozen more of the monsters seemed to appear out of nowhere.

I quickly saw the danger. Somehow, some way, these creatures were pouring out of two utility closet doors, the back of the main desk, and also out of the mailroom. A couple of the policemen spun around to face the onrush of the creatures from seemingly every direction. The heroes had been completely outflanked and the slaughter was horrible.

"Back upstairs! Now!" I screamed.

Adrenaline appeared to be the miracle drug of choice as even the oldest of my neighbors, a couple in their late sixties, had no trouble retreating upward and away from the chaos below.

"Where the heck are we going," somebody yelled from above.

"I've got to get something from my apartment," I

gasped, "then I suggest we shove every bed, table, chair, and chest of drawers we can down both stairwells."

★★★

I sprinted into my bedroom, yanked the footlocker out from under my bed, spun the dial on the combination lock, and popped the top.

"Wow," Jinny's voice sounded from behind, "you really are Travis Bickle."

I yanked out small boxes of ammunition, brown leather holsters, and three different pistols.

"Cute," I said, "now pick your weapon of choice, a matching holster, and ammo."

Jinny frowned for a moment and then scooped up an M1911 pistol and a matching shoulder holster. She then popped the clip and began loading it from a box of point forty-five caliber bullets. She then noticed my raised eyebrow.

"My dad served in world war two," Jinny said and left it at that.

I finished loading a Browning Hi-Power and fitted it to a right side hip holster, and then did the same with a Beretta Seventy and placed it in a left shoulder holster.

Two minutes later, our pockets weighed down with loose ammo, we both ran into the hallway. Our fellow fourteenth-floor residents had broken into two groups and were all dragging sofa chairs, couches, tables etc. to the two stairwells. Jinny and I split up and joined in.

Just as my group was about to shove a large couch down a flight of stairs a slim, African-American man in his late twenties entered the stairwell from the twelfth floor and sprinted up to me and the others. I quickly recognized my neighbor from Fourteen-F, Matt, a stockbroker who liked his ladies and his coke.

"I pounded on every door on every floor and told them what we were doing," he said, "about half ran up the south side stairwell."

Just then an alien scream and gargle erupted upward from the bottom of the stairwell.

"Now," I yelled in panic.

Five minutes later piles of large, heavy debris filled both stairwells between the twelfth and fourteenth floor.

The horror advanced slowly, and the terror rose with it. Jinny and I each waited in a stairwell with half a dozen of our neighbors as backup, each holding any weapon they could find at short notice, a mix of butcher knives, baseball bats, table legs, switchblades, and mace.

As the vile creatures made their way up, floor by floor, the screams from their victims became clearer. It did not take long to realize they were busting down the doors of every apartment and killing all within. The worst moment came when we could hear people from the floor below us burst into the stairwell to realize the way up was blocked.

"Help," one woman screamed, "they're all around us. We can't go back down."

"For the love of mercy," one man yelled in dire panic, "help us."

This was followed by their death screams and the sounds of the creatures struggling to break their way through our barricade.

The next two hours felt like an eternity. I knew my ammo would not last forever and so I waited until each creature would smash and worm itself upward through our barricade before unloading one to two slugs into its disgusting head. I had a couple of my neighbors working as runners between Jinny and me, confirming we were using the same tactics and making sure neither stairwell had been breached before an evacuation warning could be made to retreat to the upper floors.

Several schmucks from each of the upper floors had poked their heads into things here at the front lines, and upon seeing the nightmare interlopers from the streets, quickly accepted the quid pro quo of our defenses and ran back upstairs to spread the fear. My only worry was that some floor above might panic and start stuffing things into the stairwell before we could evacuate up above them.

I fired the last of my ammunition and then suddenly noticed a cessation of sound.

"Did we get them all?"

I turned to my neighbor Angela, a grey-haired widow in her early sixties who had been showing more bravery in the last hour than a platoon of marines.

"Your guess is as good as mine, Angela," I replied.

Just then the door behind them flew open and an East Indian, twelve-year old boy stepped forward.

"Mister David, the super wants to see you right away!"

"Okay, Dhruv," I replied. "Lead the way."

One of the building's four superintendents, Arthur Bane, a burly, married fifty-five-year-old of Irish descent, strode right up to me.

"If you're here to accuse me of some kind of hoax, Arthur—"

"Cut the crap, Dave," Arthur said, "I just saw Jinny shoot three of the ugly mothers in the south well. How are things in the north?"

"I just used the last of my ammo. But—"

"But what?" Arthur asked.

"We've got a lull. Nothing else is attacking, for the moment," I said.

"Huh," Arthur grunted, "word throughout the building is you're taking charge of things."

"Hey," I said raising my hands, "I'm just reacting. Anytime you want to take over be my guest. I haven't been giving anyone any orders, just making my suggestions."

Arthur glanced at my two holstered pistols.

"I don't suppose I should waste my time asking if you've got a legal carry permit for those . . . " Arthur asked.

I started to open my mouth but Arthur cut me off.

"Never mind, boy," Arthur said, "we got bigger problems. So tell me, you got any idea what started all this? Folks are telling me you had gone down to the lobby and everything hit the fan?"

I looked around at a lot of residents slowly closing in on the two of us and dropped my voice.

"Arthur, it was the damnedest thing," I said. "I saw an explosion down the street, thinking it might be a gas line, and then I noticed a few fires bursting up through a number of manhole covers on a lot of the streets in the surrounding blocks when those tremors hit and we all thought it was an earthquake."

"Definitely not an earthquake, laddie," Arthur said.

"I figure not," I added. "Well we make it downstairs and these monsters burst through the front doors from the street and get in a battle with cops and firemen. Heck, it looked like we were winning when the weirdest thing happened."

"What?" Arthur asked.

"A whole bunch more of them started coming from everywhere," I said, "the mailroom, the front office, those two utility doors, everywhere. And it really makes me wonder . . . "

"Wonder what?" Arthur asked.

"Why this building?" I asked. "If there are dozens or hundreds of these things, why are they converging on us? There are five other residential high-rises less than a block from here, but if I didn't know better I'd think they were all being channeled to this building . . . It just doesn't make sense."

"Actually, it might," Arthur said.

"Huh," I said.

"I've heard," Arthur said, "off the record, from a few sources over shots of the water of life down at McSorley's, they hushed up what went down when this high-rise was built. Seems one hundred feet below us is a junction of sorts, where one abandoned subway tunnel, two bypassed water mains, and a couple of large and no longer used conduit pipes crisscross each other, all of them separated at different levels by about twenty feet of soil. So maybe, just maybe, if a lot of the surrounding gas lines spilled into the surrounding subway tunnels . . . "

"The fire and explosions could have broken into all these surrounding pathways," I added.

"Which all intersect directly below this high-rise,"

C.H.A.D.

Arthur finished.

Just then, the elevator alarm rang twice.

"What the hell?" Arthur said walking toward it, and Matt, also curious, followed him. They got within five feet of the door when my own alarms starting going off.

"Careful, guys," I said.

Arthur smiled, "No worries, mate. I hit the emergency shutdown the minute those tremors struck us a couple of hours ago."

Arthur stepped right up in front of the doors and looked up at the floor number array that was lighting up randomly.

"I think this is just a feedback error—" Arthur started.

The elevator doors suddenly parted a full foot, and a monstrous green arm with unusually long taloned fingers shot outward and swiped across Arthur's neck, instantly severing head from shoulders. Arthur's skull flew through the air to land at my feet. Still standing, his corpse jetted bright red blood from its neck for a full ten seconds before tumbling over.

Matt, his right cheek and neck scored by claw wounds, staggered away in pain from the elevator doors that suddenly slammed shut.

Screams erupted from every direction and I found myself back in the stairwell yelling that everyone retreat to our agreed upon fallback on the thirtieth floor.

Ten minutes later every available piece of furniture blocked the stairwells between the twenty-ninth and thirtieth floors.

As for the elevator doors, we stacked everything

else we could find across and in front of it on the thirtieth floor and telling the other building residents to do the same on their floors. And wouldn't you know it, not one minute after the last elevator blockade was finished, the counter-attack began.

We were able to hold back the growing horde of creatures at both stairwells for a full hour, and thank fate somebody pointed out that two retired Olympic archers lived on the thirty-eighth floor and still happened to own a couple of old but still working competition bows and over two hundred arrows. The couple, in their forties, took lead on both stairwells and did their best to put Robin Hood and William Tell to shame, slinging well-targeted fiberglass missiles into the glowing yellow eye sockets of every slimy monster that dared to break through the barrier.

It was around this time we found out there were things even worse than death.

"David," Angela said, suddenly appearing at my side, "something is wrong with Matt."

I followed her back into the floor's lobby and walked up to five people who were in a semi-circle around Matt. I could immediately see why Angela was worried. Matt appeared to be in a fever of some sort, but worse than that, his skin was turning green and his eyes were actually glowing yellow, like those of the monsters that wounded him.

"He's been infected," I said. "Those things can spread their sickness."

"What do we do?" Angela asked.

As if in answer Matt snarled like a tiger and started standing up. Without pause, Alex and Barry, a gay couple from two floors above, laid into him with baseball bats, turning Matt's head into mush in less than a minute.

"Everybody back," I yelled. "Make sure you don't get any of his blood in your eyes or mouth, or even on your skin."

"David," Dhruv yelled, "something is happening at the stairwell."

Two separate mobs of creatures burst through both barricades as we finished our retreat to the thirty-ninth floor. The south stairwell that Jinny had been guarding actually ended at the thirty-ninth floor where we barricaded the door to that lobby. The north well, which I had been navigating this whole time, actually circumnavigated the fortieth floor which was a penthouse owned by some South-American multi-millionaire no one had ever met, and exited out onto the building's roof.

I looked around the main lobby of the thirty-ninth floor for a moment. Over one hundred of the building's residents were spilled out across the open floor, looking like the mother of all slumber parties. They were clearly scared, but I was actually feeling proud at how well they were all dealing with it.

"So isn't it about time we called in the A-Team to take care of these jokers," Jinny asked as we tossed the last couch into the north stairwell below the thirty-ninth floor.

"You're crazy," Dhruv cut in, "we need The Last Starfighter." Dhruv then thrust his right fist into the air, "Greetings, Starfighter. You have been recruited by the Star League to defend the frontier against Xur and the Ko-Dan armada."

Jinny laughed and rustled the boy's hair for a

moment. Our faux domestic bliss was, of course, quickly interrupted.

"They're breaking through the south stairwell," someone yelled from across the other side of the lobby.

"This is it," I yelled, "women and children to the roof. The rest of us will hold them here."

I turned toward Jinny who was holding a baseball bat that had four overly large nails pounded through its head.

"Don't even think it," she smirked.

Flipping a coin, we decided one disaster had slightly more appeal than another, and over many an objection, we tossed lighter fluid and lamp oil on both barricades and set them on fire just as the creatures began breaking through. In moments the overhead sprinklers kicked on, but the outpour of water wasn't quite enough to keep dozens of the monsters from catching on fire and lighting up like torches. Something about their skin and/or blood was very flammable.

With Jinny by my side, along with two dozen mostly able men armed with whatever makeshift club they could find or make, we slowly backed toward the stairwell exit that bordered the penthouse on the way to the roof.

"Just what the heck do you gringos think you're doing? Is that a friggin fire?" a Hispanic voice screamed out in English. "Is that beef you're burning? Are you hillbillies having a barbecue?"

Standing behind us, at the base of the stairwell, was a mean-looking, swarthy man of indeterminate age, holding an M-16 assault rifle with an M203 grenade launcher mated to its underside.

C.H.A.D.

"Mister," I yelled back, "we got bad news coming through those bonfires that are gonna kill us all if you don't get out of our way."

"My name is Tommy Melendez," he said with a thick Cuban accent, "and nobody tells me what I can and can't do, consorte . . . What the . . . "

Half a dozen of the monsters, smoking from having been burned, rushed from the south stairwell exit.

"Madre Dios, duck," Tommy yelled.

We all followed suit and Tommy launched a grenade right into the pack of hell-spawn, exploding and splattering their remains all over the far side of the lobby.

"What are those el infierno empareja?" Tommy asked.

"We don't know," I yelled back. "They're pouring up through the sewers. Some kind of gas main explosion has forced them all toward us. We have to get to the roof."

Tommy shook himself out of shock, nodded his head, and turned back toward the stairwell.

I stopped by his penthouse entrance as Jinny and the rest poured past me and up the stairwell to the roof. A moment later Tommy escorted a young and very pregnant woman into the stairwell.

"This is my wife, Sofia," Tommy said. "Help her to the roof. I'll hold these devils off."

"But," I started to say, then Tommy turned to me with a look that silenced any and all interruptions.

"Here," Tommy said, shoving a fully loaded Beretta Model 81, and two HG-78 Austrian grenades into my hands. "You know how to use these?"

I figured it wasn't worth the time to tell him I spent

two years as an unofficial weapons instructor in El Salvador, and simply replied, "Yes."

"Then move it, Tacho Pibe," Tommy yelled. "Ain't nobody or nothing gonna lay a claw on my unborn son."

I turned to help escort Sofia up to the roof but paused for a moment to see Tommy advancing on the onrushing horde of slavering monsters, unloading a clip at full automatic and yelling in rage.

"That's right you slimy Basura," Tommy shouted. "You finally come for me, eh? Gonna drag me down to hell for all my sins, eh? Well say hello to my little friend!"

Tommy engaged the grenade launcher and I just made it to the top of the stairs and started slamming the door shut when I heard the explosion. As close as that horde was to him, I knew there was no way Tommy could have survived that blast.

"Quick," I yelled out to everyone spread across the roof, "I need string, wire, tape, belts, anything you've got. We have to booby trap this door."

Two minutes later I had a grenade wedged at what I hoped was an appropriate angle to expend the majority of its force downward into the stairwell. A tripwire would set it off two steps from the door.

"Everybody huddle close in a circle and get down," I yelled.

Sooner than I would have wished, the rigged grenade went off, and with a little luck that might buy us a couple more minutes.

"Mister David," Dhruv shouted, "I'm hearing a funny noise from that shed."

I ran to the far side of the huddled group to see

C.H.A.D.

Dhruv pointing to the elevator utility shaft mounting that housed the machine drive, overspeed governor, and control cabinet.

Angela pushed Dhruv back toward his parents and walked up beside me, holding a stained bat in both hands. I had Tommy's pistol shoved in my waistband behind my belt, and held a grenade in my right hand.

It took a few moments to kick the door in. The small chamber was empty but an odd sound seemed to be coming from the semi-closed shaft cover that the elevator cables fed through.

"You got a flashlight, or a lighter?" I asked.

"Even better," Angela said, and pulled a road flare out of her purse. She lighted the end by striking it across the concrete floor and handed it to my free left hand.

I bent over the opening and looked down, seeing what I thought was movement far below.

"I can't tell," I said, "but let's see what this does," and I dropped the lit flare down the shaft. One full second later, with my eyes wide, I leaped back and yelled.

"Get out, there must be a hundred of them."

I yanked the pin out of the grenade but kept the clip clamped down tight so I could release it at the right moment. Angela backed away with me to the door when suddenly my right leg slipped out from under me, sliding across some of the creatures' blood that had dripped off of her bat and onto the floor.

This resulted in the clumsiest of athletic footfalls, where I fell backward and half out the door while my right hand fell forward and the grenade dropped and rolled toward the elevator shaft opening, but not into it.

Simultaneously, Angela saw the situation for what it was, leaped forward, grabbed the grenade and shoved it forward down into the opening.

Before I could speak a single syllable the clawed arm of one of the creatures shot upward, grabbed Angela by the shoulder and pulled her down and out of sight. Immediately the grenade exploded, dislodging the motor and cylinder that dropped down into the shaft with a sickening crunch, hopefully taking a great many of the disgusting monsters on its long fall. A small amount of the force of the blast knocked me back out onto the roof.

Dhruv and Jinny grabbed and pulled me away and back to the group. A momentary blast of flame shot upward from the shaft and just as quickly disappeared.

On the far side of the group, Alex and Barry turned toward the far ledge of the roof and slowly walked toward it.

"Hey guys," I yelled, "what's up? You see a helicopter?"

"Naw," Alex yelled back, "some noise . . . Say, maybe it's a window washer's rig. We could use it to save all of us and . . . "

Alex screamed. I stood up and saw two of the creatures reach up over the lip of the roof, grabbing both Alex and Barry and pulling them off their feet.

I staggered around the group toward that side of the roof and pulled Tommy's pistol from my belt. Two of the creatures started climbing over the edge of the roof and I dispatched them both with clean shots to their heads. Carefully but quickly I looked over the roof edge to see the two monsters strike a dozen or more of their brethren that had also been climbing the periphery, sending all of them to splatter on the pavement below. In the low light it looked like several dozen more, far below, were still climbing upward.

Feeling a sinking sensation deep inside, I ran to the nearest corner of the rooftop and looked down. At least two-dozen of the creatures were a mere ten feet from reaching this side's roof edge. I emptied three rounds into the lead monstrosities who fell and took a bunch more with them to their deaths. I spent the next two minutes expending ammo from atop the other two sides of the rooftop before running out of bullets.

Jinny and I walked the perimeter of the rooftop twice more to confirm that what looked like two hundred or more of the monsters were climbing up all four sides, and at the pace they were moving, were only minutes away.

We joined the frightened group of ninety of our neighbors.

"I don't have any inspirational speeches to make," I said with a swallow. "Ladies and kids keep to the center. Guys, we've got the periphery. We'll take as many of these rancid hunks of mucus down as we can."

Jinny grabbed my left hand. We locked eyes.

"I always wanted to ask you out on a date," Jinny said.

"And I always wanted you to," I replied with a sad smile.

Our kiss was powerful, sweet, and all too short.

"Look," Dhruv yelled.

I spun around. First one, then another, then a dozen of the creatures slowly crawled up over the outer lip of the roof. A stream of orange sunlight slipped over the horizon and shined across my back and onto three advancing menaces. Dawn had arrived.

In what seemed like moments dozens of the monsters poured onto the rooftop and closed in on our smaller group. Then I noticed it. What looked like steam was rising from their skin. Seconds later I could smell that it was actually smoke. The sunlight was burning them.

"Everybody," I yelled, "drop down and lay flat! Do it!"

With the group hugging the roof, the rising sun shot a beam of unimpeded sunlight across one whole side of the high-rise and over the rooftop. The effect was instantaneous.

Screaming in agony, every monster in sight ignited like a torch. Some collapsed in pain and death, but a dozen rained in every direction, hopefully falling off the roof.

We slowly stood up. I looked down and saw Jinny a few feet away from the main group. She must have fallen away at an angle when we all dropped down at once. I reached out and helped her to her feet.

Without notice Jinny pulled her hand out of mine and gasped.

"Jinny," I said, "what . . . "

"I can't," she said. "I just can't . . . "

"You can't what?" I asked, and then I saw, under the illumination of dawn, the changes in her face.

"One bit my ankle," Jinny cried, "I . . . I won't become one of them."

Jinny's skin was rapidly growing dark in color. Her eyes, both cornea and iris, were starting to glow a bright yellow.

"I'm sorry, Dave," Jinny said, then turned and ran from me.

"No," I yelled and reached out to grab her, but too late. Moments later Jinny leaped over the lip of the building, down to her doom.

"No!" Dhruv yelled, but his parents grabbed and pulled the sobbing boy down into their arms.

A loud growl caught my attention. One of the monsters, horribly decayed and still burning, managed to prop itself up to one leg, and then it leaped at me. Simultaneously I half fell, half jumped back away from it.

As if in slow motion, I watched it all happening. The creature was converging on my right leg as that foot moved back away from it.

Would the monster bite or claw me, or would I just fall outside of its grasp, and escape the damnation of infection? If not, I instantly knew I faced two choices.

Would I show the bravery of Jinny, and choose a quick death over the horror of being turned into one of these disgusting monstrosities, or, would my fear of annihilation prevent me from that act? Would my will to live accept this satanic gift, forcing me out of this blinding burning sunlight, perhaps to the nearby elevator shaft, where I could crawl into the blessed darkness, living on, and existing as one of these cannibalistic humanoid apartment dwellers?

One one-hundredth of a second was all that separated us now.

It was going to be close . . . much, much too close . . .

S.A.M.S.A.'S. P.A.R.T.Y.

BEN FISHER

APRIL 16, 1984

HOW MANY TIMES have you cheated death?

I don't mean exaggerated first world inconveniences. You did not, despite your butchery of the word "literally," nearly starve waiting for the pizza guy. Hyperbole aside, how many times have you genuinely expected to die?

For the first thirty-one years I meandered this Earth, my personal count was exactly one. Not that I remember it. There were complications when I was born—possibly because my mother had a fairly loose interpretation of moderation when it came to alcohol consumption during pregnancy. Or maybe I was always just a morbidity bomb, set with a nine-month fuse. Regardless, a dozen hours and a C-section later, I escaped the reaper's boney clutches for the first time.

My mother did not.

Dad raised me with a pretty tight leash. Whenever I proposed escaping his safety zone, he'd respond with a variation of the same rehearsed speech, delivered in his pedantic, droopy voice which sounded uncannily like Art Garfunkel from an alternate dimension where, instead of music, he had pursued a career as a high school guidance counselor.

"Adam, when the nurse set you on that table, blue lips and still chest, I thought I'd lost you. And I could see in the doctor's eyes that she felt the same. Your poor mother left this earth believing her only child was stillborn. But against all odds, you're *still here*. So, if you think for one second I'm letting you get your neck broken by a two hundred pound bully chasing a football, you can just think again."

Over time, the topic of conversation shifted from contact sports to motorcycles to backpacking across Europe to—well, you get the idea. The point is, I didn't often find myself on the fun side of a risky equation during my formative years.

More recently, though, I've lost count of how often I thought my time was up. It started much like the first: with a doctor stoically relaying a dire diagnosis. The topic of conversation shifted from "preeclampsia-related neonatal death" to "lung carcinoma" to "secondary malignant neoplasm" to—well, you get the idea. The medical bills ate through my savings pretty quickly and then spread to the trust funds I'd inherited after Dad passed back in '79. They gobbled up my car, my credit cards and, after I got fired from the video rental store for missing work, they finished off with the house.

I never had close friends and no immediate family, so I bounced around shelters for a bit until a failed drug test took the air out of the ball and left me on the sidelines. Maybe it's not the best sports analogy, but since I was never allowed to actually *play* any sports, it's as good as you're going to get.

Anyway, the upshot of this little pity parade is that, for the past couple years, I've been in my share of tight spots. I've been robbed at gunpoint, knifepoint and—in one particularly unfortunate scenario—with the lower jawbone of a cow. A few months back, I stuck a needle in my arm behind the dumpster of a Chinese restaurant and woke up on a ventilator. More recently, a kid wearing a *London Falling* jacket beat me unconscious with his skateboard when I suggested The Clash were sellouts. I have no regrets about that last one.

But you know what? *I'm still here.* Just like my old man said. Maybe he wasn't expecting "here" to be an abandoned subway tunnel a quarter mile from where King Kong swatted at planes, but every day I'm still breathing is a testament to that worn-out speech. That's why I bought this journal—to memorialize the fact that I'm still standing. That I'm still here. In remission, too. Or at least I was the last time I could afford a hospital visit.

I might as well be honest here, or else what's the point? I didn't buy the journal. I stole it.

But you probably guessed that, didn't you?

APRIL 19, 1984

Eliot found something strange today.

Living under New York, you find strange things all the time. A coffee mug shaped like David Bowie's head. Waterlogged baseball cards with all the players' eyes poked out. A set of instructions hastily scrawled inside a pack of matches on how to care for something called a "mogwai." And, in one particularly unexpected instance, the bottom jaw of a cow skull.

But this was something else entirely.

"It's like a dance party or somethin', man," Eliot insisted, yanking my arm. In the three months I've known him, I've never seen Eliot enthusiastic about anything. Maybe he was excitable before the Army dropped him into the jungle with a rifle, but if so, whatever he found out there in the mud and heat stole all that away. Most days, he might as well have been an extra in a Romero flick.

But today, his whole face was animating happily around his wide, toothless grin. I didn't have the heart to dampen his spirits, so I followed him through a labyrinth of tunnels lined with trash and graffiti, struggling to keep up despite my guide's awkward shuffling gait. Eliot tells everyone who asks that his knee caught some shrapnel overseas, but one night over a bottle of vodka he confessed he'd shattered it sliding into third base during a Little League game. I could almost hear my father's admonishing sigh. The air sits heavier in those deeper regions, especially with summer approaching, but Eliot seemed perfectly comfortable in his bomber jacket and sweat pants.

"Who's having a party?" I asked, mostly to break the silence. Wherever he was leading me, I wasn't anticipating a cover charge.

"The gov'ment, man! Uncle Sam's throwin' a disco!" He cackled wildly and veered left down a narrow shaft. I began to worry I might not find my way back.

A few more turns, and Eliot stopped at the

entrance of a wide intersection, pointing spastically toward the opening. There was that toothless grin again, only now it was accented by a dull green phosphorescent light, coming from the direction of his gesture. The combination of the creepy tint and flickering shadows was unnerving.

"Look! Adam, look! You see?" He clapped once and ran into the intersection, out of sight.

"Eliot?" There was no response. It occurred to me that there hadn't been an active power supply to these tunnels for years. Nevertheless, ignoring all of my father's repeated advice, I marched forward to find out what kind of party we had crashed.

The floor was recessed slightly, allowing water to pool, and I could feel the water's cold, slimy tendrils worm through my sneakers. Any complaints remained lodged in my throat when I saw the object of Eliot's excitement. Cylindrical metal canisters leaned against each other as if huddling for warmth. Their tops and sides had eroded in multiple places and a thick jade sludge oozed its way free. The slime pulsed with the sickly radiance of a dying glowstick and emitted a dry heat that contrasted with my cold, soaking socks.

Eliot swayed before the stockpile in time to music only he could hear. His arms raised and lowered rhythmically. "Isn't this rad, man? We should, like, charge admission or something!"

Maybe there would be a cover after all.

I stepped closer until I could make out the words "Contamination Hazard Urban Disposal" stenciled in white paint on a few of the canisters. The letters had a distinctly military look, a suspicion reinforced by the "Property of U.S. Gov't" printed underneath. I don't know exactly who placed the canisters under busy city streets, but I know a fancy phrase for "toxic waste" when I see it.

"We need to go," I said and stepped backward, wanting to put as much distance between myself and that glowing sludge as possible. "Seriously, Eliot. This crap will give you tumors." But Eliot wasn't listening. He was clapping his hands and circling his discovery like a witch dancing around her cauldron. I left him there, and the echoes of his mad cackling followed me all the way down the tunnels, back to the blankets I'd gathered into a makeshift bed.

APRIL 20, 1984

I can't sleep. Visions of Eliot gleefully swaying his arms against a glowing backdrop haunt my dreams. I woke to his voice, talking in hushed, urgent whispers with the others.

There are five of us in this section of the tunnels, including me. Eliot and the other three—Michaela, Franklin, and Alice—have built a shelter out of newspaper, wooden bales, and tarp. The quarters are cramped, and frankly the idea of living huddled together like sewer rats is a little too on the nose so I put down stakes a few yards away (literally, as I'm writing from inside a tent I found outside an apartment in Queens). I can't make out Eliot's exact words, but I have a hunch he's working on a VIP list.

Should I report his find? To who? If the government stashed it there, they probably won't be thrilled with some busybody dragging their secret back out into the light. Not to mention I've got at least three outstanding warrants, so the last thing I need is to start trouble. Maybe someone will come retrieve it, and the situation will fix itself.

I'm sure everything will be fine.

APRIL 21, 1984

When Michaela brought coffee around this morning, I asked about her conversation with Eliot.

"Dude was makin' even less sense than usual. Tried to sell me tickets to some party." She poured thin brownish liquid into my mug with steady hands as she spoke. Michaela's built a moderately successful enterprise selling her own unique brew made from discarded coffee filters. It isn't an especially tasty blend, but it's caffeinated, and the price is certainly right: a cigarette or a few quarters. But I happen to know of one commodity that holds an especially high value to her.

"Stay away from there. It isn't safe." I handed her a rolled up offering of brightly colored paper held together by loose staples.

"Whatever. I traded him half a cup for directions. If I get bored, I'll—" She stopped talking when she noticed what I was holding.

"No way!" she blurted and snatched it from my hand. "The X-Men are my favorite!"

For the next few minutes, I ceased to exist as Michaela flipped through the tattered, stained pages of the comic. The cover depicted a lady with dark skin and striking white hair transforming into some sort of *Alien* rip-off. I don't read the stuff, but Michaela can't get enough of it.

"All the best fiction comes from a place of truth," I noted with feigned wisdom, raising a finger insightfully. It was something my dad used to say while watching *Star Trek* re-runs.

"Dude, Claremont is, like, the *best*!"

I nodded as if I agreed or even understood. "Good enough to get coffee for the week?"

"Are you kidding? For the *month*, Mr. A!" Our transaction complete, she put the comic on top of her cart and wheeled off toward whatever section of the underground was next on her delivery route. I keep meaning to ask her how she got that thing down here.

"I'm serious, Michaela. Steer clear of that place!" I shouted after her, but she wasn't listening. She was already back inside a brightly colored world where kids like her grew up to become superheroes rather than wafer-thin runaways trading recycled coffee grounds for tobacco.

APRIL 29, 1983

Franklin shook me awake this morning, yelling frantically about a kidnapping.

He thinks his wife, Alice (or maybe girlfriend, I've never been entirely clear on that point), was abducted last night.

"Maybe she's at the mall?" I suggested dismissively, hoping to steer the conversation toward a conclusion as quickly as possible. My interactions with Franklin are, by design, limited. The man lives in a perpetual state of unbearably high energy, some of which is likely just his naturally annoying personality, and some is from decidedly more synthesized sources.

But more importantly, he's third generation homeless, and that's a whole different breed than the rest of us.

Most of the people I've met down here have aspirations of finding their way back into the fold. We share dreams of painted walls, a refrigerator, and running water. Not Franklin. He thinks about permanent housing the way you and I think about the Smurfs' village. Which is to say, almost never, and certainly not with any real intention of establishing residence. It's hard to relate to someone like that, so we tend to avoid him. Even all the way down here at the bottom of society's well, we find ways to establish hierarchy.

"You trying to be funny? 'Cause it ain't. She went off on her own and never came back." Franklin ran a hand through his disheveled beard and leaned in close. "She *always* comes back!"

I shrugged. "Sorry, man. Then I don't know what to tell you."

"I don't need you to *tell* me anything! I need you to help look for her. You know, like a search party!"

Fortunately, Michaela rolled up before I was forced to think of an excuse to avoid scouring the tunnels for an unconscious junkie. "Your cup of joe, Mr. A." She held out her pot, waiting for me to supply the mug.

I patted my jean pockets, looking for cash. An old habit. I haven't owned a wallet in years. "Sorry, I'm out of quarters."

Michaela's forehead wrinkled. "What're you talkin' about? Month's not over yet." It was my turn to look confused. She laughed. "The comic? Remember?"

Except I didn't remember. Not right away. But then the memory flooded back, as if it had been blocked behind some clog in my head. I held out my cup, grinning sheepishly.

By the time I'd finished my coffee, Franklin's enthusiastic persistence had worn me down and I agreed to search for Alice. Eliot refused to join us, claiming his stomach hurt. I didn't believe him at the time, but when Franklin and I returned from our manhunt (without success), Eliot was leaning against a concrete pillar, doubled over and puking his guts out.

I tried to check on him but had to quickly stumble away before losing my own lunch. There, in the slick pile of vomit pooling at Eliot's feet, was the partially digested remains of a rat.

MAY 7, 1984

Alice never came back.

Franklin spends every day looking for her. Nights, too. All that boundless energy is good for something, I guess.

Eliot's mostly absent as well, spending his time on a private dance floor twenty feet beneath a manhole cover on 32nd Street. He's losing hair, and an oily rash has spread up his neck and across one cheek. It must itch something fierce because he's constantly clawing at it absent-mindedly, his fingernails leaving bloody trails down his face. He talks even less than usual, and when he does, his words are slurred and thick in his mouth. I've tried telling him that whatever's in those containers is making him sick, but he doesn't care.

"It's m-mmmine! Uncle Sam g-gave it to mmmme for t-time served!" Eliot sputtered in my ear this afternoon. It caught me off guard and I jumped, spilling coffee on my *Sports Illustrated*. For years, I've read the daily paper, but the *Times* must've hired new editors, because lately the stories have been hard to follow, stuffed with too many names and places. Pictures are better. I like looking at athletes. Fit. Muscular. I like their skin.

At this close range, I noticed Eliot's complexion was turning a dark olive, as if the glow from that ooze had stained his flesh.

Flesh.

"It's not for you," I assured him. "Why don't you help Franklin look for Alice today? Change things up a bit." I leaned back as I spoke. Even to my desensitized nose, the pungent odor wafting off him was unbearable.

"F-Franklin is . . . done s-searching," he chortled dryly and shambled off into the dark. I didn't get the joke, but while he was laughing I noticed small jagged flashes of white between his chapped lips. Eliot's been all gums since I've known him. Is it possible to grow new teeth? That was exactly the weird sort of trivia that Dad would know. I should call him to ask.

Except Dad's dead. His ticker had given out at the exact same moment that he'd won fifty bucks from a gas station scratch-off lottery card. I kept that card in my pocket for years, until I ran out of ways to pay the electric bill and decided to cash it in. I cried more when I found out it was too late to collect the winnings than I did at his funeral.

How could I forget that?

Maybe I should talk to Reverend Sheppard. He might know what to do. I'm not allowed back in his shelter thanks to a certain jawbone-related altercation, but I could always swing by his soup kitchen.

The thought turns my stomach, though, and not just from the idea of drawing unwanted attention to myself. My appetite's been unreliable. I'm hungry, but nothing seems all that appealing. Just imagining myself over a bowl of broth triggers my gag reflex.

I'm terrified the cancer's returned. Maybe it's just the flu.

MAY 15, 1984

It's nott the flu.

But I don't think I'm out of remmission, either. This feels different. Some symptoms are familiar—I don't eat much, despite having an appetite, and what I do eat rarely stays down. But now there's a buzzing sound in my skull. Reverberating like someone's pressing my forehead against the side of a hornet's nest. I can hear the insects writhing around just beneath the surface. Always sscratching. Hungry.

Michelle brought me cofee this morning. I can't drink it anymore, but I still trade for it when I can. I like her coming around. Like knowing I'm not the only one still here. Normally, I wait until she's gone before I pour it out, but this morning the smell was overpowering. I dropped my mug and dry heaved over the shattered pieces. I tried to remmember the words that had been printed across its porcelain surface. *World's Best Boss*, I think. Or maybe *Is It Friday Yet?* The memmory's blurry, like trying to read with your eyes crossed.

Wait. Not Michelle. Mindy? No, Michaela. Having trouble with names.

"Cofee's no good, Mr. A?" There was genuine concern in her voice.

"It's fine. I just don't feel welll." Something was poking against the inside of my cheek. I spit and a tooth bounced against the concrete, skittering out of sight.

Mindy squatted down and helped pick up the cup fragments. Her bare arms were dirty but smooth. So smooth. "You can tell me if it's bad. I've got a business to run, and it ain't doin' me no favors to let me sell bad cofee." She scrunched up her nose, and the effect was probably cuter than she intended. In a different life, she would have broken a lot of harts. "I never drink the stuff. Too bitter."

"I said it's finne." The words came out angrier than I intended. I don't usually have a temper, but she was asking too many questions. And my head hurt.

"Okay, Mr. A. Whatever you say. Figured it wasn't the new recipe, since you haven't been complaining."

My stomach churned. "What do you mean?"

Mindy leaned in conspiratorially. "Remember when Eliot told me about that special party? Well, I took a peek and it was like somethin' out of a *Fantastic Four* comic."

My temples throbbbed. "I don't understand—"

"I'd been thinking about what you said—that fiction comes from facts, right? And then I got to thinking about how superheroes gets their powers. You know, super serums and stuff like that."

Something deep in my throat tightened. I sat down heavily to stop the world from spinnning.

"Anyways, I gotta run, Mr. A. Customers are waiting and the brew's getting cold. See you in the morning!"

SAMSA'S PARTY

As she left, I presssed my forehead into my knees, and that's when I saw it, mixed in with the spilled cofee. Traces of dark green, pulsing faintly. I wiggled an incisor around with my tongue before plucking it out like a weed.

Tommorrow, I'm going to get ridd of it. All of it.

The party's over.

MAY 16, 1984

Todday did not go as expected.

It was mid-afternoon before I worked up the ennergy to wind through the network of abandoned tunnels. At least, I *think* it was mid-afternoon. Time has a way of getting losst down here. It ripples with the darkness and humidity until marking its passage is like holding a measuring stick up to the rain. I wore a watch once, in a diffferent life. Digital. Lit up at night. I could tell you what time it was to the precise seckond. It's hard to imagine now why that ever seemed important.

What was I writting about? Yes, finding the stockpile. I had to double back a few times. The directions were fuzzzy. My head is filled with cotton. The buzzing never stops. Somewhere along those twists and turns, I tore offf my shoes and tossed them against the wall. They hugged my swollen feet too tightly, like walking inside a vice.

I paused when I finally saw the dimm green light spilling from around a corner. There was a soft noise. Like someone slurpping up thick, wet noodles. After taking a deep breath, I continued walking, this time enjoying the cool muck betweeen my toes.

The stash was still there, squatting in its own luminescence like some hulking, diseased beast. My eyes were immmediately drawn to a figure crouched nearby. The man's shoulders heaved and his head shook back and fforth violently.

Drawing closer, I recognized Eliot's bomber jacket. But the creature who turned to face me bore no resemblance to the man who told boot cammp stories between vodka shots. Its misshapen face was covered in a membrane of slime, dominated by jagged teeth and reptilian eyes. Thinn, veiny arms ended in clawed hands, a mass of sharp angles and webbed skin.

It barked a dry rasp that was both inhuman and yet somehow eerily familiar. The uttterance came again, and this time I recognized Eliot's delirious cackle. A distinctly natural sound buried under layers of something unfathomably monstrous. Like hearing an insect weep.

The thing returned its atttention to what I now saw was a body sprawled face down in the shallow water. Its jagged teeth clamped down and it shoook its head a second time, creating bloody ripples as the body rocked back and forth. Trails of sinew and skin stretched and tore, leaving thin flaps of meat against the corpse. The victim's face turned towards me, and I gasped at the sight of Franklin's damp, unruly beard.

The sound of my inhale startled the thing-that-was-Eliot, and it stood quickly. For a moment, I thought it might leapp upon me, dragging me into the water to join Frankklin. But instead it pivoted and sprinted down a side passsage, grunting and moving with the gait of a wounded animal. Its eyes glowed britely in the darkness.

SAMSA'S PARTY

I nelt down by Franklin and rolled him over. Bite marks marrred his body in a dozen places. Eliot had taken his time feasting.

Then, to my great surrprise, Franklin's eyes opened and he drew a deep, shuddering breath. Pink foam bubbled around his lips. He was scared. Conffused.

I leaned closer. "I'm sorry," I told him.

"I'm so sorry." And I meannt it.

But I was so hungry.

MAY 23, 1984

Cofee girl rong. No super herroes. Only monnsters.

Saw man in wite soot with ticking box. I tride tell man to runn. But we arre all hungry.

May be annother man in wite soot willl find jerrnal. Read my words innside. Until thenn, jernal is *still heer*.

But nott me. Nott this time.

I am gonne.

T.H.E. W.A.Y. T.O. A. M.A.N.'S. H.E.A.R.T.

TIM WAGGONER

OFFICER LUMLEY WAS about to ask June out—the words were on his lips—when he felt a prickling on the back of his neck, as if someone was watching him. He'd only been a cop for a couple years, but the streets of New York honed your instincts fast, and he'd learned to trust his. June stood behind the counter, facing the opposite direction of Lumley and his partner Proscia, who sat on stools, their backs to the diner's windows. June's gaze was fixed on a point over the cops' heads. Her eyes widened and the blood drained from her face, and Lumley knew his instinct that something was wrong was on the money.

Proscia must've sensed the same thing, for both Lumley and his partner swiveled around on their stools at the same time to see what was happening behind them. The first thing Lumley registered were glowing yellow orbs floating outside the windows. Eight of them. A split second later he realized that what he was looking at were four pairs of eyes, but eyes like nothing he had ever seen before. They looked like light bulbs that had been screwed into the empty eye sockets. The details of the faces struck him then, and at first, he refused to believe what he saw. Hairless heads, moist green flesh, pointed ears, broad noses, fang-filled mouths . . . Then the glowing-eyed creatures raised four-fingered clawed hands and slammed them against the windows, sending shattered fragments of glass flying into the diner. As the first of the four monsters began to climb through the openings they had made, June screamed, and Lumley thought, I almost did it. I almost asked her.

Lumley and Proscia had been coming into the diner for close to two months now. Not because the food was anything special, but because Lumley had a thing about June since the first time he'd seen her. She wasn't a great beauty, but then he didn't exactly look like a movie star, either. She was a slender brunette with an I-don't-take-any-crap attitude, and she wore a cute pink uniform when working. Lumley liked to put up a brash front and come across as a joker, but in truth he was shy when it came to women—something Proscia teased him about—and he'd been trying to ask June out for a couple weeks now, and when he'd finally worked up the nerve, a bunch of damn glowing-eyed monsters had ruined it for him.

The creatures—Shiners, Lumley dubbed them because of their eyes—were broad-shouldered, thick-necked, and muscular, but they moved with surprising speed, climbing into the diner with ease. The creatures made sounds as they came, animalistic roars blended with an unnatural ratcheting, like a rattlesnake's tail. They wore ragged scraps of clothing encrusted with filth and muck, and they smelled like raw sewage combined with a chemical odor that reminded Lumley of paint thinner. The stench joined with the smell of cheeseburgers cooking on the grill, a nauseating mixture that turned Lumley's stomach and nearly caused him to puke up the burger he'd already eaten.

Lumley, Proscia, and June weren't the only people in the diner. A guy in a blue T-shirt and gray cap sat a few stools away from Proscia, and he was the first to shake off the paralysis of terror that had taken hold of the diner's occupants when the monsters attacked. He jumped off his stool and ran for the door, but he only made it halfway before a Shiner lunged toward him and swiped a clawed hand at his shoulder. The creature's claws shredded the T-shirt's fabric and sliced into the flesh beneath. Blood sprayed the air, and the force of the blow sent the man sprawling to the diner floor, howling in pain. The Shiner that attacked the man fell upon him, head stretching forward on a suddenly elongated neck. The creature sank its sharp teeth into the man's soft neck-flesh, and his howl became a choking gurgle as blood filled his throat.

One of the remaining Shiners, tempted by the prospect of easy-to-get meat, broke away from the other two to join in the savaging of the man in the T-shirt, whose limbs now flailed in spastic death throes. That left two Shiners to attack Lumley and Proscia.

"Get out of here!" Lumley shouted to June, and then he jumped off his stool and drew his service revolver. He didn't turn to see if June did as he'd urged her. He didn't have time. He assumed a shooting stance and fired at one of the approaching Shiners. The .38 round struck the creature in the right pectoral, but while the bullet's impact caused the creature to jerk to the side, it didn't go down. A glowing neon-green substance oozed forth from the wound, and Lumley thought, That stuff can't be blood—can it?

The Shiner clapped a clawed hand to its wound and took a step back. It removed its hand and examined the glowing green goo smeared on its corrugated palm. It cocked its head as if confused.

Proscia had risen from his stool the same time Lumley had, and he'd also drawn his revolver. But he moved slower than Lumley—his shock at seeing honest-to-god monsters attacking getting in the way of his training, Lumley guessed—and the second Shiner rushed him. Proscia managed to get off a shot, but he only hit the monster's left ear, reducing it to a mass of ragged meat and broken cartilage. Green blood splattered onto the creature's shoulder, but unlike its companion, this Shiner didn't hesitate. It plowed into Proscia, slammed him against the counter, and grabbed hold of the man's face, the claws on its four-fingered hand penetrating Proscia's flesh. Proscia's gun hand was pinned between them, and as he struggled to angle the revolver's barrel so he could shoot the Shiner, the monster closed its hand and pulled.

Proscia screamed like a soul damned to hell as the Shiner tore his face off, taking chunks of his skull and his lower jaw with it. Blood poured from the red-raw opening where Proscia's face had been, and Lumley— dealing with his own shock now—thought that he'd never see his partner smile again. The man had a great smile, and he never had trouble getting women to talk to him. All he had to do was flash that smile, and the ice was well and truly broken. Of course, it was hard to smile when all you had left was your upper row of teeth.

Proscia's finger tightened on his revolver's trigger in reflex, and the weapon fired. Lumley couldn't tell where the bullet went, but the Shiner didn't react, so Lumley assumed the round had hit the floor. Or worse—Proscia had shot himself. *At least he can't feel it*, Lumley thought, and he felt an intense urge to laugh wildly. He fought it off, knowing that if he started laughing now he wouldn't be able to stop until one of the Shiners silenced him forever.

The one-eared Shiner threw Proscia's face to the floor where it hit with a sickening smack. Its head shot forth on an elongated neck, and it buried its face in the gaping crimson hole in Proscia's head, gripping the man's shoulders to keep his body from falling. Blood-Ear began shaking its own head back and forth, like a dog worrying a bone, making snuffling and slurping noises as it fed.

Lumley felt hot bile splash the back of his throat, but he didn't have time to be sick. Proscia and the guy in the gray cap might be dead, but June was still alive. He'd sworn an oath to serve and protect when he took this job, and by God, he intended to make good on it.

He aimed his revolver at the Shiner that had killed Proscia and which now seemed to be doing its best to chew a path to his partner's brain. But before he could fire, June—who had ignored his plea to run—reached behind her, grabbed a glass pot filled with hot coffee, stepped forward, and slammed it against the ruins of the creature's ear. Glass shattered and scalding hot coffee splashed the creature, and it withdrew from Proscia's head with a hideous squelch. The Shiner, its face smeared with Proscia's blood, howled—in pain, anger, or both.

Lumley grinned. That's my girl.

He intended to shoot Blood-Ear, but as his finger tightened on the trigger, the Shiner he'd shot in the arm recovered whatever presence of mind it possessed and attacked with a roar. Lumley spun toward the creature and fired. The round struck the creature's right eye, popping it like a gigantic boil filled with glowing green pus. The Shiner let out an ear-splitting shriek and swung its left arm toward Lumley. The creature's claws struck his upper arm, spinning him around and causing him to lose his grip on his revolver. Fire exploded in his arm, and he knew the Shiner—One-Eye—had drawn blood. Lumley's side smacked into the edge of the counter, and the impact knocked the wind out of him. He felt more than heard a snap in his chest, and he knew he'd cracked a few ribs, maybe even broken them.

He ignored the pain—the adrenaline surging through his system helped—and started toward One-Eye. He drew his nightstick and swung it at the side of the creature's head. Out of the corner of his eye he caught a glimpse of June. She still gripped the handle of the coffee pot, which remained connected to a large shard of glass, and she was using it as a weapon to slash Blood-Ear's face. Her expression was one of grim determination, and Lumley thought he'd never seen a woman so magnificent in his life.

Before Lumley's nightstick could make contact with One-Eye, the creature's hand shot out and caught hold of his wrist, halting the strike. Lumley gritted his teeth and struggled to pull free of the Shiner's grip, but the damn thing was too strong. Its neck lengthened, and like a striking snake, its head lunged forward and its fangs sank into Lumley's forearm. The pain was more intense than anything he'd ever experienced before—a hundred times worse than the claw wound on his upper arm. But along with the pain came another sensation, a warm tingling that he couldn't identify.

After several seconds, One-Eye withdrew its teeth from Lumley's arm and then backhanded him across the face. Bright light flashed behind Lumley's eyes, and he went down hard. The side of his head struck the tiled floor, and his vision blurred. He lay there, head throbbing, arm burning like fire, and watched as the Shiners that had been eating Gray-Cap stood. Their faces and clothes were smeared with the man's blood, and one of the Shiners grabbed the half-eaten corpse and threw it over his shoulder. One-Eye picked up Proscia's body and did the same, and the fourth Shiner, whose face was now streaked with glowing green lines thanks to June, knocked the coffee pot shard out of her hand, grabbed her under the arms, and pulled her over the counter. She screamed and thrashed, but she couldn't break free from Blood-Ear— actually, now Blood-Face. Lumley feared the Shiner would kill her, but it didn't. Instead, the creature put her over its shoulder, as the others had done with the two corpses, and then the four monsters crawled through the broken windows, leaving the way they'd come.

Lumley continued to lay there, waiting for his head to clear enough so he could stand. He had no idea why the Shiners had left him. He was a beefy guy, sure, but strong as those things were, they'd have no trouble carrying him. He decided it really didn't matter why he'd been spared. The things had made a mistake letting him live, and he planned to show them just how big of a mistake it was.

June continued to scream, her voice growing fainter the farther Blood-Face carried her. Lumley then heard the sound of iron scraping against iron—a manhole cover being removed, he guessed. A moment later there was another metallic scraping, and then June's screams were cut off.

They've taken her into the sewers, Lumley thought. That explained their smell.

He couldn't afford to lie there any longer. He had no idea where the Shiners would take June or how long they'd keep her alive, but with each passing second they moved farther away.

Clenching his jaw against the pain caused by his damaged ribs, he got his hands beneath him and pushed himself into a kneeling position. He took a couple deep breaths, and then stood. A wave of dizziness hit him and he almost passed out, but he managed to remain conscious. His right arm tingled painfully as if it had fallen asleep, but he could still use it. Did Shiners inject some kind of venom when they bit? As long as his arm functioned, he decided he didn't care. All that mattered was reaching June before the glowing-eyed bastards could hurt her.

He'd dropped his nightstick when he fell, and he retrieved it now. He also grabbed his revolver, which had four rounds left. Proscia's weapon lay on the floor nearby, and he holstered his gun and picked up his partner's. It had four rounds, too. He tucked Proscia's revolver into his belt, and he then headed toward the diner's door. His legs were unsteady, but they didn't buckle, and he chose to take that as a good sign.

Time to go hunting, he thought.

★★★

Even if Lumley hadn't heard the Shiners open and close the manhole in the street outside the diner, he would've been able to track them by the wide blood trail they'd left. Evidently the creatures had tossed Proscia's and Gray-Cap's bodies onto the ground once they were outside and dragged them. He hoped they hadn't done the same to June.

He pulled the manhole cover aside, climbed down into the hole, and then pulled the cover back into place. He knew it wouldn't prevent any Shiners from going to the surface if they wanted, but at least it would slow them down a little. He descended the rest of the way, and when he reached the bottom—standing in several inches of foul-smelling water—he removed the flashlight from his belt, turned it on, and shined its beam down the tunnel one direction before turning around and shining it in the opposite direction. Which way had they gone? There was no blood trail to follow now because of the water. Even the green goo that the Shiners bled would likely be diluted. He listened to see if he could hear the creatures moving, but he heard nothing but the drip-drip-drip of water falling close by.

He inhaled through his nostrils, and along with the sour stink of sewage, he detected an acrid odor, like paint thinner. He took a few steps forward, and the chemical smell grew weaker. He started back the other way, and the smell grew stronger. He knew which way to go.

THE WAY TO A MAN'S HEART

He felt warm as if he had a fever, and his right arm now tingled all the way to his shoulder. Maybe he had been poisoned. But all that meant to him now was that he had to hurry even faster.

He started jogging down the tunnel, following the Shiners' scent like a bloodhound.

Lumley had no sense of how long he traveled or where he was in relation to the city above. He'd lost track of how many turns he'd taken, and there were blank spaces in his memory, almost as if his mind had lost consciousness but his body had continued moving. The tingling sensation in his right arm had spread throughout his body, only now it felt more like an intense itching, both on the surface of his skin and inside him. Was it possible for internal organs to itch? It felt like his did. He kept scratching his arms, neck, and face, but it didn't help. He was afraid he was hurting himself without realizing it, for his nails were sharp—overdue for clipping, he supposed—and his fingers kept encountering rough patches of skin.

He was still feverish, but now it felt as if the heat was emanating from deep inside him and was being transferred throughout his body via his circulatory system. His eyes ached and his vision had taken on a yellowish tint. He thought maybe he had some kind of eye infection, or maybe it was due to some kind of reaction to the Shiner's venom. The tips of his fingers ached, as did his teeth, and his hair was beginning to fall out. Worst of all, though, was the gnawing emptiness in the pit of his stomach. It wasn't hunger. This sensation was so far beyond hunger that he didn't think there were any words to describe it. He felt as if inside him was a vast endless nothing, a yawning black void which could never be filled, no matter how much he put into it.

His thoughts had grown sluggish, too. It was becoming increasingly more difficult to think, but worse than that, thinking hurt. He literally experienced pain whenever he tried to think, and he only had relief when he let his mind go blank and operated on autopilot.

He was certain he was dying, and that was okay. He'd known the risks of the job before he'd signed on for it. Although no one at the academy had warned him that he might have to fight poisonous flesh-eating sewer monsters one day. But he wouldn't mind dying, not if he could rescue June first.

At least his ribs didn't hurt anymore, and neither did the wound on his arm where One-Eye had slashed him. That was something.

He continued putting one foot in front of the other, splashing through brackish water, holding the flashlight, but not really paying attention to what its beam illuminated. Instead, he let his nose guide him. Eventually, he began to hear noises, and what sounded like moans of pleasure. He drew his revolver with his free hand and did his best to ignore the fiery itching in his fingers as he gripped the weapon tight.

The tunnel opened onto a large chamber with a high roof, and Lumley saw a dozen Shiners or more gathered together. Half of them crouched next to Proscia's and Gray-Cap's ravaged bodies, picking at what little meat remained on their bones, and moaning as they fed. The other Shiners stood before a haphazardly arranged collection of industrial drums. The metal on several of the storage containers had corroded, and a glowing green fluid that looked exactly like the Shiners' blood leaked out, the chemical trails converging to form a single iridescent pool. The Shiners stood with their arms raised over their heads, and they were making a kind of rhythmic thrumming sound, almost as if they were chanting.

They're worshipping that stuff, Lumley thought, and winced at the pain that rippled through his brain. Following that thought came the realization that whatever the glowing green goop was, it had created the Shiners. That was why they had the same substance in their veins instead of normal blood.

One-Eye stood with the worshippers, but the creature wasn't holding its hands over its head. Instead, its clawed hands gripped June's shoulders. The woman knelt in front of him, facing the collection of metal drums as if One-Eye was forcing her to participate in the creature's obscene ritual.

As relieved as Lumley was to see June alive and apparently unharmed, he knew he had to act fast if he wanted her to stay that way. The glowing goo—not to mention the Shiners' eyes—provided enough light for him to see by, so he dropped his flashlight and pulled Proscia's revolver from his belt. He now held two guns, four rounds in each, eight total. He'd better make them count.

But as he stepped forward, weapons raised, ready to start blasting away at the monsters, he felt something inside him. No . . . he heard it, like a voice that spoke to him directly in his mind. But this voice wasn't talking. It was singing. It was the most beautiful sound he'd ever heard, the music unearthly and ethereal. It washed away his fever and the itching, along with his other pains, but even it could do nothing about the terrible hunger raging within him.

He stood there for a moment, unmoving, and he understood that what he was hearing was the song of the Green, a song that came from the drums, from the pool of chemicals, from the blood that flowed within him. He lowered his revolvers, loosened his grip and let them fall to the ground.

The Shiners turned to look at him, One-Eye included. June looked too, and an expression of profound relief mingled with hope came onto her tear-streaked face.

"Thank God you're here! I was afraid—" She broke off then, frowning, eyes squinting to make him out in the chamber's dim light.

She shook her head in denial.

"No," she said, fresh tears coming into her eyes. "Dear God, no!"

Lumley wasn't sure why she was so upset. Couldn't she hear the song? It sang of family, of togetherness, of feeding until the emptiness inside wasn't quite so empty anymore. For a little while, at least.

He scratched absentmindedly at his forearm and was only mildly surprised to see beads of glowing blood well forth on his moist green skin. The yellow tint to his vision grew stronger, brighter, more pervasive, until a bright golden light filled his entire field of vision. It was magnificent.

Part of him—a small, dwindling part which was still, for the moment, human—wondered if One-Eye had done this to him on purpose in order to get back at him for shooting out his eye. Or maybe the Shiners didn't kill every human they encountered. Maybe they infected some in order to increase their numbers. Whichever the truth was, it didn't matter. All that mattered was the song, and the hunger, and June. She looked so beautiful to him. Good enough to eat, in fact.

He bared his new teeth and started toward her.

D.W.E.L.L.E.R. M.E.S.S.I.A.H.

JASON WHITE

OSCAR DIDN T KNOW that a human body could hold so much blood until he saw it spraying out of someone's throat, felt its heat upon his face. The violence happened so quickly he stood frozen, watching long after it had happened, trying to process it, figure it out.

It was sudden, lightning quick. He'd been talking with the homeless guys when it happened. They stood on flattened cardboard boxes, cushioning for their feet.

Oscar had decided earlier in the day that he wasn't going to go home anymore. Not run away so much as just never return. He'd always seen the "filthy homeless bums" (as his father often called them) standing around the streets to and from school. They had it pretty good. They didn't have to worry about school and homework. The only thing he had to do now was figure out what to do with his school backpack and the black trumpet case he carried, the latter of which was becoming heavy and tiresome.

"Why you wanna live on the streets, little man?"

the black man with the shaggy gray beard had said. "This ain't no place for a kid. Especially a kid like you." He pointed to Oscar's tie and blazer the school forced him to wear. "Not these days."

The other man was also bearded and when he smiled there were no teeth, his mouth an uninviting entrance to a dark cave. That's another bonus for going homeless, Oscar thought. He'd never have to brush his teeth or take a bath.

His smile turned into laughter, despite no one having said anything funny. The black man went on, talking over the other man's laughter.

"If I were you," the black man said, "I'd just go on home and forget about your troubles. The troubles out here are worse."

How the homeless man could know that for a certain confused Oscar. He's never met the man before, so how could he know the nightmare of living in his apartment? He didn't know, and that was the real fact. Yet, Oscar was just as ignorant of what the homeless man was talking about. All Oscar saw was freedom. Considering the homeless man lived out here, he had to know what he was talking about.

"Winter can be rough, I'll bet," Oscar said. The comment made the second homeless man stop laughing. His expression became grim.

"You're sure right about that," the black man said. He shivered despite the heat and endless layers of sweat that glistened upon his skin. "But there's something else, something far more dangerous than any cold night, my little man."

The violent thing happened then, as though to prove the man's point. Something pushed against the cardboard upon which they stood. A hand, green with thick white claws, reached out and grabbed the laughing homeless man by his leg. The man was no longer laughing. Instead, his eyes wide with terror, he screamed. The black man screamed, too.

"It's them!" he said. He backed up, turned, and ran into the darkness of the alley.

The thing that had a hold of the second homeless man's leg pulled itself up out of the hole. It wasn't really a face Oscar was confronted with. Not a human face. Not an animal's. He had the frightening reminder of the mutated animals the kids at school liked to joke about, how giant alligators and rats crawled around beneath New York's streets. But this thing was nothing like an alligator or a rat. The skin was a sickly green, the eyes huge ovals that glowed sickly yellow light. It pulled the homeless man into the hole, but before he completely disappeared, the thing's large and white claws dug into the poor man's throat, shedding skin and meat as though it were jelly.

And then both monster and homeless man were gone. The black man was gone, too. Oscar was alone with only the honks and sirens of the traffic behind him, the dying light of the dying day.

The blood cooled on his cheeks and Oscar figured that the black man was right. The nightmare of his home was preferable to what he had just confronted. But what had he just seen? His head spun and his stomach hurt. His heart pounded inside his chest.

Home it was then. His feet pounded the pavement the final two blocks, his own mouth the opening to some cave that emitted empty, windless screams.

★★★

The elevator chugged and clanged as it took Oscar up to the sixth-floor. The entire floor was his and his family's home, so when the doors opened he was standing in the front lobby of the apartment. His heart still pounded and fluttered like the wings of a panicked hummingbird. His hand carried the trumpet with white, strained knuckles. He trembled uncontrollably and as he walked into the main living room, his breath came in gasps. The soft melody of his dad's singing along with his own recording, washing over him as he moved, offered no comfort. He feared he'd never warm up ever again. From a little beyond, a set of naked toes stuck out from the edge of the couch. They probably belonged to his mother.

"Where have you been?" It was Melinda, the live-in nanny. Oscar had been too busy staring at his mother's feet to notice her approach. She stopped before him, her eyes widening as she took in the site before her, her expression changing from rage to concern.

"My God! What happened to your face?"

"I . . . I don't know," Oscar said. "There's was a man, and . . . and . . . "

"Oh, never mind that. Your father sees you this dirty, he'll have your hide. He's in a ripe mood for it as it is. Come on."

Melinda stepped around Oscar and grabbed him by the shoulders, ushering him through the living room. As they passed the couch, Oscar's heart sank. His mother lay on her back, one arm dangling off the side so that her fingers nearly touched the plush carpeting from where an empty bottle of Johnnie Walker lay on its side. Her other arm shielded her eyes from the overhead lights. Her breathing was shallow and steady. She was in a deep sleep.

"Don't you worry about her right now," Melinda said, pushing him from behind. Her hands guided him down the hall and into his bedroom. From there, they went straight into the washroom.

"Get those clothes off, now!" Melinda took the trumpet case and knapsack from Oscar and disappeared into his room, returning quickly with a set of silk pajamas. While she was gone, he worked on taking off his blazer and shirt. When Melinda returned, she stared at the bathtub first.

"No," she said, almost to herself. "No time." She looked down at him. Her eyes were still wide and fearful. Oscar had really messed up this time. But there was love in her eyes, as well. A motherly love otherwise absent in his life.

"You should already be in bed now. If your father finds you still up and me out of my rooms, there will be a high price to pay."

She turned the water from the sink on once Oscar was out of his pants. He stood shivering, feeling sick to his stomach while she soaked a facecloth and then lathered it with a bar of soap.

"Where the Dickens were you, anyway? You had me worried sick! And what's all this on your face? Is it dirt?

The "dirt" came off onto the facecloth the color of rust. The look of it reminded Oscar of the homeless men he'd been talking to, more importantly, the spray of blood from the one's throat and his silent screams.

Tears welled in his eyes. The trembling of his limbs intensified until he feared he'd shake his bones right out from his skin. Would his own blood spray like the homeless man's if that were to happen?

Melinda paused and looked into his eyes. She knelt to Oscar's eye level.

"What happened to you tonight?"

"Th-there's something below th-the streets."

Oscar didn't get to expand. Through the bathroom mirror, Oscar saw as the door to his bedroom opened in the other room, his father stumbling through. He wore only a black pair of dress pants, the stench of whiskey radiated from him even though Oscar was in the bathroom.

"There you are!" His father's voice was loud and filled the room. It was nothing like the smooth, silky voice that came through the speakers throughout the apartment. "You're a useless waste of space. The both of you."

The fear returned to Melinda's eyes, but it wasn't fear for herself. Oscar's dad never hurt her.

"You are dismissed for the night, Melinda. Me and the boy got some talkin' to do."

He started to unlatch the buckle of his belt, then thought of something better. That better thing was his fists. He was already flexing them and cracking the knuckles as though warming them up.

Oscar wanted to cry, to fight, to hold onto Melinda and never let go. That behavior only ever managed to make things worse. He could not, however, fight back the tears. Tears of rage, fear, helplessness. Melinda couldn't fight it back either. She paused, and Oscar could tell that she wanted to stay, to do something. But that would be even worse than Oscar fighting back.

"Just go," Oscar mouthed. Melinda nodded, her face a ruin of tears, tightened muscles, and quivering lips.

★★★

"Hey, little man! What happened to your face?"

Oscar jumped. His heart picked up rhythm making his head pound and he squinted in the direction the voice had come from. It had been a couple of days since he'd been out of the apartment. He was still wobbly on his feet.

The speaker was the homeless black man with the giant gray beard from the other night. He smiled down at Oscar; the teeth that remained in his skull were different shades of black and brown.

"I thought the CHUD got you! Thank heavens it did not!" The smile grew bigger and he clapped his hands together, clasping them as he looked to the sky. "Judging by your face, you gave it a good fight."

"That thing didn't do this," Oscar said. He surprised himself at the sharp tone. He'd never talked to an adult that way before. "And what are you talking about? What's a CHUD?"

"That's C.H.U.D. for fancy folks like yourself. It's the thing we saw the other night. It took poor old Johnny away. He's the gent from the other night. The one who made no sounds when he opened his mouth. But I'm glad that it didn't take you, my little man."

What do you care? Oscar regretted the thought and was thankful he kept it to himself. The old man didn't deserve Oscar's anger.

"My name's Peter, by the way," the old man continued. "My friends call me Pete. You can, too."

Oscar liked the homeless man, Pete, but he didn't want to hand over his name to him just yet.

"What do the letters C.H.U.D. stand for? And how do you know what they're called?"

"I see my little man is skeptical. That's a good thing," Pete said and laughed. "I heard some men in these big, funky suits call 'em that just yesterday. They went down into the sewers with what looked like *flamethrowers*. Can you believe that? They never came back far's I know."

"What's C.H.U.D?"

"That's the best part, little man. These men, they called the creatures Cannibalistic Humanoid Underground Dwellers. C.H.U.D! Sounds like something you'd see on the television."

Pete's excitement confused Oscar. "If you like them so much," he said, "then why'd you run so fast from them?"

"I don't like them one bit. I just find them fascinating, little man."

"Why?"

"Because they're an abomination, a mutation. They shouldn't exist, and yet they are all over the tunnels beneath the streets. They're starting to come up to the surface now."

There was something different about Pete that Oscar didn't understand. Maybe it was that he was homeless and Oscar never talked to the homeless before because his parents told him not to, or maybe it was the scary words that came from his toothless mouth. Perhaps it was his eyes that reflected too much of the morning light. His skin wasn't as brown, either. It was paler. Greener.

"You be sure to bring your father next time he hurts you," Pete said. "CHUD will take care of him real good for you. Fix him all up, teach him how to treat kids."

Pete smiled, showing off those rotten teeth. Oscar had seen that kind of smile before. A hungry smile; it reminded him of his dad and mom opening a fresh bottle of Glenlivet or Johnnie Walker. It was the look whenever Dad's music came on throughout the apartment, two of the same voices singing the same words, and Father coming at him with the belt wrapped around whitened knuckles wearing that grin that meant only one thing.

Pain.

★★★

"What happened to your face, freak?" Paul said. He pushed Oscar into his locker, his head banging off the metal door. "Someone finally decide to show you what an idiot you are?"

The kids around Paul, his regular followers, laughed as though it was the funniest thing.

"Leave me alone," Oscar said. He tried to continue, but Paul, two years older than him, placed his hands on his back and pushed. Paul also hooked Oscar's left foot onto the back of his right at the same time, forcing Oscar forward onto his face. His trumpet case slid across the floor. He landed with a slap and a grunt, his already sore face screaming in agony. Oscar wanted to join in and shout until his throat hurt.

The laughter now above intensified. Sneakered feet and uniformed pants surrounded him.

"You're pathetic, kid," Paul said.

Oscar closed his eyes, squinting, fully expecting Paul's foot to smash into his ribcage. His father had done the same the other night. Instead, the laughter faded and was joined by the squeak of rubber soles on hardwood.

Oscar opened his eyes. Alone, he sat up. His eyes hurt and it took him a second to realize that they were full of tears.

You be sure to bring your father next time he hurts you, Pete had said to him not a half hour ago.

Clenching his fists, he wiped at the tears and got up to his feet. He ran in the direction Paul and his idiot followers had gone. They weren't very far away, just down the hall and around the corner. Other students bumped past him and someone yelled, "There is to be no running in the halls."

Oscar didn't care. He barely heard.

Only Paul was within his narrowed vision.

Once he reached the older kid, he slapped his hand onto his shoulder. He turned around to meet Oscar's fist. Paul's nose crunched beneath Oscar's knuckles. The blood came quickly as Paul fell, cupping the bloodied nose between his hands. Still, the blood seeped through.

Oscar wasn't finished. His foot caught Paul under the chin, knocking him onto his back, and then Oscar was on top of the boy, his knuckles growing bloodier with each blow he dealt.

"Leave me alone!" He shouted. "All of you! Leave me ALONE!"

★★★

"What were you thinking?" Oscar's mother said. "You're lucky your dad's in the studio or he'd have your hide."

They were sitting in the backseat of the car. Jonathan, the driver, made eye contact with Oscar in the rearview mirror for a brief second. Oscar thought he saw approval there before the man looked away, but he wasn't sure.

His mother's breath smelled strongly of scotch and it wasn't even noon yet. She kept a tiny bottle of it in her purse, which she now took out and gulped from, draining it.

Oscar didn't answer. Why should he? Looking at his swollen face reflected in the backseat window should have been enough of an answer. His mother, however, only cared about the next drink and Oscar's father's mood.

His fingers intertwined upon the trumpet case. He hated the instrument. Only played it because his father made him.

"Answer me, young man."

"Nobody is going to hit me ever again," Oscar said.

"We'll see what your dad has to say about that," she said. "Jonathan, please hurry. We must get home."

She needed more drink. She looked at the bottle in her hand the way Oscar often wished she'd look at him.

★★★

Melinda looked at him that way. She was waiting by the front door when they arrived, her eyes stained with worry and dried tears that smeared the mascara around her eyes. Her hands clenched at the bottom of her shirt.

"What were you thinking, Oscar?" she said as he'd entered. His mother stumbled past them and headed for the Johnnie Walker.

"Don't even try, Melinda," she said, pouring herself a few inches of the amber liquid. She downed it in one gulp. "He's developed an attitude. He won't listen to reason."

Melinda sighed. She placed both hands on Oscar's shoulders and knelt so that they were eye to eye.

"Are you okay?" she said.

For a long moment neither said anything. Finally, Oscar nodded.

"Okay, then," Melinda said. "Let's get you washed up and some lunch in your belly. You can tell me all about it."

Again, Oscar nodded. What he really wanted was his bed and some comics to read. A nap and maybe some early evening television. Melinda would take care of him. Until his father got home, she would see to it that he was as comfortable as possible. He realized then that he loved her. Loved her perhaps in the way he should love his own mother. There was nothing there for her, though. Or his father. Only Melinda.

You be sure to bring your father next time, the words flowed through his head, stuck there like a jingle from a television commercial. And he liked it.

★★★

The next day, on his way home from school, Oscar heard a voice that made his stomach clench.

"You don't have anyone to save you now."

He turned to peer down the alley. Full of shadows, but Paul and his goons were easy to spot. Paul hadn't been in class today, and Oscar suspected that the two black eyes and the giant splinter crudely taped to his nose had something to do with it. Oscar smiled even though he knew that it was wrong to feel pride in the violence that led to such gruesome bruising. Paul had picked on him, had physically hurt him on many occasions, since kindergarten. Time was long due that the kid tasted some of his own medicine.

Yet, the fact that they had waited here for him, all of them wearing the same grin that suggested a thirst for bloody vengeance, ruined Oscar's joy.

Fear filled the absence.

"It wasn't me that needed saving yesterday."

Shocked at himself, Oscar stuck out his chest and raised his chin as though to stand behind his words. He wouldn't be standing here too much longer. There were four of them. Despite the low grades he struggled to achieve every year in math, he knew enough to know that the odds were far from his favor. This would end badly.

Still, he held his ground. Paul sensed the difference and paused, his idiot friends stopping along with him.

"Well, you're the one who needs it now," Paul said. "Cause we're gonna gut you like a fish." He pulled out a switchblade, triggering a blade that reflected light as though it were repulsed by it.

Oscar took that as his cue to leave. His feet pounded pavement. Four sets of feet followed. Oscar ran until the muscles in his legs became rubbery and his lungs burned. He wasn't used to running, typically doing everything he could to get out of activities in gym class.

He looked back. They were getting closer.

He wasn't going to be able to outrun them. When they caught up to him, it was going to hurt. The thought made him push himself harder, his heart hammering in his chest from more than just the exertion.

As he came up to the alley where he saw the homeless man die, Pete popped out, startling him. He almost ran into the older, much smellier man.

"Follow me, little man," Pete said.

Oscar was startled to see that the man had a full set of teeth. They didn't look right. They were small with the sharpened points of a predator, like the shark from *Jaws*. His skin was paler, less brown and more white-green, the color of his eyes milky white.

Oscar followed regardless. He didn't know why, but he trusted Pete more than the fate fast-approaching from behind.

They ran down the alley. It was blocked by a brick wall at the end and just as Oscar was questioning his own judgment, Pete went off to the side and picked up a pile of cardboard. Beneath was another hole, it's insides as inky black as midnight.

"Come on, little man, jump down here."

This time Oscar did pause, but not for long as Paul and friends came to the alley's opening, screaming, "There he is! Get him!" Paul still held onto the knife. Oscar did not doubt that the kid had very dark intentions with the blade, darker than what was in the hole, so he climbed in and lowered himself until his feet touched the solid surface below. Tremendous heat assaulted Oscar immediately. It was nearly unbreathable down here.

"Back off, you little monsters!" Pete said, and Oscar thought he heard the man hiss at his enemies.

"Stay out of this, freak," Paul said. "Or you're gonna die, too."

"I doubt that."

Pete's feet followed him down. Oscar's eyes were beginning to adjust to the gloom. He was standing in a tunnel, a giant tomb of brick and mortar and dust. Something much worse, that he could smell but not see.

Perhaps it was Pete.

"This way, little man," Pete said. They went into the catacombs, the light becoming dimmer the deeper they went. Behind them, Paul landed inside the tunnel. He screamed and it sounded primal, like something from some unexplored jungle, hungry and pissed off. And then the four sets of feet were once again in pursuit.

"Down here!"

Pete led him into a darker area of the tunnel, where they again turned. They were then met by a ledge, leading down into some sort of den where sickly yellow lights floated through the murky darkness, much like the eyes of the C.H.U.D. he had seen a few nights ago.

More cries from the underground jungle, though this time it wasn't from Paul and his gang.

"Down there," Pete said.

"No!"

Oscar didn't have a choice. Pete's hands grabbed him, pulling him up onto the homeless man's shoulder in a fireman carry. Down they went on another ledge that lowered into the C.H.U.D. domain.

The eyes of the creatures offered the only light down here. Pete took him to where there were barrels stored in the corner. The barrels were everywhere, Oscar noticed, and it looked as though the C.H.U.D. were playing in some of the contents, which were slimy and glistened like oil. The words Contamination Hazard Urban Disposal were printed in white on the sides.

"Put this on you," Pete said, reaching into some of the gunk beside one of the barrels. "It'll keep you safe."

Despite Pete's advice that he put it on, the homeless man did it for him. The slime was much colder than the oppressive heat of the air that had caused Oscar's sweat to cover his entire body. The stuff on his face and hair cooled him, made his spine tingle pleasantly. Somehow, it also calmed him.

"We got you now," Paul said as he reached the top of the ledge.

The C.H.U.D. didn't move, didn't make a noise. They stood there, illuminating the den with their eyes like some creepy monsters from a late-night movie.

It was almost beautiful.

Why didn't he warn Paul about them? Was it because he had been threatening Oscar's life? Was it because the boy had been nothing but a threat to Oscar's existence ever since his father had put him in that school? Oscar didn't know, but he was still surprised at himself at the joy that exploded throughout his upper belly when the gang reached the bottom of the ramp, their own mortal souls now in danger.

"I don't like this anymore," one of the kids said. Oscar was disappointed it wasn't Paul who said it.

The joy only intensified as the C.H.U.D. began to lose their statuesque stance and moved around the gang, showing their jagged teeth. They growled and howled, the sound almost metallic, ear-piercing.

Crying came from the boys. Paul held his knife up to the new, strange threat, taking the odd swipe at any C.H.U.D. that dared get too close. His blade never found its home and the C.H.U.D.s pounced as one unit into the kids.

The weeping turned to an orchestra of agony as claws shredded skin and teeth tore into flesh. It was beautiful. More beautiful than any song his father had composed and sang to snobs in suits.

The C.H.U.D.s flayed and bit until the screams ended and their mouths were full of meat and ropey intestines, but the song they had played repeated in Oscar's head.

The slime glistened and cooled on Oscar's flesh. And he smiled, knowing now that no one would ever hurt him again.

★★★

"Where were you this time?" Melinda said. Again she looked worried sick. The jazz music of his father's orchestration and performance played through the speakers of the apartment. His father's deep and sultry voice echoed as the old man sang along to his own songs somewhere nearby.

"And what is that all over you? You're filthy!" Melinda's worry turned to anger. "You're father's deep in it. He's not going to be happy. Don't you understand?"

Oscar did understand. The throbbing of his swollen

face was a constant reminder. Cooling the hurt and physical torment, however, was the slime that coated his face and hair. It was like the aloe vera Melinda often put on his skin during family vacations when Oscar had been out in the sun too long.

Melinda touched his face. Her hands came back coated in the goo that, Oscar now noticed, was green.

"Come on," Melinda whispered harshly. "If we're quiet, maybe we can hide this from your father this time."

The echo to the singing broke from the song playing over the speakers. "Hide what from your father?"

The deep voice was indeed that of the singer's, but it had lost all its cheer, its warmth. Now the reality of what lay behind the voice was the only thing present. Melinda stood up, her eyes wide. She backed up and Oscar could tell that she wanted to turn and run for her room. Instead she straightened her back and turned to face the demon.

"Hide what from your father?" Oscar's father repeated. He held a glass with two or three fingers of amber liquid. He was smiling, but there was no friendliness in it. He took a step forward and Melinda stood her ground.

"You leave him alone," she said, her voice strong save for the tiny tremble near the end.

The smile on Oscar's father's face only grew deeper.

"Mind your own business, servant."

The flat of his palm caught her across the cheek, lightning quick, taking Melinda by surprise. Oscar stepped back. The bad situation had just gotten worse.

Father had never lashed out at anyone but either him or his mother. Mostly him. Never had he struck Melinda before.

"You leave her alone!"

This time Father's smile died and was quickly resurrected as a sneer. His hand struck out again, the knuckles catching Oscar on the nose. His head shot back, his eyes immediately tearing up. He fell hard on his rear-end, the blood already coppery in his mouth.

His father approached, the sneer a hungry rictus. He raised his fist, but then his head jerked forward, his eyes becoming glazed. This time Oscar saw the movement from behind his father, and the man's head was thrust forward a second time.

He fell to his knees, the sneer glued to his face as he fell forward onto his face.

Melinda stood behind him. In her hands was Oscar's trumpet case. She held it above her head and was about to bring it down onto his father's head, but Oscar found himself blocking the way without having made the decision to do so.

"No! Wait!" Oscar said. Melinda paused, her breath coming in large gulps. Sweat coated her forehead and her eyes held an insane look that Oscar would have once compared to his father's whenever the drink had him in a rage, as it had so often recently. Right then it didn't look anything like that. Rather, she wore the rage-filled expression beautifully. She was an angel filled with righteous anger, not some drunken monster.

"I have a better idea," Oscar said.

★★★

Oscar's mother was once again passed out. This time it was on the recliner beside the couch. Her fingers were wrapped around a near empty bottle of Johnnie Walker, a thin line of spittle or vomit running down her chin to pool and then soak into her blouse.

Oscar hadn't noticed her until they were wrapping his still moaning father up in the carpet upon which he had fallen.

"I don't know if we should be doing this," Melinda said. "We could get in big trouble."

"Nobody will know," Oscar said. He was sweating, despite the cool air of the apartment. A greenish tinge had grown across his skin, and his teeth felt sharper whenever he examined them with his tongue. He no longer cared about the mundane world he lived in. He was different now. He was becoming.

Melinda was, too.

Her skin was pale and covered in a thin coating of sweat. Her eyes burned with the desire to finish what they were doing.

Once they got the carpet up and over Melinda's shoulder, things moved very quickly.

"Where?" Melinda asked.

Oscar took her to the elevator, and from there out into the oppressive heat of the city. Nobody noticed them or the carpet strung over Melinda's shoulder or the soft moans that came from it, and if they did, no one bothered to stop them. The way people in this town cared about each other, Oscar thought they'd probably be able to get away with it even if Melinda had carried just the body without the carpet.

He led her down the alley where he had seen the homeless man die and down into the hole Pete had introduced to him earlier that day.

Melinda followed. She didn't even stop when the roar of metallic rage of the C.H.U.D.s filled the corridors below the city.

The lair was easy enough to find. The C.H.U.D.s stood in a circle. Pete was among them, Oscar was happy to see. His transformation was nearly complete. His teeth were much larger, his eyes massive ovals of glowing yellow brilliance. They parted to let Oscar and Melinda into its center. Melinda put the carpet down and both she and Oscar unrolled it until the pathetic heap of his father lay before them, bleeding and moaning. He was awake, looking at them with frightened eyes.

"Oscar?" he whispered. "Son?"

Oscar tried to remember the last time the man before him had acted like a father to him. He couldn't remember anything. He, in fact, doubted that the aging jazz singer had ever even embraced Oscar, or kissed his cheek, or told him he loved him.

No. He had only shown Oscar pain and fear.

Which was why this was going to feel so good.

Without a word, Oscar and the creatures tore into his dad. The screams were so much more welcoming than the old man's singing. Oscar was pleased to see that the tips of his fingernails had grown hard and white and sharp. They ripped into Father's stomach easily, pulling at the muscle and intestines beneath.

Melinda was still there after they were done,

though she had not participated. She hadn't mutated enough yet. That she was still here spoke widely of her dedication to him.

"Mother is next," Oscar said.

Melinda nodded in agreement and Oscar smiled. This woman who had no blood relation to him was a far better mother than anyone had ever been to him.

And now they would be together, forever.

T.H.A.T.'S. E.N.T.E.R.T.A.I.N.M.E.N.T!

MORT CASTLE

PREFACE

The show business has all phases and grades of dignity, from the exhibition of a monkey to the exposition of that highest art in music or the drama which secures for the gifted artists a world-wide fame princes well might envy.

—P. T. Barnum

PART ONE

WE USED TO be great.

It was when we had jobs.

But then we didn't have so many jobs so we weren't so great.

It was time to make America great again.

We built a wall. It was to keep out people who were coming here and taking all the good jobs, like being the CEO of General Motors or picking lettuce in California.

We had a Great Wall.

But then it fell down.

THAT'S ENTERTAINMENT

Not all of it and not all at once. Some sections just went down ker-bang. Some parts turned all smooshy when it rained.

That was sad. The wall was made of American materials and built by certified American workers.

Then we built up all these new steel plants.

The steel was pretty good.

Well, it wasn't that bad.

But most cars didn't use that much steel nowadays, so we started to make Packards with running boards and lots of steel. The new Packard looked a lot like a Kia Optima, except for the running boards, if the Kia Optima had two front ends. It cost four times what a Kia Optima cost.

Oh, and it didn't run.

You don't want to hear what happened with the coal mines.

I guess you could say some of the explosions were pretty great.

It didn't make sense to try to build up the military.

It was just way cheaper to hire Russians when we needed to invade countries or what have you. Russians were lots better at killing, too. They just naturally liked it more.

And the Russians would plant any flag you wanted in a country they invaded for you. That's how there came to be the flag of Benton Consolidated High School, Class of 1996 (Benton, Illinois, Franklin County) on Mt. Mount Tomorr-Yeltsin in Albanidonia.

Education? Most of the students who tried to get into American universities had come up through the American school system, so they couldn't read a book without hurting their lips. American universities filled up with students from India and China and Japan and Poland and Pakistan I and II and they were so smart colleges had to hire professors for them from India and China and Japan and Poland and Pakistan I and II. Maybe the students could have saved money by staying home, but they knew they could have lots more FUN in the US of A!

Fun is important.

Remember that. It is important.

All in all, things were pretty ungreat.

PART TWO:

So a whole bunch of smart brains got together. They were mostly from Amazon. Some of them were American. They had what you might call a Smartness Conference. These were the guys who had come up with AMAZON OVER THE WORLD—24 hours a day, every day, with every product you could desire (97.78% of them from other countries).

They first decided America could be great through . . . SERVICE!

Except India. Pakistan I and Pakistan II. China. Indonesia. The Philippines. The Fiji Islands. Guam. Samoa. Almost any other country where you have less than 50% indigenous leprosy produces a better service worker than the USA.

But there was one area in which America was best.

It would always be best.

That's ENTERTAINMENT!

AMERICA IS GREAT AT PROVIDING FUN!

The United States of America provides the best entertainment in the entire world.

THAT'S ENTERTAINMENT

You don't think so?

Try watching a Swedish movie.

Try dancing to French rock 'n' roll.

You want to be at a good old American baseball game or run over to Afghanistan for a nice round of Catch the Dead Goat?

Ask any German if he'd rather go to Disneyworld or Asterixland.

Maybe we don't have Macy's anymore, but we still have that great parade.

America?

America?

That's Entertainment!

That's Great Entertainment!

So what we do is make America . . . GREAT AMERICA!

Turn it into a whole bunch of regional amusement centers and theme parks.

Tried it slow at first. Made most of Florida into alligator farms, except for Disneyworld and Epcot. Alaska started up Frozen Acres, where you could be sealed in a block of ice for up to two weeks at an affordable per diem. Colorado went all weedy: "Fly the High Country." Then there was IdiotLand, Flint, Michigan, where after all the years of drinking water fortified with lead, the population had an average IQ level you could measure with fingers and toes. You'd laugh your head off at the goofy antics of all the leadheads as they went about their daily tasks, like drooling and falling over backward.

But the most popular of the original theme parks . . .

You got it!

C.H.U.D. LAND!

Right there in Chicago.

Okay, we know the first C.H.U.D. s were found in New York City, but Chicago had seven levels below the city streets, all kinds of underground-underground, and something grew a crop of C.H.U.D. s that wanted O U T—and dinner.

No brainer! The C.H.U.D. s were a natural resource to be properly utilized in the entertainment industry!

Didn't hurt anything that C.H.U.D. s are kind of cute.

They have these glowing eyes that look like headlights on the vintage Dodge Neon. They got teeth that make them look British; if they could talk right, they'd probably sound like Charles Laughton.

Kids wanted C.H.U.D. dolls, like the old Cabbage Patch kids.

They wanted C.H.U.D. lunchboxes.

There were the cartoons and video games.

There were songs about C.H.U.D. s.

They hardly ever make a sound
When C.H.U.D. s come up from underground.
They chew your guts and
Bite your butts,
And suck on your spleen
But not 'cause they're mean.

They're C.H.U.D. s—and that's what
they do-do-doodley-do, they're C.H.U.D. s!
Ally-Ally—Oxen-Free,
So's Your Mother!

THAT'S ENTERTAINMENT

Chicago gets the nation's most popular amusement center: C.H.U.D. LAND.

They went to the worst neighborhood in the entire city, where you had a one in four chance of dying of a bullet on any day of the week, except Sunday, when odds went to one in three. It was known as North Lawndale. It had the highest crime rate in the city, the country, and maybe the world. It was five miles west of Chicago's downtown, the Loop.

North Lawndale gets walled off for C.H.U.D. LAND. The walls are built of pretty good steel and do not fall down.

C.H.U.D. liners cruise the streets every two hours, day and night. C.H.U.D. land visitors are safe. C.H.U.D. liners have a Ukraine engineered and manufactured 11.3 Liter V-12 diesel engine and are equipped with Japanese Army grade laser-sighted weapons. They are shielded by Russian produced Titanium armor plating and transparent bulletproof Makroclear viewports.

C.H.U.D. LAND offers a money back guarantee: You will see a C.H.U.D. on your Urban. C.H.U.D. Safari!

Here's how it works.

Everybody wants to be in show business. Think about *Dancing with the Stars*. *America's Got* Talent. *The Voice*. *Funniest Home Videos*. YouTube.

Of course, the residents of North Lawndale want to be in SHOW BUSINESS!

No more trying to sell illegal guns or peddle Grandma's kidney or bustin' a cap on someone who wants your corner for a meth and Koolaid stand.

All you got to do is run for it when the C.H.U.D. S come out!

Sometimes you make it.
Sometimes you don't.
That's show business.
For lucky C.H.U.D. s, that's dinner.
The C.H.U.D. eyes glow and glow while everyone on the C.H.U.D. liners uses Samsung G92 and iPHONE-EXTREME(X12) to snap 3Ds for Facebook and to show Uncle Leonard back home.
So, the Chicago crime problem gets solved.
And . . .
C.H.U.D. s make America great again!

In show business, you get chewed up and spit out.
—John Aniston

Nothing is more simple than greatness; indeed, to be simple is to be great.
—Ralph Waldo Emerson

T.O.X.I.C. D.I.S.P.O.S.A.L.

DAVID BERNSTEIN

LAUREN COULDN'T BELIEVE what she had been through. Hell, what they had all been through. She stood there with George, his arms around her, as the truck and the madman behind the wheel burned. Flames engulfed the box-shaped vehicle as thick, black smoke filled the sky. Sirens blared throughout the city, some drawing near while others seemed to race away. People milled about, eyes wide, gasping in disbelief and awe.

"Is it safe to stand here?" Lauren asked, and then coughed as she breathed in fumes.

"I think so," George said holding her tightly. "There had been a lot of gas below the streets, but I guess the sewer walls held after it ignited. We don't have to worry about being blasted into space, I guess. And whatever creatures were down there are toasted."

"Good," Lauren said. "I just want to go home."

He rubbed her back and agreed.

They moved to stand next to Shepherd and Bosch.

"Is he going to be all right?" Lauren asked.

"I'm right here," Bosch said, "and can answer for myself. I'll be . . . fine. Just hurts like hell."

"Bosch is one tough cookie," Shepherd said.

"Well, as soon as we get to a phone, we'll call an ambulance," George said. "We don't mean to skedaddle, but when the authorities arrive—whoever they might be—I think the less people here the better."

"Once I radio this in, including that there is an officer down, cops and paramedics will be on their way," Bosch assured them.

"I'll stay with him until help arrives," Shepherd said. "You guys should get out of here."

Lauren and George nodded. George shook Shepherd's hand and thanked him for watching his back when they were below.

"No problem, man—" Shepherd began when the box truck rumbled, and then tipped over. A large, hulking figure with flames dancing across its body climbed out of the manhole the truck had been covering. Through the fire, iridescent orbs glowed. One of the C.H.U.D.s was still alive. It howled, whether in pain or fury no one knew. It locked eyes on the small group and marched forward.

Shepherd, who had shoved Bosch's gun back into the cop's pants after shooting Wilson, grabbed the gun again and pointed it at the monster.

"You might only have one bullet left," Bosch said. "Try not to miss or I'm a dead man for sure."

Lauren and George looked around for something to use against the flaming thing in case the bullet—if there were any left in the gun—didn't do the job.

Shepherd opened the weapon's cylinder and

checked on his ammo situation. "One shot left," he said, and aimed as the C.H.U.D. drew nearer.

George picked up a glass beer bottle and smashed the end, giving him a jagged weapon to use. Lauren was holding a pipe she had found.

When the C.H.U.D. came within two feet of Shepherd, he yelled "Eat this, you ugly son-of-a-bitch" and pulled the trigger, sending a bullet into the creature's right eye. The green sphere went dark immediately. It cried out and stumbled to the ground where it lay unmoving.

Lauren poked it with her pipe to make sure it was dead, George next to her with his broken bottle. Both the creature's eyes were dark.

"Let's hope that's the last of them," Shepherd said.

Everyone nodded as the manhole remained void of anymore emerging C.H.U.D.s.

"That one must've just been close to the exit when it caught fire," George said. "Probably would've died soon anyway."

"Can we go now?" Lauren said, dropping the pipe she held.

George tossed his bottle. "Yes, lets."

★★★

The air smelled rancid as they made their way along the city streets. There was some kind of awful chemical odor and Lauren guessed it was all the stuff burning in the sewers. She wondered how many of those creatures had been taking up residence in the underground. Her heart sank at the thought of the poor souls who had been down there when the gas ignited, now little more than smoldering ash.

"Bosch looked pretty bad, huh?" George asked.

"I hope he'll be okay," she said, grabbing his hand as they walked side by side.

"Paramedics will take care of him. Like Shepherd said, he's a tough cop."

A police car came racing along the street. The couple hurried off to the side and stood between two parked cars as the cruiser flew by.

Lauren then realized how empty the streets were. She couldn't remember the last time she'd been able to walk down the street for so long without seeing a vehicle.

As they walked on, leaving the chaotic area, the streets grew more silent. The strange chemical smell wasn't nearly as strong when they reached their block. A few young people milled about on a corner. Besides them, it seemed as if the neighborhood had been evacuated. There wasn't a vehicle parked anywhere in sight.

Just as Lauren was about to walk up the steps to the building's front door, she stopped. George smacked into her from behind.

"What is it?"

"Shit, I can't believe I forgot: one of those creatures is dead in our apartment."

"What?"

Lauren quickly told him how she had been attacked.

"Wow, and I thought me and Shepherd had it rough."

"I don't want to see it," Lauren said. "It's a mess up there. The creature's blood is pooled in our living room."

"What if it's toxic?" George asked, stopping. "Maybe we should call the authorities?"

"Are you crazy? After everything we saw tonight?"

"Right. For all we know, the Nuclear Regulatory Commission, or whatever they are really called, will want to cover all this up. Make us disappear, or have us committed so we can't go around telling people about the monsters."

"No way I'm having our place filled with those lying asshole agents."

"We'll get rid of the creature ourselves."

"But is it safe to touch it?"

George's chest rose and fell as he took in a deep breath, appearing to be thinking about something. "We'll wear gloves."

"Of course we'll wear gloves, but what about it being radioactive or toxic?" Lauren said. "The thing's blood and eyes were fluorescent green, as if radiator fluid coursed through its veins."

"We'll be fine," George assured her, rubbing her shoulder. "C'mon, let's get this over with. The faster the better."

She grabbed George's arm, stopping him. "There's a nasty mess right inside the entrance. Just want to warn you. I saw it on my way out, at least some of it. I ran so fast. It was a blur of blood."

"It can't be worse than what I've already seen," George said. He took her hand and headed up the front stairs.

As soon as they entered the building, Lauren screamed. Putting her hands to her mouth, she saw in vivid detail the human remains. Blood and guts splattered the walls and floor. Two pairs of legs with the shoes still on them lay scattered amongst the gore. A police badge glinted on the torso of one officer. A head with its jaw torn out lay next to it. A pair of arms rested a few feet away, one hand with a wedding ring attached. In the far corner was another head with half its skull missing, along with the brain inside, as if it had been scooped out. There were smaller pieces of human flesh among the larger ones, as if it had gone through a meat grinder.

George put his hand to his stomach. "I think I've seen enough of this stuff for a lifetime."

"The creature that attacked me must've gotten them first," Lauren said, still holding her hand on her trembling lips. "I mean, it doesn't even look like it ate much of them. Just tore them to shreds."

"Nothing we can do for them now," George said and nudged her forward.

As they approached the staircase, apartment 1's door cracked open and a little boy popped his head out. "Is the monster gone?" he asked.

"Justin, get in here now." The kid's mother came to the door, pulled the kid inside and shut the door.

Lauren shook her head and breathed a sigh of relief. "Thank goodness that kid didn't come out here and see the bodies. No child should see that kind of carnage."

"Or his mother," George said. "She would've certainly called the cops. We would have had to wait to move the monster."

"I'm glad her and her kid are okay."

"Yeah."

As they made their way slowly up the squeaky staircase, Lauren felt as if her legs weighed a hundred pounds each.

"We're going to have to call someone about the two dead officers," George said, "but after we clean up our place. I'd rather get it over with sooner than later."

"You're probably right, but what if someone else sees the dead bodies and calls the police?"

"Then we'll just have to wait before removing the C.H.U.D."

"C.H.U.D.?"

"That's what they're called. Cannibalistic Humanoid Underground Dwellers. It's not right referring to the poor homeless who were infected as such, but they're nothing but monsters now."

"Were, you mean, right? Aren't they all dead?"

George shrugged. "Who knows? Like the one that attacked you, I'm sure they weren't all in the sewers when the gas ignited."

"Oh, great."

Reaching their apartment, George shoved his way in, pushing aside the furniture that Lauren had piled in the way. "Wow, you really barricaded yourself in."

"Apparently not well enough." She pointed to the headless C.H.U.D. "It got in."

Despite how tired they were, the couple went to work. They'd leave the pool of green blood alone and clean it when they returned from dumping the body. Getting rid of the thing was the most important part of their cleanup.

The dead creature had a sour, chemical smell to it, like household cleaner and spoiled milk. They slipped on yellow dishwashing gloves, then grabbed the large room-sized rug they'd purchased but hadn't laid out yet. The living room furniture was moved out of the way so the carpet could be unrolled up to where the dead creature lay. George and Lauren then rolled the large and heavy headless monster corpse onto the rug before rolling it up. Lauren held the carpet in place as George stuffed the head into the hole at the top of the carpet. He then grabbed a roll of Duct Tape and secured the bundled creature.

"Okay," he said wiping his sweaty forehead with his forearm. He removed his gloves and tossed them in the garbage. Lauren did the same.

"We ready?" he asked.

"George, how are we going to carry it out of here? It's too heavy."

He rubbed his chin, the stubble sounding like sandpaper. "Hmmm."

"Do we still have that hand truck?"

"We should. Let me check."

He went to the walk-in closet, moved aside a few boxes and coats and found it at the back corner near an old tripod. The camera steadying device was the first one he'd ever purchased and he just couldn't let it go despite no longer using it. Carefully putting it aside, he maneuvered the hand truck out of the small room only managing to knock one of the coats to the floor.

Leaving the garment where it lay, he wheeled the dolly to the living room where he and Lauren struggled mightily to get the rolled up C.H.U.D. leaning against the wall. There, she kept it from falling while George slid the hand truck's lip under the end of the carpet. He then slowly let the carpet settle into place on the hand truck as he lowered his arms so he could wheel the thing around. Lauren wrapped a few lines of Duct Tape around the rug and hand truck to keep it from falling off.

"Grab a flashlight," George said. "There's one in the—"

"—kitchen drawer, I know," she said, already heading there.

Then George added, "And my utility knife."

★★★

George struggled on the stairs. A loud thud resonated with each step down, causing him to worry about someone coming to see what all the noise was. Sweat tickled his brow. Lauren stood in front, guiding him. The Duct Tape held well, making it a bit easier to move the corpse.

When the truck's wheels finally hit the first floor, he expected to see someone come out of apartment 1 and held his breath, but apparently whatever he was doing wasn't interesting enough to others in the building.

George pushed the hand truck through the blood-slick hall, the wheels leaving a trail behind that quickly filled in. Lauren opened the front door and poked her head outside. The streets were void of life, save for a plump rat scurrying across the street.

The hint of a siren could be heard far off, but other than that, the area was still.

"Ok, George," she said waving him forward. "The coast's clear."

George moved past her and down the solid cement steps, this time not worrying about waking his neighbors. When he reached the sidewalk, Lauren hurried next to him. A moment later, they were fast-walking along the cracked cement walkway. The hand truck was repeatedly jolted as the wheels ka-clunked over countless uneven slabs of cement.

The group of people that had been hanging around at the end of the block in front of the bodega were gone, the store closed. Lauren checked around the corner, then waved for him to follow. George took the bend like an elderly driver with bad eyesight, then picked up speed as he passed the graffiti decorated brick wall of the corner store. For a moment, he thought he felt the hand truck vibrate more than usual, as if one of the wheels was about to come free. Slowing, he glanced down and saw they were fine.

"What are you doing?" Lauren asked.

"Nothing." George started forward again.

They reached the alley that ran behind their building and headed down it. Inky blackness swallowed Lauren until she turned on her flashlight. Dark, red brick lined with various stains and graffiti surrounded them. A laundry line with a bra and pair of socks hung from a rope and clothespins a few feet up.

George rolled the hand truck up to a dumpster. Chest heaving, he rested his arms on the handles.

"We made it without being seen," Lauren said with glee in her voice. "Though not that it mattered since the C.H.U.D. is hidden."

"Yeah, now let's toss this sucker in the trash and scram," George said. He withdrew the utility knife that Lauren gave him back in the apartment out of his back pocket, then sliced the tape holding the rug to the aluminum dolly. With a shove, he sent the rug crashing to the newspaper, cigarette butt, and candy wrapper-littered asphalt.

"Sucker is heavy," he said, and returned the blade to his pocket.

"Um, honey," Lauren said, "How are we supposed to lift it into the dumpster?"

George put his hands on his hips and stared at the rolled up rug. "Crap. You're right. Between the weight of the rug and the C.H.U.D., we'll never do it. We're just going to have to unroll it and toss the creature and rug in separately."

Lauren's face contorted into a grimace.

"We have to touch that thing?"

"Yeah, but we'll use gloves. The creature could be diseased or worse. You run back and get them while I unroll this sucker and wait."

"Okay," Lauren said. "There should be more under the sink." She handed George the flashlight and sprinted back to the apartment.

George placed the light-producing tool on the ground so the immediate area was illuminated. Kneeling next to the rug, he withdrew his knife again and cut the Duct Tape that held it closed. He then unrolled the carpet, grunting with effort until the C.H.U.D. was visible.

George's eyes widened in disbelief at seeing the creature's head and how it had reattached itself to the body. Fluorescent green eyes stared at him. In a flash, it pushed itself up and charged at him, its mouth wide and filled with rows of razor sharp teeth.

★★★

Lauren returned to the alley five minutes later. "George?"

The flashlight was on the ground, its light shining against a worn and faded poster for Kool cigarettes that had been plastered to the grimy, gray back door of the bodega.

"George?" she called again, swallowing hard and feeling as if a stone were lodged in her throat.

No answer.

"George, this isn't funny." The hairs on her neck stood tall.

She inched down the alley, the darkness enveloping her like tar.

Something squished below her right foot, then her left as she continued toward the flashlight.

The air was a mixture of rotting vegetables and something sweet, coppery.

Reaching the flashlight, she bent and picked it up, the handle tacky with fluid. Switching the flashlight to the other hand, she saw that her palms were blood red.

Heart thumping against her breastbone, Lauren shined the light around. Each place where the beam landed revealed another piece of what could only be her husband. Blood splattered the dumpster, ground and walls, the crimson liquid everywhere.

Seeing her footprints, Lauren understood what had made the squishing sounds. She'd stepped on George's eyeballs, the orbs now flattened messes in the middle of her footprints.

Mouth agape, she screamed.

A bone-shaking growl emanated from deeper in the darkness.

Turning to see what it was, Lauren saw glowing green eyes coming her way. It was another C.H.U.D. A fraction of a second later, she realized that wasn't true. It was the C.H.U.D. she had beheaded that had come back to life. She had no idea how, but knew it to be true—and it had killed George.

"No," she roared and tossed the flashlight at the creature. It bounced harmlessly off its forehead and went out. Lauren turned to run back toward the street when she tripped on George's leg and crashed to the ground. Still-warm blood caked her frontal region.

Getting her arms under her, she pushed herself up and was ready to continue her sprint to freedom when she was grabbed from behind.

The C.H.U.D. had her by her arm and whipped her into the wall.

The force of the impact was jarring. Her two front teeth broke free and tumbled down the back of her throat.

Coughing on her jagged teeth and panic seizing her every cell, she spun around and attempted to throw a punch when she realized the appendage was gone. The C.H.U.D. had held onto her arm when it threw her into the wall, tearing it from her socket.

A river of crimson gushed from the hole in her shoulder. Frozen in disbelief, she stood there and stared.

★★★

The creature came forward, dropping the arm it held— her arm—and sunk its claws into her abdomen, then clamped its teeth around her face. As it chewed, it plunged its other clawed hand into her chest, and then ripped Lauren in half while removing her face from her skull using its jaws.

Blood and flesh exploded across the area, the C.H.U.D. lapping up what it could. It rampaged and roared as it thrashed about among the carnage. This was what it was made to do, what it was at its core. It was a pure killing machine of radioactive cells.

With its prey scattered about, the C.H.U.D. left the alley and walked down the street looking for the first manhole it came across.

M.O.N.S.T.R.O.U.S. M.E.

MARTIN POWELL

HUNGRY. Still hungry no matter how much I eat. Can't even remember the last time I felt full. I'm having trouble remembering a lot of things. I'd rather not think about that. Heh, hey, that's kind of a joke. Well, sort of. Coffee's like mud this morning. My favorite cereal tastes like I'm munching wicker furniture. Even so, the whole box goes down the hatch. Hmm. Still hungry. This's getting ridiculous.

Not sure why I decided to start up this diary again. Very junior high school of me, for sure. Maybe I'm merely lonesome since my ex moved out. Heh, that'll be the day. My fingers have gotten too shaky for keyboard, so I've devolved back to pencil and legal pad. Chicken scratchings, really. Meant only for my eyes, anyway. So, if you're reading this, you broke in and stole it. Pervert.

My ex dropped by. Again. Mouthing the same old mushy mush. I've told him over and over that we weren't hooking up again. No way, no how. He pleaded and whined giving me that wounded rodent face.

Nope, it's not happening. My bruises are almost gone from his last "aww, c'mon, gimme 'nother chance" malarkey. No more. Not ever. Never again.

Before I slammed the door, he took one last jab at me. He said I looked like something left uncovered in the litter box. He didn't put it that eloquently, of course, but that was the basic gist of it. Seriously? Was that really the best he could do? I did better, smashing his fingers in the doorframe. Broke them, maybe. I sure hope so. He swore and shrieked in the hallway till old man crab-face next door said he was calling the cops. Poof! Ex was gone in a flash, then. Good riddance. Nah, better than that. The best riddance ever.

Ex was right about one thing, though. I've looked better. That's painfully true. The mirror's not my friend. Hasn't been for a while. I do look sick, I'll admit. Pale with dark eye circles. My skin's dry and rough. Make-up doesn't glide on like all the infomercials promised, not at all like it used to. It's blotchy and fake-looking now. My lipstick is a lost cause, too. My mouth seems a different shape. Hmm. Just noticed my gums are bleeding. Great. That's just great. I'm a real charmer, no doubt about it. Maybe I have the flu? Yeah, maybe it's the flu. Or something.

Funny thing, though, I don't really feel sick. Just hungry. Really, really hungry.

★★★

Skipping lunch today, so doing diary instead. Been eating way too much lately. Where's it all go? I mean, I can still feel my ribs. Maybe I have . . . what was it grandma called it? Oh yeah. Tapeworms. Maybe I have one of those. There was a fourteen-footer pickled in a jar in high school biology. Pretty gross. But pretty cool, too. Strange, the things that pop into my mind lately.

Went into the office to get reimbursed for a few expenses. No luck. Chief wasn't there. Still out because of his divorce, they said. Lucky me. Restroom stall gossip says he's going to cancel my current assignment. The plight of the homeless is too depressing, he said. At least, they said he said it. Does sound just like him. He was never really very sold on my pitch to begin with. Minor miracle he let me go this far, all these months. Probably was the skirt I wore that day. Okay, so big deal. I'll be reassigned or maybe even fired. Yeah, maybe so, but not today. Not if he's not here.

My eyes got used to the subway tunnel quicker than the last time I was down there. I managed to find Merry Mary right away, in her usual spot. No trouble at all, not like the times before. It's a maze down there, like those silly newspaper puzzles Grampy used to let me scribble on. He always said I'd work for the newspaper someday and I sure showed him he was right. Not sure for how much longer, though. Wonder why I suddenly thought of that? They say when you're drowning your life passes before you. Is that what's happening?

Anyway, poor old Merry Mary wasn't true to her nickname today. A recent resident of the tunnels, she's usually cheery and grateful for company. Not chatty this time. Not at all. Her buddies were missing, she said. Probably gone deeper in the tunnels after being hassled by the cops. Big Nick was gone. So was Doris. And all Mary found of Earl were those day-glow tennis shoes of his, which she was wearing. Mary's never one to waste anything.

She ate the gyro I'd brought her with her usual courtesy. Afterward, we continued the interview which had me gritting my teeth till my jaws ached, telling more of her tale of how she ended up down there, forgotten even by her family. Then, she babbled about the ghosts and devils she often heard, and sometimes saw, in the deeper tunnels. Soon as she said it, she was embarrassed and giggled. So did I. We laughed and cried together all afternoon. I was sorry to leave.

Once on a school field-trip a long time ago, we went to a cave. It was cooler in the cave than outside. Much cooler. The guide said the temps stayed the same underground no matter how hot or cold it was up above. Weird, because the tunnels seemed steamy and even warmer in the past few weeks. Doesn't make sense. Mary chuckled suggesting we were in Purgatory. Yeah. Maybe we were.

Suddenly I saw what I thought were eyes. Smoldering yellow, like the eyes of a cat, but bigger and higher from the ground. In a blink, they were gone. Now I wonder if I really saw them at all. Maybe just I need more sleep. Maybe I have a tumor. Whether they were real or not, I dreamed about those yellow panther eyes all night.

✯✯✯

Chief still not at the office. I got home late. Skipped dinner. Just joking. Had a quart of frozen yogurt. Black Cherry, I think. Not sure. I couldn't really taste it. Can't taste anything these days. You guessed it. I'm still hungry, though.

Slept through the phone ringing. Maybe I dreamed that, too. Up way too early. Or is it late? Blinds still closed. Sunlight hurts. All light hurts. My jaw's sore, too. Lost a couple teeth while brushing. Just popped out. Like babies' teeth. Pointed roots or something left in their place. Shower drain is clogged with hair. Falling out in clumps now. Skin's like cracked leather boots. Mirror's not my friend. I look into it and someone . . . something . . . looks back. Not quite a face. What's wrong with me?

Fell asleep again or passed out. So hungry.

Got the phone this time. I'm fired. Beth from human resources told me. Human resources, hah. Barely said anything more. Fired, after eleven years. My insurance is gone. No doctor or dentist now.

My fever broke. Woke up in a cold sweat. Bad dreams. Very bad. The worst. Still so hungry. Writing this in the dark. Just noticed. Totally dark. But I see fine. Huh. No job, but better get to work. Got to.

That was that. Waited in the parking garage. Afraid I'd missed old Chief at first, but he showed up, all right. He jumped when I said his name. Can't blame him. Wasn't my voice from my mouth. Was hardly a voice at all. The dim ramp lights stung, but I came out of the shadows at him. He screamed saints' names I never heard of. Wonder if he believed in them? Or in anything? He didn't recognize me; I could tell from his eyes. Too bad. I wanted him to know. To know it was me. Felt acid heat from my empty belly flood my mouth.

I tore into his guts with my bare hands. My bare hands.

★★★

Last diary. Can barely hold pencil.

Didn't leave much of old man behind. He's the hollow one now. Always was. Me, I'm nice and full.

Found Mary and Nick and Doris and others in tunnel. Now all with yellow eyes and needle-teeth. Like me.

Not hungry now.

But we will be.

Soon.

S.T.E.P. A.T.E.

CHAD LUTZKE

NEARLY EIGHT HOURS had passed and the city of New York was still reluctant to send officials into the sewers of Manhattan. While there was a chance the radioactive homeless-turned-mutants still roamed the sewers in search of prey, the more pressing matter seemed to be the disposal of thousands of gallons of hazardous waste left behind by the NRC that caused such a crisis.

For Harlan Salyer, neither was a worry. For Harlan it was his ex-girlfriend, now locked in the BookStar Cafe storeroom—with bulged, glowing eyes and elongated teeth, the remnants of a large tattoo stretched across her chest the only thing left resembling the woman once known as Darlena Vasquez.

While Harlan had let himself into the cafe, Darlena chased him inside where he ran to the storeroom. Somehow—it all happened so fast—he'd made it out of the room and shut and locked the door with her behind it.

He'd met Darlena when they both dabbled with heroin. He'd turned her onto the drug. Their relationship lasted just shy of two years. Beginning with a very quick, very passionate lust and ending in Harlan acting as pimp, with Darlena being one of four different women working the streets under his thumb. Eventually things had caught up with Harlan and he served a small stint for domestic abuse and possession, then ultimately sobered up soon after.

Darlena never returned from the hole they'd dug, while Harlan strived for an honest living, now on his second year as manager of the BookStar Cafe. He'd often see Darlena through the large bay window of the cafe, begging for money, picking at her skin as though bugs burrowed under her brown flesh—half the woman she once was, both literally and figuratively.

Harlan felt tremendous guilt regarding her situation, and it was those days he struggled the most with staying clean. Not because he missed it and seeing Darlena brought back memories of them trying to touch God, but because he felt unworthy of his sobriety and everything he'd obtained, while she struggled with her demons. Demons he once fed, nurtured and groomed. While he felt responsible for her lack of teeth, frail body, and darkened eyes, he had yet to reach out. To make amends.

With the help of a treatment center offered by the state as part of his parole, he'd gotten off the "H." The arrest had been a blessing, what he needed to get him on the right path. But the same hadn't come Darlena's way, and Harlan had feared it never would, that the grave would call for her before then.

Sometimes the two would run into one another on

the street. Harlan would give a nod and a subtle smile filled with shame. Darlena would eye him with bitter resentment. She may have forgotten who she was, but she remembered Harlan: the manipulation, the beatings, the verbal lashings. A side of Harlan that no longer lived but for her never died.

Harlan sat sweating at the small table—a spent cup of coffee in front of him, the third cigarette in the past half hour lit between his fingers, his hands shaking. The pounding on the storeroom door had finally calmed to a scratch. Darlena's new elongated nails screeched against the metal. Harlan gritted his teeth against the sound.

It was Harlan's guess that Darlena had taken to living in the sewers along with much of the city's homeless, the same ones who'd been mutated into monstrosities bent on killing—devouring even—any other human with whom they'd come in contact. Harlan wasn't sure if the newly mutated Darlena had actually sought him out and this was personal, or if the cafe was the wrong place and 6:00 a.m. was the wrong time. There didn't seem to be anything behind her bulb-like eyes. No form of recognition, just blank and bright. And no voice to accompany such rage other than the growls, low and guttural with a gurgling purr. A sound Harlan would not soon forget should he live past today.

There were a few reasons Harlan wouldn't call the police. One, he was still on parole. He'd done nothing wrong, but his probation officer had been itching for a reason to report a violation. And what if somehow Darlena came out of it and brought up past sins to the police. Sins that maybe Harlan hadn't paid for.

Harlan's sponsor in recovery had spoken a few times about working his 12 steps and needing to make amends. He couldn't remember which step it was but knew it needed to be done. Even with Darlena. Especially with Darlena.

Harlan looked out the cafe window. Traffic was slowly picking up. Newsstand Larry stood across the street reading one of his own magazines, sipping on coffee from a Thermos lid and giving change for bills. Completely unaware of Harlan's predicament.

Another series of pounds against the storeroom door startled Harlan up from his chair. He put out his cigarette and went to fill his empty cup. He looked at the clock, nearly time to open. If he didn't unlock the front door the people would gather under the awning, waiting to be let in. They'd done it before, several times. Harlan was late opening at least a handful of times every month, so they knew to wait, no matter the inconvenience. People will do just about anything for some coffee and a flat surface for their MacBooks.

Harlan walked to the storeroom, put his head against the door. "Dar, can you hear me? It's Harlan." Both the scratching and the pounding stopped. "Listen, I'm not sure you can hear me but I need to say something. I need . . . I need to tell you that I'm sorry."

He felt like he wasn't doing it for her at all but for himself, to kill the guilt, so that by the time Darlena died—be it from a barrage of bullets courtesy of the NYPD or the hazardous waste itself—he was in the clear. He'd done the step, whichever one it was. He'd made amends and it'd be official. No more guilt. He was working the program.

"I got straight and . . . well, you didn't. And I guess

STEP ATE

I feel a little responsible for . . . Hell, who am I kidding? Your whole situation is because of me. I mean . . . not your cannibal, bug-eyed situation, but the homelessness and your addiction. All that."

Harlan stood silent for a moment, hoping for some kind of response, something to relieve the guilt. Maybe a slurred or a hissed "It's okay" or "I forgive you." But there was nothing, just the muffled sound of wet, nasally breathing.

"It's important to me that you know I'm sorry." The scratching returned. Scriiiich! "I wish I could go back and never have treated you that way, never have given you smack in the first place. I wish I could help you, Dar." The scratching turned to pounding and Harlan walked away, discouraged and crushed with regret.

While he thought of what to do with Darlena, Harlan swept the dirty floor of the cafe. Calling the authorities was inevitable, eventually. He couldn't leave her in the storeroom. He knew this. But he needed some time to think things through.

Harlan looked around for the dustpan. The storeroom. He brushed the last bit of dirt and trash toward the front of the cafe, unlocked the door, then swept the pile out onto the sidewalk. The city air hit Harlan, a familiar air. The same he'd breathed for forty years. He wanted to toss the broom and run, leave his job behind and curl up in a building with a needle in his arm. He went inside and shut the door before feeding the idea any more than he had. He needed a meeting. He needed two meetings.

Harlan noted a few of the tables were dirty. Along with no sweeping, the nightshift hadn't bothered wiping anything down. He went in the back to get a wet rag. That's when he heard the bells above the front door ring. He'd forgotten to lock the door.

Before he could see anyone, he heard them. "Gimme a large black. I gotta piss like you wouldn't believe."

Harlan ran from the back and saw a man with his hand on the storeroom door, attempting to twist the knob against the lock's resistance.

"Sir, don't go in there."

"Don't gimme that. Unless you want me pissin' on your floor I'm using this bathroom."

The man turned the key that jutted out from the lock and turned the knob again, pulling the door open. The creature that was once Darlena grabbed the man by the top of his head and yanked him toward her, his scalp ripping from his skull like a Band-Aid from a wound. Harlan rushed at the storeroom door, slammed it, and turned the key. The screams of the man inside died quickly and for the first time all morning, other than the sound of feeding on flesh, Darlena made no sound at all. She was content.

In an immorally twisted way, Harlan hoped the silence meant he was forgiven, that she deemed the man an offering of peace. Harlan looked out through the cafe window. More people gathered across the street, buying their papers. Some would want their coffee soon. Harlan ran in the back and got as many paper towels and wash clothes as he could find and brought them back out front. Everything else, including the mop, was in the storeroom with Darlena. Remembering the front door was still unlocked, he ran and locked it just as a short, bald man with a briefcase reached for the door.

"Not yet," Harlan said, visibly distressed.

"Are you kidding me? It's . . . " The man looked at his watch, tapped it. "I've got to be to work in ten minutes."

"Sorry, sir. Some last minute maintenance."

"Something wrong with your machines?"

"No, sir. Just something I need to attend to real quick and I'll be with you."

"Well, if nothing's wrong with the machines then unlock this door and take my order. I've got . . . " The man looked at his watch again. "Nine minutes now. I've got nine minutes before my boss chews my ass. I don't want that, and neither do you. Cuz if my boss chews my ass then I'm coming straight back here and making sure your boss chews your ass. There'll be ass chewin' all around. You want that?"

As though done on cue, like a rim shot after a bad joke, a loud snap came from the storeroom. Harlan pictured a femur breaking in half, each bright white end now busting through inches of muscle and skin. He looked toward the storeroom; a cocktail of blood and urine began to seep from beneath the door. You should have just pissed on the floor.

"Are you hearing me?" The bald man yelled.

Harlan turned back to the man. "Sir, I hear you but it's beyond my control right now. You'll have to get coffee somewhere else today. I'm sorry."

"Is this a joke? That'd take me at least another fifteen minutes. Open the door and let me get some coffee."

"No, sir. I can't do that. Now, I'm gonna go do what I need to do and if you're still here when I'm done then I'd be happy to hook you up. No charge."

"I can have your job, you know. I know who you are. You're that prison guy. You did time. You come in here late all the time, making people wait outside for you. You smokin' rock in there? You got whores in the back, all tweaked out?" The man looked around the cafe, inspecting it through the window. "How about I call the police? The 'po-po.'" The man made air quotes with one hand, the other holding tight to his briefcase. "You and your boys wouldn't like that, would ya?"

The scratching on the door returned. Scriiiich! Scriiiich!

Harlan felt desperate. Any call at all to the police would cause his P.O. to pull the trigger. He could probably explain Darlena. That wasn't his fault. She'd turned into one of those things all on her own. He'd just tell them exactly how everything happened: the guy barged in while Harlan was trying to keep Darlena contained. But with this suit-and-tie guy casting suspicion on him they wouldn't see it like that. They'd take the guy's word over an ex-con. He was sure of it.

"What's it gonna be . . . bro?" The man gave the word a mocking tone. "You gonna give me my java or do I need to spill the beans on whatever trouble you got going on back there?"

Scriiiich!

The words came out before Harlan had a chance to stop them. "Okay, but maybe you could give me a quick hand first? Free coffee every day this week?"

The bald man took a quick moment to think. "Okay. But, we gotta hurry."

Harlan unlocked the door, let the man in, then locked the door behind him.

"So, what's the problem?" the man asked.

STEP ATE

Scriiiich!

It's uhh . . . it's over here." Harlan led the way to the storeroom, trying to block the puddle growing from under the door. The man followed him, looking nervously about for whores and crackheads.

"Is it the plumbing? Cuz if it is I know a good plumbing guy, could maybe even get out here as early as lunch."

"Yeah, I think it's the plumbing. I just need you to hold this thing in here while I shut off the valve."

Scriiiich!

"I can hear it. Sounds like you may need a new gasket, maybe a whole new system."

"Maybe."

Harlan reached the door and turned the key. "Right in here. You hold the thing."

The man chuckled. "What thing?"

Harlan grabbed the man by his arm and swung the door open, shoving the guy directly into Darlena. It was the first time Harlan had gotten a really good look at her, under the light. Every bit of her hair was gone. He stared at the tattoo stretched across her chest—a heart with doves on either side. He was with her when she got it. The tattoo was a tribute to her parents who had both died. Her skin glistened with blood, pulsating in areas as though covered with boils eager to explode.

The storeroom was splattered with blood, a ridiculous amount. And on the ground, missing large chunks of his body, lay the man who'd desperately needed a bathroom. His scalp remained attached to his forehead but flipped over onto his face, covering it as though ashamed of his predicament.

The bald man screamed and then kicked at

Darlena, who then tore at his throat with her claws, allowing only one more scream that ended in a wet, bubbling gurgle. Harlan slammed the door and turned the key.

"I need you to forgive me, Dar," Harlan whined.

Harlan turned the lights off in the coffee shop. He couldn't afford for people to linger at the door, looking in, watching the piss and blood spill out from the storeroom, but the growing daylight would soon cast its bright glow on his mistakes and bring an inquisitive and thirsty crowd. It didn't matter, though. He would not be opening the café today. Not now. Not ever. He'd just fed a human being to his mutated ex-girlfriend.

Harlan sat on the floor with his back to the wall next to the storeroom door. He watched the pool of blood grow and wondered if it would congeal before it got a chance to reach the dining area. He could see his reflection in the blood and took note of his glasses. Something he'd always needed when they were together but could never afford. Now he had them, a reminder that he gained a life he didn't deserve.

"I'm sorry, Dar. I need you to believe me."

The sound of breaking bones, the ripping of skin, and the lapping of blood didn't faze Harlan. He was deep in thought, considering the turmoil of the last 24 hours for the city of Manhattan and how maybe he wouldn't go back to prison after all. The city's biggest problem was no longer drugs and street gangs but vicious cannibals that were birthed in the city's tunnels. People would come to expect carnage like this after more of them came out. These deaths would be no different than any other caused by the creatures.

STEP ATE

But that's not making amends, Harlan. That's ending lives.

Harlan no longer valued his sobriety. He didn't deserve it and knew if he left the café today he would only seek out heroin and make sure he had the life he deserved: jobless, homeless, hungry, and alone.

"I've harmed you, Dar. And I need to make amends."

Harlan stood, turned the key in the door and opened it.

Darlena was hunched down over the bald man, devouring the contents of his torso, the man now a human soup bowl. Darlena's skin stretched taut over her spine, her neck ribbed with sinew and muscle.

"Dar . . . "

The creature stopped and turned its glowing eyes toward Harlan.

"I'm sorry."

Darlena stood, then lunged.

The pool of blood grew and did reach the dining area, all the way to the front door.

Z.E.R.O. H.O.U.R.

JG FAHERTY

SEPTEMBER 6, 1995, 10:42 P.M.

THE ROAR OF the creature drowned out the angry staccato of automatic gunfire. I threw myself to the side just in time to avoid being gutted by three-inch claws. I rolled to my knees, gun up and finger on the trigger, but the target had already moved, leaping toward Gomez with another unearthly howl. Tracer fire lit up the night as someone tried to keep pace with the thing's bounding progress.

Gomez went down with a scream that quickly turned into a wet, gargling death rattle. I got to my feet and fired, then cursed as the dark shape sprinted away and the shots went wide.

"Target moving left! Nixon, Watson. Coming your way."

"Roger that, Cap." Watson's hoarse response came through the receiver stuck to my temple as clear as if she stood next to me. I fired again just to make sure the target wouldn't try to double back and then traded my handgun for the MAC-11 machine pistol strapped to my hip. I took off at a full sprint, cursing the pines that blocked much of the full moon's light.

Someone cried out. More gunfire, this time the deeper boom of a shotgun. I changed direction, homing in on the sounds, and emerged into a small clearing. The target crouched in the center, a prone form at its feet, and I skidded to a stop as it turned in my direction.

Almond-shaped eyes glowed yellow-green beneath a protruding brow. Twisted, ravaged flesh gleamed wetly in the moonlight, like the thing had just pulled itself from a fire. The C.H.U.D. growled, exposing jagged, irregular teeth that dripped blood and saliva.

The monster flexed its long fingers. The muscles in its legs quivered.

I brought my gun up and fired a short burst just as the thing leaped, the rapid drumming of the 40-caliber machine pistol beating in time with my heart.

It shrieked as the bullets caught it but still kept coming.

Claws and teeth filled my vision. Something hit me like a train and fire exploded down my side. The world went black. I couldn't move, couldn't breathe.

Jenny's face appeared in the darkness, smiling, her eyes alight. I tried to say I'm sorry. No words emerged. A deep sadness bubbled up from deep inside me. This was it. I'd never see her again, and I couldn't even say a damn goodbye.

The weight eased up and a new thought came to me.

Never let the monsters win.

I gritted my teeth and pushed, the movement reigniting the agony in my chest. The weight disappeared. My lungs came alive and I sucked life-giving air in huge, wheezing gulps. Colored spots danced in my vision, whirling in mad patterns like neon ball lighting.

"You okay, Cap?"

Watson's voice, somewhere to my left. I opened my mouth but my throat wouldn't work.

"We need a med kit!"

I recognized the second voice, too. Rich Christy, the newest member of the Double Zeroes. Everyone called him Sticks, because he was skinny as hell, and also because he kept a set of drumsticks in his footlocker.

"I'm fine." My voice sounded like a bad Christian Bale Batman imitation but at least the words came out. I tried to sit up but a twisting, grinding pain in my right side stopped me. I couldn't hold back a groan.

"Hold tight, Cap." Watson again, her tone a mix of concern and relief that let me know I'd gotten myself hurt but I probably wouldn't be dying anytime soon.

"Target?" I had to struggle to get the word out between clenched teeth. My ribs were really hurting now. Shouldn't have moved.

"Down and done. Curly and Sticks are packing it up now."

I nodded. "Casualties?"

A pause, and I suffered a different pain, this one too familiar. It never gets easier.

"Gomez and Nixon."

The sting of a needle made me turn my head. A figure kneeling next to me. How had they gotten so close? Not good. Never let your guard down. That's what I always told my men. Never . . .

The colored shapes grew larger, blending into a rainbow curtain. A cool stream ran through my body, washing away the pain. It felt good, so good. Like the ocean on a hot day. I let the waves take me, floating along, floating away . . . good to relax for a minute.

Relax . . .

SEPTEMBER 25, 6:52 A.M.

"Hello, Max."

I was just zipping my duffle closed when Colonel Martin Travers entered my room. I'd been half-expecting him to show; he'd have been informed of my discharge before the doctors even thought to tell me.

That's life in the military.

Despite our years of friendship, I stood and snapped off a salute, and not just for show. Respect for chain of command is critical in our line of business, more so than in most branches.

Travers wore his usual scowl. In the three years I'd led Task Force Double Zero—Team Animal House, as the men called it, after the famous line "Zero point zero"—I'd only seen him smile a handful of times. Either when we opened a good bottle of Scotch or he got his way with the top brass.

"At ease," Travers waved his hand at me. "How are the ribs, Max?"

Something tightened in my stomach, and it wasn't my new scar. Travers only used my first name when we celebrated a victory or he needed me for a particularly unpleasant mission.

I was betting the latter.

"Good as new." Which was pretty much the truth.

The bones had knitted perfectly and only pink scars remained where the C.H.U.D. had carved three long lines across my side, requiring some fancy laser bonding and more than fifty stitches on top of that. Even the ache was fading after almost three weeks of hospital and rehab time. I'd been hoping to relax with Jenny on a nice beach for a couple of days before resuming active duty, but it looked like that wasn't going to happen.

"Glad to hear it. Because you ship out in three hours."

"Sir?" The rapid time frame caught me by surprise. Not that the team hadn't responded to emergencies before. That was our job. But this time, knowing I'd be laid up for an extended period, I'd authorized leave for all of them.

"I already called your Animals in. The briefing's at oh-eight hundred. The newbies will be there, too."

"Newbies, sir?" I didn't try to hide my displeasure. One of my rules for accepting the Double Zeroes' Alpha position was I alone got to choose the members of my team.

Travers' scowl deepened. "Replacements for the men you lost. No time for niceties. You don't like them, dump 'em after the mission."

"Yes, sir."

"Let's go. I'll fill you in on the way."

I grabbed my duffle. Three hours barely left enough time to prep the team and do a weapons check before departure. The knot in my guts grew tighter.

This one was going to be really bad.

ZERO HOUR

SEPTEMBER 25, 1:02 P.M.

Red lights flashed in the hold of the A400 cargo plane, alerting the team to prepare for landing. I'd used the three-hour flight from Camp Blanding to Shepherd Field Air National Guard Base in West Virginia to review the little information we had on the mission and get a feel for the two rookies I'd been saddled with. I knew the rest of the Animals had done the same. Newbies made everyone nervous. This time more than most.

We'd lost two good men in the backwoods of Maine. Gomez and Nixon had been original Double Zeroes, the only two left besides me and Curly Grimes, who'd been my Beta since day one. Anytime you lost men, it shook things up for a while. But to bring in newbies without the team having the chance to train with them, to get to know them . . . that was a recipe for disaster.

And now a Level Three Search and Destroy.

The briefing had been pretty straightforward. There'd been an earthquake in West Virginia, with the epicenter near some middle-of-nowhere town called Twin Creeks. Coal mining country for decades, but back in the eighties a lot of the mines had been shut down for safety or economic reasons. Some NRC genius had decided that an abandoned coal mine was the perfect place to store nuclear waste. I guess compared to a subway, it was.

Unless the company re-opened the mine. And an earthquake caused some of the containers to contaminate the place. In the space of a few days, dozens of miners had gone missing, there'd been multiple reports of Bigfoot and alien sightings in the woods around Twin Creeks. Worse, a family of five had been murdered in their house at the edge of town, and ten people had been slaughtered at a diner in the middle of the night.

Everything about it screamed C.H.U.D.s.

"Your job is simple," Travers had said, which meant it would be anything but. "Kill the C.H.U.D.s and seal up the storage site. Then we can send a decontamination team in to clean the place up."

I thought about asking why we needed to seal the place if they were going to go in and decon it after, but then I figured what the hell. If brass wanted to do double work, let them worry about it. By then, we'd probably be on to another assignment.

Not for the first time, I wondered just how many problem sites the NRC had. We'd responded to more than twenty "incidents" since I took command, but the Double Zeroes had been around since 'eighty-seven.

That's a lot of toxic waste.

If they'd just cleaned them all up after the first incident . . .

I took a deep breath. Let it go. It wasn't my place to try and understand the workings of the government brain.

Across the aisle, Beth Watson nudged Curly and tilted her chin at the newbies, Red Peters and Dario Lopez. Both of them came from Navy Special Forces, early-thirties, with muscle to spare and the hard eyes of seasoned field pros. Neither of them paid attention to the stares from the Animals as they checked their weapons and the new comm units glued to their temples.

Curly nodded, his bald head reflecting the overhead lights. Years of working together allowed me to read the communication between my two most trusted soldiers.

We're gonna have to watch these two.

It was always the same whenever someone joined the team. No matter what you told them or how many films they watched, nothing prepared you for your first encounter with a C.H.U.D.. Even the best soldier in the world could freeze when something that shouldn't even exist came at you in a demonic fury.

"Two minutes," came the announcement from the speakers.

"Comm check," Curly said, and the others acknowledged. I mentally checked them off as they responded. Beth Watson, tougher than most men twice her size. Harley Daws, a giant of a man with a knack for explosives. Christy, who'd joined us only a few months before Maine. Jorge Lee, not much larger than Watson but faster with a gun than any of us.

They were my core team now after two missions in a row with casualties.

And me almost gone, as well.

That didn't sit well.

The idea of my own death didn't frighten me nearly as much as the fact that I'd let the C.H.U.D. totally get the jump on me. I'm better than that.

The teeth coming at me, claws tearing through Kevlar like it was cotton . . .

Only our fragmenting ammo had saved me. Even with that, it had been close. The thing had taken multiple body shots without going down. Despite the special rounds, you had to hit the things in the heart or head to stop them instantly.

I've got to talk to Travers again. We need better gear. More training.

A while back I'd put in a request to let my men train against some of the C.H.U.D.s the NRC kept at Guantanamo. I'd been turned down.

"Can't waste them on exercises," Travers had said. "The research team needs them more than you do."

I disagreed, but I was outranked on that.

The plane bumped and then smoothed out as it touched down. I brought my mind back to the present. Mission first, then worry about the future later.

Still, as I watched the Double Zeroes file down the stairs and head to the transport vehicle, a Land Rover Defender that had seen better days, I couldn't help wondering how many would make it back alive.

SEPTEMBER 25, 2:27 P.M.

My guts clenched at the sight of the crowds gathered outside the Twin Creeks police station. I'd hoped we could clean up the mess before the media got wind of anything.

I should have known better. Bad news travels faster than sound in a small town.

Humid, almost tropical air clung like a wet blanket and made it hard to breathe as I climbed out of the truck. I could almost believe we hadn't left Florida.

"Watson, with me. Curly, you and the others wait here. No interaction with the locals."

"Good luck." Curly gave me a sardonic grin.

Good luck. I'd need it. Dealing with local law

enforcement was a lot like crossing a minefield. You had to step carefully but firmly in order to get the assistance you needed without injuring any fragile egos.

I ignored the questions flung from the crowd and let Watson nimbly clear a path to the door.

Inside, the chaos was worse. I was about to grab a harried-looking officer and ask for the chief when a stocky man with gray hair and a matching mustache emerged from an office and approached us. His eyes narrowed and the angry flush of his cheeks grew darker as he took in our camo uniforms with the double skull-and-knives emblems on the shoulders, and our prominently displayed side arms.

"What in blazes is the Army doing in my town?"

"Chief Mushnik?" I held out my hand, which he pointedly ignored. So, it was going to be like that. I gave him one more chance. "Sorry for the intrusion, Chief. I'm Captain Max Kelly. This is Sergeant Watson."

"I didn't call you."

That was true. He'd called the FBI, and that call had triggered an alert somewhere that resulted in someone getting on the horn to Colonel Travers. Who he reported to remained a mystery to me. A higher up in the Army? Someone at PRC? One of the many black ops agencies that no one believed actually existed?

The answer lay well above my pay grade, and I was happy with that.

However, I still had to deal with Mushnik, who struck me as more intelligent than the typical small-town cop. That would make things both easier and harder.

"No, sir, you didn't. But someone decided you needed our kind of help."

The chief's eyes narrowed. "Help? I've got fifteen people dead and another forty missing. Last time I checked, that doesn't exactly fall under the Army's jurisdiction."

Forty missing? What the hell had happened while we were en route? And why hadn't I been told?

Watson put her hands on her hips and glared at him. "Creatures with glowing eyes and Freddy Krueger skin? Corpses that look like they fell into a tank of piranhas? Any of that ring a bell?"

For the space of two breaths, no one moved. Then some of the fury drained from the chief's eyes, replaced by a new emotion.

Fear.

He motioned toward his office.

"Maybe we need to talk after all, Captain."

★★★

An hour later, Watson and I exited the station. As we left, I heard Mushnik shouting orders to his officers. He sounded the way I felt: frustrated, confused, and a little scared.

It turned out a lot had gone down while we were in the air. More miners missing, bringing the total to more than forty. One Robert DeWitt, Regional Manager for Consolidated Mining, had been in Mushnik's office when we arrived. A kind of weaselly fellow with the nervous habit of clearing his throat each time he spoke. After fifteen minutes, it was driving me nuts. He'd seemed more frightened about having to explain to his superiors why the Army would be shutting down his mine than why the men had disappeared.

Mushnik also showed us the security cam footage of the diner attack. A dozen figures breaking through the plate glass window. The grotesque features, the bright, shining eyes.

The mayhem.

Some of the patrons had tried to fight back, burly men with generations of mine workers and farmers in their blood.

They'd gone down in seconds, their silently screaming faces captured in all their pain and terror.

The waitress and two old men in a back booth hadn't even lasted that long.

Mushnik had kept his gaze turned away until the video ended. I understood where he was coming from. He'd just watch people he knew get butchered and eaten by things that shouldn't even exist. That wasn't supposed to happen in a town like Twin Creeks.

Hell, it wasn't supposed to happen anywhere outside of the movies.

He wanted answers, and I'd had to skate around the facts in order to appease him. Just enough so that he'd help us, without me having to reveal state secrets.

We'd been lucky the C.H.U.D.s in the video had clearly been wearing Consolidated Mining coveralls. That allowed me to use our stock cover story. We'd tracked down a shipment of chemical warfare product from the nineteen fifties the Army believed had been stored in the mine. If it was leaking, it would cause hallucinations, psychotic breaks, and skin burns.

I blamed the eyes on bad camera equipment.

DeWitt was happy to accept my story. Mushnik's

expression told me he didn't believe or trust me, which raised my estimation of him a few points. But he agreed to help. His men had located tracks leading from one of the murder sites to a trail in the woods that ran up to an old cave, which DeWitt said connected to one of the mine's many unused branch tunnels. Since no one at the main entrance to the mine had reported anything suspicious, it seemed likely the cave was the C.H.U.D.s egress point. I decided we should go in that way as well, allowing us to take out most, if not all, of the C.H.U.D.s before we sealed up the storage site. Mushnik and one of his officers would accompany us as guides. Since we'd be on mine property, DeWitt insisted on coming, as well.

I didn't have time to argue with him, so I allowed it, with the stipulation he did as he was told and stayed out of the way.

Curly stepped out of the truck and raised an eyebrow as we approached.

"Well?"

I thought about what we'd seen and heard in Mushnik's office. Forty-something C.H.U.D.s hiding in caves. Compared to that, Maine was a cakewalk.

"Tell them to suit up for bear. We're gonna need everything we've got."

Hopefully, it would be enough.

SEPTEMBER 25, 5:43 P.M.

The entrance to the cave gaped like an open mouth. Waves of cold air drifted from it like corpse breath and I couldn't shake the unwanted image that the hill was alive and waiting to eat us.

Just like the creatures inside it.

"This cave is hot, sir." Lopez showed me the Geiger meter on his wrist. We all wore them. The digital needle hovered close to the yellow, indicating background radiation at the high end of normal.

In town it had been solid green.

Curly caught my eye and nodded. The team was ready. We wore our standard Kevlar vests under our shirts. The three civilians had on lighter police versions supplied by Mushnik. The Animals all carried MAC-11s loaded with fragmenting rounds. Mushnik and his officer, a young man named June, carried their service pistols. DeWitt had nothing; apparently Mushnik trusted him with a weapon about as much as I did.

I signaled for Lopez and Christy to take point.

Weapons in hand, we moved forward, Watson and me on either side of the civilians, Curly and Peters holding down the rear.

Darkness enveloped us within a few feet. The darting blue-white beams of our flashlights couldn't drive it away; instead they teased the eye, making shadows dance and alternately revealing and hiding any details.

According to DeWitt's maps, we'd follow the cavern—which narrowed to something more like a tunnel—for about a klick. Then we'd have to cross a natural cavern, almost three hundred meters, before taking another tunnel which would lead us up to the section of mine where the missing men had been working. That matched closely with the waste dump coordinates Christy had programmed into his GPS unit.

As we walked, I marveled at the cave structure. Pink and white quartz deposits glittered in the rock. Jagged splits marred the walls in several places, some large enough for a man to walk through. DeWitt had mentioned that the hills through the region were like Swiss cheese, with probably hundreds of undiscovered caverns, despite all the mining and exploration.

He also mentioned that we'd be crossing a cave system the company had considered opening to the public, until the EPA nixed the idea.

"Too close to the mining operation." DeWitt's voice held a note of annoyance. No doubt because of the revenue loss.

I said a silent thank you to the gods of government regulations. C.H.U.D.s popping up in the middle of a tourist attraction? It would've been like New York all over again.

Lee's voice came over the comm. "I think I heard some—incoming!"

Oh, hell. His words sent a cold spear through my guts. I spun around, already knowing what I'd see.

Two C.H.U.D.s appeared out of nowhere, like they'd been born from the darkness. Shaped like men but larger, with eyes that glowed yellow-green like neon lights.

I stepped in front of the civilians, my MAC up and firing. Next to me, Watson did the same. The metallic chatter echoed off the walls and pounded my eardrums. Phosphorescent explosions painted the stone walls in abstract shapes.

The C.H.U.D.s fell over, heads reduced to dripping stumps.

A barrage of reports reverberated like fireworks

farther back as Curly and Lee faced off against more of the creatures. Voices shouted and a bestial roar answered them.

More C.H.U.D.s materialized, growling as they emerged from the stone.

Not the stone, the crevices! An ambush!

I blasted another monster into oblivion. Then a heavy weight slammed into me from behind. I hit the cold stone and rolled, losing my flashlight in the process but hanging on to my gun. I got to my knees in time to blow the head off another C.H.U.D. right before it could gut me.

Someone screamed. I caught a glimpse of Officer June going down, a C.H.U.D. clawing at his chest. I got off two quick bursts. The first flung the creature off him and the second removed half its face.

Two more went down as Watson fired a long volley. I slammed another clip home and joined her.

Dozens of demonic eyes filled the tunnel, blocking the way to the cave's entrance.

"Fall back!" I ordered, hoping the team would hear me over the din. They did. We retreated deeper into the cave.

Everyone except DeWitt, who had curled up in a ball on the floor, arms over his head.

Lopez cursed and ran back for him while we provided covering fire. He grabbed DeWitt by the arms, yanked him up, and dragged him to safety.

We fashioned ourselves into two lines, back to back. I covered our forward movement with Watson, Peters, and Christy while Curly, Daws, Lopez, and Lee guarded the rear, with the civilians in between us. In that fashion, we headed deeper into the tunnel. The

C.H.U.D.s paced us, staying just out of range but never to the point where their luminescent orbs disappeared.

As we walked, I tried to grasp what had just happened. C.H.U.D.s were not supposed to work as a group. Sure, some of them seemed more intelligent than others, but that was because the mutagenic effects of the radioactive sludge were unpredictable, based on factors such as length and method of exposure. The brains in Guantanamo had been trying for years to achieve predictable outcomes, with the ultimate goal of controlling the mutagenesis effect.

Secretly, I hoped they'd never succeed. Mindless C.H.U.D.s were bad enough. The idea of intelligent ones terrified me.

Gunfire clattered. A C.H.U.D. roared.

"Dammit. They won't go down." Lopez's voice came in gasps, too heavy for the little exertion we'd done.

He's panicking. Damn newbies. "Lopez, remember rule number one. Aim for the head." I kept my tone even, despite the sweat running down my ribs.

"I thought rule number one was don't drink the radioactive Kool-Aid," Curly said. That brought a few nervous laughs.

"Can it." My response held no rebuke. A little humor was good to ease tensions and we both knew it. That's why I'd given him a standard set up line.

"Just don't bottle—Oh, hell!"

More gunfire, and then Curly's voice rose above it. "Run!"

I tried to urge more speed from my legs but they wouldn't obey. A weapon barked in the darkness behind me. One short burst. Too short.

Someone screamed, the long, throat-tearing wail of a man suffering unimaginable agony.

"They got Peters." Beth Watson's words came out in harsh exhalations.

The kid's first assignment and he's gone. I would have cursed but I didn't have the air to waste.

We were running blind and deaf, the worst possible combination. We'd been hit twice more by surprise attacks from the sides and, while we all carried plenty of extra cartridges for the guns, we were down to two flashlights. The only thing that had saved us was there didn't seem to be any more side branches. That, and the tunnel narrowing until it was just barely wide enough for three people to move abreast.

I expected to barrel into a sea of voracious C.H.U.D.s at any moment, but so far they all seemed to be behind us. DeWitt had reported forty missing. We had to have killed half of them. Unless more of DeWitt's men had been contaminated than he knew of.

Based on what we'd seen, that seemed distinctly possible.

Someone cried out up ahead, my only warning before the tunnel opened up and I stumbled over a two-foot drop. I landed badly, twisting an ankle before catching myself on a block of damp stone. The rest of the team tumbled out behind me. Christy and Daws shined their lights around us as we regrouped.

We'd reached DeWitt's tourist cavern.

Massive conical shapes turned the floor into a

forest of rock, while more of them hung from the ceiling like giant fangs.

"Take cover." I crouched behind a stalagmite as thick as my waist. Mushnik pulled DeWitt behind another, saving me the trouble.

Two beams of light focused on the tunnel opening. My finger hovered over the trigger of my MAC.

"First sign of movement, light 'em up," I said. A chorus of affirmatives came back to me.

A minute passed. And then another.

"Did we lose them?" someone asked. It sounded like Lopez.

A stupid question. No one bothered answering and he had the good sense not to repeat it. C.H.U.D.s could run forever and had a sense of smell like a bloodhound.

They knew where we were. So why weren't they attacking?

I waited another two minutes before speaking.

"All right, we're going to keep moving to the target. But stay alert. We already know they've got alternate routes through this damn mountain."

Curly took point. We wove our way between the pillars, light and shadows creating mysterious shapes that danced around us, a constant distraction that pulled our eyes in too many directions at once. The ominous silence grew as if the world held its breath.

The way it did when a predator was nearby.

Five minutes passed. Ten. The tension between my shoulders refused to ease. I trusted that feeling. We weren't safe yet, not by a long shot.

"Shhh." Curly slowed his pace.

A snuffling, grunting sound, barely audible. Curly

motioned for Daws, Lopez, and Lee to move around to the left. The growling grew louder. Something snapped, the brittle sound of a branch breaking. I paused. A wet, almost slurping noise. It reminded me of something . . .

Jenny's dog, Clyde, wolfing down a bowl of food.

Another step. The noises stopped.

We rounded a column and someone gasped. Illuminated by Christy's light, three shapes crouched over a body, its chest ripped open, organs on grisly display. Bones littered the floor around the beasts, some still with bits of meat on them. Too many for just the one carcass.

The creatures snarled, displaying jagged teeth. They rose up in unison, big as football players, their disfigured faces covered in blood and fluids.

DeWitt screamed.

Mushnik fired, the pop-pop of his .9mm high and flat compared to the dull, rapid thud of military-grade weapons. The creatures didn't even flinch. Growling like rabid dogs, they leaped forward, arms outstretched, clawed hands ready to disembowel their prey.

Us.

Curly shouldered Mushnik to the side and let go a short burst that caught the lead C.H.U.D. right in the face. Fluorescent goo splattered the rocks and it fell to its knees with a guttural croak. The two behind it paused and Curly emptied the rest of his clip into them.

After a few tense moments waiting to see if anything else attacked, the team lowered their weapons.

"Look at the clothes." Curly prodded one of the C.H.U.D. corpses with his foot.

"Those are Consolidated work uniforms," Mushnik confirmed.

"Impossible," DeWitt muttered.

"Impossible's a word we don't use much anymore." That shut him up. I took a moment to glance at my wrist gauge. The needle rested just below red. We had to be getting close. C.H.U.D.s tend to establish their nests close to the initial source of the contamination.

"Christy, spot us."

The earnest ex-Marine tapped the GPS strapped to his forearm and eyed the digital readout. "The storage chamber is about a half-click east and forty meters above us."

I glanced at DeWitt. "A different level?"

He nodded. Just when I thought my dislike for him couldn't get stronger. What else hadn't he told us?

"All right, let's move out. Eyes and ears open."

I motioned for Christy to take point, since he had both a light and the GPS. At the same time, a muffled growl reached us from somewhere way off to the left. Another answered from our right.

We double-timed it across the cavern.

The eyes of our unseen enemy burned the back of my neck. An attack now would be disastrous. There was no doubt we were being followed. Hushed grunts and an eerie keening made the continued presence of the C.H.U.D.s known. I recognized the ploy from my days in jungle combat. Intimidate the opponent, frighten them to the point where they make mistakes.

A sure sign of intelligence.

Another first to add to the list. What the hell was going on in these caves?

The C.H.U.D.s' tactics were working. I saw the eyes of my men darting back and forth, their fingers twitching near their triggers. The way we were speed-marching faster than was safe in the current conditions.

Dammit, we had enough weaponry to take out a small village and the C.H.U.D.s were winning the mental battle.

"Cap, over here." Christy waved his light. "I found the tunnel."

The opening in the stone lent a burst of strength to my aching legs. A short hike up to the next level and then all we had to do was locate the storage cavern, set the explosives, and leave.

Oh, and kill a couple of dozen C.H.U.D.s along the way.

The final tunnel was even narrower than the last one. My breathing sounded harsh in my ears as I followed Lee's vague shape ahead of me. Behind me, the fabric of Daws' uniform made a constant shushing against the walls as he squeezed himself along.

And we emerged, with more than a few sighs of relief. Flashlight beams reflected off chiseled walls and ancient wooden beams. Lopez and Lee took up positions guarding the tunnel mouth while the rest of us watched Christy turn in a slow circle, his eyes on the GPS.

"C'mon, Sticks, where is it?" Curly asked. Christy shook his head.

"According to this, we're right on top of it."

"Everyone look around." I took the opportunity to

examine the layout of the room. A rough square that I judged to be about thirty feet long and half as wide. Some old supply bags piled along one wall, a string of cheap lights hanging from the ceiling, the bulbs broken or missing. On the other side from where we'd entered, a wide opening that DeWitt indicated was the exit to one of the main mine tunnels that led to the surface.

Two entrances meant planting two sets of explosives. Not a problem; I had enough C-4 with me to take down a couple of buildings.

"Over here." The team converged on Daws. A trickle of yellowish-green liquid snaked across the stone by his feet. It emerged from a massive vertical gap in one of the walls.

I took his flashlight and peered through the opening.

On the other side was a cave, slightly smaller than the one we stood in, the walls covered in cracked cement. Stacked in the center were at least two dozen metal drums, several of them on their sides. Puddles of liquid, which looked a lot like radiator fluid, surrounded the barrels and formed tiny rivers that flowed across gullies and down into fissures in the stone, which led to who-knew-where.

It was by far the largest storage setup I'd come across since joining the C.H.U.D. cleanup program. No wonder there'd been such an outbreak. The only surprise was that it hadn't happened sooner.

"This is it." Any doubts were erased when I checked my Geiger. The needle had pinged way into the red. I backed away from the opening, taking care not to step in any of the liquid. We'd come prepared for battle, not decontamination. "Curly, take everyone toward the main tunnel. I'll set the charges and we'll get the hell out of here."

"Yes, sir."

I took two small bricks of C-4 and two timers from my belt. Using the soft glow from my Geiger, I attached the timers and set them for thirty minutes. That would give us more than enough time to put a safe distance between us and the explosions.

Then it would just be a matter of placing men at each entrance and picking off the C.H.U.D.s as they came in or out. Not quite as easy as target practice, but still a lot safer for my men than fighting in caves.

And that was all I cared about.

"Let's move," I said, joining the team in the tunnel. "We've got thirty and counting."

Unlike the previous passageways, this one was completely man-made, hewn from the rock by modern machinery. It was also wider, a good twenty feet across, making our exit relatively easy despite only having two lights.

Until about ten minutes later, when Watson edged up next to me.

"Hey, Cap?" Something in her whisper raised the hairs on my neck. "You smell smoke?"

I took a deep breath. Sweat, the rancid odors of C.H.U.D. gore on my clothing . . . and something else. I sniffed again. There. A hint of diesel fuel and . . . wood smoke?

Watson was right.

"Hold up. Something's burning."

"That's probably the coal fires." At DeWitt's words, everyone turned and looked at him.

"Fires? What are you talking about?" Jorge Lee's voice rose half an octave.

"That's why my men were in the mine to begin with. The earthquakes triggered some fires in the coal veins."

"You idiot!" Watson grabbed DeWitt by the shirt and slammed him into the rocks. "Why didn't you tell us?"

"I told the chief!"

Daws advanced on Mushnik, who held up his hands and backed away. "I didn't think it was important."

"Oh, for the love of—"

"Stand down, both of you." I understood their fury, felt it myself, only mine had a different target.

Me.

None of the intel from Travers or Mushnik had mentioned what the missing men had been doing. And I hadn't asked.

"What?" DeWitt looked from me to Watson and back. Mushnik seemed just as confused, but he kept his mouth shut. "Coal fires happen all the time. It doesn't take much to set them off. We're very careful about putting them out before they spread."

Fear rose inside me like a vengeful spirit. Fire and radioactive waste. That explained how so many men were contaminated so quickly.

"It doesn't take much to set them off."

Those fires had been going now for days. And I'd just planted explosives. If they spread farther . . .

"I have to go back and deactivate those charges." We still had plenty of time. We'd just have to think of another way to seal the contaminated area. Kill the C.H.U.D.s and bring in spray foam, maybe.

"I'll go with you," Lopez said. "As backup."

"Okay. The rest of you keep heading for the exit. We'll rendezvous there."

Daws handed Lopez his flashlight and we took off at a fast walk. We hadn't even gotten halfway back when an all-too-familiar snarling reached us from up ahead.

We stopped and raised our weapons. A dozen pairs of eyes appeared. And then another dozen.

I opened fire on them. So did Lopez. Cries of pain and howls of fury overwhelmed the sound of our guns.

The C.H.U.D.s rushed forward.

I don't know how many we killed, but it wasn't enough. My clip ran out and they were on us before I could reload. I dropped the MAC and pulled my service pistol. Burning fire flared in my left arm. I shoved the gun into the mouth of a C.H.U.D. and pulled the trigger. Hot fluids exploded across my arms and chest. Strong hands grabbed me. I turned the gun that way, saw it was Lopez. Blood streaked his face. He pulled me backward and together we ran. I shouted a warning for the others.

We rounded a corner, C.H.U.D.s roaring and thundering along behind us, and the Animals were lined up. I don't think I've ever been so happy to see guns pointed at me. We squeezed past and fell to our knees, gasping for air, while the team let loose a deafening barrage.

A high-pitched scream cut the air, followed by more rapid hammering of automatic weapons. Someone shouted that Lee was gone. Inhuman growls and more of the terrible keening.

Then everything went silent.

I forced myself to take deep breaths until my head cleared. Then I let Curly help me up.

Before I could take a damage report, an awful sound rose up, a gibbering cackle unlike anything I'd ever experienced in all my dealings with C.H.U.D.s. It took me a moment to understand what we were hearing.

Laughter.

Something landed by our feet with a wet thump.

An arm.

Corporal Lee's.

"What the hell?" Daws went white as a ghost, something I'd never seen him do, not even when an infant C.H.U.D. bit off two of his fingers.

"To the exit. Now."

"What about Lee?" Watson asked. I hated my answer.

"He's gone and this place is gonna blow in ten minutes. Move!"

"Yes, sir!"

The Animals took off, running as fast as the flashlights allowed. Rocks threatened to trip careless feet. The tunnel widened until we couldn't see the sides, allowing us to make good time until Christy shouted something and came to a stumbling halt. Lopez, following too close, ran into him. The rest of the team crowded around.

"Jesus." DeWitt put his hand over his mouth but to his credit, he didn't puke.

Lee's body—what was left of it—lay on the ground. All its limbs gone, chest and belly split wide open like he'd swallowed a grenade.

"How . . . ?" I didn't need to hear the rest of

Mushnik's question to know what he meant. How had the C.H.U.D.s planted the body so far ahead of us? My own question was a little different, and more frightening.

Why had they done it?

That's when the noises started again. Snuffling, growling. And something else. Whispers that turned my blood to ice.

"Diefoodeatyoudie."

"They're trying to surround us." Curly brought his gun up but held his fire. I patted my belt. One clip left plus whatever was in my Glock. I tried counting clips in my head. Each person had started with ten. Thirty rounds per clip for the MACs. We'd been pretty much shooting indiscriminately. So if they each had one or two left . . .

Even with side arms, those weren't good odds.

"Keep moving for the exit." I nudged Watson to take point with me. "Curly, Daws, cover our asses."

"No." Lopez stayed still.

"That's an order, soldier." Damn gung-ho newbies. We were wasting precious seconds.

"You go. I'll cover you." He slapped a new clip into his gun. His last one, I noticed.

"We don't need heroes, mister."

"Someone has to hold them off. It should be me. I'm not making it back anyhow." He lifted his arm and I saw the dark stain covering his entire side. Glimpses of white bone showed through the hole in his flesh.

"Dammit, Lopez." I shook my head. He'd never said a word. "Give 'em hell."

I gave his shoulder a squeeze and then did the hardest thing a commanding officer has to do.

Abandon one of their own.

It only took me a few moments to catch up with Watson, who'd slowed up to wait for us. When she saw my face, she just bit her lip and picked up the pace.

A minute later, we heard the sound of gunfire.

And then the screams.

★★★

We almost made it to the main entrance before the C-4 blew. A deep rumbling alerted us to the detonations. The ground trembled and gave a violent shake. Earth and rock cascaded down on us and clouds of dust made it impossible to see anything. Someone cried out, "My leg! My leg!"

Then the back of my head exploded and everything went dark.

SEPTEMBER 30, 10:17 A.M.

The door to my room opened. Colonel Travers entered, only this time without the doctors who'd been an almost constant presence since I woke up chained to a hospital bed. I caught a glimpse of the two guards in the hallway before the door closed.

"Any word on when I'm getting out of here?" I didn't bother with formality anymore. Five days of medical detention will do that to a person. The fact that Travers didn't care only confirmed my fears.

I wasn't leaving anytime soon.

He'd debriefed me via a secure line on an iPad. I'd told him everything, including the whispers and the fires.

My first taste of fear for my freedom came when he didn't express any surprise.

Instead, he'd told me we'd all been quarantined. There'd been concern my team and I had been contaminated by radioactive steam released into the air when the liquid waste dripped onto burning coal. But when I showed no signs of changing after three days, he'd ordered the chains removed and he and the medical personnel started entering the room without protective gear.

However, I hadn't been allowed out. And the guards never left.

I assumed the rest of the Double Zeroes—along with Chief Mushnik and DeWitt—were in similar isolation. Every day, Travers told me they were fine, I'd get to see them soon. Just like he kept telling me we'd be released in a "couple of days."

I wasn't sure what hurt worse, being kept as a prisoner or the fact that he'd lied to us from the beginning of the mission.

"We've hit a snag." He dropped a photo on the bed.

DeWitt. Only all his hair had fallen out and patches of skin had peeled off on his cheeks. His eyes looked larger, too. And cloudy.

"Damn." What else could I say?

"We don't know if you're all going to be affected. But . . . "

"Yeah."

Travers took a deep breath. Let it out slowly. He pointed to the laptop on my end table.

"I've lifted the internet restrictions. You can watch whatever you want. Email Jenny. Just, you know."

"I know." My oath. Don't reveal anything. Not that I could. All emails would be reviewed before they went out. I still appreciated the gesture. His way of apologizing.

He nodded. "See you tomorrow."

I waited until the door shut before booting up the laptop. The first thing I did was check the news. I found what I was looking for right away.

The massive coal fire continues to burn underneath the town of Twin Creeks, West Virginia. The government declared a state of emergency and quarantined the area. Due to the potential release of toxic gasses, all residents had been transported to a nearby military hospital for treatment. The National Guard . . .

I closed the page. All those people. A new type of exposure, one that seemed to have solved the brain boys' biggest problem.

Those whispers in the cave, the ones I kept hearing whenever I tried to sleep.

"Diefoodeatyoudie"

All those people. What was going to happen to them? To my team?

To me?

An angry growl rumbled in my throat and I forced it down.

I had a feeling we were going to find out soon.

T.H.E. D.E.U.C.E.

PHILIP C. PERRON

TIMES SQUARE, AUGUST 7TH, 1985

"**IT WAS A** wild ride," Leanne said, circling her arms above her head for emphasis. She gave Margaux a look over followed by a frown. "Hey, what's wrong with you? You take something?"

Margaux, or better known back home in Rhode Island to family and friends as Camille, clasped her hands around the coffee mug. Her fingerless black-laced gloves kept her palms protected from its heat. A blended smell of burnt hamburger and stale cigarette smoke made her want to vomit. She brought the mug up to her lips and took a swig of the typically flat coffee that this greasy spoon always served around three in the morning.

"So darling," Leanne asked again, "did the dragon bite?"

Margaux's eyes fluttered down to her sleeveless left arm and its exposed syringe marks. She pulled her arm tight up against her side in shock. "No," she said with a scowl, "I never mix the junk with work. Too many freaks and psychos out at this hour."

"The truth," Leanne said. Her Polish accent always betrayed her foreign origin. Margaux thought it ironic, being ethnically Korean yet born in Rhode Island, that the johns always seemed to think she was the foreign born while Leanne the native.

"Do you have a light?" Leanne asked.

Margaux slid her book of matches across the table and watched as her friend . . . acquaintance . . . associate . . . inhaled the first puffs of her Marlboro. As she took in the sweet smell of the fresh cigarette, Margaux also took in her surroundings. Five people . . . the Puerto Rican waitress . . . the Puerto Rican cook . . . a black cop just off duty . . . and a twenty-something couple that oddly didn't fit the scene. Just outside beyond the oversized floor to ceiling windows was 42nd street and the Apollo Theater across the way. The marquee flashed brightly, promising the thrills of the showing of a double feature of *Night Has a Thousand Desires* and *Black Venus*. People traveled . . . in cabs . . . on foot . . . up and down the street looking for the next trick, the next hit, or the next high.

"Next week," Leanne said, breaking Margaux's train of thought. "That's when I head back home to visit."

"Poland?"

"No, silly," Leanne guffawed. "Back to Pittsburgh . . . for two weeks to visit my daddy and sister."

"Oh, right," Margaux said. "I forgot."

"Wow, you really are out of it tonight. Why don't you head back to your apartment and crash . . . regroup . . . start over tomorrow night?"

Margaux shrugged. "I just may do that."

"If you do," Leanne added, concern in her voice,

"when you get there, don't jolly pop, and promise me you'll take a cab and not the '4' train home, you hear me? Way too many . . . undesirables."

Margaux nodded. "Yeah, I hear you."

Outside a woman laughed loudly. Margaux watched the group of hookers that had been hanging just outside the diner's door turn their attention toward 8th Avenue. A tall blonde pointed and the group hurried along in their stilettos and miniskirts past the diner's window and out of view.

"Would you like something else?" the middle-aged waitress asked.

"Pie," Leanne asked. "Do you have cherry pie?"

"We do."

"A slice . . . and a scoop of vanilla ice cream."

The waitress left leaving Margaux without a refill of coffee.

"Go figure," she mumbled.

"What's that?" Leanne asked.

"I know the coffee is crap, but you'd figure she'd—"

"Chud," a husky sounding chain smoker's voice interrupted the otherwise quiet diner. "They're here."

Leanne followed Margaux's gaze, pulling her chair back and turning to look. An unshaven blonde man with a ratty checkered flannel shirt stood by the door, the buttons hanging open revealing a Culture Club T-shirt underneath. His eyes looked crazed . . . a look Margaux was all too familiar with. Chasing the dragon.

"We're becoming like . . . they're coming for . . . for us all," he said, his voice slowly cracking before filling with despair. "We've turned our back on God. They've come to the—"

"That's enough," the cop said. As he put his hands

on the table to stand up, the crazed man reached around his back and pulled out a handgun. Before anyone could react, the barrel was already pointed at the officer's forehead. The shot echoed through the diner. Blood . . . brain . . . skull splattered across the floor and up the legs of the well-dressed woman.

"Dios mio!" the waitress shrieked.

The chair the police officer sat upon tipped backward sending his body to the floor. The crazed man walked over, stood above him, pointed the gun and fired three more times.

"Jesus wept," the well-dressed woman, her stiletto feet covered in red, said through tears.

"It's the end of times," the crazed man shrieked. He raised the handgun above his head and shook it in anger.

Gun smoke and the metallic iron smell of blood filled Margaux's nostrils. She clenched her teeth hard upon the side of her cheek, hoping not to throw up. Soon the taste of her own blood filled her mouth as she bit too hard upon her inner cheek.

"Chud," the crazed man said again. "Down below. They have awoken. They are us." He cocked the handgun, put it to his own chin, and fired. Once more, blood, skull, and brains sprayed from the top of his head, painting the ceiling red. His lifeless body stood for a few seconds before tumbling over onto a table, spilling it, his corpse, and all the table's contents to the floor. The seconds passed. Only the sound of the rotating ceiling fan whooshed its tune in the otherwise quiet restaurant.

"Officer Cleveland?" A walkie-talkie clipped to the officer's belt crackled. "We have a 10-15 on West 42nd Street. Over."

The waitress took a few steps around the body of the crazed man. She leaned over the policeman.

"Officer Cleveland," a man's voice crackled again, "repeat, we have a 10-15 on West 42nd Street. We need you to head over to the Selwyn Theater. Do you copy? Over."

"What's a 10-15?" the waitress asked through her sobs.

"A civil disturbance," Margaux answered. Working the streets, she knew the codes all too well.

"And?"

"Probably a fight," the well-dressed man answered. "I'd say it was—"

"Officer Cleveland," the radio crackled again, "if you are near, have everyone get inside whatever stores . . . theaters . . . buildings that are near. Have them lock the doors. Officer Cleveland, please copy. Head over to the Selwyn Theater immediately. Over."

"What's going on?" Leanne turned back to Margaux.

Margaux looked about. The shorthand cook had come to the front. Everyone, including the well-dressed woman, seemed fairly calm. Having witnessed the murder of an officer of the law followed by a suicide, there was no hysteria.

Margaux knew what each and every one of them was thinking . . . and what they all knew. The well-dressed couple couldn't hide the fact they were locals. She perceived they weren't some out of town couple just in for the weekend. They all knew. The Selwyn Theater was but two doors down, separated only by an adult bookstore.

"Close the grates," she said. She looked over at the cook. "Close the grates . . . now!"

The shorthand cook gave her a confused expression, but he followed her eyes out the diner's window. His face changed and he hurried out to the sidewalk. Margaux watched as he quickly looked up and down 42nd Street. The road seemed suddenly empty. Vehicles were no longer passing and foot traffic was scarce. He reached above the window. As he pulled, the chained grille rolled down into place. Distant sirens sounded a few blocks away.

Oscar, Margaux remembered from her many times in the diner. The cook . . . his name is Oscar.

"What's going on, Rick?" the well-dressed woman asked.

"Maybe a riot," Rick answered.

Oscar re-entered the diner and locked the door behind him. He pushed the waitress aside and grabbed the police officer's walkie-talkie.

"Over here," Margaux said, holding her hand out.

The cook seemed to have some sort of internal debate, but he hurried across the room and handed the walkie-talkie to Margaux.

"Hello?" she asked. Static came from its speaker.

"Sometimes if you hit it hard," Leanne suggested.

Margaux spoke again. "Hello? Anyone there?"

"Who's this?" a woman asked.

Ease spread through the room. "Hi," Margaux answered. "We need to report a murder-suicide."

Oscar came over and placed upon the table the officer's identification, his gun, as well as the crazed man's gun.

Margaux picked up the identification. "Officer . . . Officer Reginald Cleveland was murdered."

"I repeat, who is this?"

"My name is Margaux," she stopped herself. "I mean, my name is Camille Park. We are at the Sinclair Diner. A crazed gunman came in, shot and killed Officer Cleveland, and then killed himself."

"Okay, Camille," the woman on the other end responded. "That's the greasy spoon next door to the Selwyn, right?"

"Two doors down," Margaux corrected. The others took seats alongside Leanne.

"So who else is there?"

"There's myself," she said while scanning her companions. "Also my friend, Leanne . . . I don't know her last name."

"Wojciechowski," Leanne yelled over.

Margaux made a hand gesture as if writing.

The waitress pulled out her receipt pad and wrote. Afterward she handed the pen and pad to Oscar. When it arrived back to Margaux, she read off names.

"There's six of us. Myself, Leanne, two employees, Oscar Cuellar and Juanita Ibanez, and two other customers, Richard Levine and Naomi Sokoloff."

"Okay, this is what I need you to do," the woman said. "I want one of you to go over to the perpetrator and look under his shirt."

Margaux looked confused.

Oscar nodded. "I'll do it."

"What are we looking for?" Margaux asked.

"Any deformity," she said. "Anything such as discolored skin. Scaly or bumpy skin. Anything that doesn't appear . . . normal."

Oscar stood over the dead man. He reached across to the counter and grabbed a butcher knife. Cutting from the bottom of the dead man's T-shirt straight through the printed face of Boy George, the shirt parted to reveal green and blackened skin. "What is this?" he asked, taking a step back in shock.

"Okay," Margaux asked, "are you still there?"

"Yes," the woman said. "Does the perpetrator have any deformities?"

"Skin," Margaux stuttered out. "It's black . . . grayish . . . maybe green."

"Scaly?"

Oscar nodded.

"Yes," Margaux answered. "And he was mumbling something . . . something like chud."

"Okay, Camille," the woman said, "hold on for a moment." The walkie-talkie went to static.

"Did they say anything about staying put?" Rick asked.

"No," Margaux said shaking her head. "But before . . . earlier . . . remember they said to have everyone go inside . . . into stores or buildings . . . and lock the doors."

Leanne lowered her head in despair. "This is more than just a crime scene now."

"Is it some sort of terrorist thing?" Naomi asked. "Like in that movie *Back to the Future*. The Libyans?"

The walkie crackled. "Okay," the woman said. "Camille, I need you and your companions to stay put. Make sure you lock the doors—"

"We did," Margaux interrupted. "We even pulled down the grates to cover the storefront."

"Okay, just stay put. Don't go outside. Don't leave the diner. Do you understand?"

Margaux looked about at her companions. Each nodded.

"We do," she said. "We understand. No worries.

THE DEUCE

We'll stay put. But can you tell us what's going on? What's happening? What's a chud?"

"We'll get back to you. Stay put." The walkie went to static. Silence followed.

Margaux stood.

"Where're you going?" Naomi asked.

"Just looking outside the front door." As she walked by the dead body of the murderer, the walkie crackled. "Anyone there?" she spoke into the radio. By the time she got to the diner's front door, the walkie went dead again.

"Do you see anything?" Juanita asked.

"Nothing," she said, looking back and shaking her head. "It's . . . it's quiet outside. Like one of those side streets in the Meat Packing District."

"What do you mean?" Leanne asked as she led the others over to where Margaux was. "No one's out there? No cars?"

"No one," she said. "Nothing." She slid to her left so the others could get a look out through the glass door.

"What about the Selwyn Theater?" Oscar asked. "Do you think that's where this guy," he pointed over at the body of the murderer, "came from? Did he kill someone there too you think?"

"I don't know—" Margaux stopped as the walkie lit up with static. Just as she was about to speak, she looked over at the others.

"What is it?" Rick asked.

Margaux turned and stared at the radio in her hand. She put her arm out and lowered it toward the body of the murderer. As the walkie got closer to the corpse, the noise of static rose.

"What the heck?" Rick pushed his way over and yanked the walkie from Margaux's hand. He lowered it and pulled it back and repeated the process three more times. Each time the static rose as the radio was lowered toward the body.

"What's going on?" Naomi asked.

"Shhh," Rick demanded. He lowered the walkie to the body again. The static rose to a steady pitch. Rick slowly carried it from feet to head. The crackling remained firm. He looked over at the others.

"What is it?" Naomi demanded.

His eyes turned away and followed the splattered blood across the length of the floor. After a brief pause, he lowered the walkie and traversed the trail of gore along the tiles. The walkie continued to crackle until finally stopping as the blood thinned out and ended. "Naomi, stay there for a moment."

She looked at him confused.

Rick walked back and bent down on one knee beside her. He lowered the walkie to her open toe stilettos. Immediately once more it began to static.

"What?" she said, her voice cracking with fear. "What is it?"

"It's the blood," he said.

"But the blood on her feet isn't the murderer's," Leanne mentioned. "It's the cop's blood."

"The cop?" Juanita asked.

"No . . . way," Oscar said. He hurried over to the body of Officer Cleveland and rolled him to his back. The top of the man's head was intact even with the large bullet hole in the middle of his forehead. Oscar reached down, pulled apart the dead man's shirt. Buttons ripped from fabric and scattered across the floor.

THE DEUCE

Margaux and the others stepped forward to get a better view. There, just as with his murderer, the officer had greenish colored skin that was covered with small scaly bumps.

"Oh my God," Naomi shrieked. She took a seat upon one of the counter stools, not caring that anyone who wanted could get a look up her miniskirt. She unbuckled her pink stilettos. With disgust, she tossed them across the room. Pulling napkins out of a dispenser, she wiped furiously away the wet blood that caked between her toes and that painted her ankles.

"What's the static mean?" Leanne asked. "And the . . . deformities?"

"Radiation maybe," Margaux said, almost choking on the words. "I remember seeing that Jane Fonda film, *China Syndrome*. And also some documentary on PBS."

"Like in *Back to the Future*," Naomi said. "Uranium . . . the Libyans wanted it."

A loud bang shook the storefront grate. Everyone stood motionless waiting. A number of rasps followed.

"Someone's out there," Naomi said.

The walkie crackled. "Camille, are you there?"

Rick handed the radio back to Margaux.

"We're still here," she answered.

"Did you hear anyone outside?"

"Someone just knocked on the diner's grate."

"Okay," the woman said, "I'm in direct contact with them now. They're going to come to the door. Don't be alarmed."

"Alarmed?" Margaux asked. "Alarmed about what?" Before the woman answered, two figures . . . men . . . appeared covered head to toe in yellow latex suits. Their faces showed out through clear plastic shields. The shorter held a silver metal case. The taller raised one of his gloved hands and waved.

"Oh . . . my . . . God," Naomi said through tears. "It is uranium. It is terrorism. It is the Libyans."

"Camille," the woman said, "I need you to let them in."

"What's going on?" Margaux asked.

"I need you to let them in," the woman repeated. "They're going to help."

Oscar walked over to the glass, gave the new arrivals a Mona Lisa smile, and proceeded to unlock the door.

The taller man waved him away. Oscar stepped back and took a seat on the stool next to Naomi.

"What's happening here?" Margaux asked.

The men looked at her but said nothing. Instead, they went and examined the corpses.

"CHUD?" the taller asked, his voice sounding flat through the latex.

"Very soon," the shorter one answered.

"The cop, too?"

"Same," the shorter responded.

"Typical?" the taller asked.

"I'd say not," the shorter said. "He may have not even known."

"How so?" the taller asked. He leaned over to get a view of the police officer. "It looks as if it progressed."

"Possibly twelve hours in development—"

"What's going on here?" Naomi asked, almost yelling. She jumped off the stool and stood on her tippy-toes.

"Ma'am, please," the taller man said. "Bear with us."

"Don't you think we deserve some answers?" Margaux asked. "I mean, there's been a murder-suicide. One's a policeman. And there's something besides that weird color . . . that skin . . . "

"How so, ma'am?" the taller man asked.

"Well," Margaux said pausing a moment to take a breath, "they may be . . . they may be radiated . . . if that's even a word."

The shorter man looked to his companion and waited. The taller pointed one of his gloved hands over at one of the booths. The shorter man picked up the metallic case and placed it on the table.

"What makes you think that?" the taller man asked.

"The cop's walkie-talkie crackles near the bodies," Rick said.

"Could just be interference—"

"You're wearing monkey suits," Rick almost yelled.

"Okay," the taller man said raising his hands in protest, "these are suits for—"

"Terrorists then," Naomi yelled. "Like the Libyans!"

"Before we go on with this line of talk," the taller man said, "I need to know where the weapon used in the murder is. It will have to be collected as part of the crime scene."

"Over there," Oscar said, pointing to the table on the other side of the room. "And the policeman's gun is there too."

"Okay, good," he said. "Now Dr. Avsec will answer some of your questions."

"That's a start," Leanne said.

The shorter man, Dr. Avsec, undid the latch of the

case. "Now, what I have in here is a Geiger counter." He pulled out a small device that looked like a wand. "If it beeps we'll know whether radiation is indeed—"

"What's a chud?" Juanita interrupted.

The taller man looked at her.

"Well, Dr. Avsec just said it a moment ago," she explained. "And the crazy guy kept saying chud were coming . . . right before he shot himself."

Dr. Avsec and the taller man's eyes met.

"Go ahead, Dr. Avsec."

Dr. Avsec looked down at the metallic case. "Well," he said, "it means a couple of things. The government was planning to remove waste . . . radioactive waste from Manhattan, but there was a hiccup you could say. Government agencies disagreeing . . . things like that, and it's been stuck down below . . . right here . . . in the middle of Times Square . . . or the Deuce."

"But what's chud mean?" Naomi asked.

"It's an acronym for Contamination Hazard Urban Disposal."

"Hold it," Rick said, "that doesn't make any sense."

"Well, it has another meaning," Dr. Avsec said as he reached into the case a second time. "It's also an acronym for Cannibalistic Humanoid Underground Dwellers."

"Cannibal-what?" Rick asked.

"Oh my God," Naomi cried, understanding seeming to cross her face.

"Indeed," Dr. Avsec said revealing a pistol in his hand. He immediately fired two shots. Rick and Oscar both fell upon the tiles. Their bodies motionless.

Naomi shrieked in terror. A third shot and silence.

"I'm sorry," the taller man said, his voice filled with

regret. "This is not a personal decision. You folks were unfortunately at the wrong place at the wrong time. You've been exposed. You know too much. I'm sorry."

Margaux huddled herself beside Juanita and Leanne and the three embraced as if already reaching the fifth stage of grief . . . that stage simply being acceptance.

"I'm so sorry," the taller man said once more. "Dr. Avsec, please."

"Indeed," he said while raising the pistol yet again.

A.L.L. A.T. S.E.A.

ROSS BAXTER

WHEN MAJOR JOHN Reynolds got to the bridge of the tug it was already crowded with people gawking out of the windows. The burly Royal Marine pushed himself forward, moving towards the tug's captain.

"There she is!" exclaimed the captain, stating the obvious. "The Delta Star."

Reynolds said nothing, silently appraising the build, condition and access points of the huge vessel which loomed out of the mist ahead. Although he had been studying the engineering plans and layout since embarking on the tug earlier that day, he was still slightly surprised at the sheer scale of the cargo vessel.

"Are you sure your little tug can actually tow that thing?" he muttered.

"Normally it would take three tugs to handle something that size," wheezed the elderly captain, "but in the interests of speed, the Ministry decided that one would be enough. I don't think it'll be an issue given the current sea state and the fact that we're only forty nautical miles from Belfast, though."

ALL AT SEA

Reynolds nodded but said nothing; the crew of the civilian tug had not been told the full story, and until he got on board Reynolds would not be able to make a decision about what the next step would actually be.

"She's still making a steady five knots and I can't see any sign of damage despite the distress call they made. I'm assuming their power must be down as they're not answering VHF, but the surprising thing is that I can't see a single soul on deck even though I've fired off two flares—you'd think their lookout would have spotted us by now?" the captain went on with a scowl.

"Well, they'll know soon enough," said Reynolds. "Position the tug five hundred yards from her stern and tell your crane operator to make ready to lower our boat."

"I can get a lot closer than five hundred yards," boasted the captain.

"Five hundred yards is the minimum," muttered Reynolds, stalking off the crowded bridge to collect his equipment.

★★★

The boat transfer proved quick and they were soon powering across the calm North Atlantic waters towards the gigantic container vessel. Reynolds and his team of five Royal Marines had to crane their necks to see up the slab sides from the small inflatable, but getting on board was not what concerned him. The US-registered vessel had set sail from the port of New York fifteen days earlier, bound for the Chinese military port of Dinghai with a cargo that neither the Americans nor the Chinese would share any information on. Neither of the two countries were keen for a British investigation team to board the vessel, both insisting they would send their own teams instead. But the bizarre nature of the distress call and the fact that the ship was drifting in British Territorial Waters had spurred the authorities to act quickly. The six Royal Marines and the tug were the first response, having the objective of securing a tow to the vessel to ensure it did not flounder on the rugged Ulster coastline.

"This looks like the spot, Sergeant!" Reynolds shouted to his helmsman as the inflatable coasted the final distance towards the dark blue hull of the cargo ship.

The sergeant nodded and killed the engine, letting the two marines on the port side tether the boat securely using two magnetic fetters.

"Boat secure, Sir!" called the nearest marine.

"Very good," Reynolds acknowledged. "Now listen up! I'll go first up the line, followed by Sergeant McKinley, Corporal Frost, and marines Hanson, Brown, and Letts. As per the earlier brief; from the distress call we're not actually sure what's happened on board, but be prepared to use your weapons. Happy?"

"Aye, Sir!" McKinley answered in his broad Scots accent on the behalf of the others.

Reynolds waited whilst the corporal fired the grappling line upwards and pulled until it soundly snagged. After a final check of his weapon he grabbed the heavy cord and heaved himself upwards, his boots connecting loudly with the slick hull. The others quickly followed, rapidly ascending up the sheer stern of the cargo vessel. On reaching the top Reynolds grabbed the railing, then took a quick look before flipping himself over to the deck. McKinley, Frost, Hanson, Brown and Letts followed in quick succession, all crouching low with weapons ready on the empty after-deck.

The major swiftly scanned the deck but saw nothing. He silently made the sign for the others to shadow and cautiously moved to follow the starboard railing towards the white painted stern superstructure which housed the accommodation section and the bridge. Ignoring the first entrance he continued stealthily forward along the deck to the front of the section to get a view of the vast cargo area. He peered over the bulwark and blinked in surprise; sitting on one of the colossal cargo deck hatches sat an American military helicopter.

"Looks like the Yanks got here first," whispered Sergeant McKinley.

Reynolds nodded; the SH60 Seahawk could not be seen on the deck from below due to the size of the ship and he figured it must have landed unobserved in the mist before they arrived on the tug. "It will have come from a US warship out in the Atlantic. I think their Ticonderoga and Perry class carry them. Whitehall will be livid if they don't know about this."

"It won't be the first time," grinned McKinley.

"We'll check out the Seahawk first, and see what the score is," Reynolds briefed the five Marines. "You'd better slope arms as we don't want to surprise anyone."

Reynolds slung his Sterling submachine gun over his shoulder and stepped down onto the silent upper cargo deck. There was no-one around the helicopter but he expected the pilot to be on-board, which was the usual drill. He walked up to the rear of the grey-painted aircraft, noting the US markings and name of its parent ship, USS Yorktown, painted on the side of the fuselage. Then he saw the cockpit door was open.

"Hey!" he shouted, amiably so as not to startle the pilot. "Anyone home?"

He received no reply so strode over to the door. The sight which met him stopped him dead; the pilot was indeed still on board, but only parts of him. Blood seemed to cover most of the inside of the cockpit. The body lay sprawled across the seat and centre instrument panel, its tattered flying suit shredded and torn to reveal a bloody and empty rib cage. An eyeless face regarded him from inside a gore-soaked helmet, the flesh appearing to have been ripped off in great chunks.

"Christ!" uttered McKinley from behind him. "A grenade?"

"There's no damage to the helicopter," Reynolds replied, unslinging his weapon. "It was no grenade."

"Check inside!" McKinley snapped to the marines. He peered closely at the glistening bone showing through the remains of the pilot's face; the marks in the few shreds of skin left on the cheeks appeared to be bite marks, as if the pilot had been savaged by a ravenous wolf.

"Clear!" Corporal Frost shouted from within the Seahawk. "Nothing amiss back here."

"Sir, check this out," called Letts. "Footprints. Human."

Reynolds looked to the deck where Letts was

pointing and saw the bloody prints of bare feet leading away from the Seahawk back towards the bridge and accommodation block. He moved to the now-open fuselage door with McKinley and summoned the others. "It looks like the pilot has been ripped apart, but not by gunfire or a grenade. The ship is still steaming towards the coast and will be aground within the hour. I'm not sure what we're facing, but we've got to get to the bridge and change course, or kill the engines and get a line across to the tug. Follow me, formation one, and fire at will if you need to."

The marines nodded and fell into a single line behind the major, who led them to the bulkhead door directly under the towering bridge structure. Reynolds paused at the half open door, studying the blood streaked door handle. He pointed for the others to see, then cautiously pulled open the steel door with his boot whilst keeping his submachine gun pointed at the opening. The door groaned on its hinges, the sound magnified in the silence pervading the ship. Inside, a lit stairwell led upwards, with a corridor off to the right. Bloody handprints extended both up the stair handrail and along the corridor walls.

Reynolds signaled for them to all proceed upwards. As soon as they stepped inside, each was struck by the sickening stench of decay and human waste, eye-wateringly strong and enough to make Frost and Hanson retch. Reynolds paused to let the two get their breath back, vigilantly scanning the stairs and the corridor. Suddenly a dark shape loomed out of a doorway at the far end of the corridor, peering at them. All six marines saw the figure at the same time and brought their weapons to bear, awaiting the signal to open fire from the major. In the few seconds that followed Reynolds strained his eyes forward, trying to make sense of what he was seeing. The figure appeared to be a parody of a human, its facial features all bloated and exaggerated. In place of a mouth was a yawning maw, all razor-sharp incisors and drool, whilst the eyes were wicked and seemingly glowed white. It held its hands upwards, showing grotesquely misshaped fingers which extended like wicked talons. The creature appeared to be part-naked, the grey flesh uniformly darkened and slickly glistening, with multiple lesions and swellings.

"Sir?" whispered the sergeant.

Reynolds hesitated a moment, unsure if by holding up its distorted hands the figure was trying to surrender, but suddenly it emitted a blood-curdling howl and rushed shrieking towards them. He hesitated no longer and fired a short burst, the rounds smashing through its chest and ricocheting off the bulkhead behind. Although slowed, the figure continued bounding towards them and the other marines simultaneous opened fire. Knocked backwards by the heavy gunfire the figure convulsed on the floor, writhing in agony despite having its chest blown open by the multiple volleys. Reynolds took a careful aim and sent a single round into the side of the skull, instantly ending the convulsions.

"To the bridge!" Reynolds ordered, turning his attention back to the stairs.

The marines followed in practiced fashion, each marking the major's steps whilst the rear marine covered their backs. On reaching the top Reynolds rolled over the threshold onto the landing, finger on trigger. The landing appeared clear, but two bodies lay sprawled on the once-white linoleum of the adjacent corridor. A glance told him all he needed to know; both were American sailors, and both were very dead. Blood and gore covered the area, the corpses ripped apart like the unfortunate pilot of the helicopter, with much of the flesh and internal organs missing.

"Upwards!" Reynolds yelled, jumping to his feet. "Two more levels to the bridge."

He made the top of the next stairs in just six leaps, again rolling over the threshold. This time it was not clear, and two shapes hove down onto him. His Sterling instantaneously barked rounds, followed by fire from McKinley's SLR, the rounds sending the assailants careening into the wall. Frost finished them with two well-placed headshots, whilst McKinley lifted the major to his feet.

"You're wounded!" McKinley shouted, his ears ringing from the gunfire.

Reynolds ignored the sergeant, looking instead to the end of the corridor where two armed figures crouched over a third. The two stood slowly, both keeping their weapons lowered.

"Keep the stairs and my back covered," the major ordered, ignoring his bloodied shoulder and walking quickly towards the two Americans. From the uniforms, the standard-issue weapons and the lack of body armour they appeared to be sailors, likely part of a non-specialised team that had been embarked on the Seahawk. The third sailor was obviously dead.

"I'm Major Reynolds, Royal Marines."

"And I'm glad to see you," panted the sailor on the left, a tall black NCO whose uniform was ripped and blood-stained. "I'm Chief Petty Officer Rucker, this is Seaman DeWinter and Wiggins."

"Wiggins is dead," said Reynolds.

"Yeah," breathed Rucker, "I thought we were, too."

"What happened?"

"We were sent to answer a distress call. They told us to be careful but we weren't expecting this," said Rucker.

"Obviously," muttered Reynolds, looking in disdain at the empty pistols the sailors carried. "What are we facing, and how many?"

"I don't rightly know. It looks like the crew has turned into some sort of monsters!"

"How many have you killed?"

Rucker shook his head. "Two, maybe three. They jumped us, we had no chance."

"Given a crew of eighteen on the vessel, that probably leaves at least twelve. We've got to get to the bridge to change course or the ship will hit the Ulster coast. I suggest you two come with us," Reynolds barked.

"Yes, sir!" replied Rucker. DeWinter nodded eagerly behind him.

"Take my Browning," said Reynolds, handing Rucker his pistol. "It has nine rounds. My sergeant will give DeWinter his sidearm. Stay close and do what I say."

The two American seamen nodded and followed the major to the marines poised by the stairwell.

"No time for introductions, but this is Rucker and DeWinter. The bridge is the next level up—we need to secure it and change course. We'll use the VHF radio to request further assistance, and then hold the bridge till we're relieved."

ALL AT SEA

"Major, our Lieutenant had a portable VHF and before he died he called the Yorktown to say we'd been overrun. I'm hoping they'll send reinforcements," offered Rucker.

"That'll be difficult without another chopper," muttered Reynolds. "We'll have to hold the bridge until a detachment arrives from Belfast. The Army has a brace of troop-carrying Puma helicopters that could arrive within the hour. Now, sergeant, lend DeWinter your Browning."

"Sir," replied McKinley, unstrapping and offering his 9mm to the sailor.

"Rescued by the army? I'd rather bloody swim ashore!" quipped Corporal Frost.

"How many do you think are up there?" Reynolds asked the sergeant.

"From the sounds, I think at least five," McKinley replied. "They're just behind the bulkhead waiting. We can't get a clear shot from down here so we'll have to engage them their side of the opening."

"This is the only way onto the bridge," said Reynolds, lowering his voice and withdrawing a grenade. "Fall back ten yards, cover your ears, and then follow me as soon as it goes off."

"What about your shoulder, sir?" McKinley cut in.

Reynolds looked down at the ragged bloody tear in his olive green tunic, having quite forgotten the pain. "Just a flesh wound. Now, on the count of three, two, one!"

The major lobbed the grenade up the staircase as the others swiftly cleared backwards. Two seconds later a blinding flash lit the stairs followed by the hollow thud of denotation, shrapnel pinging wickedly off the steel surfaces.

"On me!" Reynolds yelled, leaping up the stairs.

He flung himself up through the acrid smoke and leapt through the bulkhead door, firing short bursts at the dark figures beyond. McKinley and the others followed, weapons barking at anything that moved.

"Clear!" yelled McKinley from the port side of the bridge.

"Not clear!" shouted Frost from the starboard side.

With a meticulous movement that only comes from years of practice, the marines instantly fanned to cover the right side of the bridge, each low and making use of the available cover. Through the thinning smoke and cordite, they saw movement in the chart alcove but held fire for a clear shot and the major's cue. A few short moments passed and then a figure leapt from behind the cabinets, evilly glowing eyes fixed on Frost who was the nearest. The marines fired as one, the head of the apparition exploding as multiple rounds impacted in close groupings.

"Clear!" shouted the corporal.

"Hanson and Letts, secure the stairwell!" ordered Reynolds, scanning the scattered corpses. "There's probably at least another seven of these things unaccounted for."

He moved forward towards the bridge steering console, glad to see it was undamaged from the grenade. The layout looked standard but he took a moment to familiarise himself with the position and course.

"I can take the wheel, Sir," Rucker offered. "I'm acting helmsman on the USS Yorktown."

ALL AT SEA

"Thanks," Reynolds grunted, glancing at the quickly approaching coastline. "Bring her hard about, starboard thirty!"

The ship stirred as Rucker forced the wheel with all his strength. Reynolds pushed forward on the engine levers to increase the speed of the turn, desperate to avoid the imminent grounding.

"Major, this one's still alive!" McKinley shouted from the port side.

Reynolds locked the levers at Full Ahead and told Rucker to steer out to sea before joining his sergeant. McKinley warily covered the creature with his SLR, his finger tight on the trigger. It lay groaning on the grubby floor of the bridge, dark fluid leaking from multiple gunshot wounds to its chest and abdomen, its yellowy eyes regarding them savagely.

"Look at the clothes," said McKinley in a low voice.

Beneath the dirt and blood the clothes were obviously seaman's attire, probably the uniform of a deck officer of the cargo ship.

"Bastards!" muttered Brown. "They killed the crew and dressed in their clothes!"

Reynolds shook his head, his eyes firmly on the creature. "No, they are the crew."

"What?" Brown exclaimed.

"Look at the wedding ring and watch on the left arm."

"I don't understand, Sir," said Brown.

"Neither do I, but they're beyond help now," replied Reynolds. He took careful aim with his Sterling and fired a single shot between the creature's eyes. The round exited the back of the skull with a spray of dark green fluid and globules of gelatinous brain matter, and the groaning stopped.

"Delta Star, Delta Star," came a voice over the VHF radio speaker at the front of the bridge. "This is the USS Yorktown. Are you receiving, over?"

Reynolds turned and strode over to the radio. "Yorktown, Yorktown. This is Major John Reynolds of 3 Commando Brigade, Royal Marines. We have control of the bridge of the Delta Star and are turning the vessel away from the coast. Over"

A slight pause followed, and a new voice came over the radio. "Major Reynolds, this is Commander Eric Hughes of the USS Yorktown. Do you have the status of the US Naval boarding party? Over."

"Chief Petty Officer Rucker and Seaman DeWinters are with us, but I'm afraid the rest of your men didn't make it. We'll hold our position on the bridge until relieved by the garrison in Belfast, and will evacuate Rucker and DeWinters once relieved. Over."

"What is the status of the merchant crew? Over."

"Eleven dead, the rest likely still on board. Over," Reynolds replied.

Another pause followed. "Major, the ship has been categorised as a Category Alpha Biohazard. You must exit the vessel now. Over."

Reynolds looked at the radio in puzzlement. "This is Major Reynolds. Negative. We will hold our position until relieved. Over."

"This is Commander Hughes. The vessel is US flagged and as such is deemed to be US sovereign territory. You, your men, Rucker and DeWinters are all ordered to exit the vessel right away. Over."

Reynolds shook his head. "Negative. This ship is in UK Territorial Waters and is under UK jurisdiction. We will hold our position until relieved. Over."

ALL AT SEA

A moment passed before the Yorktown replied, "Major, we are about to launch a Harpoon missile strike against the Delta Star in order to neutralise the biohazard threat. Estimated time to impact is two minutes. There will be no further communications. Out."

"Rucker!" Reynolds shouted across the bridge to the US Navy Chief Petty Officer. "How likely is your Commander Hughes to follow through?"

Rutter frowned nervously, a worried look on his face. "I think he's serious, major."

Reynolds took up the VHF microphone again. "Tug Charlie One, tug Charlie One, this is Major Reynolds. Did you copy the last transmission? Over."

"We did," replied a voice over the bridge loudspeaker.

"Move to a position two hundred yards off the starboard quarter, just in case," ordered Reynolds.

"Sir!" McKinley shouted from the ship's radar. "Four fast moving objects closing fast from red-zero-nine-five degrees. Missiles!"

"Everyone onto the starboard bridge wing!" Reynolds yelled, pointing towards the door on the right-hand side of the spacious bridge.

Hanson and Letts looked up questioningly from the top of the stairwell.

"There's loads of them ready to rush up, sir!" cried Hanson.

"Get to the bridge wing now!" barked Reynolds, running over to relieve them at the stairwell.

Hanson and Letts sprinted off as soon as the major reached them. He saw the grey skinned creatures massing at the bottom and lobbed a primed grenade down. The explosion came an instant later, a severed arm and foot flying by him as he raced back towards the bridge wing.

"Jump!" Reynolds screamed.

The five marines immediately launched themselves over the railings, leaving Rutter and DeWinters staring at him blankly.

"It's your only choice!" Reynolds yelled. "One of the missiles will be locked onto the bridge!"

Rutter and DeWinters gingerly clambered over the railings, but both stopped, looking down in panic at the size of the drop. Reynolds leapt forward, hitting both men hard in the back and sending them screaming over. He looked over his shoulder to see a dark shape shooting towards the opposite side of the bridge, and was suddenly hit by a shockwave which flung him spinning over the railings. He saw a huge flash then only darkness.

★★★

Sergeant McKinley had not been to Haslar Royal Naval Hospital in Portsmouth for a number of years, but the place was familiar to him. He followed the directions from a naval nurse and finally found himself in a very unfamiliar part of the rambling Victorian building. After many twists and turns he eventually arrived outside the ward, checking his appearance in the glass of a nearby notice board before pressing the call button for admittance. After a short wait, the door was opened by a medical orderly who inspected his identification and led him through to meet the consulting physician, who waited for them in the austere corridor.

ALL AT SEA

"Morning, Sergeant," said the doctor, shaking McKinley's hand. "I'm Surgeon Commander Collins."

"Thanks for letting me see the major, Sir," said McKinley. "We've served together for the last seven years."

"So I understand. Falklands and Northern Ireland?"

"That's right, Sir," McKinley nodded.

"Well, it's not good news I'm afraid," sighed Collins, beckoning McKinley to follow him. "He was severely injured by the explosion and the fall from the bridge wing. He's been here two weeks now, and every day gets worse."

"But he was conscious when we pulled him from the water, and despite the broken legs and dislocated shoulder he seemed in good spirits," countered McKinley.

"The problem is the wound he received before leaving the ship," Collins said, holding the door of a small anteroom open for the sergeant. "The wound contained some foreign matter and an infection has taken hold. As a result, Major Reynolds is in a sterile isolation ward and I can only let you see him through the glass. I must also tell you that this will be your only chance to see him."

"Why?" asked McKinley, his voice tinged with confusion.

Collins closed the door then moved to a curtained window. "Here's why," he answered, opening the heavy curtain to the side.

Behind the glass a glistening grey shape leapt against the armoured glass, misshaped hands clawing frantically whilst yellow glowing eyes regarded them both with hungry intent.

Y.O.U. W.I.L.L. N.E.V.E.R. L.E.A.V.E. H.A.R.L.A.N. A.L.I.V.E.

JONATHAN MABERRY AND EUGENE JOHNSON

-1-

SHERIFF BOSCH ROLLED to a slow stop on the gravel turnaround in front of the cabin that was the getaway place for state senator Alvin Joseph. Bosch had met the senator a couple of times and thought he was a cookie-cutter blowhard rich cocksucker. No different than the politicians of large and small caliber he'd met while working homicide in New York. Or, maybe the difference was that a blowhard with that kind of money seemed to matter more way the hell out here. Joseph probably had more cash and owned more property than everyone in the town combined, with enough left over to buy, say, Mars. The senator was from one of those families who owned oil, coal mines, manufacturing plants, research and development facilities, and had government contracts up the wazoo.

Must be nice.

YOU WILL NEVER LEAVE HARLAN ALIVE

Bosch had been out this way a few times, mostly to clear out the disused mines that were favorite spots for meth labs and moonshiners. He even ran off a group of squatters who were trying to turn one of the mines into one of those weirdo religious cult communes. He'd never been to the senator's cabin before, though, but one of his deputies had called in a backup request. Unfortunately, the radios in the department's cruisers were twenty years old and the reception was for shit. All the dispatcher could tell Bosch was that it was Deputy Singer and he wanted a backup car. Bosch had been cruising the roads doing nothing much but killing another day and took the call.

He killed the engine and got out. A ray of late afternoon sunshine broke through the branches and leaves from the west, striking his eyes, and making him blink. Birds chirped by the thousand and there was the soft buzz of lazy honeybees. The cabin was nestled against a dense stand of trees beyond which the Appalachian hills rose like a backdrop for a movie about getting away from it all.

Shit.

It was rustic. Bosch hated rustic. Where were the sounds of the city? Cars and horns and heels clicking on concrete and people yelling at each other? Proper sounds. Normal sounds.

The big bad city was a long way from here. The world itself seemed far away. Too far.

But . . .

On the other hand, this part of Eastern Kentucky was pretty damn far away from those things. The monsters. Actual motherfucking monsters. He shuddered.

He knew that he should be grateful to have survived, let alone escaped what had happened in New York. This town might be in the middle of nowhere, but it was light years away from the bureaucrat bastards who covered everything up. Escape had become necessary. The bureaucrats spent a lot of money to sanitize the situation and tie up all loose ends so that none of them got painted by the blame brush. Bosch knew that he was a loose end and at first he tried to make some news, make a crusade out of what he knew. But the big shots beat the shit out of him with depositions, regulations, threats, and the endless process that sucked the life out of him. They cost him everything after the investigation. He was lucky that he was even able to get this job as a county sheriff, even way out here.

Bosch rubbed his chest, still able to feel the scars from the 'incident' compliments of the bureaucrat fucker for the NRC, Wilson. The incident. Shit. They could all burn in hell along with that bastard Wilson.

That's what the papers called it. The fact that the news whitewashed it was proof they were in the pocket of the mega-million, circle jerk of politicians and corporate fat cats. Nobody wanted the real story out there.

Bosch wasn't even sure he did. Certainly not enough to try and fight them over it. The evidence was gone, the victims buried, the whole thing blurred into a conspiracy theory and urban legend.

"What the hell did you expect?" he asked himself. He felt a twinge and touched the scars beneath his clothes. They hurt nearly as bad as the memories. Above him, an eastern meadowlark tried to cheer him with a lovely song. Bosch gave it a lethal stare. "Yeah, well why don't you go fuck yourself?"

The bird stopped singing and then flew away. Bosch nodded.

There were three other cars in the turnaround. Deputy Singer's patrol cruise and a pair of black Lincoln Town cars. The car on the left was the kind of late model used by government agencies and some private security firms; the other was a new 1989 Lincoln with smoked windows. Bosch didn't recognize either and it was no use calling in the plates because the radio reception was nonexistent. So, who were these people and why did Singer need backup?

Mysteries were another thing Bosch didn't like. People—the great unwashed herd of civilians—never quite grasped that about real cops. Being a cop was all about maintaining or restoring order. It wasn't about trying to channel Sherlock Holmes. It wasn't the thrill of the chase. Cops were anal and OCD. They wanted things to work smoothly and make sense. They became offended when some asshole fucked with the order of things and dumped the puzzle on the floor. Putting it all back together was part of the job but not the point of it. Denting the heads of the idiots who messed things up was punishment for disrupting harmony. Why was that hard to understand?

He trudged toward the cabin but slowed as he approached, frowning as he saw something that immediately set the temperature of the day to 'wrong.'

There was blood on the porch floor.

Not a lot, but some. Enough.

He rested his hand on the butt of his holstered pistol and studied the bloodstains for a few careful seconds. Smears like this on the porch of someone living in the city was absolutely bad news. But this was the country. Every-damn-body out here hunted or fished, or both. Everybody was killing something out here and folks were always dragging some or all of the bodies back to eat or hang on the wall and brag about. Bosch was not a sportsman. He liked hunting people, but shooting a sixty-pound deer that didn't have a fucking chance and no claws or fangs felt too much like felony murder to him. Maybe Senator Joseph killed something small and defenseless and brought it inside to gloat over and whack off to.

He squatted down and looked at the blood.

There was a fair amount and he didn't like it one damn bit. He pivoted on the balls of his feet and looked around. There were scuff patterns in the dirt and on the flagstone walk up to the porch, but they were in poor shape. Most likely messed by whoever came in those two black cars. His own deputy—he hoped— would have taken care not to pollute the scene. If, in fact, this was a crime scene.

Bosch straightened and sighed, his hand still on his gun. An hour ago he'd been on his couch watching baseball on Television, but something told him that he would not be getting back to the game and his beer anytime soon.

The door was wide open. From where Bosch had parked, that wasn't evident because of the deep shadows thrown down by the porch roof. Now he could see it. Without thinking he used his thumb to unsnap the retention strap and fitted the gnarled handle of his old Smith and Wesson five-shot Chief's special.

The door stood a few inches ajar but neither it nor

the frame showed signs of forced entry. No obvious scratches on the lock, either. There was a partial footprint on the threshold. Too small and narrow for the senator. A teenager, maybe, or more likely a woman. The print was odd, though, as if someone was carrying their weight awkwardly. Through the door, Bosch could see more footprints continuing down the hallway.

Before he could go inside, the bushes at the corner of the cabin shook violently. Bosch turned and with one smooth move drew his pistol and raised it in a two-handed shooter's grip.

"Whoa!" said a familiar voice as a bulky figure stepped out of the bushes. "Hold on there, sheriff, it's just me. Singer."

"Dammit, Singer! You could've got yourself shot," he growled, shoving his gun back into its holster.

The deputy was a middle-aged man who carried too many pounds and not enough common sense. The kind of law officer who had risen to the rank of deputy early on but never higher because of equal parts low ambition and middle skills. Decent enough, though, in most ways. He gave Bosch a smile that was half greeting and half wince. "Sorry, Sheriff, but I found something I think you need to check out."

"What is it?"

"Come look and you tell me." Singer turned and headed back into the bushes the way he had come. After a brief two-count, Bosch followed his deputy into the bushes, around the cabin and then out to a clearing on the far side.

"I know it's your day off, and I'm sorry and all, but I figured you might want to see this," Singer said, as they emerged from the bushes.

Bosch stopped dead in his tracks.

There were two people in the clearing. One was a stranger dressed in a dark suit, squatting down with his forearms on his knees and his shoulders hunched. His body blocked most of the second person, who lay sprawled on the ground. The weeds, the shrubs, the grass, and the wildflowers were all dappled with afternoon sunlight and bright red blood.

-2-

Bosch pointed his gun at the stranger. "Put your hands on your head, fingers laced, and stand up. Do it now."

"Sheriff—," began Singer, but Bosch ignored him. All Bosch could see of the dead man was a shoulder, a portion of a blood-streaked male face, and the torn cloth of a suit. The weeds and the stranger hid the rest. The man in the dark suit turned to look at the officers. He had a thin sharp-featured face, with dark eyes and an unsmiling mouth. He did not look particularly nervous staring down the barrel of a gun. He didn't have any expression at all.

"I won't tell you twice," warned Bosch.

The man rose to his feet and placed his hands on his head. "Always happy to cooperate with the authorities," he said, his tone dry and condescending.

"Pat him down," ordered Bosch, and Singer took a half step forward.

"Sheriff," said Singer, "this is Mr. Lynch. He works for the senator."

"I don't care if he's the senator's live-in lover. Pat him down."

"I have a gun in a shoulder holster," said Lynch. "I'm licensed to carry."

Bosch had Singer frisk him anyway. The deputy removed the small automatic and tucked it into the back of his own belt, then took Lynch's wallet and held it up so Bosch could read the details on the driver's license and an official card that said Peter Lynch was employed by Blue Diamond Security. Bosch had heard of them. Private contractors who worked for big corporations, in the U.S. and in other counties where ever there was a need. Mercenaries and hired muscle.

"May I put my arms down?" asked Lynch.

"Go ahead. But stand there and don't touch anything," said Bosch as he lowered his gun, but did not holster it.

"What happened here?"

"A dead body," said Singer.

"Well, gosh, Singer," said Bosch. "I guess that solves the whole thing."

"I—"

"Please, tell me it's not the senator?" Bosch said as he rubbed his temple that was tightening just at the thought.

"Your guess is as good as ours, Sheriff. We just found him a short time ago," said Singer.

"What's your story, then?" asked Bosch trying to piece things together.

Lynch gave one of those bland professional smiles that gives nothing genuine away. "I was scheduled to meet with the senator today to assist him with some business matters. I arrived to find the cabin door open and the deputy here searching the property. We found the body about two minutes ago. There's no sign of the senator. There is, however, a wallet on the ground, but I didn't touch it."

"Me, neither," said Singer.

Bosch could see a black leather billfold half hidden by tall weeds.

"Step away from the body," repeated Bosch.

Lynch held up his hands in a no-problem gesture and moved a few feet to the side. "I think we can all agree this isn't a hunting accident," he said quietly, trying for a joke. It landed flat.

Bosch stared at the mutilated body and his mouth went dry as paste. He felt dizzy, but he took a breath and forced himself to study the corpse. To understand it, to read it and listen to it and know it. Evidence always wanted to speak, even if in a whisper. The poor bastard had been ripped to shreds. Literally, to shreds. The missing skin revealed the jagged ends of broken bones and purple coiled intestines. The body was missing most of both legs below the knees. One of its arms was completely gone, torn violently from the socket. The other was nearly untouched. Bosch stepped closer, aware that the world suddenly seemed too bright. Bosch could see savage bite marks all over.

"I think a bear got at him," said Singer.

Bosch licked his lips. His heart was racing and his hand trembled as he slid his gun back into the holster. His palm was sweating. "Bear . . . ?" he echoed.

"Had to be," said Singer. "Or some kind of animal? I mean, god, it ate his darn face off. Ain't nothing else up here big enough to do it."

Bosch said nothing. He wasn't sure he could form words.

"Sheriff? Sheriff, you okay?"

"Your boss doesn't look so good," said Lynch.

That snapped Bosch out of it. He took a handkerchief from his pocket and wiped sweat from his head. "So, is this the senator?"

"I'm pretty sure it's not," said Lynch. "His driver, maybe. Hard to tell, that's his new Lincoln out front. Plus, the cheap suit is a giveaway. No way the senator would wear anything like that."

Bosch knelt, took a pen from his shirt pocket and used it to open the wallet. There was a driver's license behind a plastic window. "Christopher Allan Gates."

"That's him," said Lynch. "Shit. Gates was okay. Did his job, kept his mouth shut."

Bosch looked at the dead man's body. What was left of it. Then he leaned over and peered at the details on the license. "Says he was six-one."

"So?" asked Singer.

"Footprints on the porch are too small." He squinted toward the house. "Have you been inside? Either of you?"

"No," said Lynch. "I just got here. I had some papers for the senator to sign. I got here and saw some bloody footprints on the porch and the door was open. I called for the senator but there was no answer, so I started looking around and . . . well . . . found Gates here. So I drove back to the road and flagged down your deputy and told him to follow me back here. We just got back to Gates when you showed up."

"That how it is, Singer?" asked Bosch, and the deputy nodded.

"You go into the house?"

"No, sir," said Singer.

"Lynch, you see the senator anywhere?"

"No. And I didn't touch anything inside. I only went as far as the living room. When no one answered my call I figured something went south around there so I left to get help. And that's all there is."

Bosch didn't like it, but Singer was nodding in support of the story. He looked down at the body.

"Figure this poor guy's been dead for less than an hour."

"Look, fellows," said Lynch, "the senator's somewhere around here and we need to find him."

"We will," Bosch assured him. "Okay, Lynch, I need you to go back to your car and wait until we know what the hell's going on around here. Give me your keys."

"I'd be more use in a search," he began, but Bosch was already shaking his head. Lynch shrugged and handed over his keys.

"Don't go back into the house and don't wander away." Bosch turned to Singer. "We need to check the house. Get the shotgun out of your cruiser."

Singer went pale and cut a nervous look at the house. "Wait . . . you think the bear's in there?"

"I don't know, but get the shotgun."

Bosch looked around taking in the crime scene as Singer trotted back to the turnaround. It wasn't long before Singer was back with a big Winchester model 1300. It was a twelve-gauge with a seven-shot capacity, with extra rounds on the heavy leather strap. Singer, for all his deficiencies, was an experienced hunter and a better shot than Bosch with long guns.

Bosch looked around. "Who else lives out here?"

"There is nothing around here for miles," said Lynch. "It's all the senator's land. He likes his privacy."

"Well," said Singer, "there is the old McKinney

farm way over to the northwest, and a few empty farm houses spread out around here. People who lost their places to the banks. And there's some old mines nearby."

"All on the senator's land," said Lynch.

"Shit, that's a lot of area to cover," muttered Bosch as he looked up at the house. "We're going to need to get some more people up here. Maybe some state cops."

The town was tiny in terms of population but, typically of farm country, it was huge in acreage. The whole town covered as much square mileage as Manhattan, but most of it was crop fields, cattle pastures, hills, and abandoned mines. Bosch had a ten-man department, but there were only ever three deputies on shift at any given time. One of his men was working traffic detail, cruising the roads for speeders, and the other was in the office to deal with walk-ins, phones, and paperwork.

Lynch, who had not yet complied with the order to return to his car, said, "Sheriff, I agree. We need to make finding the senator a priority. He is a very important man."

"You don't say. Well I am glad we agree, but—"

"But, I am going to have to insist that because the senator is involved, we need to handle this delicately," Lynch interrupted.

Bosch almost smiled. "You're going to have to 'insist?'"

"I'm head of security for the senator, Sheriff. This is his property."

Bosch walked over to him and kept walking until Lynch was forced to give ground. Then he jabbed the man in the chest with a stiffened forefinger. "Let's get a few things straight, son. First, this is a crime scene, which means I'm in charge and you are, at best, a civilian and, at worst, a suspect. The only reason you're not cuffed in the back of my cruiser is that my deputy knows you, but my patience has a short sell-by date."

Lynch said nothing. Bosch gave him another jab.

"Second, this is an active crime scene, which means I will call in back-up, emergency services, and forensics. I expect that the press and the public will get wind of all that. We will do our best to keep details confidential, but your security needs and mine are likely to be different. We're going to do it right and by the numbers. You reading me?"

"Loud and clear," said Lynch, his mouth tight.

"Good." Without turning, Bosch said, "Call it in, Singer. Get everyone out here. Our boys, the staties, everyone. Do it now."

Singer hesitated for a moment and then trudged back to his cruiser to make the call. Bosch and Lynch waited in silence. While it was being done, Bosch looked inward at his own emotional reactions. He knew, despite what he'd said to Lynch, that he was already doing things wrong. The sight and condition of the body had shaken him to his core. He could feel his skin crawl. He should have cuffed Lynch and cleared the house by now. Instead, he was screwing around out here. He knew why. There were bloody footprints going into the house. Maybe it was in there.

It.

He wanted to yell. To scream. To run away.

This is a bear, he told himself. Just a fucking bear. Lynch was watching him, and Bosch saw something flicker in the man's eyes. Doubt, sure, but something else, too.

Bosch spoke quietly so that Singer could not hear, "If you know anything about what happened here you'd better tell me right now."

Lynch shrugged, "I have no idea."

Bosch studied him. "God help you if you're lying to me."

"Sheriff," said Lynch quietly, "I can assure you that Senator Joseph had nothing to do with what happened here."

"We'll see. Tell me, Lynch, is there anyone who would want to possibly harm Senator Joseph? Does he have any enemies that might have done this?"

"No one comes to mind," said Lynch. "Senator Joseph is well-liked, both by the people and his peers. Both in the political and the business world. I really don't know who would want to do anything to him."

"What about the driver?"

Lynch glanced at the corpse. "Chris was a good guy. Didn't have an enemy in the world, far as I know."

"You telling me the truth?"

"I am, Sheriff, and stop trying to scare me. I'm not the bad guy here, and you're not that impressive. Look, let me put it in plain terms. You need to find the senator. If you don't, it won't matter that you have only been sheriff for a few months. I can promise you will be looking for a new job and this time no one will hire you."

"'This time?' What's that supposed to mean?"

Lynch gave him a few millimeters of a cold smile. "I run security for the senator. Don't you think I would have checked out everyone who matters in this town?

I know who you are, Sheriff Bosch, and I know about your troubles in New York. I know about the wild claims you made about—what was it?—alligators in the sewers?"

"It wasn't fucking alligators."

The smile told Bosch that Lynch knew what it was. "You were lucky to get a job as anything above dog-catcher. That's not me insulting you. That's the talk."

Bosch wanted to pistol whip the smug smile off the man's face. He could feel his face getting hot.

"They're on the way," called Singer from the other side of the house.

Bosch stepped back from Lynch and pointed toward the turnaround. "Now."

They walked through the bushes and out onto the side yard and around to where Singer waited by the car, the shotgun in his hands. When they were still out of earshot, Bosch leaned close to Lynch. "I think a little later you and me are going to have a meaningful chat."

"Sure," said Lynch, "whatever you say." He walked away and got into his car, leaving the door open.

Singer came up to Bosch. "I don't have any bear shot, but double-buck ought to do it."

Bosch drew his pistol. The .38 caliber felt like a cap pistol in his hand and he didn't have a shotgun in his own cruiser. The department only had two of them, and the other was back at the station. "Let's go."

-3-

Bosch thought about what little he knew of Senator Joseph. The politician had a fairly solid reputation as a family man, as a man for the people. A clean-cut image. But in Bosch's experience, no one was that clean. Even so, he hadn't heard anyone speak ill of the man, and if this was a murder and not a random animal attack, what was the motive? On the other hand, black bears were plentiful and they could get nasty. They seldom attacked humans without provocation, but it wasn't unknown. What disturbed Bosch was the degree of mutilation. Black bears were omnivores, but tearing up an adult male and either eating half of him or carting the rest off for a late snack, was bizarre.

If it was a bear, that could be a real problem if the damn thing was actually inside the house. Adult males grew to about five hundred pounds. He nodded to Singer to take point, and the deputy moved onto the porch with the shotgun up and ready.

Singer pushed the door open with his toe and they went in fast, cutting left and right, checking corners and behind the door. The living room was big, wood-paneled, furnished in leather and wood, with a huge stone fireplace.

It was empty.

The bloody footprints wandered awkwardly toward the adjoining den, and they followed it, clearing that room, the dining room, and the kitchen. There was no one there. They took the stairs slowly, and Bosch was all too aware that every goddamn step had its own unique and piercing creak. Caution seemed absurd with all the noise, but they kept mum and moved into the short hall. There were two bedrooms and two bathrooms. All empty.

The cabin appeared to be perfectly crafted. Considering that the senator owned it, Bosch guessed it was the best money could buy. While Senator Joseph always claimed to be a man of the people, he was also among the wealthiest businessmen in the state.

"I didn't see any footprints on the stairs," said Singer. Bosch agreed and they went downstairs. The last of the bloody prints faded out in the kitchen. One of the cabin's back windows caught Bosch's eye. It had been broken. The torn curtain hung in limp tatters, moving sluggishly in the gentle breeze. The kitchen door was wide open and they went outside, raising their weapons again.

"Look," said Singer, and Bosch turned to examine the outside wall of the cabin. It was crisscrossed with deep claw marks.

"Bear?" he asked.

But Singer frowned. "I . . . guess . . . ?"

"Well, are they or aren't they?"

"Really not sure," said the deputy. "They're big enough, but they're weird."

"Weird how?"

"Spacing's wrong. I think," said the deputy. "Look, boss, I'm a deer hunter. I know some guys who hunt bear, and I've seen plenty of places where bears have marked their territory by clawing up the trees. This is as deep as that, but it almost looks more like a cat claw than a bear. See the angle of the cuts?"

"We don't have mountain lions around here," said Bosch.

"There's some say we do. There was a cougar shot in Bourbon County back in 2014. And there have been some sightings. Most of 'em are probably methed-out dopers too high to tell the difference between a house cat and a mountain lion, but it's not impossible. But there's a problem with that, too, 'cause even though the marks look like a cat's, there ain't ever been a cougar with claws that big. Not in Harlan, Kentucky. Maybe a Siberian tiger or something. Cougars are only a little bigger than wolves. So . . . like I said, these markings are weird."

"Weird," echoed Bosch. "Well, that's just fucking great."

There was nothing else to find. Bosch told Singer to circle the house to see if he could pick up the bear's trail, and the deputy moved off, walking in the low, careful crouch of an experienced tracker. Bosch went around to the cars, and halfway down the side yard he found a torn purse lying among the debris of some shattered flowerpots, but there was no wallet.

"Lynch," he called, and when the security man appeared, Bosch said. "There's no one inside, but there's a purse and some fingernail scratches on the back wall. Was the senator's wife up here with him?"

Lynch avoided eye contact with Bosch for a moment, staring into the forest, before turning back to the Sheriff. "Excuse me?"

"I asked if Mrs. Joseph was up here with the senator?"

Lynch cleared his throat. "She's in D.C. at the moment, for a charity function."

"What was he doing up here at the cabin? Was he with anyone else?"

Again, Lynch hesitated. "Well, that's complicated."

"Un-complicate it for me. Was the senator up here banging some campaign worker or—" He stopped and whirled as a sound rose from within the shadowy woods. Lynch's hand darted toward his holster before he realized it was empty.

The sound had been a scream.
A woman's scream.
High pitched and filled with bottomless terror.

-4-

Bosch froze, and for one full second he was not in
Harlan County but was instead back on a blood-
streaked New York street while all around him
nightmare shapes tore the world apart.

*Please God Please God Please God Please God
Please God Please God*. That was all that went through
his head.

For one full second.

And then he was running. He had no memory of
going from motionless statue to a flat-out run.

"We're coming!" yelled Singer behind him.

They reached the edge of the woods and plunged
inside, following the screams through the dense
shadows thrown by the tall trees. Thorny bushes
plucked at him and boulders seemed to rise up out of
nowhere to try and ambush him. He heard Singer's
footfalls and the huff of the deputy's breath, and Bosch
cut a look to see the man angling to his left.

The screams were terrible. Not pain screams,
Bosch thought. Pain had a different frequency, they
were sharper and thinner. This was the full-throated
scream of total horror. The kind of scream he had
heard before but never thought he would ever hear
again. Not in a place like this. Not in a small town
where the worst crimes were usually Friday night
drunken bar fights or speeding along country lanes.
Coming here, taking this job, had been his escape, his

salvation. A haven. Even the nightmares had begun to fade and lose their reality out here. His life had become a wonderful series of lazy green days and cool purple nights. The color of boredom, of safety, of sanity.

Those screams painted the day in different colors.

"Over there," yelled Singer as he began moving toward where the ground dropped sharply down. There were hundreds of slash pines and maple saplings, but Bosch bulled his way through them. Briars tore remorselessly at his uniform and skin, but he did not notice. Everywhere he looked were trees, ivy, and undergrowth, no sign of a person. No distinct landmarks gave him any sense of direction, and to make matters worse, the sun was almost down.

They ran down the slope and found a game trail that allowed them to run faster. Bosch was in front, with Singer puffing behind him. Bosch's lungs were burning and he had a stitch in his side that was as painful as a knife cut.

The next scream came from their left and Bosch whirled. There was a clearing eighty yards ahead and red-gold sunlight slanted down between the trees. But the sky was darkening and he knew that the mountains would kill the useful light.

The screams stopped. Bang. Just like that.

Bosch faltered, suddenly unsure of the direction the last one came from. Singer nearly collided with him.

"Where?" asked Bosch in a tense whisper.

The deputy seemed uncertain and stepped away, peering into the woods, lips compressed. "I . . . I'm not sure, boss."

The forest fell into stillness and silence. They

continued the way they had been going, but now neither of them was sure they were going in the right direction. They searched for fifteen minutes and found nothing. Not a footprint, not a drop of blood. Nothing.

Finally Bosch stopped, holstered his gun, cupped his hands around his mouth and yelled. "This is the police. We're here to help you. Tell us where you are so we can find you."

Nothing.

Singer tried it next; then both of them. Their calls bounced off the walls of trees and fled high into the darkening sky and faded out. No one answered their call. They stood together, panting, hearts pounding, sweat running cool on their faces, fists balled in frustration.

Something nagged at Bosch. The forest around them seemed too still. He heard no nightlife, no animals moving around. No crickets chirped. Nothing moved at all in the dark but the tree branches in the night breeze.

"Is it always this quiet in the woods at night?" he asked Singer.

The deputy shook his head. "No, sir, it ain't. Maybe all that screaming spooked everything."

Bosch heard the uncertainty in the deputy's voice, though.

"Shit," said Bosch, "I can't see a goddamn thing out here." He took a flashlight from his belt and swept the beam through the trees. He saw absolutely nothing except goblin shapes thrown by the shadows of rhododendron bushes.

"Backup should be here soon," said Singer. "Maybe we can get a line of guys with lights and someone with a bullhorn." But he didn't sound hopeful. Searching a forest at night, with landscape as steep and treacherous as this, was risky.

"Singer," said Bosch, "you're the hunter—those screams, were they stationary?"

The deputy shook his head. "No. I think whoever it was, was running. Fast but maybe not in a straight line. Panic running, maybe, which is why we can't find the natural path. The last one I heard was from around here, but the others were off to the east. I think she was running west or northwest."

"What's over that way?" asked Bosch, pointing to the west. "I'm all turned the hell around. Could she have been making for the road?"

Singer considered, then shook his head. "The private road, the one we used to get here, is behind us. There's nothing over that way but an old mining road that was officially abandoned like twenty years ago or better."

There was a soft crack of a twig and Bosch drew his gun. He whirled as a vague shape moved through the shadows to his left. Singer had his shotgun socketed against his shoulder. Bosch cocked his hammer back and was starting to slip his finger inside the trigger guard when a figure stepped out into the fading light.

"Did you find them?" asked Lynch.

"You have got to be shitting me," snarled Bosch, lowering his gun. "I told you to stay back at the cabin. I could have shot you, asshole. The fuck's wrong with you?"

"Whoa, calm down, Sheriff. I thought you could use the help. It is my job to look after Senator Joseph and his interests, and that includes finding him."

Lynch kept his voice calm and even wore an ingratiating smile.

Bosch studied Lynch with narrowed eyes. "What did you say?"

"I said you could use some help and—"

"No, before that," he interrupted. You said 'them.' Who else was up here with the senator?"

"Caroline Golden, Senator Joseph's assistant." He paused.

"His 'assistant?'" said Bosch. "He brings his assistant all the way the hell out to the middle of nowhere? Just the two of them? So this place is what? A backwoods fuck-pad and she's his piece of ass? And you were going to tell me when?"

"Sheriff," said Lynch with asperity, "family values are very important to the senator's constituency. If word got out that he is not the family man they elected, it could ruin him. It is my job to look out for his interests, so I made a judgment call that it wasn't important for you to know."

Bosch got up in his face. "You didn't think a woman's life was important? That votes are more important? I am so close to kicking your ass. Actually, I'm close to handcuffing you to a tree and forgetting I ever saw you."

Lynch began to smile that oily smile of his, but it faded as he saw something in Bosch's eyes. "I apologize, Sheriff, and—"

A fresh scream tore through the twilit sky. This time it was not a mindless shriek but a desperate plea. "No . . . no! God! Get away from me!"

"That's Caroline," cried Lynch.

"It came from down there," yelled Singer and he

was off into the woods, chasing the beam of his own flashlight. Bosch bolted after him, and he heard Lynch running behind. The cry had been maybe two or three hundred yards away. The three of them ran as fast as they could manage, but the landscape was littered with boulders and there were rabbit holes and deadfalls.

Then the woods suddenly thinned and they saw a big old farmhouse squatting and faded in a field of corn that had grown wild and become withered with some kind of leaf blight. Ivy crept up the walls and hair vines choked the brick chimney. A fallen oak tree had crashed down on the roof and smaller, younger trees had pushed up through the warped boards of the front porch and completely blocked the door. Off to the right were the remains of an old barn.

"Who owns this place?" Bosch asked as they pushed through waist-high grass.

"The senator bought up all the land in the area," said Lynch. "He was looking to build a waste processing plant, but decided to go a different direction."

As they closed in on the barn they saw an old wooden sign that read McKinney Farms, over which was tacked an official notice.

Eviction Notice
By Order of the Governor
Land Transferred to The Joseph Corporation

"Man of the people," muttered Bosch. "Your boss is a real saint."

A cold breeze blew out of the east and made the diseased corner rustle and whisper. There were no new screams. Bosch knew that they should have rushed inside by now. Should have.

But fear made him drag his feet. Singer and Lynch seemed no more eager to rush in than he did. The barn creaked as the wind shoved at it. Everything else was as still as the grave.

They raised their weapons as they approached the barn door.

-5-

They braced the barn door and held there while Bosch surveyed the area. The withered grass was trampled outside of the door but even Singer couldn't make much of that.

"Okay," said Bosch in a hushed voice, "we go in just like we did with the house. Lynch, you stay out here."

"Can I have my gun back, Sheriff?"

Bosch began to tell him to go piss up a rope, but the heaviness of the night pressed down on him and he relented. Lynch took the weapon, checked the magazine and racked the slide to load a bullet into the receiver. He did it with such professional competence that it relieved rather than disturbed Bosch.

Lynch must have sensed his reaction and said, "I know what I'm doing. Eight years in the army. Rangers. Worked for Blue Diamond ever since. I've been to the dance before, Sheriff. And I've cleared a building before. You tell me what to do and I'll do it."

Bosch nodded. "We go in first and cut right and left. You cover the door. Once we're in, you enter and take up a covering position next to me. Hold that while I clear the room. Can you do that?"

"Yes," said Lynch.

And that was how they did it.

Bosch pulled open the door of the old barn while Singer covered him with the shotgun. They went in fast, yelling, announcing who they were, owning the moment.

"Don't shoot. Oh god, don't shoot me," cried a terrified voice. Bosch snapped his light upward and there, leaning over the edge of the hayloft, was the pale, wide-eyed, dirt-streak face of the most beautiful woman he had ever seen. Her hair was a mess, her eyeliner was smeared and tear tracks glistened through the dirt on her cheeks, but she was stunning.

"Caroline," called Lynch. "These men are police. You're okay."

"Is it still out there?" she called. "Did you kill it?"

"There's no one else here," said Singer, but Bosch stood rooted to the spot. The word hung in the air.

It.

Did you kill it?

Bosch helped her climb down the rotted old wood ladder. He could feel that she was trembling, likely from both fear and exhaustion. She wore a short, very green knit dress over darker green tights. In any other circumstance, she would stop traffic. She was tall, with superb legs and a stunning figure that looked athletic and strong as well as gorgeous. Her hair was honey blond and she had eyes the same forest green as her tights. Bosch figured her to be twenty-three or four, which made her less than half the age of Senator Joseph. Her clothes were torn and she had blood on her legs, but he could not see any injuries.

"Are you hurt?" asked Bosch. The woman shook her head, but her eyes were glazed with fear and shock. She looked like she was a half-step away from total collapse, and she leaned on Singer, who—more of a gentleman than the other two—had removed his windbreaker and draped it around her shoulders.

"Caroline, where is Charles?" Lynch demanded.

Tears filled her eyes. She shook her head, unable to answer.

"Caroline, where-"

"Hold off a goddamn minute," Bosch interrupted, motioning Lynch away while trying to calm Caroline.

"Caroline, could you please tell us what happened? Where is Senator Joseph?" Bosch asked, gently holding her by her arms.

Caroline cried, "Oh, god . . . Charles. They took him. They took Charles," she said, her words coming so fast they tripped over each other. "They took Charles. They took him. They took Charles."

She went on and on like that, and it chilled Bosch. She did not meet the eyes of any of the three men but instead kept drifting toward the barn door, then darting away, and drifting back again.

Lynch kept trying to connect with her, and his words came out sharper and sharper. "Caroline, focus. Is the senator hurt? Where is he? Who did this?"

"They took Charles," she said. "They just came and took him."

The woman was way out on the ragged edge of hysteria. Her eyes were huge and wet and she kept blinking as if trying to clean them of what she had seen. Up close her pale skin was a sickly gray beneath a spa tan, and her rubbery lips hung slack. But her hands twitched and spasmed like dying birds.

Singer leaned close to Bosch. "She's going into shock. We need to get her out of here."

"We need some answers, damn it," snapped Lynch, and Bosch was caught between agreeing with him and his deputy. On the other hand, he did not want to leave the relative safety of the barn without knowing who or what was out there.

"Look, miss," said Bosch, "we're here to help. We're the police. We will protect you."

"They took Charles," she said, then stopped and blinked her eyes clear for a moment. "W-hat?"

"I'm Sheriff Bosch and this is my deputy. We're here to help you and we have plenty of back-up on the way. You're safe."

"Safe?" She sounded amused by the word, as if it was one of those made-up words from a Dr. Seuss book. "They took him."

"Who took him?" asked Lynch. "Can you tell us that, Caroline? Who took Charles? You need to tell us what happened so we can help him."

Caroline lifted her head up out of her hands, wiping away some of the tears with her palms. She took a deep breath and let it out in a series of shuddering gasps, took another and exhaled more normally. It wasn't clear to Bosch if she was really getting herself together or if this was another level down the stairway to shock. When she spoke, her voice was eerily calm and conversational. "Charles and I had come to his cabin for the weekend," she said. "We were tired and hungry and I went into the kitchen to reheat some food we'd brought in with us. Chinese food. Charles was in the living room. He put the news on. While I was taking plates out of the dishwasher I thought I saw someone looking in the window. It scared me. I . . . I guess I screamed and Charles came running in, but he didn't see anything. He . . . he laughed at me. Said I was too much of a city girl and it was probably a deer. But it wasn't. It wasn't a deer. It wasn't any damn deer . . . "

Her words started tumbling faster again and a new note of hysteria crept back. Singer, who Bosch knew was the father of two teenage girls, put a reassuring hand on her shoulder. "It's okay, miss. Take a breath. Good. Take another, let it out slow. Good, good. Now go ahead and tell us the rest. It's okay. You're safe. We're all safe."

That seemed to calm Caroline and it impressed Bosch. He gave Singer an approving nod as Caroline continued.

"I told Charles that I definitely saw something and he got a little mad at me. I started to cry and he told me I was being stupid. He opened the door to prove there was nothing out there. Nothing out there. Nothing . . . "

Fresh tears broke from her eyes and fell down her cheeks.

"They were right there," she said in a tiny voice. A little girl's voice. "They were right outside in the dark and they . . . they took him."

"Who did?" asked Lynch.

"Them," she said.

"Who?"

"*Them*," she repeated as if that would explain everything. "They tried to come into the house, so I got out. I left. I had to get out. I had to. I ran and ran and then I saw the barn. All the time, though, everywhere I looked, I could see those *eyes*."

"Slow down, tell me what you mean," asked Bosch. "What about the eyes?"

She shook her head and grabbed Singer's arm with two small, desperately strong hands. "No one has eyes like that. They were wrong. The eyes were wrong."

"Wrong *how*?" asked Bosch.

She swiveled her head to look at him. Bosch could see that there were mad lights there, as if the house of her sanity was burning down.

"Their eyes . . . they were wrong. They weren't people eyes. They were yellow. Not like cat eyes. Bad yellow. And . . . and . . . they were on fire."

"What?" asked Singer. "What do you mean?"

"They were all wrong," she said. "They had claws and fangs and their eyes glowed in the dark. I think they were demons. I think demons came and took Charles away to punish him. He's a bad man. I know that. He knows I know it. And the demons know. They were waiting for him and they came with their claws and their teeth and their fiery eyes to take him down to hell."

Caroline suddenly began to laugh. It was a terrible, cracked, shattered laugh that began deep in her chest and rose into the air, high and shrill.

Bosch cried out and stumbled back from her. Not because of the laugh. No.

The claws. The fangs. The glowing eyes.

"No," he breathed. "No, no, no, no fucking way, no!"

Behind him the barn door swung inward as if shoved by tremendous force. It caught Bosch on the shoulder and sent him sprawling onto the ground. He landed hard and badly and his gun went skittering away. Pain detonated in his shoulder and down his arm and for an irrational moment he thought he was having a heart attack.

When he looked up the irrationality of that paled. In that instant he longed for something as simple, as normal, as real as a heart attack.

There, framed by moonlight in the open barn doorway, was a figure out of a nightmare. His nightmares. It stood on wide legs, huge and powerful against the night sky. A massive chest and shoulders and arms so packed with swollen muscles that they hung crooked, like an ape's. The shreds of a shirt and a pair of blue workpants clung to its slime-covered body. And just as Caroline had said, and just as Bosch had remembered, its huge eyes glowed an unnatural yellow. It looked just like the ones he had encountered back in New York.

"No . . . " he whispered again. Ragged, hoarse, filled with absolute terror.

It was a C.H.U.D.

-6-

The world jumped the rails and crashed.

Bosch lay on the floor of the barn and stared at the monster. He saw other shapes moving in the field behind it. More of them.

More.

Of.

Them.

"God almighty . . . " he breathed.

Singer said, "Jesus Christ . . . what the hell's that?"

The creature bared its teeth. Hot drool dripped thickly from them and splashed on its misshapen chest. It had been dragging something, but dropped it outside the barn.

"No," said Lynch, "no fucking way."

He raised his gun and fired.

The monster threw back its head and howled with such fury that it shook the rafters of the old barn. Rats shrieked and ran from the corners, fighting to escape through holes in the wall; they snapped at each other in their panic.

Caroline screamed.

Bosch did, too. He could not help it. The sound was torn from him.

Lynch fired again, but Bosch couldn't tell if he was hitting anything. The monster did not go down. It didn't even stagger.

Bosch scrambled onto hands and knees and scuttled toward his gun, recovered it just as the monster stepped inside the barn. He spun around and got to one knee, leveled the pistol and fired. The bullet caught the monster in the shoulder and this time it did react, turning halfway around. Green sludge oozed from the wound.

"Head for the house," Bosch yelled. "I'll cover you."

The C.H.U.D. hissed, more in fury than pain, and Bosch shot it again. Behind him, Singer and Lynch took Caroline's arms and half-dragged her toward the back of the barn. The cart door was closed and the hinges rusted, but Singer fired two shots and blew them to splinters. The door bowed outward and fell with a muffled thud in the grass.

"Come on, boss," he yelled.

Bosch got to his feet and fired three spaced shots at the C.H.U.D., who was advancing slowly, as if unsure what it was facing. Bosch had no idea how intelligent the monsters were, but suspected they were operating at a level just above pure instinct. The lizard brain driving them and their human brain turned to mush. All the creatures had a savage drive to kill. And to eat what they killed.

The bullets punched into the thing's chest and it slowed the monster's advance, but the goddamn thing did not go down. He raised his revolver at the C.H.U.D., firing as Lynch and Caroline ran through the thick grass toward the old farmhouse. He landed at least two shots squarely at the center of the creature, but the shots only slowed it down a little. Then the hammer clicked hollow on a spent shell.

"Reloading," he roared as he backed away. He had two speed-loaders on his belt, a total of ten more rounds. One loader held only the standard 158-grain round-nose loads; the other was a more powerful set of hollow-point bullets. And he had a box of ammunition in his car. But he'd already shot this fucking thing five times and it was still coming. He fumbled for the hollow-points. "Singer," he bellowed.

The deputy was halfway through the door, with Lynch and Caroline already outside. He turned and ran back to Bosch to offer cover while the sheriff reloaded. The C.H.U.D. lumbered forward, slashing the air with its claws. Singer fired once and the twelve-gauge buckshot caught the monster in the hip, spinning him, knocking him down.

"Go, go, go," yelled Singer, firing even as he backed up. He aimed the second shot at the open doorway, where more of the damn C.H.U.D. things were pressing forward. At that distance the buckshot was in a wide spray pattern and did little more than make the things flinch.

Then he spun, grabbed Bosch's arm and shoved his boss toward the back door. They burst through and saw Lynch and Caroline already more than halfway to the old farmhouse. It was something they could maybe defend, but only if they got inside with enough time to barricade the doors. Bosch thought about his cruiser and the other cars, but they might as well have been on the far side of the moon.

Bosch never ran so fast in his entire life. Singer, who was fatter and slower, began falling behind, but Bosch slowed to keep pace. Their guns were reloaded but the monsters were coming. They were not fast, but they were coming.

"What are those things?" gasped Singer. His eyes were fever bright.

Bosch didn't answer. He saved his breath for running.

-7-

Lynch was wrestling with the front door, which was mostly blocked by the tree that had grown up through the porch. He pried it open just enough to let Caroline slip inside and then he followed. Bosch and Singer got there as the Blue Diamond agent vanished into the house.

Singer paused and looked back in the direction of the senator's house, frowning, actually thinking about it.

"Don't," warned Bosch. "The woods could be full of those bastards and we need your shotgun here."

"But the backup . . . "

"Is probably there, but we can't risk it. Maybe

there's something we can use inside. Something to make torches, or a fire axe. Anything to give us a chance. You saw how hard it is to stop them."

"What are they?" Singer asked again.

"Get inside. I'll tell you when we're safe." He looked at the house. "I have a feeling our friend Lynch knows more than he's telling. And, believe me, Singer, he is going to tell us or I'll feed him to those motherfuckers."

They squeezed inside. They were both thicker in the middle than either Caroline or Lynch, but fear is a wonderful incentive. They managed it and Bosch slammed the door.

There were heavy storm shutters on the windows and most of them were in pretty good shape. Bosch didn't know how long they would hold, but he was certain the creature did not have the intelligence to figure out how to unpin them. The doors were the weak spots. "Singer," he said, "push some furniture in front of the door. Lynch, come with me. If there's a fridge we can use it to block the back."

Outside they heard the distorted roar of the creature. One roar, which was a small comfort. The others must not have reached the farmhouse yet. The roar was not right outside, but coming closer. Singer set his shotgun down and grabbed the arm of the dilapidated old couch. After a moment Caroline joined him and they clumsied the thing against the door. Bosch and Lynch went into the kitchen and pushed the heavy appliance in front of the back door only seconds before they heard the creature crash against it. The barricade shuddered but held. The stove was disconnected from the disused gas line, and they pushed that against the fridge. Then they returned to the living room and helped stack two heavy armchairs atop the couch. The C.H.U.D. began pounding on the doors, but even though the farm was old it had been solidly built. They were all safe for the moment.

"Be careful of the floor over there," said Singer, pointing to a spot near where they'd built the mound of furniture. "It's rotted out. Nearly put my foot through it. Smells nasty, too. Like eggs. God only knows what's down there."

Bosch bent and sniffed. "Methane," he said. "And coal gas. We must be over part of the mine."

Singer nodded. "Guess so. They dug mines all through this area. Something like a hundred miles of it, going this way and that."

The pounding on the door continued.

"I think there's only one of 'em out there," said Bosch, peering through a crack in the wall. "Check your weapons. Give me an ammo count."

Singer had eleven extra shells for the reloaded shotgun. Lynch had one spare magazine. Bosch hadn't fired any of his hollow-points, so his five-shot revolver was fully loaded and he had the second speed-loader. Singer also had an old-fashioned Smith and Wesson model 10, a six-shot, but he did not have any hollow-point rounds for it and only one additional speed-loader. It wasn't a lot of firepower, but it was better than nothing.

Bosch considered the smell rising up through the rotted floor and Singer seemed to read his mind.

"We got to be careful," said the deputy. "One spark from the guns and we could blow ourselves sky high."

Bosch nodded. It was not an encouraging observation.

"Look, boss . . . what are those things?" repeated Singer, pointing to the door.

"C.H.U.D.s," said Bosch and Caroline flinched at the word. Lynch's expression did not change. "Cannibalistic Humanoid Underground Dweller. C.H.U.D. really stands for Contamination Hazard Urban Disposal, but the people who lived on the streets back in New York gave it a different spin. C.H.U.D. was a bullshit plan to dispose of hazardous materials by dumping them in disused parts of the New York subway system."

"I don't understand," said Singer. "New York?"

"Yeah," said Bosch, eyeing Lynch. "Some devil's bargain made between corporations and local government. Dump the shit where no one can find it. Cheaper than the more expensive and time-consuming method of proper disposal. The barrels leaked, the contents got out, and a bunch of homeless people were mutated into . . . well, into monsters. No other word to use."

"That's . . . that's . . . "

"'Fucked up' is the phrase you're fishing for," said Bosch. "A lot of people died."

"I didn't read about nothing like that in the news."

"Two words," said Bosch. "Cover up. And the funny part is that they probably spent more on spin control than they would have by following the hazardous waste disposal methods protocols."

"Do you think Charles is alive?" Caroline asked. Now that they were safe she seemed to be regaining her composure very quickly.

"I don't know," Bosch admitted. "These things eat people as their main source of food, but if they took him alive, we still might find him. Honestly, though, his odds aren't good."

"The senator is too important, Sheriff," Lynch said. "If there is any chance we can find him, then we have to do it. We're not leaving without him."

"We have to save him," agreed Caroline.

"Right now," said Bosch, "I'm a bit more interested in living through the next ten minutes than mounting an expedition. We need to get back to the senator's house. If the state cops are here, they'll have more firepower. We need a lot of muscle because those sons of bitches don't go down easy. And we need to stop them before they get out of these woods and find their way into town."

"Wait, wait," said Singer, "I'm still trying to wrap my head around this. If these things were in the New York sewers, then how are they here? Did they follow you or something?"

"No," said Bosch. "Maybe the senator knows and . . . " His words trailed off as he caught Caroline eying Lynch, who was shaking his head. "Hold on, what is it you two aren't telling us?"

"Nothing," said Lynch a bit too quickly. "I agree, we need to get back to the cabin, get help, and then come back for the senator."

"Do you know something about this?" asked Bosch.

"Of course not," said Lynch.

But Caroline said something that changed the frequency of the moment. "He needs to know," she said to Lynch.

"Shut up," Lynch yelled.

"We have to tell him," she insisted. "Charles may be alive."

"What the hell are you two talking about," Bosch demanded.

The hammering was now so hard the old walls shook and the ancient bones of the house groaned. And it wasn't one set of fists, Bosch realized. There were more of them. Hammering on the doors, the walls.

"Jesus Christ," he breathed.

There was panic in Lynch's eyes. "Those things are about to get in. We need to make a break for it while we still can. Let's go out the back door and try to run around the things. We've seen that we can outrun them."

Bosch looked back at Caroline. "Caroline, you know something. Whatever it is, you need to tell me now before that thing breaks in and we have no chance of saving Charles."

She looked once more at Lynch, who continued to shake his head at her, then closed her eyes and turned back to Bosch. "Charles and I aren't just sleeping together. I also work in his office. Not just for him, but with him."

"And . . ." Bosch prompted.

"Shut up, shut up, shut the fuck up, you stupid cow," snarled Lynch as he stepped suddenly forward and raised his hand to strike her.

Bosch caught his wrist and spun the man around but Lynch, quick as a cat, tore his arm free and began to bring his gun up. Then Singer was there, pressing the barrel of the shotgun against Lynch's cheekbone.

"Don't," said the deputy. "Listen up, asshole. I got two daughters at home. I'd like to see 'em again and right now you have information that could make that happen."

If Lynch was impressed, he didn't show it. "Shooting me won't help you or them," he said calmly.

Singer moved the barrel from Lynch's head to the side of the agent's knee. "Say that again."

That made Lynch twitch. He looked into Singer's eyes and then at Bosch and saw that he had no friends in the room. Bosch took Lynch's gun away for the second time that day.

"Don't be a fool," said Caroline. "Tell them."

It was clear Lynch did not want to, but he was smart enough to know that he had no cards left to play. "Ah . . . fuck it. Okay, the senator was bidding on a contract to build a waste processing plant out here, but the project didn't get funded. He'd already bought all this land, though, and he'd already had a contract with the Nuclear Regulatory Commission, so he leased the old mines around here to the NRC for toxic waste storage."

Bosch shook his head. "Okay, that blows, but it also doesn't make sense. But there would have to be people around the toxic waste for a long time to turn into those things. Back in New York, the homeless had been exposed for years."

"Squatters," said Caroline. "In the mines. We tried to clear them out. I think they even had you and your deputies come out and move them along. Charles didn't want a repeat of what happened in New York. He wasn't part of that disaster, and I know it hurt him to think about all those people being hurt."

"They weren't hurt, goddamn it," growled Bosch. "They were killed."

"I know, I know," she said, dabbing at her eyes. "We wanted the mines cleared. We thought they were clear. But . . . "

"It was those idiots and their meth lab," said Lynch. "My boys ran them off half a dozen times, but every time they would show up again in another part of the mine system. No way to find them all; the mines are huge and they go on for miles."

"If you knew people were going back to the mines," said Singer, "why'd you dump that stuff there?"

Lynch did not answer. After a long moment Caroline said, "Charles said it was worth the risk. And . . . well . . . "

"Well what?" demanded Bosch.

"They were criminals, weren't they?" Lynch said coldly. "Bikers and hillbillies cooking meth."

As if in protest of those words the C.H.U.D. began pounding even harder on the door. Plaster fell from the walls.

"You crooked son of a bitch," Bosch yelled and punched Lynch in the stomach. Hard. It doubled the man over for a moment, but then he straightened and swung on Bosch. The smaller man was very fast and he could hit. The blow sent Bosch staggering back, against the piled furniture. He stepped down too hard on the rotted floor and his foot crunched down, momentarily trapping him. Lynch used that advantage to pivot and kick Singer in the balls. The deputy dropped his gun and sagged to his knees, vomiting onto the dirty floor.

"Stop it!" screamed Caroline, but Lynch was in gear now. He kicked the shotgun away from Singer, grabbed Bosch's hair and pinned him back against the couch and punched him again. Same spot, every bit as hard.

Bosch was hurt and he was caught off guard, but

he was New York born and bred. He tore his foot free, tucked his elbows in and hunched his head and took the next punch on the bunched muscles of his arm. Then he counter-punched with his left, popping Lynch over the eye. It jolted the man and Bosch pushed off the couch and head-butted him, exploding Lynch's nose. The agent staggered back and Bosch followed with a flurry of punches, hitting Lynch in the mouth, the floating ribs, the right eye. Each punch was powered by all of Bosch's fear and rage. Years of it. Memories of terror and blood put steel into the sheriff's fists. And with each blow Bosch yelled his rage out. "You and your fucking boss have probably killed us all. You son of a bitch!"

Outside the C.H.U.D. howled with rage. Maybe they could sense the violence or smell the blood that flowed from Lynch's nose and mouth. He hit the door with such incredible force the lock splintered and the door jerked inward against the barricade. The whole stack of furniture moved. An inch. Another blow and it slid another inch.

Bosch and Lynch froze, staring at it.

Singer looked up from where he knelt on the floor.

With a shriek of inhuman fury the C.H.U.D. finally tore through the door and pushed the couch and chairs out of its way. The stack of furniture collapsed and the topmost chair crashed down on the rotted section of floor—it plunged straight through, sending up a cloud of noxious mine gasses. Caroline staggered back, coughing and gagging. Singer stumbled to his feet and backed away, casting around for his shotgun as the C.H.U.D. pushed its way inside.

Everything went to shit.

Everyone did exactly the wrong thing.

Caroline tried to help Lynch up, but he was dazed and too heavy for her to lift and it took her one second too long. The C.H.U.D. reached out for Lynch, missed, and its claws raked Caroline, ripping red lines down her lovely face, turning beauty to red horror. She screamed and punched at the monster. Lynch shoved her toward it and twisted around, tried to crawl toward Singer's shotgun. He closed his hand over the stock at the same time Singer grabbed the barrel. They fought for the weapon, wrestling with each other in a freakish tug of war as the C.H.U.D. lunged for the agent's legs. In the same split second that the monster buried its terrible claws in Lynch's calves, the agent grabbed the middle of the shotgun and tried to pull it free of the deputy's grip with a final, savage tug. His finger slipped inside the trigger guard.

The blast seemed to shatter the world.

Bosch watched in horror, caught inside a broken fragment of a moment. Singer's body stood over Lynch, hands still grasping the barrel of the gun, but the man's face and the top of his head were gone. Just gone. The buckshot had struck him in the forehead and everything above the deputy's nose was a red pulp.

On the floor, Lynch screamed as the C.H.U.D. clawed its way up his thighs and buttocks and lower back. The man's scream reached the ultra-sonic as the monster dug its claws deep into his back, curled around his spine and tore it halfway out of the house of flesh.

Behind him, Caroline leaned back against the wall, hands pressed to her bleeding face. But the slash marks were only half the damage that turned her from beauty to horror. Fully half of the heavy lead pellets from the shotgun had struck her in the upper chest, throat and right side of her face. Bosch could see the white edges of chipped bone and exposed teeth and then a geyser of bright arterial blood jetted from her throat and painted the living room in nightmare colors.

All in one second.

All of that horror, that damage, that destruction, in a second.

Bosch got to his feet and stood there, swaying, drunk with pain and shock. He did not remember drawing his pistol. He was not even aware that it was in his hand until he felt it buck as his finger pulled the trigger. He saw the bullets punch into the C.H.U.D. It roared.

And then it screamed and collapsed, its face torn away and those hellish yellow eyes blown dark. Bosch heard a sound and turned toward the kitchen as the fridge toppled and crashed down. Another C.H.U.D. pushed through the door. And another behind that.

His gun clicked empty.

Beneath him the rotting floor creaked and the foul breath of the mine exhaled at him.

The C.H.U.D.s lumbered toward him. Six of them. Seven. Eight. Ten.

Bosch's hand went through the motions of reloading his pistol. The last rounds. Not the hollow-points. Regular rounds.

The creatures surrounded him.

He looked down at the hole in the floor, breathing in the methane and coal dust.

Bosch looked at the monsters who were reaching for him.

"Fuck you," he said.

And fired down into the dark.

Flame spat from the barrel.

The world turned yellow and there was a roar louder than all of the C.H.U.D.s. Louder than anything. Bosch was smiling as the fireball lifted him into the night, away from the claws, hurling him upward at the starlit sky.

INTERVIEW WITH PARNELL HALL

BY ERIC S BROWN

How did you get involved with C.H.U.D.?

Hall: In 1978 I wrote a girls basketball movie for a pornographer who'd gone through EST training and decided he had to make a legitimate movie. I was an actor then, and I answered a casting call in *Back Stage* magazine for a movie called the *Magnificent Five*, about a girls basketball team competing in a men's tournament. I told an actress I was going up for it, and she said, "Oh, I know the producer. He's a pornographer. I went through EST training with him. He doesn't have a screenplay. I'll tell him about you." So when I went for the audition he pulled me aside and said, "You're the writer, right? Well, these girls want to save their school so they enter this basketball tournament to win the cash prize, but they don't know how to play so they hire this coach to teach them, only they don't have any money to pay him so they're all sleeping with him." I said, "Huh?" He said, "Write it." I said, "What?" He led me over to a typewriter, sat me down, and said, "Write it." I banged out a five-page treatment and he hired me on the spot.

The man he hired to direct it was a producer named Andrew Bonime, who had just come off legitimate projects like *The Harrad Experiment* and *The Bell Jar*. He was doing the movie for the same reason I was, to get the screen credit. We worked on the script all summer, trying to turn it into a teenage sports comedy.

The movie never got produced, but Andy hired me for other projects. Over the next year I wrote screenplays for *This Perfect Day*, based on the book by Ira Levin, *The Thousand Dollar Cup of Crazy German Coffee*, based on a short story by Warner Law that was once owned as a star vehicle for Cary Grant, and an original sci-fi time travel love story. I asked Andy which one he was going to do first, because I was young and naïve and I thought if you wrote a screenplay it was because you were going to make a movie. He said, "It's probably going to be a movie called *C.H.U.D.*" I said, "What's that?" He said, "It's a horror movie about monsters that live in the sewers of New York and come out and eat people." I said, "Why would you want to do that?" He said, "Because that's the one I can get the money for."

A few months later he came to me with a problem. He had investors willing to put up a million dollars for *C.H.U.D.*, but they wanted to see the screenplay, and he didn't think it was in any shape to show them. He asked me to read it and see if I could fix it. I read it and told him no. It wasn't my type of movie, I didn't have any feel for the project, but I suggested since he worked so well with writers that he go back and work with Shepherd Abbott, the original writer of the screenplay, and I was sure they could make something of it.

A few months later he called me back, desperate. He needed a screenplay, and he had to have it by next week. Could I just write something called *C.H.U.D.* he could show the investors? If I would do him this favor, he'd never ask me again.

Three years and fourteen drafts later they made that movie.

What was it like to work with Andrew Bonime?

Hall: Andy was a dream to work with because he was a creative producer, and he cared about the script as much as he cared about the bottom line. As opposed to some producers who give notes because they want to justify their jobs and they feel they should, Andy had genuine creative ideas. He and I agonized over scenes in that movie. It wasn't that we couldn't agree on them, it was that we were desperate to get it right. Every screenwriter should have the experience of working with a producer like Andy Bonime.

What was the experience of writing the movie like for you?

Hall: Writing the movie was like being on an emotional roller coaster for three years. The fourth draft of the movie went to Avco Embassy. We managed to get ahold of the coverage. For those not in the industry, producers don't read scripts, they hire readers who reduce a screenplay to a plot summary and evaluation.

The coverage for *C.H.U.D.* read: "This is the best written horror movie I have ever read for Avco Embassy. The characters are three-dimensional, witty, and likable. The jeopardy is continual and nearly unbearable. I see a lot of money in this."

Avco passed on the project. They turned it down. They didn't want it. Of course, they had every right to do so, still, I couldn't help wondering what their coverage would have had to say to get them to take it.

What was the most difficult part of scripting the movie?

Hall: After three years of futility, the movie was finally a go project, and the director and actors had been hired. The three actors were John Heard and Daniel Stern, established stars who would later appear in the Home Alone movies, and Christopher Curry, an unknown but excellent actor they had worked with. John Heard was cast as the photographer you see in the movie, Christopher Curry was the police captain you see in the movie, and Daniel Stern was his right-hand man, a rookie cop who becomes a hero. Remember him from the movie? I didn't think so.

We were in preproduction when one night I got a call from Andy Bonime. He was as upset as I've ever heard him. And for good reason. Danny Stern didn't want to play his part. Danny had just played a rookie cop in *Blue Thunder* with Roy Scheider, so he wanted to play something else. "What?" I asked. His answer floored me. "He wants to be a hippie who works in a soup kitchen on the Bowery."

Danny had written a five-page treatment of the

Reverend, the character he wanted to play, and had just dropped it off with Andy. He was messengering it over to me, and wanted me to read it and tell him what I thought.

I read the treatment and it wasn't encouraging. The character was great. I could see why Danny wanted to play him. Only he didn't work in the treatment. Danny had the Reverend walking into the police station to report a lot of homeless were missing. This was bad on several counts. We've already been in the police station for several scenes with Captain Bosch, and then for several more with John Heard who is there to bail out a bag lady who tried to steal a cop's gun. The Reverend just duplicated John Heard's action, which was boring and repetitive. It also kept us in the police station forever when we ought to be moving the camera. And he's got to explain who he is and that he runs a soup kitchen on the Bowery, so we get a lot of talky exposition.

As I read the treatment, I could understand Andy's point of view. He's muscled this film along for years, finally got the money, attracted stars, and he could see it all slipping away.

So could I.

I called him back, said I thought it might be possible, but it wasn't there yet. If he wanted, I would work on it and meet with Danny and the director in the morning, and see if we could work something out. He told me to give it a try.

I stayed up all night figuring out how to work the Reverend into the existing script, then met Danny and Doug Cheek, the director, at Doug's apartment.

I explained that Andy was not disposed to be

receptive to the proposed script changes, but if the three of us could come to an agreement, I would be willing to advocate for the idea and try to get Andy to let me do a rewrite to include the character of the Reverend.

I then went over the treatment, pointing out the problems I found in it. I began by explaining why having the Reverend show up at the police station was a bad idea. "The first time we see the Reverend, we want to see him in the soup kitchen, ladling out soup to the homeless people. That way we don't have to explain who he is and what he does and we can get right into the action." Danny pointed out that in my version the Reverend didn't appear until fifteen pages later in the script than in his version. I said, "Yes, but to make up for it I added a scene where he breaks into John Heard's darkroom and steals the photos he uses to bluff everyone to a standstill at the scene in the Commissioner's office."

In the end, I got them to agree to let me do a rewrite, and then I got Andy to let me do a rewrite. I took a week and rewrote the whole script, adding the character of the Reverend.

I showed it to Andy first. His reaction was instantaneous and typical. "I love it," he said. "Even if Danny dropped out of the movie I would still use it." As much as Andy didn't want the changes, as soon as he saw they helped the movie, he was all for them. God bless a creative producer.

So Danny wound up playing the Reverend, and the rest is history.

INTERVIEW WITH PARNELL HALL

What's your fondest memory of C.H.U.D.?

Hall: One of my favorite moments on the movie was coming up with the character of Val, which I owe entirely to Danny's desire to play the Reverend. When Captain Bosch first comes to the soup kitchen to investigate the underground people that are disappearing, he wants to talk to one who's left. The Reverend points him to Val, a man sitting alone eating soup. Bosch tries to talk to him, and Val suddenly slams a large knife into the table. Bosch jumps back in alarm and wants to know where he got a knife like that. The Reverend tells him all the underground people are looking for weapons. That registers with Bosch, who had just been dealing with Mrs. Monroe, the bag lady John Heard just bailed out for stealing a gun. He rushes out to have her followed.

The character of Val was wonderful. Danny improved on him by adding biblical quotes and lines about shutting the sky. Though only a small part, Val became one of the more memorable characters in the movie. When Andy read the script, he just loved the moment of Val producing that huge knife. Doing the rewrite, he felt, was worth it for that one moment.

Do any other moments stand out?

Hall: We were in pre-production getting ready to shoot—it seemed we were always getting ready to shoot—when Andy had another problem. In the screenplay, the monsters were caused by radiation from nuclear missiles hidden under the city. It turned out some of the investors had defense contracts and weren't happy with the missiles. So the missiles had to go.

The missiles were the big reveal. That was what our heroes found down in the underground at the end of the movie. They'd been told it was radioactive waste that caused the monsters, but they didn't know it was from missiles. Without the missiles there was a big hole in the script. I asked Andy what he wanted to put in their place. He suggested toxic waste. I wasn't happy. They'd already been told it was radioactive waste, so finding out it was toxic waste instead? Big snore. It made me cringe. I needed something else.

For years I had been saddled with the fact I was working on a screenplay about Cannibalistic Humanoid Underground Dwellers. I mean, the movie hadn't come out and become a cult classic yet, and when I told people what C.H.U.D. stood for, they didn't treat me like Paddy Chayefsky.

That's when I created the term Contamination Hazard, Urban Disposal. And that became the big reveal. Our heroes had been told that C.H.U.D. stood for Cannibalistic Humanoid Underground Dwellers, but that was a lie, to keep them from finding out what C.H.U.D. really meant. C.H.U.D. was actually a government project to store toxic waste under New York City on the theory that there was so much stuff down there no one would notice. So at the end of the movie instead of missiles, John and Danny would find the boxes labeled Contamination Hazard, Urban Disposal. It was what Andy had suggested, toxic waste, but it had the kicker of being an alternate meaning of C.H.U.D.

The New York Times review of C.H.U.D. said:

INTERVIEW WITH PARNELL HALL

"If you believe the advertisements, C.H.U.D. stands for cannibalistic, humanoid underground dwellers, but it is one of the pleasant revelations of this enjoyable horror film that C.H.U.D. also stands for something else." Amen.

ABOUT THE AUTHORS

After thirty years at sea, **Ross Baxter** now concentrates on writing sci-fi and horror fiction. His varied work has been published in print by several publishing houses in the US and the UK. He won the Horror Novel Reviews' Creation Short Story Award in December, 2014. Married to a Norwegian and with two Anglo-Viking kids, he now lives in Derby, England.

Ross has an author page on Amazon, and his website is: https://rossbaxter.wordpress.com/

David Bernstein is originally from a small town in Upstate New York called Salisbury Mills. He now resides in NYC and misses being surrounded by chainsaw-wielding maniacs and wild backwoods people that like to eat raw human flesh. He's grown used to the city, though hiding bodies is much harder there. He is the author of *Witch Island*, *The Unhinged*, *Damaged Souls*, *Apartment 7C*, *Goblins*, *Relic of Death*, *Skinner*, *Amongst the Dead*, The Machines of the Dead trilogy and more. David writes all kinds of horror, from hair-raising ghost stories to gore-filled slashers and apocalyptic tales of terror. He loves hearing from his readers.

"Renaissance Man" is a term used to describe individuals with multiple talents, skills, and abilities, who accomplish great things using all of them. **Andrew Bonime** was certainly one of these people. Born in the Bronx, New York on March 29, 1948, Andy moved with his family to suburban Long Island when he was four years old. Growing up in the town of Wantagh, he began showing musical talent at an early age, and by his freshman year in high school, was leading a successful rock group and consummating the first of his many deals in show business.

Called "The Abstracts," this classic rock band was cutting demos and playing steady gigs within two months of being formed. They were also playing original songs composed by Bonime and a classmate who wrote lyrics. While other bands were playing sock hops in the gym, the Abstracts were performing two-hour concerts to packed audiences in auditoriums. Bonime also masterminded a recording session at Columbia records in Manhattan, and a record deal that won 'The Abs' their first single. He was just 17 years old at the time.

Graduating high school in 1966, Bonime enrolled at Boston University and entered the exciting world of cinema, also making his first venture to the west coast to attend film courses at USC. This led to his connections in the movie industry, and in 1973 he became involved in project development for the movie *The Harrad Experiment.* Next came Bonime's role as Co-Producer for the movie *The Bell Jar* in 1979, and then in 1984, the movie he produced that has become synonymous with his name—*C.H.U.D.*, initially a 'Grade B' sci-fi thriller that has today become a true cult classic with a worldwide following.

Bonime moved on from his film career to fully

embrace the new digital age, co-authoring the book *Writing for New Media*, and teaching a constantly sold-out digital media course for The New School, a division of The College of the Performing Arts. It was there that Bonime met Diana Ross, and he was once again back in the studio as Vice President of Motion Pictures and TV for the superstar.

After the tragedy of 9/11, Bonime relocated to Los Angeles to run his film development company, Cloudshine, LLC, and in 2006, produced a Grammy-nominated independent album with female vocalist Laura Pursell. During his later years, Bonime began battling serious medical issues and finally succumbed on March 26, 2017, just three days shy of his 69th Birthday. He leaves a legacy of achievement in music, film, and digital media spanning more than five decades.

In a writing career that began in 1967 with the publication of *Esp Attack*, his first novel, **Mort Castle** has written about many monsters including The Walking Dead, Leatherface, The Nefarious Dr. Valentine of Paris, The Iron Swastika, young women with dirty feet, and now, oh, those CHUDs. Castle's next book is entitled *Knowing When to Die*, a short story collection and not a non-fiction "how-to."

Nick Cato is the author of the novel *Don of the Dead,* the novellas *The Apocalypse of Peter, The Last Porno Theater, The Atrocity Vendor, Chew Toys* and *Death Witch*. He has one short story collection, *Antibacterial Pope,* with a second on the way October of 2018, and also a non-fiction film book titled *Suburban Grindhouse* coming in 2019. He runs the popular review site *The Horror Fiction Review* and hosts the

Suburban Grindhouse podcast. Nick's nonfiction film articles appear on the *Cinema Knife Fight* website and in the recently re-vamped *Deep Red* magazine. When not writing Nick is a slave to two radical dachshunds. He can be found on the usual sites and at nickyakcato.blogspot.com.

David Drake was born in 1945. He has written or co-written more than 60 books published by major publishers. In addition he has published more than a hundred shorter pieces of fiction as well as many essays and introductions, like this one published in *C.H.U.D. Lives.*

A life-long resident of New York's haunted Hudson Valley, **JG Faherty** has been a finalist for both the Bram Stoker Award® (*The Cure, Ghosts of Coronado Bay*) and ITW Thriller Award (*The Burning Time*), and he is the author of 5 novels, 9 novellas, and more than 60 short stories. He grew up enthralled with the horror movies and books of the 1950s, 60, 70s, and 80s, which explains a lot.

Follow him at www.twitter.com/jgfaherty, www.facebook.com/jgfaherty, www.jgfaherty.com, and http://jgfaherty-blog.blogspot.com/

Ben Fisher is an author of comic books and prose spanning a wide spectrum of genres, from monster-filled horror titles such as *Smuggling Spirits* and *Hexen Hammers*, to the critically acclaimed post-apocalyptic series The Great Divide, to the bestselling, kid-friendly Misadventures of Grumpy Cat & Pokey. Underlying all his work is a common thread of shared hope and humanity, relayed with unmistakable dry wit.

Ben grew up in rural North Carolina where he discovered a love of genre fiction through the models of Harryhausen, the panels of Kirby, and inside the legendary Dungeons & Dragons "red box." He currently resides in Portland, Oregon with his cat and an increasingly unwieldy collection of board games.

When things get too quiet, he writes and performs music under the name Tesla Deathray Survivors Anonymous.

Christopher Fulbright and Angeline Hawkes are a husband and wife writing team whose fiction spans many genres, including horror, dark fantasy, and thrillers. Christopher is a former journalist turned technical writer with fiction published by DarkFuse, PS Publishing, Delirium Books, Elder Signs Press, Bad Moon Books, and several others. He is a recipient of the Richard Laymon President's Award given by the Horror Writers Association, and is an active member of the International Thriller Writers organization. Angeline holds a B.A. in Composite English Language Arts and Secondary Education from Texas A&M University-Commerce. A Bram Stoker Award nominated writer, Angeline works or has worked for such publishers as Delirium Books, Chaosium, Elder Signs Press, Dark Regions Press, DarkFuse and many others. For more information, please visit their individual web sites at http://www.christopherfulbright.com and http://www.angelinehawkes.com. Follow them on Twitter @FulbrightHawkes.

Parnell Hall is the author of over forty books, including the Stanley Hastings private eye novels, the Puzzle Lady crossword puzzle mysteries, and the Steve

Winslow courtroom dramas. With Stuart Woods, he writes the New York Times bestselling Teddy Fay series and Herbie Fisher series. Parnell is a Shamus Award winner, and has been nominated for the Edgar and the Lefty. He is a recipient of The Eye, for lifetime achievement, awarded by the Private Eye Writers of America.

Michael H. Hanson created the ongoing Sha'Daa shared-world anthology series currently consisting of *Sha'Daa: Tales of the Apocalypse*, *Sha'Daa: Last Call*, *Sha'Daa: Pawns*, *Sha'Daa: Facets*, *Sha'Daa: Inked*, and the as yet to be released *Sha'Daa: Toys*, all published by Moondream Press (an imprint of Copper Dog Publishing). Michael has three collections of poetry in print (*Autumn Blush* and *Jubilant Whispers* published by Racket River Press, an imprint of Copper Dog Publishing and *Dark Parchments: Midnight Curses and Verses* published by MoonDream Press) and is presently compiling his fourth poetic anthology, *The Great Soap Rebellion*, an illustrated collection of poems for children. In 2018, Michael's short story C.H.A.D." will be appearing in the Eric S. Brown edited anthology *C.H.U.D. Lives!* and his short story "Rock and Road" will be appearing in the Roger Zelazny tribute anthology *Shadows and Reflections*. Michael also has stories in Janet Morris's Heroes in Hell (HIH) anthology volumes, *Lawyers in Hell*, *Rogues in Hell*, *Dreamers in Hell*, *Poets in Hell*, *Doctors in Hell*, and the recently published *Pirates in Hell*.

Bram Stoker Award®-nominated **Eugene Johnson** is an author, editor, and columnist of horror, science fiction, fantasy, children's books, and supernatural thrillers. He has written in various genres, with his stories appearing in anthologies such as *The 3rd Spectral Book of Horror Stories*, *C.H.U.D. Lives*! tribute anthology with a story co-written with Jonathan Maberry, and more.

Eugene created anthologies such as *Appalachian Undead* (had an honorable mention in *The Best Horror of the Year Book 6* and picked by FearNet as one of the best books of 2012) with Jason Sizemore, *Drive-in Creature Feature* with Charles Day, the Bram Stoker Award®-nominated non-fiction anthology *Where Nightmares Come From: The Art Of Storytelling In The Horror Genre* with Joe Mynhardt, and more.

He is currently working on several projects including his children book series Life Lessons With Lil' Monsters; his new fiction anthology *Fantastic Tales Of Terror* featuring stories from Christopher Golden, Elizabeth Massie, Bev Vincent, Tim Waggoner, and many more (due this summer from Crystal Lake Publishing); and more.

He is a member of the Horror Writers Association where he serves on multiple committees.

Eugene is a graduate of Marshall University with a master's degree in Mental Health counseling. He lives in Appalachia with his family.

Born and raised in the coastal English town Lowestoft, it should come as no surprise that **Alex Laybourne** became a horror writer.

From an early age, he was sent to schools at least 30 minutes' drive away and so spent most of his free time alone, as the friends he did have lived too far away for them to be able to hang out with them in the weekends or holidays. Stories became a way to pass the time and soon developed into a life-long love for the art of writing.

Married with five wonderful children; James, Logan, Ashleigh, Damon, and Riley. His biggest dream for them is that they grow up, and spend their lives doing what makes them happy, whatever that is.

Chad Lutzke lives in Battle Creek, MI. with his wife, children. For over two decades, he has been a contributor to several different outlets in the independent music and film scene, offering articles, reviews, and artwork. He has written for *Famous Monsters of Filmland, Rue Morgue, Cemetery Dance*, and *Scream* magazine. His fiction can be found in a few dozen magazines and anthologies including his own 18-story collection *Night as a Catalyst*. Lutzke is known for his heartfelt dark fiction and deep character portrayals. In the summer of 2016 he released his dark coming-of-age novella *Of Foster Homes and Flies* which has been praised by authors Jack Ketchum, James Newman, John Boden, and many others. Later in 2016 Lutzke released his contribution to bestselling author J. Thorn's *American Demon Hunter*, and 2017 saw the release of his novella *Wallflower*. His latest, *Stirring the Sheets*, was published by Bloodshot Books in spring 2018.

Jonathan Maberry is a New York Times bestselling author, 5-time Bram Stoker Award-winner, and comic book writer. V-WARS, his vampire apocalypse series of novels and comics is being produced for Netflix starring Ian Somerhalder. He writes in multiple genres including suspense, thriller, horror, science fiction, fantasy, and action; and he writes for adults, teens and middle grade. His works include the Joe Ledger thrillers, *Glimpse*, the Rot & Ruin series, the Dead of

Night series, *The Wolfman*, *X-Files Origins: Devil's Advocate*, *Mars One*, and many others. Several of his works are in development for film and TV. He is the editor of high-profile anthologies including *The X-Files*, *Aliens: Bug Hunt*, *Out of Tune*, *New Scary Stories to Tell in the Dark*, *Baker Street Irregulars*, *Nights of the Living Dead*, and others. His comic book work includes Black Panther, Captain America, Punisher, Wolverine, Bad Blood, and a prequel comic to George Romero's last film, *Road of the Dead*. He lives in Del Mar, California. Find him online at www.jonathanmaberry.com

Greg Mitchell is a screenwriter and novelist and author of *The Coming Evil Trilogy* and *Infernal City*. His eclectic career includes eight novels, several short stories, two Syfy Channel Original Movies—*Snakehead Swamp* and *Zombie Shark*—and a co-writing credit on the non-fiction work *Back in Time: The Unauthorized Back to the Future Chronology* with Rich Handley. He lives with his wife and two daughters in Northeast Arkansas.

Philip C. Perron was born in Lowell, Massachusetts. He is the founder, producer, web designer, editor, and co-host of the Dark Discussions Podcast, which discusses genre film, novels, and all things fantastic. Also included on the network is You Know Nothing Jon Snow: A Game of Thrones Podcast; Bullets, Brothels, and Bots: A Westworld Podcast; and Searching for American Gods: An American Gods Podcast. He is a reviewer of films on the site Cinema Knife Fight where he writes a number of articles. His fiction has been included in many anthologies including the award-winning *Chiral Mad 2* (from

Written Backwords Press) and *Bugs: Tales that Slither, Creep, and Crawl*. He now lives in Amherst, New Hampshire with his wife, two children, and dog. You can find Philip on Facebook and www.darkdiscussions.com

Martin Powell has written hundreds of stories in numerous genres for Disney, Marvel, DC, Dark Horse, and Capstone Books, among others. Nominated for the prestigious Eisner Award for his work with Sherlock Holmes, he has written many of the most popular characters in the industry, including Superman, Batman, Popeye the Sailor, Dracula, Frankenstein, and Tarzan of the Apes. Currently, as the author of almost a dozen different ERB online comic strips, and the critically acclaimed *Jungle Tales of Tarzan* graphic novel from Dark Horse, Powell has written more Edgar Rice Burroughs characters than any other contemporary writer. He received the coveted Golden Lion Award from the Burroughs Bibliophiles in 2017 for his on-going contributions to the legacy of Edgar Rice Burroughs.

https://www.facebook.com/martin.powell1
http://www.amazon.com/Martin-Powell/e/B001JRXRSU

David Robbins has had over three hundred books published, both fiction and non-fiction. He is a member of the Science Fiction and Fantasy Writers of America, the Horror Writers Association, and others. He's had books published under nine different pen names. His latest include the Angel U series; *A Girl, The End of the Word and Everything*; *Battlefield Mars* and *Hit Radio*.

Under his own name he is best known for

Endworld, a science fiction series with a post-apocalyptic setting, the first of which came out in 1986. He has also written a spin-of series called Blade. As David Thompson he has been writing the popular Wilderness series for over twenty years. It's the generational saga of a Mountain Man and his family in the rugged Rockies of the 1800s.

Robbins has written a number of Horror books under his own name, among them *The Wereling* and *Prank Night*. He also penned *The Return of the Virginian*, a sequel to Owen Wister's masterpiece. As Jon Sharpe, he's written over a hundred of The Trailsman books. As well as seventeen books in The Executioner and Mack Bolan series.

He started writing relatively late in life, and over the past several decades has averaged ten published books a year.

Ryan C. Thomas is the author of several novels including *The Summer I Died, Born to Bleed, Scars of the Broken, Bugboy, Hissers, Hissers 2: Death March, Salticidae, The Undead World of Oz, Hobbomock, Ratings Game, Origin of Pain, Red Ice Run*, as well as several novellas and short stories. He lives in San Diego with his wife, children, and two dogs. Visit him online at www.ryancthomas.com.

Tim Waggoner has published close to forty novels and three collections of short stories. He writes original dark fantasy and horror, as well as media tie-ins, and his articles on writing have appeared in numerous publications. He's won the Bram Stoker Award, been a finalist for the Shirley Jackson Award and the Scribe Award, his fiction has received numerous Honorable Mentions in volumes of *Best*

Horror of the Year, and he's twice had stories selected for inclusion in volumes of *Year's Best Hardcore Horror*. He's also a full-time tenured professor who teaches creative writing and composition at Sinclair College in Dayton, Ohio.

Robert E Waters has been publishing science fiction, fantasy, and horror stories since 2003, with his first publication in *Weird Tales*. Since then, he has published over 50 stories in both online and print magazines and anthologies. He is a frequent contributor to *The Grantville Gazette*, an online magazine dedicated to stories set in Eric Flint's Ring of Fire Alternate History series. His most recent novel, *The Cross of Saint Boniface*, an historical fantasy set in the 16th century and featuring Catherine of Aragon, is currently available on Amazon. Robert lives in Baltimore, Maryland with his wife Beth, their son Jason, and their cat Buzz.

Jason White is a factory dwelling writer and podcaster from the frozen lands of Ontario, Canada. He has interviewed many writers for The Darkness Dwells Podcast, including Laird Barron and Ramsey Campbell. He is the author of 20 short stories, published in various magazines and anthologies, and the novel *The Haunted Country*.

THE END?

Not quite . . .

Dive into more Tales from the Darkest Depths:

Novels:

Beyond Night by Eric S. Brown and Steven L. Shrewsbury

The Third Twin: A Dark Psychological Thriller by Darren Speegle

Aletheia: A Supernatural Thriller by J.S. Breukelaar

Beatrice Beecham's Cryptic Crypt: A Supernatural Adventure/Mystery Novel by Dave Jeffery

Where the Dead Go to Die by Mark Allan Gunnells and Aaron Dries

*Sarah Killian: Serial Killer (For Hire!)*by Mark Sheldon

The Final Cut by Jasper Bark

Blackwater Val by William Gorman

Pretty Little Dead Girls: A Novel of Murder and Whimsy by Mercedes M. Yardley

Nameless: The Darkness Comes by Mercedes M. Yardley

Novellas:

Quiet Places: A Novella of Cosmic Folk Horror by Jasper Bark

The Final Reconciliation by Todd Keisling

Run to Ground by Jasper Bark

Devourer of Souls by Kevin Lucia

Apocalyptic Montessa and Nuclear Lulu: A Tale of Atomic Love by Mercedes M. Yardley

Wind Chill by Patrick Rutigliano

Little Dead Red by Mercedes M. Yardley

Sleeper(s) by Paul Kane

Stuck On You by Jasper Bark

Anthologies:

Tales from The Lake Vol.4: The Horror Anthology, edited by Ben Eads

Behold! Oddities, Curiosities and Undefinable Wonders, edited by Doug Murano

Twice Upon an Apocalypse: Lovecraftian Fairy Tales, edited by Rachel Kenley and Scott T. Goudsward

Tales from The Lake Vol.3, edited by Monique Snyman

Gutted: Beautiful Horror Stories, edited by Doug Murano and D. Alexander Ward

Tales from The Lake Vol.2, edited by Joe Mynhardt, Emma Audsley, and RJ Cavender

Children of the Grave

The Outsiders

Tales from The Lake Vol.1, edited by Joe Mynhardt

Fear the Reaper, edited by Joe Mynhardt

For the Night is Dark, edited by Ross Warren

Short story collections:

Frozen Shadows and Other Chilling Stories by Gene O'Neill

Ugly Little Things: Collected Horrors by Todd Keisling

Whispered Echoes by Paul F. Olson

Embers: A Collection of Dark Fiction by Kenneth W. Cain

Visions of the Mutant Rain Forest, by Bruce Boston and Robert Frazier

Tribulations by Richard Thomas

Eidolon Avenue: The First Feast by Jonathan Winn

Flowers in a Dumpster by Mark Allan Gunnells

The Dark at the End of the Tunnel by Taylor Grant

Through a Mirror, Darkly by Kevin Lucia

Things Slip Through by Kevin Lucia

Where You Live by Gary McMahon

Tricks, Mischief and Mayhem by Daniel I. Russell

Samurai and Other Stories by William Meikle

Stuck On You and Other Prime Cuts by Jasper Bark

Poetry collections:

Brief Encounters with My Third Eye by Bruce Boston

No Mercy: Dark Poems by Alessandro Manzetti

Eden Underground: Poetry of Darkness by Alessandro Manzetti

If you've ever thought of becoming an author, we'd also like to recommend these non-fiction titles:

Where Nightmares Come From: The Art of Storytelling in the Horror Genre, edited by Joe Mynhardt and Eugene Johnson

Horror 101: The Way Forward, edited by Joe Mynhardt and Emma Audsley

Horror 201: The Silver Scream Vol.1 and *Vol.2*, edited by Joe Mynhardt and Emma Audsley

Modern Mythmakers: 35 interviews with Horror and Science Fiction Writers and Filmmakers by Michael McCarty

Writers On Writing: An Author's Guide Volumes 1,2,3, and 4, edited by Joe Mynhardt. Now also available in a Kindle and paperback omnibus.

Or check out other Crystal Lake Publishing books for more Tales from the Darkest Depths.

Hi, readers. It makes our day to know you reached the end of our book. Thank you so much. This is why we do what we do every single day.

Whether you found the book good or great, we'd love to hear what you thought. Please take a moment to leave a review on Amazon, Goodreads, or anywhere elsc readers visit. Reviews go a long way to helping a book sell, and will help us to continue publishing quality books. You can also share a photo of yourself holding this book with the hashtag #IGotMyCLPBook!

Thank you again for taking the time to journey with Crystal Lake Publishing.

We are also on . . .

Website:
www.crystallakepub.com

Be sure to sign up for our newsletter and receive two free eBooks: http://eepurl.com/xfuKP

Books:
http://www.crystallakepub.com/book-table/

Twitter:
https://twitter.com/crystallakepub

Facebook:
https://www.facebook.com/Crystallakepublishing/
https://www.facebook.com/Talesfromthelake/
https://www.facebook.com/WritersOnWritingSeries/

Pinterest:
https://za.pinterest.com/crystallakepub/

Instagram:
https://www.instagram.com/crystal_lake_publishing/

Patreon:
https://www.patreon.com/CLP

YouTube:
https://www.youtube.com/c/CrystalLakePublishing

We'd love to hear from you.

Or check out other Crystal Lake Publishing books for your Dark Fiction, Horror, Suspense, and Thriller needs.

With unmatched success since 2012, Crystal Lake Publishing has quickly become one of the world's leading indie publishers of Mystery, Thriller, and Suspense books with a Dark Fiction edge.

Crystal Lake Publishing puts integrity, honor and respect at the forefront of our operations.

We strive for each book and outreach program that's launched to not only entertain and touch or comment on issues that affect our readers, but also to strengthen and support the Dark Fiction field and its authors.

Not only do we publish authors who are legends in the field and as hardworking as us, but we look for men and women who care about their readers and fellow human beings. We only publish the very best Dark Fiction, and look forward to launching many new careers.

We strive to know each and every one of our readers, while building personal relationships with our authors, reviewers, bloggers, pod-casters, bookstores and libraries.

Crystal Lake Publishing is and will always be a beacon of what passion and dedication, combined with overwhelming teamwork and respect, can accomplish: Unique fiction you can't find anywhere else.

We do not just publish books, we present you worlds within your world, doors within your mind, from talented authors who sacrifice so much for a moment of your time.

This is what we believe in. What we stand for. This will be our legacy.

Welcome to Crystal Lake Publishing—Tales from the Darkest Depths

CPSIA information can be obtained
at www.ICGtesting.com
Printed in the USA
LVHW021027201020
669251LV00004BA/425